PRAISE FOR SAM LLEWELLYN'S
DEAD RECKONING

"OUTSTANDING DEBUT THRILLER . . . A new reputation is on the rise here. Llewellyn does for boats what Dick Francis does for horses."
—*Literary Review* (London)

"It isn't often that you pick up a mystery, set in an unfamiliar milieu, that grabs your attention so quickly and continuously. *DEAD RECKONING* HAS ALL THE ELEMENTS OF A GOOD MYSTERY OR A GOOD RACE—SPEED, ENERGY, COMPETITON AND DANGER."
—*Morning Pioneer Press Dispatch* (St. Paul, MN)

"SLICK, READABLE, RACY AND PUNCHY."
—*Sunday Express* (London)

"Violence, adultery and the struggle between 'old' and 'new' Pulteney inhabitants lead to the climactic . . . cross-Channel race. . . . LLEWELLYN PULLS IT OFF SMOOTHLY."
—*Publishers Weekly*

"THE WRITING IS CLEAR AND EFFORTLESS AND THE MYSTERY CAREFULLY PLOTTED. . . . one can feel the sting of the wind, the spindrift, the little humans trying themselves against the elements. MAY MR. LLEWELLYN SAIL ON FOR A LONG TIME. . . ."
—*Newgate Callendar, The New York Times Book Review*

DEAD RECKONING

SAM LLEWELLYN

POCKET BOOKS

New York   London   Toronto   Sydney   Tokyo

POCKET BOOKS, a division of Simon & Schuster Inc.
1230 Avenue of the Americas, New York, NY 10020

Copyright © 1987 by Samson Llewellyn
Cover art copyright © 1989 David Loew

Originally published in Great Britain
by Michael Joseph Ltd, 1987
Library of Congress Catalog Card Number: 87-18025

ISBN: 0-671-64659-1

First Pocket Books printing April 1989

10 9 8 7 6 5 4 3 2 1

POCKET and colophon are trademarks of
Simon & Schuster Inc.

Printed in the U.S.A.

DEAD RECKONING

1

I woke suddenly in the dark. The clock said 4:03, and the wind was moaning round the slates. Behind it there was a lower, duller roaring. It was then that I knew why I was awake.

As I rolled out of the warm bed I started to shiver. Woollen underwear, jeans, oiled-wool jersey, thick oiled socks. Downstairs into the kitchen, last night's dishes piled in the sink. A look at the kettle; no comfort there, no time for coffee, because I was already in the porch, hauling on calf-length boots, yellow rubber with non-slip soles, yellow oilskin trousers and coat, woolly hat and sou'wester over the top.

Outside the front porch the wind hit me like a wet sack. It nudged at me, clearing my head, as I ran down Quay Street and into Fore Street. Tarmac and shopfronts gleamed with rain under yellow street-lamps. It could have been any small town in England at four o'clock in the morning, except for the smell of the wind, which was salty, and the drubbing roar that grew louder as I scuttled across Fore Street and down to the Front. And what had woken me up.

It was bad; I had learned to judge how bad during twenty-five years of watching Fore Street. On a calm day in July, Fore Street looked like a travel poster: Come to Sunny Pulteney, white houses stacked up the hill above a blue sea fringed with lacy foam. Now the lace was angry clouds of spray that hissed across the formal beds of tulips and a car that some idiot had left on the inland side of the road. Head down, I ran towards the corrugated iron structure two hundred yards to the left, under the shelter of the Customs House.

A salt-rotted Cortina whipped past, fans of spray hissing from its tyres. I kept running. In front of the corrugated iron was a bright white light. It lit two men as they got out of the car and ran through the doorway. I was a minute behind them, blinking under the hard lights that illuminated the white upperworks and navy-blue hull of the *Edith Agutter*.

"Last one," said Chiefy Barnes, the coxswain, large eyebrows knitting under the rim of his sou'wester.

"What have we got?" I said, struggling with the braces of the RNLI-issue wet-gear. It had taken me four minutes since the maroon.

"Yacht," said Chiefy. "The Teeth." He turned away. "Starting engines."

In the bowels of the boat, the twin diesels coughed, turned over, and started sweetly on the first revolution of the flywheel. I wanted coffee. I did not like yacht jobs. Too many of my friends were mixed up with yachts.

"Doors open," said Chiefy. "Stations."

The wind's drubbing turned to howling, and the far end of the shed changed from wood to rain and wind. I clipped on my lifeline. The lights went out.

"Let go," said Chiefy.

There was a dull chunk as the wedges came away. The lifeboat started to move. As she passed the doors the wind staggered her. Beneath her keel the carriage rumbled briefly for that moment of weightlessness, twenty tons of machine and twelve men doing exactly what gravity asked; then the pressure in the knee joints as the boat hit the water in a giant flower of spray, shook herself, and began to move.

I went below to try for some coffee. George was jammed in his corner, muttering at the radio. It smelt of paraffin and bilge down here; the *Edith Agutter* was an old boat, overdue for replacement. She was named after my grandmother, and my grandmother had been dead for forty years.

Jerry gave me a mug of coffee and I drank. It was sweet and scalding.

George said, "Transmissions ceased."

It did not sound good. It felt bad, too, from the lurching corkscrews of the old boat as she wound her way among the swells. An hour later, when we got there, it looked even worse. I was on deck by then; we all were.

The wind whipped sheets of water across the cockpit. Through the spinning circle of the windshield the waves were black in the growing dawn, except where the Teeth chewed them to a horrible creamy froth that extended a mile along the southern horizon, broken here and there by black fangs. They looked bad that morning, the Teeth.

"Not a bloody hope," said Jerry. He glanced at me and looked quickly away again.

Chiefy massaged the twin throttle levers, and we crept closer, into the fringe of the broken water, where the spume blew like shaving-foam. I found myself swallowing nothing, dry-mouthed. Chiefy's face was mildly interested; I knew from past experience that he would be humming monotonously. I also knew that if anyone could get to whatever was happening in the middle of those rocks, Chiefy could.

Foot by foot, feeling her way, the *Edith Agutter* closed in. The movement of the deck became arbitrary and jerky. Heavy spray rattled on the plate-glass and streamed wobbling down.

9

"There she is," said Jerry.

It was not difficult to see her, once you knew what to look for. The difficulty had been looking for something that looked like a ship. This was a slab of white stuff, like a giant eggshell rolling among the granite chunks, lifting a stub that became a broken mast trailing a web of rigging.

"There'll be nobody in that lot," said Chiefy.

As always, he was right.

We watched the sluggish roll of the shattered hull, and I listened to my heart beating very hard and very slowly.

"Maybe there's a raft," said Jerry. But he knew as well as anyone else that if there had been a raft it would have been blown onto the stones too, and its inmates would have had about as much chance as if they had gone swimming in a concrete mixer.

"Better wait for the tide," said Chiefy.

He brought the *Edith* round in a wide, slow arc that took her out of the robbly backwash and into the rhythm of the swell. Then he started a steady cruise to leeward of the reef.

It was calmer in here, and the wind was dropping for the dawn lull. To seaward, a fog of spray hung above the reef like a curtain.

As usual, it was Chiefy who saw it first.

Out of the curtain of spray floated a yellow survival raft, a little rubber tent over an air-filled tube with a rubber floor. The deck heeled under my boots as Chiefy shoved the throttles forward, and we took positions. I was on the starboard bow, so it was me that caught it with the boathook. Two of the inflated sections were punctured, and it was nearly awash. We walked it back to the waist. The boat's side was level with the tent's door, but the shadows made it hard to see in. I did not have to see in, though. I knew.

We brought out two bodies. The first one had been lying face down in a foot of water, and would have drowned if he had not already died of a fractured skull. The second one was still alive, which was a miracle. We brought him out on a stretcher, very gently. He was semi-conscious, but his legs flopped limply, because he had a broken back.

Once they were below, we called up the choppers for the injured man and set out for home.

"She'll come off that ledge and go down," said Chiefy. "No point waiting for the tide." He was speaking to me, and me alone. I knew why.

The yacht on the Teeth, which would sink at high tide, was called *Aesthete*. I had conceived and designed her myself. And the dead man was called Hugo Agutter. He was my younger brother.

2

There is an odd quietness that comes over Pulteney when the lifeboat is in after a bad night. At first it is apprehensive; the *Edith Agutter*'s predecessor is scattered among the crevices and tide rips of the Western Teeth. Then the apprehension changes to suspense, as the chopper hacks its way overhead when it has picked up the bodies. And the suspense gives way to a sort of miserable calm once the word has gone around: one dead, one broken back. The dead man from the town, the broken back a yachter. The word travels fast: from a shower where a tired lifeboatman is soaping off the salt before he starts his day's work; to his wife, frying fish fingers for breakfast; from his wife to the milkman, from the milkman to the postman, and so through the narrow streets of white houses where the holiday people and the yachters live; up to the council estate tucked over the back of Naylor's Hill, and down to the old warehouses by the harbour where the sailmakers and yacht designers are starting their day. And eventually, once the village knows, the news spreads outwards to the rest of the country.

I went down to the garage. My rusty BMW sneezed at me, and started. Grey rain drifted onto the windscreen and the cobbles and the window-boxes my neighbours liked to set against the whitewashed granite of their holiday homes.

It was a road Hugo had known well. He and I had learned to ride bicycles on it, in the days before Pulteney became a yachters' haven. In those days, the traffic had been Yeo's lorry for the fish that came off the boats that unloaded in the harbour every morning. But in those days, there had been fish to be caught in the Western Approaches. In those days, there had been no need for the signs banning cars from the village street. I drove past Maginnis' window. In those days, the window had been made of wood, with panes that distorted the dusty sweets inside. Now it was plate-glass—a memorial to Hugo's first attempt at teaching himself to drive. I had been his instructor, and I vividly remembered sitting in a pile of newspapers, shrimping nets and sherbert fountains, laughing hysterically as bricks rained on the car roof from the lintel of the devastated window.

The new houses on the edge of the village came up and fell behind. Out here the roads were wider and faster. I felt the tears rise for poor old Hugo. But he was past crying for; it was Sally who was in trouble.

She had got engaged to Hugo while I was at Southampton, doing a Naval Architecture course. Ridiculously early, the parents all said. Hugo loved to win; I think that had been it. But it had worked, and they had been very happy. Yes, very happy.

Until this morning.

Hugo's house—Sally's house, I should say—was long and low, grey granite tucked under a hill of wind-thrashed oaks. The gates were open; they had never been closed, as far as I remembered. But the house looked closed, its windows blind and wet in the drizzle. There was only Sally's Peugeot van, parked untidily by the front door.

Sally herself came to meet me. She was dressed as

usual in a blue jersey and jeans that were unfashionably tight but showed her long and beautiful legs. She had a good face: Egyptian, with a slab of black hair on either side, hollows under finely-modelled cheekbones, and a wide red mouth. Her eyes were long, and beneath their thick black lashes, astonishingly green. She was pale, her face sunk back over the bones. She had not yet started to cry; perhaps she did not yet know. But as I came closer, I noticed that her eyes had a dazzled look and her head moved not with its usual grace but with a slow, awkward swing. When her eyes fixed on me, they were suddenly full of pain.

"Let's go inside," I said.

We went in. The house was full of her junk, Chinese and London art-gallery. An Elizabeth Frink bird stood on the hall table, crowned with a yachting cap. Hugo's.

"Amy rang," she said. "Henry's got a broken back."

"I know," I said. I was going to continue, but she interrupted.

"And you came out here to tell me. Well thanks, Charlie, but I already know."

I put her in a chair. The muscles at the corners of her jaw were knotted. She would not want sympathy.

"Charlie," she said, "why don't you go and make yourself some breakfast."

The kitchen was big and bright, with an oilcloth-covered table and paintings above the dresser. The paintings were mostly of boats; there was an Alan Lownes of steam drifters and an Alfred Wallis of St. Ives harbour with schooners. I was tired, my stomach sick and acid. I dropped eggs into a frying-pan, thinking of the times we had come home after sailing all night, me and Hugo, and had breakfast in this room, with the salt still on us. Sally's voice murmured on the telephone in the next room. It was scarcely possible to comprehend that Hugo would be away for ever.

Sally came back in as the coffee boiled up in the percolator. She had herself under control again.

"I'll look after . . . things," I said.

She laid her hand on mine, cold and dry. Then she left.

I finished my coffee. The sun came out and I watched the blackbirds hopping after the worms on the lawn and the heaving of the rhododendrons in the wind. The telephone rang. I picked it up.

It was a woman's voice, brittle and full of raw nerves.

"Sally?" it said. "Darling, if there's anything I can do to help—"

"I'm afraid Sally's not here," I said.

"Who's that?"

"Charlie Agutter."

"Oh." There was a pause. I knew the voice. It belonged to Amy Charlton, wife of Henry with the broken back. "I suppose you were on the lifeboat," she said.

"Yes."

"Well, Henry's conscious," she said, tightly. "But he's paralysed."

"I'm sorry."

"And so you bloody well should be," said Amy, her voice rising suddenly. "Last night, I had a perfectly good husband. This morning, they're taking him up to Stoke Mandeville and you know what that means. He'll never walk again and I'll have to spend the rest of my life changing his damn nappies."

"They're very good at spinal injuries," I said, as gently as I could.

"Don't tell me who's good at what, Mr. bloody yacht-designing Agutter. You designed that boat and the boat cracked up, and you killed your brother and Henry's a cripple. Well, don't think I'm going to sit around and do nothing about it. You Pulteney bastards, you're all pirates. You saw Henry coming and

15

you took his money and built him a deathtrap." The line went dead.

I put my end down quietly and tried to catch my breath. My legs felt rubbery. She's right, I thought; it is my fault. If the boat did crack up, I killed them.

Then my eyes went to the colour photograph above the telephone: an ocean racer, decks cluttered with sails and ropes and people. *V.Ex*, winner, One Ton Cup, the ultimate testing-ground for state-of-the-art sea sledges. Designer, Charlie Agutter. Designer of good boats, that won races. Not deathtraps. There were more reasons for hitting rocks than your boat cracking up.

3

Fifteen years ago, Pulteney was what is known as a nice little fishing village. It had a long, windy beach, from which wise people did not bathe, and a horseshoe-shaped harbour jam-packed with wooden fishing-boats. Its situation, in the unfavoured part of the South Coast between Bridport and Torquay, meant that the crowds left it alone.

Then everything changed. The cause of the change was the death of Lord Cerne and the subsequent sale of Bollard Row, a picturesque slum above a cobbled alley too narrow for cars. The purchaser had been a 25-year-old Deptford scrap dealer called Frank Millstone. Though young, Millstone had a vision of the future which included himself as feudal entrepreneur. Under the hands of his builders and interior decorators, Bollard Row became a little epic of seaside quaintness. Soon after, he had brought a load of yachting journalists into the harbour aboard his fifty-foot catamaran, pointing out its advantages as a yacht haven. The journalists saw the advantages, through a fog of Millstone's Bollinger. The Pulteney boom was on.

More streets came on the market, and the people

17

who had lived in them for years moved to the council estate over the hill. The new owners of their homes were also the owners of the sleek yachts which had taken the place of the fishing-boats in the harbour. Spearman's boatyard, long one of Pulteney's main employers, moved to new premises and doubled its workforce.

One of the few houses in Pulteney that Millstone was unable to get his hands on was ours. It was a white Georgian town house, long and low, with two floors and a huge bow-window. It clung to the hill, overlooking the harbour. It had been built in 1817 by my great-great-grandfather, an extremely lazy man who had spent most of his life in the bow-window with a telescope, spying on the shipping. It was one of those houses that, while it is by no means beautiful, is exactly right in every detail, and it had inspired in successive generations of Agutters a love amounting almost to obsession. Millstone had also been affected by its spell. He had lost no time in making an offer for it, and the Agutters had lost no time in refusing.

Despite our resistance to Frank Millstone, the Agutters did pretty well out of the Pulteney boom. My father owned a decaying line of coasters, one of which he had driven himself. The line's assets were four 1,000-ton rustbuckets and a warehouse down by the quay.

The ships were sold to a Greek coal merchant, and the warehouse was converted into offices for companies who wished to bask in the glamour of the new Pulteney.

One summer, I drew a boat for a merchant banker whom I had met in the new Yacht Club Millstone had built on the site of a net shed by the harbour, and he sailed it into the Captain's Cup team. That year, the British team had come second, which was encouraging, as the Captain's Cup is one of the four most important yacht series in the Northern Hemisphere.

Pulteney was now feeding racing-boats into the off-shore racing circuit in Australia and the U.S. as well as Europe, and I was doing a good share of the designing.

My mother had died while I was at university, and my father and I lived one in each half of the house. My father's only condition in this arrangement had been that he was to have the side with the bow-window, since he was now of an age where an armchair and a telescope on a busy harbour were the only amusements left.

In this bow-window he spent most of his days, his legs wrapped in a loud tartan rug, ministered to by the bulging but extremely efficient Nurse Bollom. Nurse Bollom lived in a hot, scrubbed room in the attic, and I had learned not to mind the fact that she disapproved of me intensely.

I parked the BMW on the quay beside the office door and went into my office past Ernie, the draughtsman.

My workroom occupied much of the ground floor of the warehouse. It was a large, bare room, with a huge blow-up of *V.Ex* on the whitewashed wall, a computer on a black desk, and a drawing-board lit by a vast window overlooking the stone horns of the harbour. It normally dwarfed people who weren't used to its echoing spaces. But Frank Millstone went a long way towards filling it.

He was an enormous man, with an enormous face and little blue eyes in nests of wrinkles that made him look as if he was permanently on the point of breaking into a big grin. He was wearing a navy blue pea-jacket and a pair of faded blue O.M. Watts trousers. If you had seen him rolling down Quay Street, you might have taken him for a jolly nautical tramp.

You would have been wrong.

Frank bought and sold money and commodities on a huge scale. He was also Life President of the

Pulteney Yacht Club and a keen buyer of racing-boats. Two years previously, he had won the Half-Ton Cup with *Pallas,* designed by one of my principal competitors, Joe Grimaldi. This year, he had designs on the Captain's Cup team. The series of offshore races that served as trials for the Cup were due to start in June. Three months previously, he had said that he wanted Charlie Agutter to design him a contender. Whether or not I liked Millstone, that had been good news.

"Charlie," he said. "How are you?"

"Fine." Frank was not a man to confide in about a lost brother, or even a lost night's sleep.

"How's my boat?"

"Going for finishing on Monday."

His eyes twinkled in their nests of wrinkles like twin refrigerators in need of defrosting. "Yes. Charlie, I'm coming straight to the point. I'm worried about the rudder."

I thought about my talk with Amy, and goose-pimples pricked my skin. "What's wrong with the rudder?"

"It's not a normal rudder."

What he was trying to say was that the rudder was a thing I had designed myself, using research lifted from the Royal Navy and NASA. Most rudders slowed a boat down when they steered her. Not this one: theoretically, it should make her faster.

"Charlie, Hugo's boat had one of your new rudders. I think we want a normal rudder," said Frank.

"There was nothing wrong with the rudder," I said.

"I said I would like a normal rudder," said Frank.

It was only now that I realised that what we had here was not the standard client-designer debate. This was the professional relationship teetering on a knife-edge, aggravated by Frank's suspicion of me as Old Pulteney, and my suspicion of him as New Pulteney.

I said, "Hold on—"

"Will you change that rudder?" said Frank.

"No, I bloody well will not," I said. "Now, why don't you tell me your problem?"

"I suggest you go and talk to Henry in hospital," he said.

"You have been speaking to Amy."

"Perhaps."

"It's not like you to listen to gossip, Frank."

He got up. His eyes were definitely not smiling. "Go and talk to Henry," he said. "And please stop work for the moment. I've suspended payment."

"What?" I said. I couldn't believe my ears.

"We'll wait for the salvage report," he said, and rolled heavily out.

I sat there for a moment, feeling as if I had swallowed a big cold cannonball. If Millstone and Amy had the idea that the boat had a design fault, it would not be long before the rest of the world got it too—which would be a disaster.

Contrary to popular belief, yacht designers do not make a lot of money, unless they are very successful. I was on the way up, but I was not at the top. I was designing Frank's boat as a contractor, overseeing the building myself and taking my fee out of the price I had quoted him at the beginning. It was an unusual arrangement, but it was attractive to owners because it put the risk firmly on me. It was not the only risk I had to take.

In order to get to the top, I needed to get some boats of my design into the Captain's Cup. The trials for the Cup were now some four weeks away, and invitations to compete had been issued by the National Offshore Racing Federation to thirty likely entrants. Some of these entrants had been training for months. Others had not yet got boats. What they had in common was that they were very rich and very competitive, and prepared to spend six- and seven-figure sums to make sure their boats got into the three-boat team.

The fact that they were very rich meant that a lot of

people listened to them, very closely. If I was getting on the wrong side of my owners, I was in deep career trouble. I had sunk a lot into getting into the Captain's Cup. In fact, I had sunk everything I had, and more besides, and I was broke. I also had my father to support, together with Nurse Bollom, not to mention my own boat, *Nautilus*.

I sat at my desk and tried to think. It was not easy, because my brain was operating in the thick fog that always descends when I am very tired. All I could decide was that the sooner we got *Aesthete* off the bottom and into a yard, the better.

Outside the window, the wind was wailing in the halyards of the moored boats. It was being a bloody awful April, and with a wind like that there was no chance of salvaging the wreck from the middle of the Teeth. But I have never been good at sitting still and waiting, so I picked up the telephone and dialled Neville Spearman.

There had been Spearmans in Pulteney for longer than there had been Agutters. Spearmans ran trips round the bay, set lobster-pots, worked in supermarkets and ran estate agencies. Neville was easily the most successful Spearman. He had played the Pulteney boom very cleverly, expanding a yard that used to turn out good, heavy fishing-boats into one equipped to build state-of-the-art racing-yachts. He was a gloomy old devil, though, who always managed to give the impression that the Pulteney boom was too good to last, and that he expected a general collapse imminently. But he combined this quality with a shrewd perception of what side his bread was buttered, so as long as things were going well, he could be relied on. The telephone rang for a long time. Finally, he answered. I could hear the whine of sanders in the background.

"Morning," he said.

"Have you got that salvage barge in the water?"

He got my drift immediately. "Yes. But not in this weather. Charlie, I was about to ring you."

"Yes?" Chilly winds of disaster drifted from the receiver.

"Sir Alec Breen was on the blower. He's asked me to stop work on *Windjammer* till . . . things are cleared up. He's writing you a letter."

"Is it the rudder?" I said.

"He seems to think so."

"You told him you thought they're okay? That NASA and the Royal Navy are using the materials?"

"Do me a favour," he said. "You know what owners are like."

"I'll find out what really happened," I said.

"That would be nice. Then we could all do some bloody work."

"Book that barge to me as soon as we get a calm day."

"Will do," said Spearman.

Sir Alec Breen was another of my clients. We were a week into finishing a one-tonner of my design at Spearman's yard. She was a nice boat and another strong Captain's Cup possibility, and Breen had come to me only after some hot competition. Boat designers like me are as much slaves to public opinion as pop stars. The difference is that our public is smaller, consisting of the couple of hundred men who can afford to spend a quarter of a million pounds on a boat every three or four years.

Under the right circumstances, Breen was my favorite kind of owner. He was no more addicted to sailing fast boats than he was to synchronized swimming. What he enjoyed was organization. Presumably he was not getting enough of it in his everyday life, most of which he spent running the chain of a hundred and twelve gravel-pits that brought him in an income reckoned by City analysts to be between three and five million pounds a year. Having organized a designer and builder for his boats, Breen liked to organize a crew, then sit back and wait to see his name in the papers. He was seldom disappointed.

He had a reputation as a cold fish. I rather liked him. He was small, with a slight Northern accent, heavy-lidded eyes and a perpetual cigar. He was one of those people who will sit in the corner of a room, unnoticed until he opens his mouth—at which point it is apparent that he is the focus of everything that is happening in that room. The first time I had gone to see him, he had taken me on a tour of one of his gravel-pits, and identified seventeen different fossils, with an evident appreciation of the excellent organization of the evolutionary process.

One of the things he admired about evolution was the principle of the survival of the fittest. For Breen was one of the most competitive people I have ever met, both in business and in the small world of offshore racing, which was where my problem lay. Breen was not a sentimentalist about his employees. If they didn't deliver, out they went, and he was not shy of advertising the fact. In the boardrooms, clubs and other expensive places where the owners of offshore racers meet and talk, the word would be out that Agutter had problems. Disaster is the favourite topic in such places, and Agutter would be the disaster of the week, this week.

I tried to call him. He was not available, which was no surprise. If Breen was writing a letter, Breen was writing a letter.

I was tired, I felt sick, and I wanted to go to bed. But it was too early. I decided I needed air. I was at the door when the telephone rang again.

"Charlie," said the voice. It was the voice I had been going for a walk to avoid.

"Archer," I said. "Can I help?"

"In a way," said the other voice. It was level and sounded slightly amused, but that didn't mean anything. "I heard about *Aesthete*. I'm very sorry about Hugo." He paused. "Are we still sailing tomorrow? Because we should talk."

"Of course," I said, and rang off.

Jack Archer was the design manager of Padmore and Bayliss. P and B produced eight hundred yachts a year, and I had just negotiated the contract to design a complete new range for them: seven models, from racers down to bilge keel cruisers. It was a lovely job, and not the least lovely part was the royalty P and B had agreed to pay me on each boat.

One-off racing-boats establish a designer's reputation, provided they win. But they do not pay the milk-bill. It is the fleet-boats that pay off big, and fleet contracts are like hen's teeth. I had sweated nails going after this one, and I was very, very worried about what Archer was going to say when we had our little chat tomorrow.

"Hell," I said. I took the phone off the hook and marched out the side door of my office.

Chiefy was in his usual corner at the Mermaid, with a glass of rum in his hand and a pint of bitter at his elbow. He was usually there after the lifeboat had been out. Ashore, he was smaller than you would have guessed if you had only seen him at the wheel of the *Edith*. He was an ordinary-looking man, baldish, with bushy grey eyebrows and square brown hands. It was only the eyes that gave him away, blue and very sharp, with a distance in them that went beyond the smoke-mottled walls of the Mermaid and onto horizons saw-toothed with big seas.

"Have a drink, boy," he said.

I accepted a pint of bitter.

"Won't light no fires with that," said Chiefy, reprovingly.

"I've just been out to Sally," I said.

Chiefy nodded. "It weren't Hugo at the helm."

25

The same thought had occurred to me. Hugo was a beautiful helmsman and he knew Pulteney backwards. If he had been at the wheel, he would never have gone anywhere near the Teeth on a night like last night.

"Unless something did go unseemly on that there boat of yours." Chiefy's idea of a good boat was the *Ark Royal,* reinforced wherever possible with lengths of railway line. "Not what I calls seaworthy," said Chiefy. "Not properly. None of your bloody racing-boats. Look at Edward Beith."

I was getting tired of people telling me my boats were unseaworthy. "Why don't you shut up?" I said.

Chiefy darted a glance at me. His eye was less sharp than usual; he was far gone in rum. He had loved Hugo, too. "Beith didn't look too happy when I saw him at Spearman's yesterday. Trouble with *Crystal,* I reckon."

Ed Beith was more Old Pulteney. He, Hugo and I had been friends since before we could walk. Pulteney regattas, in the days before the big money had arrived, had been contests between Beith and his crew and the Agutter boys. We had sailed 505s, very hard. We had smoked illicit Capstan Full Strengths in Chiefy's net shed. We had pursued girls, among them Sally. In short, we had had a gang.

When Ed's father died, he had inherited the farm, inland from Pulteney. It had once run all the way to the cliffs, but Millstone had bought the cliffside bits cheap, by setting-up a cousin of Ed's. The cousin had begged the land from him to give him a start in sheep-farming. Ed had sold it to him cheap and Millstone had paid off the cousin and built chalet bungalows.

It was a gesture typical of Ed, who, outside a racing-boat, was incapable of subterfuge. He had a lot of land, but he was known to be in hock to the bank. His forty-foot sloop *Crystal* would not be helping. She was a fast boat, but her hull was made of a heat-bonded composite of resin and aramid paper that didn't like staying together. There were rumours that he was finding her expensive to run.

"Did you talk to him?"

"He said to tell you to drop in," said Chiefy. "Well, I'm off. You ought to check that bloody rudder of yours, though. I've heard a lot of nasty talk about it."

"No checking anything till we can pull up *Aesthete*. But I'm off to see Henry Charlton in Stoke Mandeville, just in case he remembers anything."

"You'd better have a lie-down first," said Chiefy. "It's a bloody long way." His rock-hard hand clapped me on the shoulder. "And when you've finished popping about, we can have a drink about Hugo."

"I'd like that."

I finished my pint and trudged up the steep cobbles, thinking: I'd better ring Hugo and talk about *Crystal*, see if there was anything we could do. Then I remembered that Hugo was dead.

4

At the house I wearily made the bed and did the washing-up. Then I poured myself a Famous Grouse, put a John Coltrane record on the turntable and moved round in a dreary trance, straightening the pictures. I stopped in front of the little glass case which held my bronze medal from the Montreal Olympics, trying to remember the surge of power that I had felt there, the confidence that nothing could go wrong from now on. The glass reflected a thin face, fair hair sticking out in harassed spikes above low cheekbones and sunken cheeks, the eyes sunk into gloomy pits above deep pouches. Not the face of an Olympic medal winner, but of a man under suspicion of professional incompetence which had caused the death of his brother.

"Ugh," I said. The face in the mirror's glass bore no resemblance to the Charlie Agutter seen by readers of the *Yachtsman,* or the viewers of the BBC yachting programmes. That Agutter was a bronzed, fit optimist. Grey pessimists, like the one in the glass, did not have successful careers.

"Ugh," I said again. I turned off the stereo, tipped the whisky down the sink, and took a shower. Then I got the BMW out of the garage and started inland, trailing flakes of rust.

It was twelve miles to the A303, and from there on it was a matter of keeping foot to floor until the outskirts of London.

I had rung the hospital. They had said that Henry was conscious, and able to talk. As I pushed the BMW through the traffic, I tried not to worry about what he was going to say. He did not like me, I knew; and, to tell the truth, I didn't much like him. He always managed to give the impression that the world had been invented expressly for his convenience, and that his fellow beings were there to do his bidding or, alternatively, to be beaten in competition. I don't think I have ever met a man who needed to win as desperately as Henry. He was by turns rude and patronising to Chiefy, and had behaved towards Hugo as if Hugo was his invention.

It was dead on two o'clock as I came to Stoke Mandeville Hospital. Apprehensively, I followed a bright nurse along sunny corridors floored with green linoleum.

"He'll be pleased to see you, I expect," she said. "Only five minutes, though."

He had a room to himself. His face looked big and red against the pillow and the white plaster of paris that encased his upper chest. My eyes strayed to the mound of his body under the blankets. In most bodies, there is a sort of tension. In Henry's, there was none. He was like a sack. Only his eyes moved, glazed and bloodshot.

"Henry," I said. "I came to say how sorry I am about all this."

"Thanks," said Henry, in a blurred voice.

"What happened?"

"I hit my head. Can't move." He sounded drugged. It seemed unlikely that the hospital would have told him the full extent of the damage.

"The race," I said. "Can you manage to think about it?"

"Who won?" said Henry.

"Beeston."

"Sod," said Henry. His eyes cleared for a moment. "What are you doing here?"

"I want to know how . . . what happened," I said slowly. There was no sense in pretending to Henry that we liked each other.

"Tell you," said Henry. "Had the Teeth to leeward. Doing nicely, opening the Quay Light." He frowned. "The steering went. No helm, wouldn't answer. Don't remember. How's Hugo?"

The nurse came in. "Now then, Mr. Charlton, we'd better get you ready for the doctor."

"How's Hugo?" said Henry, again.

"Never mind Hugo," said the nurse.

"That's it," said Henry suddenly, in a loud clear voice. "It was Charlie Agutter's bloody rudder. It broke."

My stomach clenched like a fist.

"Charlie—bloody—Agutter," he said again, in a voice hideous with scorn and anger. Then the tears began to roll down the big, red face.

The nurse said, "You'd better go now," and I backed away, watching her put the screens round and hearing dimly her cheerful chatter. Life went on, said the chatter; Doctor Amin was ever so nice, Bernie in the next ward was in a wheelchair now, wasn't that nice?

I said, "Sorry," but nobody heard me. Then I turned round and left the hospital.

I drove home like a robot.

Hugo ran one of the world's most technically advanced sail lofts. He had just taken delivery of a new computerised cutting-machine, and he had made *Aesthete* a new mainsail. He and Henry had gone off to try out the mainsail in the Boulogne Bracer, an early season Pulteney race. It was sailed as a two-hander and had been designed as a trial for long-distance racing. Nowadays, it was used by the Pulteney owners to test new gear and helmsmen before the season started in earnest. The Bracer took yachts up-Channel to within sight of Cap Gris-Nez and back again to Pulteney Quay. The start is on the morning tide and the boats come in two days later. This time, they had gone up-Channel on a dead run with a force five westerly behind them. The westerly had then backed southwesterly and freshened to force six, eight later. This was convenient, since it meant they did not have to come home with the wind dead against them, tacking hard with a tired crew.

The main problem with a sou'westerly would be the Teeth.

The approach to Pulteney is nice and easy. All you have to do, assuming you know where you are, is to stay eight and a half miles offshore until you open the harbour—or, at night, until you are due south of the harbour light. This brings you along the southern fringes of the Teeth, which run like a wall parallel with the coast. Then you pay off for the light. Races are won by good navigators, who shave it close even on a night like last night. It is reasonably safe, provided your steering-gear holds out: but then you would hardly give a second thought to your steering-gear, because holding out is exactly what it is built for. If the gear failed in a southwesterly wind, of course, the tendency would be for you to be pushed to leeward— north-east, towards the rocks.

I winced, imagining it. Rain and wind howling up from Biscay. Heavily reefed mainsail and storm jib, the deck heeled steeply towards the roaring white shadow a few hundred yards to the northward. Henry braced at the wheel, his mind working at the problem of shaving between wind direction and the reef. And

31

then, suddenly, the wheel slack in his hand and the yacht slewed head to wind, everything flapping and roaring, and the wind pressing her back into the teeth of the rocks . . .

It was unimaginable. But it had happened. I thought of the life raft, and what had come out of it. And now the tears ran in earnest.

It was nine o'clock when I got home. The sun was hanging over Beggarman's Cliff, pulling a trail of orange blotches across the bay. Far to seaward, the Teeth blew plumes of mist that the sun turned to gold.

My feet seemed impossibly heavy as I staggered up the crooked stairs. I washed my face, fell onto the bed, and went to sleep.

5

The telephone was ringing. My mouth felt as if it had been swilled out with glue. I grabbed the receiver.

"Charlie," said a smooth, cheerful voice. "Archer here. Just ringing to see we're still all right."

"All right?" I said muzzily.

"For this morning."

"Oh." I could picture him, pink and scrubbed, anxious to do the right thing. Archer was a great one for doing the right thing. "Of course," I said.

"Ten o'clock all right?"

"Ten o'clock."

I put the telephone down, swung my feet out of bed and sat looking at them. Bloody Archer. Must keep up appearances, though.

The stairs seemed hard to negotiate, and the power lead would not fit into the kettle. Two spoonfuls of instant coffee in a little water improved things. The world began to tick. I dressed in canvas trousers, oiled jersey and Docksiders, and went down to the office. There was about three times the usual amount of mail. Perhaps it was from people who wanted me to build new boats. Then again, perhaps it wasn't.

There was one letter I did open because I had been

33

expecting it and I wanted to get it over with. The envelope bore the Consolidated logo. There were no surprises. It was from Sir Alec Breen, and it said that, while he realised that in ocean racing accidents did happen, pending full investigation of the *Aesthete* wreck he was sure I would understand that he could not continue with the project currently in hand at Spearman's yard. Had I any comments to make?

I had. I dialed his number. The secretary who had told me yesterday that he had been unavailable put me through.

"Yes," said Breen.

"I got your letter," I said. "I don't think you're being fair."

"Oh?" said Breen.

"You're assuming the boat's unseaworthy before you've any evidence," I said.

"True," said Breen. There was a pause: I could imagine him taking the cigar out of his mouth. "I'm allowed to."

"But is that a fair assumption?"

Breen paused again, the pause of a man so powerful he did not give a damn about leaving embarrassing silences. "I don't have to be fair," he said. "I just make assumptions, never mind whether they're fair or not."

I played my final card. "If we stop work now, you won't have a boat for the Captain's Cup trials. We've only got four weeks."

"You salvage that boat, and we'll see," said Breen. "There's always next year. Well, Charlie, nice chat. Bye, now."

He put the telephone down.

He was right. He could wait. I was the one who was in a hurry. I had to get a boat in the Captain's Cup to impress Padmore and Bayliss and the rest of them. That would be why Archer was so keen for a sail.

I looked at my watch. Ten to ten. Time to forget

about bankruptcy and poor old Hugo, and put on a nice grin and go and be the life and soul of the joyride.

Jack Archer had arranged for my boat *Nautilus* to feature on *Age of Sail,* a TV programme dealing with classic yachts. All I had to do was provide a crew, look noble at the helm, and bask in the free publicity, though I was by no means clear what good publicity would do a yacht designer with no yachts to design.

The TV crew were waiting on the quay outside. I pointed out *Nautilus,* her long bottle-green hull blade-like and elegant among the more plebeian boats lying against the quay. The director started setting up long shots, and I leaned against my office wall and waited for the day's guests.

The first to arrive was Johnny Forsyth. Johnny was tall and thin, his leathery jowls pocked with old acne scars. He was not quite Old Pulteney, but he was not quite New Pulteney either. He had been in the Special Boat Service, from which he had emerged resolved to spend the rest of his life as a marine painter. With this in mind, he had moved with his wife to Pulteney perhaps five years before the Millstone invasion.

It soon became apparent that Forsyth was better at building and sailing boats than at painting them. In fact, he was a brilliant racing tactician, if a little aggressive. During the season, he picked up fees as a consultant to various offshore racing campaigns. For the rest of the year, he freelanced—doing a little broking, designing the odd boat and doing detail work and rebuilds for Neville Spearman at the yard. His wife ran the restaurant at a pub called the Lobster Pot, near Spearman's yard on the Coast road. Frankly, she was not much of a cook. But she rubbed along, and Johnny rubbed along, and they were nice people. Personally, I always found him a little puzzling. He could do a lot of things, and if he had done one at a time he could have done very well. But as it was, he never rose beyond a sort of mediocrity, punctuated with flashes of brilliance.

This morning he said, "Sorry about Hugo."

"Can you come to the funeral?" I said.

"Sure." He clapped me on the shoulder. "What's happening this morning?"

I told him. "Scotto's aboard. And Georgia."

"Ah," said Forsyth, with his lipless grin. "Sweet Georgia, the chocolate charmer. I'll pop across and give them a hand."

I looked after him, reflecting that Georgia, who came from Trinidad, might not have enjoyed the description. Johnny was full of little awkwardnesses.

Now that Forsyth had gone, another man got up from a bollard. He was slim, too beautifully dressed in a blazer and flannels, with a tan too brown and even to be genuine.

"Hi there," he said, with what he probably thought was a boyish grin. "Hector Pollitt, *Yachtsman,* and you're Charlie Agutter. Have you got a spare minute?"

I looked down the quay. A Mercedes had drawn up in the car park and a stocky figure was picking its way over the tarry rubble that separated it from the quay. "No," I said.

Pollitt's eyes followed mine, and lit up. "That's Jack Archer!" he said. "You're building a boat for him?"

"Not for him personally."

"Ah," said Pollitt. "Contract job, is it? For P and B? Listen, could we have a comment from you on the *Aesthete* tragedy?"

"Hugo was my brother," I said. "I'm very upset and I'm not about to discuss my private life with the trade press."

"Ah . . . Yes . . . Of course, we're all very sad . . . you designed *Aesthete,* didn't you?" He knew damn well I had. "There's a rumour that they had trouble with the helm."

"Who told you that?"

"Oh, you know, scuttlebutt. But my readers would like to know."

"Naturally, I'll be on the salvage barge, as and when we pick up *Aesthete*. I'll be in a better position to make a statement at that time."

"Of course you will," said Pollitt, nodding brightly. He did not put away his notebook. "Good morning, Mr. Archer."

Archer was solid, brown and economical. He had won an early STAR—Single-handed Trans-Atlantic Race. He had rapidly earned a reputation as a hard man and a formidable helmsman and he was much in demand on the international offshore racing circuit. But nowadays he mixed his racing with Padmore and Bayliss. He professed to dislike the commercialisation of Grand Prix racing. When he wasn't putting contracts on hold, I liked him.

He gave Pollitt a practised smile and shook me by the hand. His handshake was warm, dry and hard.

I said, "Shall we go straight out to the boat?"

Pollitt said, "Is this a professional visit, Mr. Archer?"

Archer smiled at him. He had to sell five hundred boats a year, so he smiled at a lot of journalists. "What exactly do you mean?" he said.

"In Cowes they're saying that you're talking series design with Charlie."

"Do they really?" I said. What I meant was different. The only way of salvaging my P and B contract was to keep it dead quiet until I could prove *Aesthete* had gone down from natural causes.

"I have a tremendous admiration for Charlie's work," said Archer.

"How about the rumours about *Aesthete?*" Pollitt winked at me, as if we were having a little laugh instead of trying to wreck my livelihood for the sake of his story.

"I've heard them. But grown-up people don't listen to rumours, do they? Nice to see you, Hector."

Hector persisted. "But you believe them enough not to sign the contract." He simpered at me apologetically, then said, "Would you have another designer in mind, if this . . . fell through?"

I found myself itching to clout him. Archer smiled and shook his head, and said, "We ought to get going."

Pollitt said, "Of course," and walked away.

"Look out," said Archer. "Here comes another."

This time it was the Yachting Correspondent of the *Morning Post*. We ran along the quay and down the steps to *Nautilus'* deck.

"Phew," said Archer, and grinned. His grin was boyish and attractive, and good for at least a hundred sales a year to Padmore and Bayliss.

Nautilus was a converted twelve-metre and the light of my life. Hugo and I had found her fifteen years previously, on a mud bank near Burnham. Rebuilding her with Hugo had taught me more than any naval architecture course. As well as paint and timber and screws, we had given her part of our souls. Now she was a poem in dark green with a gold stripe, and the beauty of her was almost as good as seeing my brother again. Almost.

We slipped the mooring and went past the quay head under sail. I felt the familiar tug of the water on the wheel, and squinted up at the tower of the mainsail. Every time I came aboard *Nautilus* it was like coming home.

"Okay," said the TV director. "Now, Mr. Agutter . . . er . . . Charlie, if you could tell us who's who?"

I introduced him to Forsyth, and also to Scotto and Georgia. Scotto was an amiable blond gorilla from Christchurch, N.Z., who worked around Pulteney as a freelance boatnigger or paid hand, which meant that he spent a lot of time on *Nautilus*. Georgia, his girlfriend, had worked her way across the Atlantic from Trinidad, and was as handy on a boat as Scotto.

"Right," said the presenter. "Let's do it."

He asked me a lot of questions, and I answered them without thinking about them, because my eyes kept moving about the boat, and my mind was saying: that was the bit of deck Hugo was going to put in next week, and that was the Turk's head Hugo had tied last time we sailed up to the Skagerrak.

When he had finished with his questions, he went away to ask the crew questions about what sailing on a twelve-metre meant to them, or something. Archer came alongside me at the wheel.

He said, "Charlie, you are not going to like what I am going to tell you." I looked across at him. His blue eyes were worried in his fair-minded brown face, but his chin was stuck out, as if he had decided to do something and he was not going to be deterred.

"What," I said.

"We've decided to review our contract situation," he said.

"You mean cancel it." *Nautilus'* great white wing of sail dipped in a puff, and I brought her up delicately, delicately, till the luff shivered like a maiden's thigh.

"Don't make it awkward," said Archer. "We're holding it up pending enquiries into the *Aesthete* wreck." He spat it out as if to say, there, that's it, let's leave it.

I did not want to leave it. "You've been listening to rumours," I said. "Archer, you're a friend. What have you been hearing?"

"They're saying the rudder dropped off," Archer said. "They're saying that you won't have a boat in the Captain's Cup trials this year."

"I thought grown-up people didn't listen to rumours," I said bitterly. *Nautilus* dived into a wave with a comfortable sploosh.

Archer's blue eyes were definitely worried, now.

39

"Look," he said. "If those rumours cost us two sales, they've cost us fifty thousand quid. And they could lose us two hundred sales. See?"

"So you're dropping the contract."

"Delaying it. If you can convince us and the press that *Aesthete* was not a design problem, and if you can get a boat or two through even as far as the Captain's Cup trials, we'll all be happy. I can't say fairer than that."

"Cruel but fair," I said, ironically.

Archer said, "Don't be bloody childish, Charlie. We're bending over backwards."

"Sure," I said, and began to pass the wheel through my hands. "I think we'll go home now."

The director said, "Another twenty minutes, till the light changes?"

"Get stuffed," I said.

Scotto eased sheets, and *Nautilus'* razor nose settled on the tiered houses of Pulteney. I knew I was behaving like a madman. But now there was no Hugo and no work, I was suspended over an abyss with no visible means of support.

Except my friends, I thought. Scotto and Georgia were looking worried, and Johnny Forsyth's pock-marked face was bent to the TV director, explaining something. Explaining that I was a little jumpy, death in the family, poor fella? Or possibly doing a little hustling for a spot on the box himself.

It was always hard to tell what your friends were up to, in the sportsmanlike world of offshore racing.

6

Nurse Bollom rang down when I got home. "Your father's a bit better," she said briskly.

I went up the stairs to his part of the house.

"Barnes was here," he said. "Told me about yer brother." His eyes were pinkish blue and bright. "Yer mother would have bin terribly upset, poor gel." He paused. "Poor chap." He raised his thin shoulders in a heavy sigh. "Let's have a drink." He filled two tumblers from the bottle under his rug and gave me one. "I remember you two little beggars the day you sank that Admiral who came to open the Regatta. Pinched his bungs, didn't you?" He shook his head. "Good chap, Hugo. Damn sad." A tear formed at the corner of his eye and fell into his whisky. He drained the glass, and watched me as I did likewise, like a priest overseeing a fiery sacrament. The subject was closed.

I forced myself to tell him about the problems with Archer, concentrating with an effort. He shook his head at the mention of the name.

"Archer!" he said. "Used to be damn good when sailing was sailing. Pity to hear he's gone professional." I waited dully. The routine was a familiar one.

"'Course, when I was a lad there was none of this

money rubbish," he said. "You sailed because you ruddy well wanted to sail. Nobody gave me any money when I built *Petrel.*" He had sailed single-handed in *Petrel* from San Francisco to Yokohama in 1926. "And racing used to be fun then, as ye know. Now it's all thugs on the deck and lawyers in the cockpit. And ye can't recognize those things as boats."

"What things?"

"Those things." My heart sank as his bony liver-spotted hand rose in its familiar groping gesture. He was slipping again. "Those silver-paper canoes ye call boats. I hear one of your plastic rudders fell off."

"Who told you that?"

"Can't remember. Someone. In my day we made rudders out of oak and bound 'em with iron. Stands to reason. Where's your brother anyway? Haven't seen him for a while." I squeezed hard at the arm of the chair. "If it was me, I wouldn't give my brother a duff rudder. He's dead, someone said."

I sat there in a small personal hell as he lapsed back into his muddle, where history was tied in knots and the only fixed point was that he had someone he could trust to pay the nurse and look after him.

If things carried on as they were, I had a nasty feeling that my father's trust might be none too well placed.

I spent most of the afternoon in the office—not that there was a lot to do. But I sat at my drawing-board and tried to make a set of lines for a motor-sailer that now would probably never be built by Padmore and Bayliss. And when I had had enough of that, I gazed out of the window and watched Chiefy red-leading rust spots on the pot winch of his lobster-boat, anchored between the stone horns of the harbour. It would be a lot simpler to set lobster-pots.

The telephone rang. It was Sally. Her voice sounded as if she had a scarf wrapped hard round her neck.

"It's Henry," she said. I waited. "At the hospital. The doctor told him he'd be paralysed from the chest down. He—" Her voice disintegrated into something between a croak and a sob. I heard her take a deep breath. "He put a plastic bag over his head and killed himself," she said.

Out there, in the whip of the breeze, Chiefy's lips moved, and I knew he was singing as he chipped away the brown rust.

"I'm coming over," I said.

There was a Subaru pick-up in the drive. I walked in without knocking. A murmur of voices came from the drawing-room, and Hugo's hat was gone from the head of the Frink bird. His coats were gone from the hook by the door, too. I was looking at the place where they had been when Sally's voice came from over my shoulder.

"Has anybody found anything?" She had been crying.

"Not yet. Too much sea."

"I suppose there is. Poor Charlie, it must be hell."

"Don't worry about me," I said fatuously.

A smile broke through, making her cheeks small and round and giving her momentarily the face of a little girl. "It's better than worrying about me. I hear they think it's the steering. Come on in. Ed Beith's here."

"Horrible about Henry. How's Amy taking it?"

Sally shrugged. "Raging. You know Amy. Only—" She hesitated.

"Yes?"

"Well, she might . . . God, what a horrible thing to say. But she and Henry weren't getting on at all well. I think she might even be secretly relieved."

I thought back to my conversation with Amy. Changing his damn nappies, she had said. "You might be right."

Sally shivered, and I could see that she was close to tears again. "Come on. Drink."

It was good to be in the same room as Sally and Ed again, though it made the gap left by Hugo's absence all the more painful.

Ed was a large man with crinkly hair, dressed as usual in a dirty boiler suit. He was sitting on the sofa, clutching a glass of whisky. None of us could think of anything to say. In the end, I asked him about his problems with his boat *Crystal*. He said that she was fine, but he did not sound altogether convinced.

"But Frank Millstone wants to buy her," he said.

"I'm not surprised," I said. "She's fast."

"If she stays together," he said. "That bloody hull keeps coming apart."

"So sell her," I said.

"I don't much fancy selling anything at all to Millstone," he said. "Not after that land business."

He seemed to want the subject changed. So I told Sally about Millstone and Breen, though not about Jack Archer's big contract.

"Bastards," she said. "They can't."

"They have."

"What you need," said Ed, "is a PR trip. A junket. Take them out in some other boat with one of these rudders and convince them."

It was about the first positive suggestion anybody had made since the lifeboat had come back. It lightened the gloom perceptibly.

I laughed. "Ed wants me to convince them that Agutter's boats are fine, so Millstone will leave him alone."

"Well . . . yes," said Ed. "Why don't you borrow *Ae* off Billy Protheroe?"

"Call him now," said Sally, infected with the sudden purpose in the room. "Go on."

Ae was *Aesthete's* sister ship. She had come out of the same mould, and she was the only other yacht in the world that had *Aesthete's* revolutionary rudder technology. She was a very fast boat, and Billy Protheroe was confidently expected to sail her in the Irish Captain's Cup team.

"What will it prove?" I said. "The rudder won't cave in to order."

"It will prove you're not worried," said Sally. "Anyway, I'd like a weekend in Kinsale." She smiled, and the smile squeezed two tears out, one on either side of her small, straight nose. "The funeral's tomorrow."

So, as much to keep from thinking about funerals as anything else, I rang Billy Protheroe at his house in the dirty green hills behind Kinsale, and asked if we could borrow his boat for Saturday. Protheroe was a bloodstock dealer and loved a little gamble. The idea appealed to him greatly.

After that, all I had to do was charter an aeroplane. Then I had to issue the invitations, and hope that I had enough money left over to buy petrol to get me to the airport.

7

In films, it rains at funerals. At Pulteney, it blows. That is why the tombstones in the graveyard on top of the cliffs are propped up with piles of stones, and the church itself hides in a hollow, behind a bank of azaleas and rhododendron. The azaleas were just coming into flower, yellow against the green of the leaves, the day Hugo was buried. I stood and watched, numb, feeling the ache that the coffin's weight had produced in my shoulder, as the earth rattled on the lid. The grave was in a little forest of Agutter head-stones, in a corner near the grave of two Frenchmen blown off the French 74-gunner *Cinna* during the Napoleonic Wars.

There was a big crowd, but nobody looked at the stones. The inhabitants of Pulteney knew them off by heart, and the yachters do not care much for things like tombstones. Chiefy, who had been carrying the coffin too, said afterwards that he did not reckon many of the yachters had come out of respect for the dead; it was because they wanted to make certain sure that the town's best helmsman was nailed under six feet of earth.

They had also come to gossip. I was catching a lot of

meaningful glances from out of the corner of my eye. I found I was beginning to get angry, because this was Hugo's funeral and all these yachters were using it as a cocktail party.

Neville Spearman, owner of the yard, sidled up to me afterwards, looking, as always, haggard and a little shifty.

"Sorry about . . . all this," he said. "Look, Charlie, I had a word with Alec Breen and Frank Millstone, and they're making time to pop over to Ireland with you."

"That's very kind of you," I said.

"Oh, no," said Neville. "Self-preservation, mate. I don't want to lose the work for the yard."

"Thanks anyway, Neville," I said.

He shrugged gloomily, and shuffled away into the crowd spilling from the lych-gate. I stood there for a moment, watching people failing to catch my eye, feeling tired and hollow.

"Hi, Charlie," said a voice behind me. It was Hector Pollitt, the journalist, grinning, his expensive teeth white against his expensive tan. "How's things?"

My irritation bubbled up and spilled over. "How d'you think?"

He shook his head. "Bad business."

"Yes. Now, if you'll excuse me?"

Sally was hemmed in by men in expensive sailing clothes. She caught my eye, and I saw the whites of hers. Pollitt persisted.

"I hear you're off to Ireland for the weekend."

"True," I said.

"Would you mind if I came along for the ride?" He stood there grinning at me. You little bastard, I thought. He knew and I knew that what I was looking at was not Hector Pollitt, but a gun levelled at my head. Nothing I proved to my planeload of customers would do me any good if Hector Pollitt was not convinced.

"No," I said, with a smile that hurt my face. "Welcome aboard, Hector." Then I walked quickly away, to stop myself beating his head against a tombstone.

I found Sally with my father, in the middle of a press of people. Sally was crying. She was not making a sound and her face was quite composed, but the tears were pouring out of her long green eyes, down her cheeks and splashing off her chin onto her grey silk double-breasted jacket. My father, crouched in his wheelchair wearing a blue serge suit, looked completely lost. He was staring at a yachter standing in front of him and saying in a distant, reflective voice, "What an enormous arse!"

I took them away. We were meant to go and drink tea at Sally's house, with the rest. But we left the tea ladies to dish out the tea, collected Ed Beith and Chiefy and some other very old friends, and went back to my house, where we sat out of the breeze in the sun, and drank whisky till we all wept.

During the days that followed, the wind continued to blow and the seas to roar among the Teeth. The telephone in my office remained silent, except for journalists looking for quotes on what they now referred to as the *Aesthete* disaster. My father had taken a violent turn after the funeral, and his confused roarings were making the house miserable. Furthermore, I knew that Nurse Bollam needed paying, and that I was good for about two more months' salary. The trip to Kinsale, which had started by resembling an unpleasant duty, was beginning to look like a holiday in the sun.

I arranged to pick Sally up on the Saturday morning at eight-thirty. A thin drizzle was hissing in from the sea, and the met. report spoke of Atlantic lows. But she waved cheerfully from the doorstep, and jumped into the car with a happy anticipation that was a joy to

48

look at. At the funeral, she had looked grey and ghostly; this morning, she looked as fresh as a glass of orange juice. Her amazing skin was shining, her eyes gleamed, and her short dark hair was crisp and bright against her neck.

"So," she said, "what's the timetable?"

"Rendezvous Plymouth airport, 10 A.M., for coffee and dirty looks. Personnel: Archer, Breen, Millstone, Pollitt, first class. Steerage: you, me, Gloria, Scotto. Lunch Protheroe, so he can get the gossip. Sail, subjecting boat to cruel and unusual punishment."

"What do you mean?"

"As tour guide, one likes to keep a little something up one's sleeve."

"All right. Next, please."

"Drinks and dinner with my friend Protheroe, bloodstock man and owner of *Ae.*"

"Must we?"

"Public relations," I said. "Protheroe's keen on the new rudder. He'll make the others jealous and there's nothing as convincing as jealousy."

"Oh," she said. "In that case."

The rest of the journey passed in sprightly vein, despite the drizzle that continued to fall and the grim suburbs of Plymouth that climb the hill to the airport. We got out of the car in an extremely good mood. Unfortunately, the mood did not survive the atmosphere of the private waiting-room I had engaged.

The First Class and the Steerage were already there. Frank was talking to Archer and Pollitt.

Breen looked up from the corner where he was making notes on a copy of the *Financial Times* with a gold pen. He was small and thick-set with a shock of wavy grey hair and his inevitable Romeo y Julieta.

"Charlie!" he called, and came forward and shook my hand in his chubby, dry hand. As he shook, I could feel myself being pushed backwards into a corner. Breen never did anything without a reason.

When he had me in the corner he took his cigar out of his mouth and fixed me with a cold eye.

"Charlie, I must tell you I needed some persuading to come along," he said. "Let's sit down." We sat. That made us both the same height. "I've come because I think you're good, and I want you to get through this bad patch, and I believe in supporting talent. As long," he said, "as it delivers. Okay?" He smiled and clapped me on the back. "That's all," he said, and walked back to his FT. I went over and ordered coffee.

Pollitt grinned.

Archer said, "Morning, Charlie," and bent his diplomat's ear back to what Pollitt was saying.

Millstone shook hands with his unnecessarily powerful grip and said in a soft, confidential voice, "Word in your ear, Charlie. What are you up to, then?" The eyes were blue chips in the nests of wrinkles, and his mouth an unfeeling slot full of teeth.

"Up to?"

"We were sorry not to see you after the funeral."

"Were you?" I said. I had no idea what he was getting at.

"Yes," he said. "Very sorry. You know, in a way death is a . . . community occasion. And in a community like Pulteney, close-knit as it were, we've got to all pull together."

"Have we?" I could feel myself getting angry.

"Yes. We all liked Hugo," said Frank. "We all wanted to . . . rally round. But you weren't there. Amy Charlton had lost Henry, after all. But you persuaded Sally to go home with you."

"Frank," I said. "Hugo was Sally's husband and my brother. Don't you think you should mind your own bloody business?"

"Pulteney is my business," he said. "Where would it be without me?"

"Money can buy houses. Some houses. But it can't

50

buy people, Frank," I said. And as soon as I said it, I knew I had gone too far. Millstone fixed me with those icy eyes, and his enormous torso swelled and shrank, swelled and shrank, as he took two deep breaths. Then he turned and went to the coffee tray and poured himself a cup and drank it in one gulp.

Public relations, I thought. Agutter, you stupid bastard.

"This way, please," said the stewardess.

On the plane, Sally gripped my hand. "You look terrible," she said. "What's happened?" I told her. "Pretentious oaf," she said. "Pay no attention."

The Twin Otter accelerated down the runway and jumped into the air. We bumped up to five thousand feet, and I calmed down. When we were at our cruising altitude I went to the table, where the First Class were sitting, and said, "Before we get to the other end, has anyone got any questions?"

"A little detail on *Ae,* please," said Breen.

"*Aesthete*'s sister ship. Same number of hours afloat, same layout and equipment, including steering gear. I want you, as owners—"

"Potential owners," said Frank Millstone, with a sullen shifting of his great body in the seat.

"—as potential owners, to see for yourselves how the system works. Naturally, Hector will be telling his readers about it, too."

"For better or worse," said Pollitt, and giggled.

8

Returning to a yacht you have built yourself is an odd sensation. It was high water, and *Ae* was tied up alongside the quay, a huge grey plastic willow-leaf against the dirty green of the Kinsale water. The deck of an offshore racer is almost flat. Aft is the trench, a long waist-deep slot in the deck with a companionway at its forward end, flanked by the big barrels of the winches that control sails, halyards and runners. Below is a cabin, with the most minimal galley that can be got away with under the International Offshore Rule, radio and navigating gear, ten pipe cots made of nylon webbing on aluminium tubing, a lot of sailbags and nothing else. Give or take a winch, most offshore racing-boats have a pretty similar layout.

Sally was very quiet as we went below, stored our gear, and came up again. *Ae* was *Aesthete*'s double; she was being reminded of things best left.

Protheroe had come down to see us off and, incidentally, to give his wandering hands a walk over Georgia. He was a long, gloomy-looking man, with a convivial red nose and a cold eye.

Standing on the dock with his hands in his pockets, he said, "Well, I'd say you know your way round.

Don't break her, now. We had the steering checked the day before yesterday at Hegarty's yard." He climbed the iron ladder up to the quay.

The engine whirred, and *Ae* turned slowly. Then she got the ebb under her nose, came round, and started towards the open sea. Her halyards slapped the metal of her mast. The wind tried to get under her bow and swing her. She lurched a little in the wavelets it made on the tide. It took a cold twenty minutes to get to the channel end buoy. The wind-speed and direction indicator read 26 knots, S.W. It drove low grey squalls of cloud over the humpback of the Old Head of Kinsale three miles away, and streaked the dirty grey Atlantic with lines of foam.

Scotto looped the halyards onto the cabin winches and heaved up main and genoa. I gave the helm to Archer. Above, the unsheeted sails roared. I wound her genoa sheet onto the winch and took up the slack. The sail rippled hugely. I cranked the winch, Scotto heaved on the mainsheet, and Archer eased the wheel a fraction to starboard. The wind snapped into the sails from over the starboard bow. *Ae* dug her port rail into the grey Atlantic and surged forward.

Frank Millstone's big face was already red and blue with cold. He dived below and came back wearing yellow wet-gear. The others already had theirs on. *Ae*'s sharp bow met the first of the Atlantic waves from the open water beyond the lighthouse which stands at the tip of the Old Head. Spray whizzed astern, and I heard Sally laugh.

Ae was as close to the wind as she would go. The lighthouse was coming up abeam.

"I'll take her," I said to Archer. He stepped aside.

"Hold tight," I said.

And for the next hour I took *Ae* and knocked hell out of her. First, we went a couple of miles out to sea. Then, by way of crescendo, we came in under the Old Head. There is a heavy tide-race off the Old Head, and today the wind was setting against the tide, raising a fierce short sea. Scotto and I flung *Ae* at it, and she took it like a railway engine running over a beach of boulders. She crashed into the waves, and the water flew in sheets, and the passengers shut their eyes and hung on. Finally, well past the Head, I turned her quarter to sea and Scotto flew the big spinnaker. A gleam of sun pierced the overcast sky and lit the green-and-orange belly of the sail. Glittering fans of water swept from under the flare of her bow and turned to rainbows in the sun as she tobogganed down the face of a wave. The log needle swept up and round to eighteen knots.

Sally's face broke into a sudden, dazzling smile. She dug Hector in the ribs and said, "Write that down."

Hector leaned over the side and vomited. Frank Millstone shook his head, smiling; his eyes were no warmer. Archer caught my eye and winked. The next wave came under the stern.

"I haven't finished," I said. "Scotto, fly us the number four genny."

Spray from the next wave squirted from under the bow as Scotto wrestled with the billowing sail. The spinnaker came down. Beyond it, the clouds were separating, revealing ragged-edged patches of blue. The anemometer read twenty-five knots. As I turned the wheel and laid *Ae* on the wind, the iron-taut rigging began to scream. Down went the lee rail, and the water began to arrive aboard—not the fine, hissing spray of the downwind leg, but blustering lumps of Atlantic as *Ae* stuck her nose into the tide-race. The lighthouse came up over the bow.

"Action replay," I said. "That lighthouse is the Teeth. Round we go."

Millstone, Breen and Archer were torn between watching me and watching the foaming cliffs of the Old Head two hundred yards away. They knew that *Ae* was doing exactly what *Aesthete* had been doing a few seconds before the end. Pollitt must have realised, too, because he was sick again. And Sally—well, I didn't look at Sally. She had a good imagination, and it would be working on Hugo.

Ae plunged into the waves, kicking. The lighthouse was close abeam now.

"Easy," I said.

A big wave came under the boat; I felt her go up. The wind battered at us, the anemometer needle swinging to thirty knots. We were so close to the Head that I could see the individual tufts of bladder-wrack. Hector turned away and retched over the side again.

"She takes it nicely," I said. "No problem."

"This is bloody stupid," said Millstone. "There wouldn't be, would there? Can we go home now?"

Breen said mildly, "I'm finding this most interesting." His Romeo y Julieta had gone out, doused by a wave. His eyes and the cigar end stared at me, three disconcerting black holes.

The lighthouse was past the sightline scored on the deck.

"Paying off—" I said.

I never finished the sentence. *Ae* toppled sideways off the slope of the big wave, landing in a cushion of spray. The wheel kicked hard. There was a slight jolting sensation. Then everything happened at once.

The sails began to flap and drum, and the nose swept up and round, head to wind. *Ae* rolled forty-five degrees back on herself. Pollitt slumped to the cockpit floor and I saw Millstone's mouth, wide with surprise, as it went underwater and came back up again, spluttering. Breen was halfway up on one knee as we went, and the lurch knocked him over. There was a vicious crack as his head hit a winch and I saw Scotto grab his ankle, wrapping his own leg round a stanchion with an extraordinary octopus-like movement, as the side went under. Georgia's arms embraced a winch and she stuck to it, eyes tight shut. Archer

55

staggered, caught himself, and came back on his feet like a tennis-player preparing for the next shot. Sally had grabbed my waist, and the wind whipped her hair back into my eyes.

I could hear a sort of dim roaring that was not the sea; human voices, panicking. But I could not do anything. Millstone's face loomed before mine, red-eyed and blue-veined, yelling. *Ae* rolled back on herself, then to leeward again. But there was nothing I could do except spin the wheel, port then starboard, and think: some bloody PR trip.

Millstone's face came up again. This time, I could hear what he said. "What are you doing?" he bellowed.

I answered him so the others could hear. "It's the steering," I said. "It seems to have failed."

9

For a split second, there was complete silence, as it sank in. I heard Archer say quietly, "Christ." Then Millstone started to shout, and so did Pollitt, and the clamour gained a new and sharper edge as their eyes shifted from the boat. What they were looking at was the high black cliff fifty yards downwind. They were measuring the time it would take us to hit it. And they were coming to conclusions.

Pollitt, on his knees, started to yell. So did Millstone. I shouted, "Shut up!" and hit the engine starter-button. Nothing happened.

Archer and the other three were already moving into position.

"Everybody quiet," I said. "Archer, mainsheet." I willed my fingers not to freeze on the wheel. The noise of wave on cliff was a dull, stunning rumble. But the heart started beating again, as it does, and the knees strengthened.

We were in half a gale, on a lee shore. Overhead, the sails, unsheeted, walloped at the wind. Hector was still staring at me, silent now, the colour of putty. So was Frank Millstone. I felt frightened and responsible and very silly. At that moment, I have to say that I did not much care if the cliffs got me. But there were the others and in particular Sally, who was crouched over Sir Alec. But there was no time to worry about how I felt, or how anybody felt.

I yelled up to Scotto, "Back the jib!"

He understood, retrieved the flailing sheet and hauled in. The nose came off the wind. Archer was hauling on his mainsheet, and as the nose came off the main filled.

"Bring the jib across when I say," I shouted to Scotto. "Frank, crank the engine! Sally, flares! Georgia, radio!"

It is by no means difficult to sail a boat without a rudder, if you know the boat well. The secret lies in the fact that the mainsail, being aft of the keel, tends to pivot the boat into the wind while the jib, being forward of the keel, tends to pivot it away from the wind. It is an exercise that most dinghy sailors can perform, in harbour in a light breeze. In a force six and a sea that has travelled all the way across the Atlantic for the express purpose of slamming itself into the cliffs of the Old Head, it is not so easy. But I stood there and shouted orders to Scotto and Archer, while Georgia and Sally dragged Breen down to the cabin, followed by Millstone. The motion eased as soon as the sails were full; pitching and yawing, *Ae* began to creep ahead. But by this time the cliffs were a mere forty-five yards away, and we were in the fringes of the white water from the backwash.

High on the cliffs, I could see the tiny figure of a man, looking down. He waved. I waved back, praying that he would get the message. But he stayed and watched the fascinating spectacle of the little yacht floundering in the boiling foam. Then Sally came up with the flares, and the first red comet whizzed into the sky. Still the man stood.

The cliffs of the west coast of the Old Head run

northwest for perhaps half a mile before they fall away northward. If we could make that half-mile without being pulped on the cliffs, we would have plenty of clear water between us and the shore.

Millstone appeared at the hatch. "Bloody thing won't start," he roared.

I could hear Georgia below, giving the boat's name and position. And I could imagine the news spreading from the aerial at the transom: steering failure on yacht *Ae* after a similar accident a week previously on her sister ship; designer Charlie Agutter claims no problem with steering-gear; it'll be better for old Agutter if he hits the cliffs and doesn't get home. But there was no point worrying about that, for the moment.

"Can you take her, Archer?" I said. "I want to go below and have a look."

"Sure," said Archer, squinting at the sails, then at the cliffs. We had made perhaps two hundred yards. But the cliffs were only forty yards away now. "Mend it if you can, old boy." Even now, he managed to exude reassurance.

"I will."

The steering-gear was housed under the cockpit sole. I grabbed a torch and wriggled in. It was a very simple mechanical steering-gear, steel wires running from the wheel across pulleys to the rudder stock. Protheroe had not been fibbing when he said he had had it checked. It was gleaming with grease, and it looked exactly as it had when I had passed it out of the yard the previous autumn. I followed it through to where the stock of the rudder disappeared through the yacht's bottom.

It was in excellent shape, which was a disaster, because the novel parts of the system were outside the hull—as far away as China in this sea. And it was that part of it that had gone wrong. The full implications

59

didn't bear thinking about, but I thought about them anyway for perhaps five seconds, lying in that greasy, little plastic coffin. Then I wriggled out into the cabin.

Sally was bending over Breen, who had lost his menace and now looked small, white and sick. She glanced up at me. Her skin was like paper and there were tears on her face. She said, "He's all right. Concussion, I think. Charlie, I am sorry."

"The lifeboat's on its way," said Georgia, from the radio.

I smiled at Sally, with difficulty. It was typical of her that she had not mentioned what she was thinking: this was just what had happened to Hugo.

As I came through the hatch, I was deafened by the shriek of the wind and the thunder of the waves at the foot of the cliff. We were thirty yards off now, and as I stood up I saw the wave that had passed under us turn white ten yards to starboard and collapse in a smother of foam.

Millstone had been watching it, too. He shouted, "Why don't we anchor?"

"Because if the hook doesn't hold, we'll pile up."

Millstone said, furiously, "You crazy bastard, I never thought you'd bring her in this close."

"Unlash the life raft," I said. "Get it ready to go." I put my head down the hatch and said, "On deck, all of you."

The man on the cliff above had been joined by others. They were no longer waving; they were watching, motionless. There was nothing they could do. No rocket-lines: nothing. And we had two hundred yards to sail to the point and the wind was blasting out of the southwest. The masthead lurched crazily against the sky, which was now as blue as blue; and *Ae* sailed on, staggering, but moving forward.

Archer said, "I think we'll make it," conversationally, as if discussing a walk in the park. And it looked as if we would, just, if we could keep her on her heading.

When I lined mast and forestay against the point we had to round, I saw that we were about ten yards clear.

"Keep her sailing," I said, unnecessarily.

Then it happened.

The tiny figures on the clifftop disappeared behind a rock, and I remember thinking: there must be an overhang. Then everything flapped and *Ae* came onto an even keel as the wind bounced downwards, rocked her back to windward, and knocked her sails empty. In the tiny silence that ensued, Scotto's voice said, "Whoops!" A wave shoved the stern shorewards, pointing the nose up towards the wind.

"Back your sail, Scotto," I said, equally quietly.

Then the wind came back with a roar. Scotto scrambled forward like a giant ape and grabbed the leech of the sail in his vast hands. Millstone's mouth yelled curses from his doughy face. *Ae*'s nose came round and we were sailing again. But she had lost ground. Now the nose pointed not at the open sea, but at a big, black cliff with a tangle of foam-lashed boulders at its foot.

I got her sailing again. The wake bubbled from her stern, mixing with the white foam. The cliff raced up to meet us. We would hit bang on the point . . .

Bang on the point.

The stern lifted under the next wave. The wave broke as soon as it had passed under her bottom. The next one would take us with it.

"Let go genoa!" I shouted to Scotto.

As he let go, I joined Archer on the mainsheet, giving it a final crank that brought *Ae*'s nose hard onto the wind in a lurching luff that carried her over the top of the wave. But the rock was on us now. Scotto crouched in the pulpit with the spinnaker pole, the cliffs reeling round his head. I found I wanted to laugh. Crazy idiot, I thought; did he think he could fend off forty-nine feet of surfing boat with that thing?

We were so close that I could actually smell the

weed and see individual winkles. Someone, probably Millstone, was bellowing in the far distance about life rafts. It was too late for life rafts. The backwash from the last wave swirled in the ten-foot gap between the boat and the rock. I drew breath, to have air in my lungs when the moment came. The next wave, the fatal one, hunched ugly grey shoulders to seaward.

The backwash pushed us off. The gap widened to forty feet.

I yelled, "Genoa, Scotto!"

Scotto heaved in the sheet and *Ae* shot past the headland with six feet to spare. As we passed, there was a dreadful crash and a jolt that knocked me flying. Then the land fell away and we had a hundred beautiful yards of clear water to starboard and everyone was talking at once because the lifeboat was round the point and cruising down to take us in tow.

I talked and laughed with the rest of them, lightheaded with relief.

Scotto and Archer banged each other on the back.

"Brilliant," I said. "Nicely done."

10

When I went below, Sir Alec was on a bunk. He was pale, but his eyes were open, and the tautness had come back into him. He didn't say anything, but those eyes rolled over at me like gun barrels. Sally was dabbing at the side of his head with a wet rag, and his wavy, grey hair was plastered to his skull. She looked at me and then down at my feet, pointedly. I had already seen it: a couple of inches of water over the cabin sole. The pump handle was clipped to the bulkhead where the head would have been if there had been a head. The waves boomed in the hollow cavities of the stripped-out hull as I slotted in the handle and began pumping.

The rhythm was lulling, a metronome for the thoughts; the thoughts were not. Hugo, Henry, *Aesthete, Ae*, Millstone, Archer, Alec Breen. Round and round the names went, marching to the beat of the pump. The water level stayed constant.

Breen said, "Well, Charlie, this looks like the finish, eh?" Then he moved slowly and ponderously onto the deck; I could hear him being sick. And Sally unclipped another pump handle and pumped too, with her knee touching mine.

"I'm sorry," she said.

"Can't be helped," I said. But it could have been helped. Somehow. The names kept marching. And, as they marched, there rose before my eyes the structural engineers' reports on the rudders. And the conviction grew in me that something was not right. In fact, something was very, very wrong.

Protheroe was waiting on the quay, dressed in a tweed suit and a Lock's felt hat, sad-eyed and impassive, every inch the bloodstock man. The others waited in a soggy group, watching as he came up to me. His eye was cold as a gull's. I steeled myself.

"What's happened?" he said.

"Rudder failure." There was a pause; he nodded, and I could read in that nod what he thought of new-fangled rudders that failed. "I want to take her round to Hegarty's at Crosshaven for a full inspection."

"And it's not just the rudder, I hear." His voice was cold and deliberate, but there was a hiss in it. He was very angry. I couldn't blame him.

"No. We hit a rock. The keel bolts are sprung."

"Ah," Protheroe fingered his chin. "Sounds like it'll cost the odd quid."

"That's down to me."

"Ah," said Protheroe. "Well, now. Your lot'll be wanting to get back, and I'll take them, so."

They started to climb into the minibus. They all made way for Breen. Frank Millstone was issuing loud instructions to someone to turn on the damned heater, and Hector Pollitt was muttering into a portable dictaphone.

For the first time since I had known him, Archer seemed embarrassed. He came and planted himself in front of me, and seemed about to say something, and to stop himself at the last minute. In the end, he clapped me on the shoulder and said, "Sorry," and climbed in. Scotto winked and Georgia came and squeezed my hand. It was all very awkward and embarrassing—not unlike a funeral. My funeral.

Sally hung back.

"Come on," said Frank Millstone irritably from the bus.

She took my arm. I looked down at her and she smiled at me out of her long, shadowed eyes. The pressure of her hand on my arm was the warmest thing I have ever felt.

Hector Pollitt stared at us, his face inward-looking and calculating until he caught me looking back. Then he put on his false smile and waved.

"Hurry up! I'm freezing," said Frank Millstone.

Sally held my arm for a moment longer. Then she said quietly, "I can't face that lot tonight. I'll hire a car and bring your stuff to Crosshaven. The Marine Bar." Then she went over to the minibus.

The sun had come out now, and the shadows of herring gulls flicked across her as she walked across the stones of the quay. Hector Pollitt put out a hand to help her into the bus. The doors slammed, and streets swallowed the noise of its engine. I turned away, thinking of Pollitt's Judas grin.

It looked like Charlie Agutter might be in need of industrial retraining.

They put a motor pump aboard *Ae* and we towed her round to Crosshaven behind a fishing-boat. At Hegarty's, they pulled her out on the crane and wheeled her into the shed.

Billy Hegarty, who ran the yard, was an old friend, a small man like an exceptionally well-dressed gnome. When I asked if I could take a look at the boat, he said, "Well, I don't know about that," and avoided my eye.

Billy had easily built a dozen boats for me. Now his small, rumpled face was more than usually creased, and I could guess why.

"You've heard the rumours then, Billy?"

"I have."

"And old Protheroe's worried I might be fingering this and that to hide the evidence."

"That's about the size of it, now."

"So he rang you to say not to let me in."

"Right."

"Okay." I couldn't ask Billy to go against Protheroe. Protheroe was a ruthless bastard, and he was worth good money to Billy. "Well, I'd say I'll just have to lump it."

The cracks in Billy's face deepened. "Jesus, Charlie," he said in disgust. "'Tis a bad business, so." He lit a Sweet Afton and puffed at it like a steam engine. Finally, he said, "I'm away to the wife's sister's wedding. Protheroe's coming too. It's above in Bandon, and we'll be away in a half-hour."

"Well now," I said, understanding that loyalty to me had triumphed over loyalty to Protheroe. "Look out for yourself, Billy."

"And the same to you. The fella'll come and let out the guard dog in a couple of hours." He handed me a Yale key. Then with a level glare from his dark blue eyes, he marched away to his car.

It was six o'clock. Dinghies were scudding in the harbour, and gulls wheeled over the Marine Bar's dustbins. I turned away, as if to walk along the beach. When I was in dead ground behind a thicket of gorse and old oil drums, I doubled back.

I came up on the blind side of the sheds. The door of Shed C said PRIVATE—NO ADMITTANCE. My feet rang on the concrete inside. *Ae* sat like a big, silver whale on the cradles, gleaming in the pale light from the perspex sections in the roof. I stopped. The shed was cool and quiet as a cave; the only sound was the drip of water from her hull.

I walked across to her, and pushed the rudder. It rotated free on the stock, which did not move—which should have been impossible.

My rudders are moveable-silhouette aerofoils. When the helmsman turns the wheel, the first five degrees of movement turns a cam inside the rudder, which distorts the flexible surface of the side of the rudder opposite to the one in which he has turned the wheel. This reduces the water pressure on that side, producing lift, so the stern half of the boat is actually sucked in that direction; the bow, of course, turns in the direction intended. Each time a helmsman steers with a conventional rudder he baffles the water and obstructs the boat, slowing it down. With my system, the baffling effect is enormously reduced—with the result that my boats are faster and demand less muscle-power from the helmsman.

I lugged across a step-ladder, borrowed a toolbox from one of the workbenches and went to work.

The rudder is an aerofoil of foam and carbon fibre. It fits snugly onto the stock that bears the cams, held in place by a pair of flush-head bolts.

The bolts were in place, their tops gleaming in the late sun from the rooflights.

I attacked them with a big screwdriver, removed the fin and laid it carefully on the concrete floor. Then I returned to the shaft. What I saw froze me solid.

The titanium bolts locking the cams cost twenty pounds each. Perhaps that was why someone had taken them out and replaced them with ordinary quarter-inch aluminium bolts.

All the aluminium bolts had broken, allowing the rudderstock free play in the cams. That was why the steering had gone. It was amazing it had lasted as long as it did.

Carefully, I replaced the shattered bolts in their holes, hoisted the rudder blade back into position and fastened the top bolts. Then I let myself out of the back of the shed, drew the door behind me, skirted back to the beach and walked slowly towards the Marine Bar.

Around me, the steep banks of the harbour were green in the late sun, and gulls screamed. I walked through them in a trance. Sabotage. A word from the Second World War. Not one generally used in connection with sailing races.

I pushed at the frosted glass door and entered the stale tobacco fug of the Marine Bar. Sally was waiting in the window, beside a pile of seabags. She took one look at my face, ordered a hot whisky, and moved herself to a chair beside the coal fire. I realized that I was still wet, and freezing cold.

She said, "What happened?"

"Somebody sabotaged the rudder," I said. Her glass stopped dead, halfway from the table to her mouth. I watched her face go still and pale as it sank in.

"Does that mean someone sabotaged *Aesthete?*"

"It might, mightn't it?"

"So Hugo was murdered? And Henry?"

"It would amount to that," I said. "Not that it would be a very clever way of doing it. Unreliable."

She nodded.

"Two boats," I said. "Both with my new rudder. Both with steering failure. What does it add up to?"

"Someone doesn't like your rudder."

"Which is bloody stupid."

"Or somebody doesn't like you."

"Which is likelier." I meditated for a moment. "Because it doesn't matter that it was only the rudder that went. What they'll be saying is that my boats won't take a hammering. And once word gets round . . ." I laughed, without being amused. "It's already got round. You heard Breen. I'm finished."

"Until you show someone those bolts."

I drew strength from her level green eyes. "I can't get the bolts," I said. "Billy Hegarty would be crucified if anyone knew he'd let me in. And the dog's on duty by now, so I can't go back."

"So," she said. "Someone's killed Hugo and Henry

and is trying to wreck your reputation. But you're not allowed to tell anyone." She finished her drink. "Who'd do a thing like this?"

"It's either an incompetent murderer, or someone who hates my guts on general principles, or someone who doesn't want me in the Captain's Cup team, or someone who thinks I don't deserve to design for Padmore and Bayliss . . . Hell's teeth, this is offshore racing. You can't help making enemies."

"*Aesthete* could have been an accident."

"It could have been," I said. Neither of us believed a word of it.

"Will you go to the police?"

I finished my whisky. "No," I said.

"What, then?"

"I'm going to get one of my boats into the Captain's Cup team," I said. "And I'm going to find out who's behind all this."

"I hired a car," said Sally. "And I booked us in to the Shamrock, in Kinsale. I thought you wouldn't want to see Protheroe."

"Telepathic," I said. "But I want to ring Protheroe first."

Irish telephone boxes always make me laugh with their emergency services instructions: dial 999 for Gardai, ambulance or clergy. I grinned into the telephone as the ringing tone sounded; then I realised that it was the first time I had been amused by anything for days. An answering machine asked me to leave a message after the tone. I told it my whereabouts and went back to Sally.

News of the accident had evidently gone round Kinsale like a bush fire. Even the receptionist at the Shamrock commiserated as we signed the register.

"Fierce bad luck," he said, and told us about his life, which had been spent following offshore racing. "Sorry for your trouble," he said to Sally, in the time-honoured formula of the Irish funeral.

We dined at Ballymaloe. It was hard to feel as if we were living under the shadow of sabotage and murder, with lobster and Pouilly Fumé on the table and Sally on the far side of it. We had an almost light-hearted evening. Partly, it was the removal of uncertainty. But partly, it was something else; something I did not feel like admitting to myself, because it made me feel disloyal to Hugo; but something that Sally felt too, because on the way back to the hotel she wound her fingers into mine, and we walked very close from the carpark to the lobby. It was the need for mutual comfort, I told myself after I had kissed her goodnight outside her room. The world had shown itself big, cold and deadly, and humans will crowd up for warmth. That was all.

Next morning, the telephone rang at eight. It was Protheroe.

"I had your message," he said.

"I'd like to be there when they strip down the rudder for you." I could feel a new confidence in my voice.

"Of course," said Protheroe, mildly. "The fella from Lloyd's wants to see too. He's coming in to Cork at 11:30 and I'm picking him up after Mass, God help me. So will we say half-twelve?"

11

It was a lovely morning. The wooded shores of Crosshaven had their feet in the water as the hired car snaked along the lane above the harbour, and the sun was turning the oaks a brilliant green.

It was cool in Billy's big corrugated iron shed and the high roof blurred the voices of the three men standing round *Ae*'s stern. There was Protheroe and Billy Hegarty and André Martin, the man from Lloyd's. I had met him before, when I had been trying to convince the underwriters that my rudders were an insurable proposition. He was smooth and rotund, with upward-slanting eyes that never held any expression. He had been hard to convince, I remembered. Still, that was his job. There shouldn't be any trouble this morning.

After we had exchanged greetings, Martin took charge.

"So you think it's sabotage," he said. "We've taken the liberty of examining the parts that show."

I shrugged. "Fine."

"So now we'll dismantle the rudder itself." He peered at the retaining bolts. "I take it we're agreed that there are no marks of violence here?"

We looked after him. There were no scratches on the retaining bolts. Whoever had sabotaged the rudder had been careful, and so had I last night.

"Billy?"

Billy Hegarty took out the retaining bolts and lowered the rudder blade. We closed in to examine the shaft. Billy put up his hand and pulled out a fragment of a bolt. "Them's the fellas went," he said.

"Well?" said Martin. "Have you anything to say, Mr. Agutter?"

I stared at the broken pieces of metal in Billy's hand. "Impossible," I croaked, from a dry throat. For the bolts that last night had been made of aluminium had somehow, unbelievably, changed. Now the splintered fragments in the calloused palm of Billy's hand had the bright, satiny sheen of titanium. "Impossible," I said again.

"'Fraid not," said Martin. "Mr. Agutter, I think that, pending tests of these bolts, you should tell your clients that Lloyd's are refusing a certificate to craft fitted with this type of rudder. And the same will, I suspect, go for the International Offshore Rating authorities."

Protheroe fixed me with his gull's eye. He said, "You've let me down, boy," turned and walked away beside Martin. I knew that was the last I would see of Protheroe, client. The shed door closed with a tinny slam. I sat down suddenly on a crate.

After a decent interval, Billy said, "They shouldn't have gone, not titanium bolts."

"They didn't," I said. I told him what I had found the previous night. "So somebody must have had them out and put them in a vice and smashed 'em, and switched the bits back last night after I'd gone. Did you see anyone?"

"Sure I was at the wedding." Billy's dark blue eyes shifted away from mine. I could see he only half believed me.

"You mentioned a guard dog."

"Ah, when I came in this morning the bloody thing was asleep."

"Where is it now?"

"I couldn't say."

We walked round to the back of the shed. A large alsatian was lying in the sun, sleeping. Billy went up to it and prodded it with his foot. It opened an eye, then went back to sleep.

"Funny," said Billy. "Normally he'd have the leg off you." He prodded it again, harder, and shook it for a bit. This time, the dog did not even open an eye.

"Was there a watchman on?" I said.

"There was. But he does spend all the night in the Marine, below."

"Great," I said, with irony.

"Which isn't so stupid when you think there's only the one road," said Billy. "If there'd be a car or a man he wouldn't recognise, he'd be out of there like a shot."

"Could we ask him?" I said.

"Sure he'll be on his bed," said Hegarty. "But I'll ring him." He walked across to the wall phone above the littered workbench and spoke at length. Finally he came back. "There was nobody," he said.

"It's what they call an inside job, then?"

Billy made a face. "I bloody well hope not," he said. "There's something wrong with that dog, though."

"Yes." I looked down at my feet, bowed under a grey weight of gloom. "If you could do a stress test on the bolts, and a dope test on the dog? And you'd better mend the boat and send me the bill."

Billy nodded.

"And you might ask around a bit among your men, you know."

"I will," said Billy. His wrinkles conveyed worry and distaste. "But they're good lads."

"See what you come up with," I said. "I've got to get back to England. I'll be back, though. Soon."

We shook hands. I walked slowly back to the car, looked at the OS map, then drove among the tiny lanes to the top of the cliff to the west of Crosshaven. It was a forlorn hope—the nearest approach to Crosshaven by road without actually passing through the village.

The beach path started here. The wind bent the plumes from the tall chimneys of Whitegate oil refinery across the water. The ground was soft in the parking space at the end of the lane; a couple of disused coastguard houses crouched among blackish-green gorse bushes. I stooped, looking in the peaty, black mud. There were footmarks, not too blurred, small, a woman's probably, with domed hobnails. They led down to the beach and back. On the beach, they were lost in soft sand. I walked back to one of the houses and knocked on the door, then tried the other. They were empty, waiting for the season. Their black panes watched me impassively as I got back into the car and drove away.

I told Sally. She took it in silence. Last night had turned leaden. We were both occupied with our own thoughts and the silence continued as I carried her bags down and went to pay the bill.

The ocean racing receptionist was on duty. I had no desire to discuss yesterday's events, but he had.

"And I heard about that other trouble you had, in England, with Mr. Charlton getting killed and all. The poor woman," said the receptionist. "But I'd say she's a brave one."

"What on earth are you talking about?" I said.

"Mrs. Charlton. Oh, she looked great this morning. I followed it in the English papers."

"Amy . . . Mrs. Charlton was here?"

"Surely you saw her?"

"No."

"Well now. She's just after checking out herself."

"Is she really?" I said. What the hell had Amy been doing here? Then I thought about footprints and said, "What was she wearing on her feet?"

"On her feet?" said the receptionist.

"Yes." I felt a complete idiot.

"Wellingtons. Green ones. Them ones with the studs," said the receptionist, frowning. "I'd say you'd meet at the airport. That'll be nice, won't it?"

But we did not meet.

I told the Protheroe party to go back without me. I did not feel I could face them for the moment. Before Sally and I caught the afternoon flight, I checked at the information desk that Amy was not on any of the rest of the day's passenger lists. Perhaps she had gone by boat, or by Dublin.

All the way home, Amy's green wellingtons marched through my thoughts.

No, I kept telling myself: it was absurd, far too much like a real coincidence. I wished I had had time to hang about in Ireland, and make some serious inquiries. But time was passing, and the Captain's Cup trials were looming close, and I had to do something about getting in there.

As everyone knows, the Captain's Cup is much more important than little niggles about sabotage and murder.

12

I dropped Sally at home that evening. Halfway back along the high-banked lane to Pulteney is the turning to Brundage, where Henry Charlton had lived. A hundred yards past it, I slammed on the brakes, reversed, and took the Brundage road. I had to talk to Amy. It was going to be nasty, so I wanted to get it over with.

She lived in a converted water-mill. The gates were shut and there were no cars on the smoothly-raked gravel of the drive. I crunched across the gravel and knocked on the door. The housekeeper, fat and solemn, said Mrs. Charlton wouldn't be back until late tonight, poor thing. I told her to say I'd called, and went home.

My father was making a mess of a soft-boiled egg, watching *Songs of Praise* with every evidence of enjoyment. I wanted to talk to somebody; but he was obviously not on form. So I went through to my own quarters, decided not to drink any whisky, and rang Georgia.

She came at about eight, with shopping bags, looking like an Indian temple sculpture in paint-spattered jeans and an old blue guernsey. We sat at the walnut table eating fried chicken she had cooked.

I said, "Tell me what happened in Ireland after we left."

"We went back to Protheroe's. Protheroe had to go out, but we sat around, had a few drinks, you know. It wasn't a very jolly party."

"Did anyone go out?"

"Are you kidding? Nowhere to go. Anyway, old Breen was feeling pretty bad. Well, we all were."

"So you just hung around and went to bed."

"We played poker," she said. "Archer was hassling me a bit. He always does, me and anyone else who happens to be female. It's real flattering." She made a face.

"Really," I said. "Archer? He's always seemed so, well, statesmanlike."

"Anyway, I went to bed soon after that, and Scotto came too. The other guys stayed up late. Then this morning nobody said much at breakfast and we all came home in that plane."

"And as far as you know nobody went out last night?"

"Not in a car, anyway. I was sleeping at the front of the house."

"You're sure?"

"Yes. Because I heard Hector Pollitt coming back in."

"Back in?"

"He got out of the bus in Kinsale. Said he had people to see. He came back in a taxi, after midnight."

"Did he," I said. "Did he really?"

Georgia was looking at me very hard. "Charlie, what is all this about?"

"Oh, nothing. What were they talking about, in the house?"

"You, mostly. They kind of went over your career

and, well, I guess reappraised you is the right word."

I nodded. I was thinking about Pollitt. Him and Amy, on the loose in Kinsale. But why would either of them have wanted to sabotage *Ae?*

After Georgia had left, I went to bed and lay staring at the ceiling. Amy in her green gumboots still marched round the inside of my head. But this time she was with Hector Pollitt, dressed in wet clothes and slinking about in the dark. I worried at the events of the day. And slowly but surely, the cast grew. Why had Millstone said, "I never thought you'd bring her in this close"? And Archer. He never said much, but there was sometimes a coldness that came across his face and made him look capable of just about anything. Even Sally could have done it; she'd had the opportunity . . . But at this rate, I'd be believing that I'd done it myself.

The telephone woke me at eight o'clock the next morning. It was Amy. I felt muzzy in the head, ill-equipped to deal with her.

"What do you want?" she said.

"I wanted to talk to you."

"That's what you're doing now. Could you hurry it up? I've got more important things to do."

Sleep was still drugging me and I couldn't think of the tactful way to ask what I wanted to ask, so I asked it anyway. "Look, Amy, I want to know what you were doing in Kinsale."

I heard her breath zip between her teeth. I could imagine her face, tight and foxy. "What on earth are you talking about?"

"You were in Kinsale," I said.

"Who says?"

"I do."

"Mind your own bloody business."

"Amy, I'm trying to find out what happened to *Aesthete.*"

"I thought we all knew. Particularly you," she said. "Have you seen the *Daily Post?*"

"What's that got to do with it?"

"Read it and see. Oh, they're going to see to you properly, you bastard." The receiver went down, no doubt with a crash. I put my end back slowly. I could still hear the raw edge of hatred in her voice. Amy seemed very keen on the wreck of Agutter's career. Keen enough to sabotage my boats?

Apprehensively, I dressed and slunk out.

I knew it was bad from the way old George Maginnis looked at me in the shop. But I had not imagined how bad it could be.

The *Daily Post* had headlined it ESCAPE FROM DEATH BOAT NO. 2 and went on to give heavily-slanted biographies of me and my guests for the day. Sir Alec Breen and Frank Millstone were by way of being public figures, and the *Post* treated them with its normal toad-eating deference. They had no such scruples about me. They pointed out that the wreck confirmed suspicions that my new rudders (which they managed to make sound subtly unsporting) were a danger to the public. They also pointed out that their reporter, in pursuing me, had discovered that I had checked in to the Shamrock Hotel with a woman named Mrs. Agutter. I was known to be unmarried. The story was echoed with varying degrees of stridency by most of the other newspapers, some of which also carried a quote from Protheroe saying that he never wanted to see me again except in court, where he planned to sue me for my last cent. As far as I could see, the only glimmer of light was that, by the time the court got around to awarding damages, I'd be bankrupt anyway. Hugo had always thought what newspapers wrote was a huge joke. I missed him badly, because I found I was taking them very seriously indeed.

The telephone rang steadily as I worked my way through the pile of newsprint. Mostly it was reporters. I managed to divert them by pretending I was somebody else. The last call, however, was from a voice that sounded heavier than the normal Fleet Street model.

"I'd like to speak with Mr. Charles Agutter," it said.

"Who's that calling?"

"Detective Inspector Nelligan, Plymouth CID."

"In connection with what?"

"I think I'd better speak to Mr. Agutter."

"You are."

"Ah." There was a pause. "Could I pop over?"

"If you like."

"In ten minutes," said the voice. "If that's convenient." He did not sound at all bothered whether it was convenient or not.

"By all means," I said, and he rang off.

I called my solicitor, and told him to buy the newspapers and see if he could find anything that was actually libellous. He expressed horror, mixed with eagerness as the sums involved sank in. I went through to see my father, who was watching the test card on the television and picking his nose. He didn't recognise me. Nurse Bollom said he had been very bad.

"He messed himself this morning," she said.

"It's not unusual."

She pursed her pillar-box red lips. "Er, Mr. Agutter," she said. "Have you any idea when my cheque might be coming through?"

"I'm sorry," I said. "Completely overlooked it."

She administered a measured dose of red-smudged teeth from over her starched bosom and fragments of powder fluttered on her small moustache. "Not at all," she said. "I know you have a lot on your mind." There was a copy of the *Daily Post* on the table, next to her coffee cup.

I wrote her a cheque for an enormous sum of money, and left. As I entered my part of the house, the telephone was ringing again. I took it off the hook, and put four cushions on top of it. It was twelve o'clock. I do not normally drink at lunchtime, but I thought that a morning like this would have been enough to make Job drink at lunchtime. So I opened a beer and sat with it, reading the newspapers again and trying not to be sick.

Ten minutes later, the doorbell rang. I opened the door to a small, slender man with eyes hidden under a low brow-ridge.

"Nelligan, CID," he said. "Nice place you've got here." He glanced round the garden, with its tulips and early geraniums shining in the sun, and twitched his little moustache appreciatively at the scent of the honeysuckle. I invited him in, and he sat down.

"Do you mind if I smoke?" he said. I did, but I didn't want to start on the wrong foot by telling him so. So he lit a John Player Special and glanced furtively about him. "Nice paintings," he said.

"Have a beer," I said. He was meant to say not while he was on duty, but actually he accepted.

"Nice beer," he said, looking at the tin of Budweiser I gave him. "I like that American beer."

"Good," I said, wishing he would stop acting like a house clearer's appraiser. "Now, what's the problem?"

"Problem? Oh, I see." He had a slight West Country accent. "Well, we had a rather funny telephone call, from one of those newspapers in London. They asked would we comment on the fact that . . . well, it's rather personal."

"Say it anyway," I said. A chill had descended on the room. Something dreadful was about to happen.

"What they said was you'd been staying the night in a hotel in Ireland with the widow of your brother, recently deceased in a boating accident."

"True," I said. Then, seeing what he was leading up to, "In separate rooms."

"I am told there was a connecting door."

"Who told you this?" I said, thinking: Amy.

He smiled and shook his head. "Sorry."

"So what did you tell them?" I said.

"No comment. I mean that was what we told them. But the thing is, is it true? About Mrs. Agutter, I mean."

"No," I said. "It is a shameful bloody lie."

He nodded. "But . . . well, pardon my asking, are you sure you weren't having an affair with her?"

"Quite sure."

"Not before the . . . er . . . accident with the boat?"

"No." I was beginning to get angry. But getting angry would be unprofitable.

"So this was in the nature of a . . . er . . . one night stand?"

Profitable or not, I lost my temper. "If all you can do is sit there and make insulting suggestions, you can bloody well get out."

He made no effort to move, but stroked his small moustache and had the grace to look faintly embarrassed.

"Yes. Well, you've been very frank, Mr. Agutter. We'll want to look at that boat when she comes up. Because, of course, this opens new lines of thought for us."

"If you will excuse me, I've got better things to do than—"

"Help the police with their enquiries? Yes, well. Sailing yachts is a rough sport, isn't it? Accidents happen. Just say you'd been having an affair with Mrs. Agutter before your brother's death. Then you could have a motive for, well, causing the accident." He raised his small, soft hands as I got out of my seat. "No, no. Don't get upset, Mr. Agutter. But you do see that we have to follow everything up? Because it looked like an accident at first. But now, of course, it could be murder."

"Listen," I said wearily. "I've just been shipwrecked in Ireland, exactly the way my brother was shipwrecked in England. I was on the boat at one time. Do you think I'd murder myself? If I were you, instead of coming up here making comic suggestions I'd go and look for whoever it is that's trying to wreck my career, bankrupt me by sabotaging my boats, and frame me for bloody murder. Have you got that into your thick head?"

"Language," said Nelligan, mildly. "You said sabotage. Have you got proof?"

"No," I said. "But I'll get it." My ears were ringing with fury.

"Well," said Nelligan. "I'll look forward to seeing it, Mr. Agutter. Meanwhile, don't disappear, will you?"

He squashed his cigarette out with great concentration and walked out into the wind that had not stopped blowing since the black night of *Aesthete's* wreck.

13

I went down to the office that afternoon, and tried to work on the lines of the Padmore and Bayliss motorsailer. But I was so restless I could hardly stay in my seat. Unless I started to take positive steps to get into the Captain's Cup, working on the Padmore boats was a waste of time.

After half an hour, I gave up and picked up the telephone and rang the Shamrock Hotel. I got hold of the knowledgeable receptionist and asked if Mrs. Charlton had had any visitors on Saturday. The receptionist said she had not, none that he'd seen anyway. She had gone out to dinner and come back alone. I put the receiver down. Well, she might have been dining with Pollitt. But what would that prove? It was too much to hope for that Pollitt's late arrival at Protheroe's should be linked with Amy's gumboot prints on the cliff top. If, indeed, it was Amy who had made those footprints.

My next call was to Spearman's. I got hold of Neville. He sounded even more depressed than usual.

"That boat of Alec Breen's," I said.

"Yes." He was always wary. This time, he sounded actively suspicious.

"It must be using up shed space."

"Yes, it bloody well is," he said. "Are you going to give me the go-ahead with it? I've got a queue of stuff that needs building."

"I'd like you to finish her."

"Good idea." I knew what was coming next. There was a long pause, during which I could imagine him screwing up his face and running his hand over his dark-socketed eyes. "We've known each other a hell of a long time, and of course I admire your work and everything, but, well, who's paying?"

This was the tricky bit. "Neville," I said. "As you say, we have known each other for about thirty years. And thank you for your kind remarks about my work. Would you consider doing it on spec? Breen'll come round. If he doesn't, we'll sell her to someone else."

I could hear him breathing into the receiver. Finally he spoke. "Charlie," he said. "Let me tell you the facts of life. Number one, you won't get that boat finished in time for the Captain's Cup trials. Number two, nothing personal, but your name has gone actively poisonous, cocky. Finishing that boat without a definite commission is throwing away money, because she won't sell. Even if she's a good boat, you're too late. I'll do you a favour. She can stay in the shed for another week. But after that she's on the heap. Okay?"

"A week," I said.

"Good luck," said Neville, and rang off.

I made a list of possible buyers, and sat looking at it, trying to crank myself up to start selling. It was like standing barefoot at the bottom of Everest. Also, Neville was right. She'd missed the bus for the Captain's Cup.

I was just picking up the telephone again when Ernie, the draughtsman, stuck his head round the door and said, "Sally rang. Said she'll see you at the cocktail party tonight. Mr. Beith's going with her."

I was pleased to hear from Sally, but perhaps a little

disappointed to hear that Ed was taking her to the party. The memory of that moment of closeness in Kinsale had been popping up quite frequently these last few days. But of course, it could never lead anywhere. At the moment, both of us were probably best off around old friends like Ed.

Nonetheless, I indulged in a little private swearing. If anything was needed to put the lid on a lousy day, it was the Cocktail Party. It is the official beginning of the Pulteney sailing season. It takes place in the white clapboard clubhouse, with its terrace built out over the harbour, and an appearance is *de rigueur* for serious competitors. I had to assume I was a serious competitor, even without a boat.

I spent the afternoon failing to make a sale. At six, I climbed into a blazer and an RORC tie, took a deep breath, and walked across to the Yacht Club.

A few of the younger drinkers were braving the breeze fluttering the flags on the mast above the balcony. Older salts were already tucked up near the bar. Several pairs of eyes rested on me for a second too long, then swivelled pointedly away. I went out onto the balcony, leaned on the railing and contemplated *Nautilus*, green and glossy against the blue evening sky. The wind seemed to be moderating. I gulped my whisky, and thought about myself and *Nautilus* and Hugo. All of us built for racing, and none of us going to race again, for our various reasons. I did not want to start thinking about Hugo here. I took another pull at my glass, and it was empty. I would have to be careful not to get drunk.

When I went back in, the bar was three-quarters full. Again I had the sensation of being brushed by dozens of eyes. Archer vouchsafed me a nod and a grin before returning to his conversation with a public relations adviser from the NCB. Johnny Forsyth winked conspiratorially, then answered a summons from the other side of the room. Forsyth the freelance, I thought. Like all freelances, always on duty. I looked around for a friendly face; Sally wasn't there. Instead I saw the synthetic tan and flashing teeth of Hector Pollitt bearing down.

"Hello," said Pollitt, with a large, insincere smile. "Recovered from the other day?" I nodded. "Bad luck, that. How d'you rate the chances of getting one of your boats in the Captain's Cup now?"

I felt myself begin to bristle; then I thought, hold on a minute, he must have had a couple, to say a thing like that. Perhaps I could get him to talk.

"Have a nice evening with Protheroe?" I said.

Pollitt gazed at me with slightly bloodshot eyes. "Didn't go back till late," he said. "Things to do, people to see, y'know."

"On a story, were you?"

He laughed. "You might say so."

"Did I see you at the Shamrock?"

He wasn't as drunk as all that. "I don't know," he said. "Did you? Seems unlikely, because I wasn't there." He laughed again.

"Oh God, it's you," said a woman's voice at my elbow. I looked down. It was Amy, in a high-necked dress that was black, for mourning presumably, which managed to emphasize the jut of her pointed, little breasts and the sharpness of her aggressive chin. Her mouth was an ugly red line, and her eyes were creased with spite. "I'm surprised you've got the nerve to show your face."

Hector laughed. I said, "Hello, Amy," as pleasantly as I could.

"Don't you hello me," said Amy, in a high, carrying voice. "I had the bloody police round asking nosey questions. I told them they should have been talking to you." Hector was nervously smoothing his glossy, brown hair with a nicely-kept hand.

There was silence in the bar, now. A lot of rich, new

Pulteney faces were looking worriedly in our direction or staring hard at the floor. A big hollow had opened where my stomach was meant to be. Then I smelt perfume, and Sally's voice said, "For God's sake, shut up, Amy, you're making a fool of yourself."

Amy's eyes narrowed to slits, and she whirled on Sally. "And as for you, you scrubber," she said. "How you can stand there, next to your boyfriend, and—put me down!" For I had picked her up and carried her out of the room.

Ed Beith was in the hall. He raised his eyebrows, grinned, and said, "Is this wise, Charlie?"

Too angry to answer, I carried her through the hall and onto the quay. She hammered at me with her fists and screamed. Outside in the air, she stopped screaming, and I put her on her feet. A small crowd had followed us out, glasses in hand, to watch. Her make-up was smudged, her face twisted with rage.

My own heart was thudding unpleasantly. "Tell me one thing," I said. "Was it you taking walks on the cliffs near Kinsale on Saturday night?"

For a moment her face smoothed out and she said, "How on earth . . . ?"

"And Hector," I said, pressing home my advantage. "Did you have him with you? A quick stroll on the beach, down to Crosshaven?"

Her eyes were black, and they flicked like windscreen wipers between me and Pollitt. The surprise in her face abated, and the tensions of rage and calculation returned. She laughed, a high, ugly laugh that bounced round the stone faces of the harbour, and said, "Well, you can bloody well find out."

"What about it, Hector?" I said.

He flashed his teeth, spread his hands and said, "Like she says, old boy."

"Let's go," said Amy. "I don't like the company."

I turned back towards the clubhouse. As I entered the door, Frank Millstone stepped in front of me.

"Agutter," he said. "We don't like chaps who lay hands on ladies in this club. Maybe you'd better get off home and think about that."

I looked up at the jovial face with the cold, satisfied eyes. Then I shrugged my shoulders and walked off along the quay, head down. The Yacht Club was everything that stank about the new Pulteney.

A voice at my elbow said, "Take it easy, Charlie."

I looked up. It was Johnny Forsyth, his leathery neck incongruously trapped in a white collar and a Pulteney Yacht Club tie. I said, "I should keep away, if I were you. I'm not nice to know."

"I just thought I'd tell you I know how it feels," said Johnny. "It's not much fun, being at their mercy, is it?"

"No," I said, screwing up my eyes against the dazzle of the late sun in the harbour.

"But look at it like this. Some years you work, some you don't. Like us. This year, the wife's doing okay with the restaurant, I've got a bit of work, and if Frank can find a Captain's Club boat, I'll be doing the tactics. Oh Christ, sorry Charlie, I'm not trying to rub your face in it."

"No," I said. "Thanks."

"I just wanted you to know."

"Thanks," I said again. "Look, you'd better get back to the party." And I trudged off up Quay Street.

It has always been one of my difficulties that I am constitutionally unable to accept defeat. My main emotion was one of intense anger, and by the time I was brushing under the honeysuckle that overhung my front gate, I knew what I had to do to get into the Captain's Cup. I pulled the Famous Grouse out of the cupboard and tipped quite a lot of it into a glass. It was a scheme that required a certain amount of Dutch courage. Then I heard the squeal of tyres on the cobbles and the creak of the gate, and Sally and Ed Beith were coming down the path.

"That bitch," said Sally. "Are you all right, Charlie?"

"I feel a bloody idiot," I said. "I shouldn't have touched her."

"You should have dropped her in the harbour," said Ed.

"It was nice of you to . . . defend my honour," said Sally, avoiding my eye. "That scrubber."

"Scrubber?"

"She used to lead Henry a dance. She even made a dirty great pass at Hugo once." Sally was calm and matter-of-fact, but I could see that she was very angry. "She's really got an itch, that one."

"Do you think she's scratching it with Hector Pollitt?"

Sally looked surprised. "Hector? It's possible, I suppose."

"Because they were off on Saturday night, in Ireland. And I found what could have been her footprints on the cliff top. So she was at least close at hand when sabotage was being covered up."

"Sabotage?" said Ed. "What's this?"

"Tell you later," I said. "And if she covered up that sabotage, what's to stop her covering up the sabotage of *Aesthete* to get rid of Henry?"

"Pretty unreliable method," said Ed.

"It's you they're after," said Sally. "Why should Amy want to ruin you?"

"God knows," I said. "But she's doing a grand job."

"It's not so good to be on the wrong side of Millstone," said Sally. "What are you going to do about him?"

"Sail the bastard under the water and forget about him."

"But he hasn't got a boat," said Sally. "Nor have you."

"I'm getting one," I said. "A revelation came to me on the way home tonight. And Millstone's expecting to find one. Johnny Forsyth told me as much, tonight. Know anything about it, Ed?"

Ed was staring at his whisky. "He's looking for one, all right," he said, without looking up. "I don't know what's come over this town. I reckon he'll make me an offer for *Crystal* any day now."

"Would you sell?"

"Oh, I don't know really," said Ed, and fixed me with a steady eye above a big grin. It was the eye I remembered from teenage contests in Pulteney regattas. "So what are your plans?"

"Oh, I don't know really," I said, and looked him straight back between the eyes. We had been playing these games for twenty years and we both knew exactly what we were planning to do.

Ed finished his whisky and stood up. "I must pop off and transact this and that," he said. "Sally?"

"Could you drop me home?"

She put her hand on mine. Her fingers were warm and dry. "Take care, Charlie." It was no good trying to hide it from myself. I liked it.

They left. It was only eight o'clock. I picked up the telephone and dialled Billy Hegarty in Ireland.

The lines were in their usual demented state, and when I got through I had had to chase him from his home, via two pubs, to Jury's Hotel in Cork. He sounded slightly drunk, and there were convivial noises off.

"Charlie," he said. "Cripes, aren't I after trying to get hold of you all day?"

"What's the problem?"

"Well, after you went I had the vet over to take a blood sample out of that dog. And you were right, the brute was full up with sleeping pills."

I could feel my face stretching in a grin, and the horror of the cocktail party receded. "You're a great man, Hegarty," I said. "Now, listen to this. I want you to tell the story to one man, and I can promise you that he's a boat owner who wants to win, and the only way he'll win is if he never tells a soul." Billy was making doubtful noises at the far end. I cut him off. "And, Billy," I said. "Would you ever find out if there was anything peculiar the day Protheroe had the rudder checked? Any strangers in the yard, sleeping dogs, you know?"

"Ye're a hard man," said Billy. "I'd say I'll have to."

After he had rung off, I started to look for Breen.

He was not easy to find. First of all, I rang his office and there was no reply. Then I rang his home, and someone who might have been a butler said that Mr. Breen was out, and had, as far as he knew, gone to a party, but it was hard to say where. The manservant then began to show signs of extreme discretion, and put the telephone down as I was in the middle of asking him to go and look in the boss's diary.

At this moment, I had an inspiration. About six months previously, when we had been making early drawings for Breen's boat, he had had occasion to give me the number of his car phone. So I ran out of the house and down to my office, and looked under the diary entries for last November. And there it was.

I was sweating as I waited for the call to go through. This was the last throw between Agutter and Queer Street. The ringing tone sounded twice, then someone picked up the receiver and said, "Hello." It was not Breen.

"Hello," I said. "Jack Danforth here. Would you mind coming half an hour late? I'm a bit tied up at nine."

"What?" said the voice on the other end. "Er . . . Mr. Danforth . . . nine when?" The man sounded like a chauffeur.

"Tonight, of course," I said, gaining confidence. "Bloody hell, man. He can't have forgotten."

"Forgotten?" said the chauffeur, sounding nervous.

"Well, he'll just have to fit it in," I said. "We're only in Nottingham for the night. Could he drop by?"

"Nottingham?" said the chauffeur. "That's a very long way. He won't be able to do it. We're in Lymington, in Hampshire."

"Know it well," I said. "Not at old Harry Foster's?"

"It's a dance," said the chauffeur. "At Mr. Birkett's."

"Oh, well," I said. "That's that, then." I put the telephone down. It had been almost ludicrously easy. I only hoped that Breen would not find out, or his chauffeur would be out of a job.

After that, all I had to do was ring up my friend Harry Chance in Lymington. Harry knew everyone there was to know and specialised in big shots. He informed me that Septimus Birkett was giving a fund-raising dance for someone's America's Cup challenge, and that he lived at Reynolds' Stone Hall, three miles out of town.

All that remained was for me to stroll back to the house, climb into my dinner-jacket and take a couple of deep breaths for my nerves' sake. Then I was on the road for Lymington.

14

Two hours later, I parked the BMW under some trees on the verge of a wooded lane. I straightened my bow-tie in the driving mirror. My face was what I had to call haggard. I climbed out, walked up the road to the tall gate-pillars, and turned into the drive.

The drive was gravel, beautifully raked. It led between banks of rhododendrons to a house, large, white and latter-day Georgian, nestling under the eaves of the New Forest like a cuckoo chick in a wren's nest. The night air was cool on my face as I skirted a gravel sweep with perhaps fifty expensive cars parked on it. From the gardens on the other side of the house came the thud of a bass guitar and a muffled roar of voices. I walked round. There was a lawn, grey in the moonlight, surrounded by high black trees. Attached to the garden front of the house was a marquee, lit yellow from within. I walked down a turf walk between two flowerbeds, pulled back the flap and slipped inside.

The air inside was hot and the noise deafening. At the far end of the tent, a band was playing, but it was nearly drowned by the voices. The men looked smooth, and some of the women wore tiaras. There was a fair sprinkling of New Pulteney. It was what Hugo would have called the Royal Yacht crowd.

I stood for a moment with the sweat breaking in my palms. Now all I had to do was find Breen. The crowd stretched before me like a sea. I dived in.

If I had been a terrorist, I could have wiped out a good slice of the royal family. But I was only a yacht designer in search of an owner, and for five minutes I patrolled the groups of expensive men and women without any success. Then I saw a pair of square shoulders topped by a head of close-cut brown hair and a brown neck, sitting at a table with four young women, all of whom were laughing. You could feel the charm radiating from him like heat from an electric fire. Archer.

I went up and touched him on the shoulder. He looked round, flushed and smiling, his blue eyes sparkling in the light, and I remembered what Georgia had told me about Archer and the ladies. The smile stiffened a little when he recognized me.

"Archer," I said. "I must have a word."

He stood up. "Of course," he said. We walked away into a corner. As we went, he said in a low voice, "What are you doing here?"

"I've come to see Breen."

"Breen?" Archer said the name as if he did not know what it meant. "Look, Charlie, if old Septimus Birkett sees you, he'll have you tossed out. Millstone's here. A lot of people from that cocktail party. He's been spreading the word about you. Forgive me for saying so, but you were a bloody fool earlier on this evening."

"Possibly," I said. I was keyed up past the point of listening to anything except what I wanted to hear. "Where's Breen?"

"He was in the house earlier," said Archer. "Having

dinner. For Christ's sake, Charlie. You know I'll do anything for you in the normal way. But tonight . . . you're out of order, mate."

"Everything I do, I do for Padmore and Bayliss," I said, with a smile whose ugliness hurt my face. Archer raised his hands; on your own head be it, the gesture said. Then he turned away and walked greedily back to his table of lovelies, a pint-sized ball of sexual fire.

I moved quickly to the green-and-white striped tunnel that led into the tent from the house. A crowd of men and women were coming down a passage lined with paintings of Dutch sea-battles. The men were smoking cigars. Breen was not among them. I walked on, looking into doorways. The first was a drawing-room. A very old man was talking to two middle-aged women by the fire. I said, "So sorry to interrupt. Have you seen Alec?"

"Washing his hands," said the old man.

"Oh," I said, and went back into the passage.

At that moment, Breen came out of a door under the staircase, looking chubby and well-scrubbed. I saw his eyes flick towards me, move away, then flick back. I walked quickly up to him.

"We have to talk," I said.

He put his cigar in his mouth, and sucked. "I've got nothing to say," he said. He advanced down the passage. "Excuse me."

I was standing by a door. Inside was a small room that might have been a library, with books on the walls, and armchairs and a desk. On the desk was a telephone.

As Breen passed me, I grabbed his wrist with both hands, and heaved him in. He looked solid, but he fell with surprising ease, and we both landed in a heap on the library floor, Breen uppermost. I got out from under him, and slammed the door. Breen had got as far as his knees, and was staring at me with a face frozen with shock and anger.

"I'm sorry to have to do this," I said. "But would you mind sitting down?"

He got up, brushed the dust from the knees of his dinner-jacket trousers, and retrieved his cigar from the Bokhara rug. Then he said, "Let me out of here, Agutter." His eyes were more than ever like gun barrels in his mild, podgy face. Nobody I have ever met, having been thrown on the floor by a surprise attack, could have turned round and dominated the room twenty seconds later. But Breen managed it.

"No," I said. There was a key in the door. I turned it, and dropped it in my pocket. "Not until we have had a little talk."

"Brute force does not speak to me," said Breen.

"Be reasonable," I said. "You were about to walk straight through me. You've done worse, in your day. I just want you to make one telephone call. After you have made it, you can turn me over to the police, or do whatever you want."

Breen pondered a moment. He took out another cigar, cut it and lit it. When it was burning to his satisfaction, he took a deep breath and shouted, "Help!"

His voice was surprisingly loud. I had not imagined that he would shout. The sweat began to pour inside my shirt.

"Help!" shouted Breen, opening his mouth wide.

I pulled out my handkerchief and stuffed it between his gaping jaws. Tasselled cords hung by the curtains. I tied him to the chair with one, and put the other round his face to keep the gag in place. He struggled, but he was a desk man and his strength was in his will, not his body.

When he was tied up tight, I picked up the telephone and dialled Billy Hegarty, in Ireland. As the telephone rang, someone knocked on the door and said, "Are you all right in there?" The knob rattled. "It's locked," the voice said.

97

"It shouldn't be," said another. "I'll get the spare key."

Billy answered. I said, "Billy, it's Charlie Agutter. I want you to explain exactly what's been going on round your yard, as far as you know. It'll go no further." Breen's eyes stared at me, cold and distant.

I held the telephone to his ear while Billy said his piece. When his voice stopped, I said, "Goodbye, and thanks."

The voices were back at the door, now. I said, "We're fine," and slipped my key into the keyhole, half-turning it so they couldn't put theirs in. Then I returned to Breen.

"Billy Hegarty runs the yard at Crosshaven," I said. "Somebody's been drugging his guard dogs in order to get in and sabotage *Ae*'s rudder. Someone removed the original titanium bolts and replaced them with aluminium. Then they reinstated the titanium bolts in time for the Lloyd's inspection, having first broken them with a mechanical hammer. Billy has told you enough to wreck his reputation as a secure yard and I can now be charged with assault. Consider this before you decide what you want to do when I take off the gag."

A voice outside the door shouted, "Security! Open up!"

I went to Breen, untied him from the chair, and took the gag out of his mouth. Then I poured him a glass of whisky and soda from the tray in the corner, and said, "You'd better open the door before they break it down."

Breen pulled his small, thick body out of his chair and walked slowly across the room. He ran a hand across his iron-grey hair, turned the key, and opened the door.

A big man in a dinner-jacket said, "Why did you lock this door? We're security."

"We're having an important meeting in here," said

98

Breen. The sweat was sticking my shirt to my chest, and my heart was banging. "Could we have a little peace?"

And the balance of power shifted, as it always did, from the big men in dinner-jackets, back to Breen. They melted away.

Breen took a drink of his whisky and soda, and sat down behind the desk. Then he leaned forward and hissed, "I have ruined men for less." He held his position, face suffused with blood. Then he relaxed. "Now, then, it strikes me that this story of yours is even odder than the way you have chosen to tell it. You'd better explain."

My throat was so dry I could hardly speak. "Nothing to explain," I said, reaching with shaking hands to pour myself a drink. "Some bastard's trying to wreck my business and keep me out of the Captain's Cup."

"So your brother's death was not an accident."

"It would appear not. But we won't know for sure till we pull up *Aesthete.*"

"So there could be murder involved."

"Yes."

"You must be angry."

"I am." But I was beginning to relax. For the first time ever, Breen was talking to me like a human being, not a machine paid to give results.

He leaned back in his chair, and smoke wreathed his head like clouds wreathing a small mountain. Finally he said, "I used to build motor-bike sidecars. With my own hands." He held them up. They were small and thick. "I had a workshop in Coventry. I rented it from a bloke called Purdue. Well, I had a new suspension system, and I knew Purdue wanted it, and sure enough he found out I was in trouble at the bank and then he quadrupled the rent. Thought he'd bankrupt me as principal creditor. But I got angry and I got organized and I raised some money and bought out his lease and I booted him into Station Road." He took the cigar out of his mouth and opened his eyes and looked straight at me. The whites showed all the way round. "It was being angry made me win," he said. "I wouldn't have, else." He paused. "But you have to learn to control it. You controlled it tonight, I suppose."

I said nothing. Dealing with clients has given me a sort of extra sense that tells me when we are getting to the heart of things. I knew, now, that this was the pivot of matters between me and Breen.

"It could be any of those people out there who are doing this to you," said Breen, gesturing towards the distant hum of voices. "Millstone included. Did you know he's going for the team?"

"Yes," I said, "but he hasn't got a boat."

"He'll get one," said Breen. "He's in the process just now. Determined man, Frank Millstone."

He sucked at his cigar for a moment. The dance band was thudding away in the garden. Finally he said, "I won't finish the new boat. We've lost a week; it's too late. Besides"—the eyes came up like gun barrels—"I'm only ninety-eight per cent sure you're on the level." My heart sank. "Hold on," he said.

He picked up the telephone and dialled a number. I went and mixed myself another drink while he spoke in a low voice. After five minutes, he put the receiver down. "Well, there you are," he said. "You can sail for me in the Captain's Cup. In *Sorcerer*."

"Sorcerer?"

"I've just bought her," he said. "Well?"

Sorcerer was a fast boat I had designed the year before last, for an owner who had subsequently got himself killed in a helicopter crash. That was elderly by Captain's Cup standards, but she was a good hull. In fact, it was a good offer.

"New sails," I said. "And you take care of that unfinished hull at Neville Spearman's. I'll organize the crew."

100

Breen's chubby face stretched into a grin like a ventriloquist's dummy. "You have quick reactions, Charlie. Very well." I got up. "Wait a minute," he said. "Get angry enough to win. But don't get angry enough to . . . take liberties with me. You're on my time, now."

He placed his fists softly on the desk and leaned forward a fraction. The smile disappeared, and once again I could feel the strength of his will and his gun-metal eyes boring into mine. "And don't ever tie me up again."

Then he got up and spread his arms, waving his cigar in his blunt, cheque-signer's hands. His face came alive and his voice sounded almost springy. "Now, let's go through and meet some people."

I followed him, slightly dazed. At least I had a boat to sail. At least I had designed her myself. But she was two years old . . . He forged a path down the passage and into the marquee. More people were dancing, now. This time, I was calm enough to take in some details. The band was playing on a dais. It was a full dance orchestra, with sequined music stands, playing under full-sized date palms.

Breen paused in front of them, and turned to me, and, for an insane moment, I thought he was going to ask me to dance. Instead, he said, "Let's go!" and jumped up on the stage. The leader looked round and Breen said, "Stop." Then, without looking back, he stepped over to the microphone and waited. He was stocky and intensely energetic and his cigar jutted over the dancers like a gun barrel. The band stopped playing.

Breen said, into the microphone, "May I have your attention for one minute? I'm sorry to stop the music, but I know you'll all want to hear that Charles Agutter is sailing *Sorcerer* for me in the Captain's Cup trials. Good luck, Charlie!"

He began to clap. Some of the other dancers followed his example, then others. I saw Millstone, not clapping, and Hector Pollitt, clapping with a cynical grin on his even brown face, and several Pulteney people. Not Archer, though. It was the second party that night where all eyes were on Agutter, and a lot of these people would have heard about the first one. The sweat of embarrassment broke out on my temples and I forced a smile. The clapping was ragged, itself slightly embarrassed. Breen put his arm round my shoulders, standing on tiptoe to do so. I waved, and we climbed down from the stage.

"Drink," he said. I needed one badly. People came and talked. I answered as best I could, scarcely conscious of what was said. I kept thinking that to be thrown out of one party and to be the hero of another, all on the same night, must be some kind of record. As soon as I could, I detached myself from Breen's circle and went out onto the lawn and beyond the marquee.

The air was heavy with the scent of azaleas, and behind it the invigorating tang of pine trees. Above, the sky was clear.

"Hello, Charlie," said a voice at my shoulder. "Congratulations." I turned. Light shone from the speaker's shirtfront and from his glistening white teeth.

"Thank you, Hector," I said, with as much enthusiasm as I could muster.

I could smell whisky on his breath. "Seen Amy?" He seemed very drunk.

"No," I said. "I was just going for a walk."

"Ah," said Hector. "Yes, it's a nice night. I'll join you."

This was by no means what I wanted. But I could not politely tell him to go away, so we strolled across the lawn under the stars.

"We haven't had a chat," said Hector. "Nasty scene on the quay, there. 'Motional lady, Amy."

"It's understandable."

"Understandable? Oh, I see. Henry and everything." He paused. "Charlie, what do you think happened to your rudders?"

Drunk or not, Pollitt was on duty. "No idea," I said. "If I hadn't seen it with my own eyes, I'd have said they had been interfered with."

Hector chuckled. "Who'd do a thing like that?"

Abruptly, I said, "What were you doing on Saturday night in Kinsale, Hector? You weren't at Protheroe's."

"No, I was . . . seeing some people." His voice had changed. It was defensive, now. "Is it any of your business?"

"But were you with Amy?"

The whites of his eyes glared in the moonlight. "What if I was?"

"You could be of help."

He was quiet, then. We walked on across the lawn, under a yew arch and into a rose garden. The turf paths of the garden converged on a cone-topped summer-house with lattice windows. In the summer-house, a woman's voice said, "Oh!"

It was not a startled sound. In fact, it was quite the reverse—as if the woman had got something she had been expecting for a long time, and was pleased about it. More sounds followed it. The maker of the sounds must have been quite unconscious that she was making them, probably because she was concentrating on whoever was in the summer-house with her. They developed a rhythm, and the rhythm accelerated until it was an incoherent moaning working up to a high animal pitch, and the woman cried out a name. Then the sounds stopped.

I stood and listened; not through prurient curiosity, but because I recognized the woman's voice. It was Amy's and the name she had cried out at the moment of climax had been, "Archer."

When I turned to go away, Hector was no longer at my side. Sound travelled well in the shelter; I heard the thud of running footsteps receding across the lawn, the slam of a car door, and the howl of tyres in the gravel. Then the scream of an engine disappearing down the long tunnel of rhododendrons.

Soon after that, I went home myself.

15

Next day, I felt almost human. I called in on Sally, and over breakfast told her about the party and Breen. She laughed, and her cheeks went small and round and pink, like a little girl's. As I left, Ed Beith's Subaru was turning in at the drive gates. Good old Ed, I thought. Solid as a rock. Not like those perpetual adolescents at the party.

I went down to the office and rang around for a crew. I loaded up Scotto and another couple of hands and drove over to Lymington, where the marina already had *Sorcerer* in the crane. I looked her over. She was in terrific shape, crisp and clean as the day she was built. She'd spent most of the previous year in a shed.

Scotto spat out his chewing gum. "Not bad," he said. We dropped the mast in, and by four o'clock we were nosing into the Solent under the eyes of the Isle of Wight ferry passengers.

The shipping forecast for Portland, Plymouth and Wight was force four to five, southerly. We made very good time down the coast. *Sorcerer* went well; she needed a new mainsail and a couple of genoas, but if we could get her worked up in the very short time available, she had a good chance for the Captain's Cup team. Actually, she was better than good; and I could see that Scotto thought so too.

At midnight, the flash of Portland Bill light was well astern, and Scotto had up a kite and a blast reacher. I had forgotten how to be tired as she hurdled the long black seas under a high half moon. I had sailed this course dozens of times with Hugo, and now, tired as I was, I could almost feel him standing at my shoulder. He would perch on the weather deck and the red ends of his bloody awful Players would glow against the black hulk of him, and he would talk. He was a much better hand at talking than me, and what he really excelled at was in stripping people's polite actions down until the bare motives showed, like gears, slippery and dirty. I wondered what he would have made of *Aesthete* and *Ae,* and all these broken rudders. Myself, I didn't know where to begin. Last night had complicated matters still further.

What the hell was Amy up to? Assuming that she had been with Pollitt in Ireland, that she'd been having an affair with him, and that she'd been cheating with Archer in the summer-house, why should any of it be connected with the rudders?

By four A.M., we were off the Teeth, opening Pulteney Harbour light. Scotto was watching the suck of foam among the rocks. I was trying not to, because there was no Hugo smoking next to me, and the Teeth were the reason.

"Wind's dropping," said Scotto.

We arrived off Pulteney in the last ghostly whisper of breeze. I put *Sorcerer* on a mooring in Lower Pulteney, just around Beggarman's Point from Pulteney proper, and went home. First I rang Neville Spearman to arrange the salvage barge. Then I had four hours sleep. When the alarm went off, I stumbled into the garden. The wind had dropped and the midday sun glittered off a sea smooth as satin. I went down to the quay and collected my diving gear. Then I went looking for Chiefy.

He was in the bar of the Mermaid, as usual. Ed Beith was with him. I ordered a pint and drank it; I was parched and tired. Then I said to Ed, "I'm sailing *Sorcerer* for Breen."

"Sally said," said Ed, in what I thought was a lack-lustre manner. "Glad to hear it."

"Don't see why," I said. "It'll be my regrettable duty to sail the pants off you."

He smiled. Again, it seemed a little forced. "You may not get the chance," he said. "Millstone made his offer for *Crystal* today."

"Crystal?"

"A big offer. For boat and crew."

"Tell him to get stuffed," I said.

Ed finished his whisky. "My exact words to the bank manager only this morning." He rose stiffly to his feet, ape-like in his foul boiler suit. Presumably he had worn it to see his bank manager. "Well, see you around." He walked out of the bar.

"Ed's not too happy," said Chiefy.

"He'll never let Millstone have the boat, though."

"Ed'd be well shot of her, if you ask me," said Chiefy. "Better off farming than sailing them things. Come on, then. Today's the day."

We went round to Spearman's to pick up the salvage barge. I humped my mask, bottles and weight belt across to where Johnny Forsyth was watching a couple of Spearman's men buffing the hull of a forty-foot sloop he looked after for its absentee owners, ready for Regatta Week.

His eyes flicked to the diving gear. "Hear you're sailing for old Breen," he said. "Nice work, if you can get it."

"Thanks," I said. "Who told you?"

"Frank Millstone."

"I hear Frank's getting close to a boat."

Forsyth looked at me sharply, his narrow eyes gleaming above his lunar cheeks. "Is he?" he said. "Wish I was getting the broker's commission."

"Aren't you?" I said.

He laughed, not very humorously. "Some chance," he said. "Frank likes to do his own deals, or he uses the big boys up the coast." He jerked his acid-stained thumb in the general direction of Lymington and the Hamble. "It's hard to scrape up a general purpose longshore living these days."

"You do okay." I was edgy. A lot of questions were due to be answered today. "I've got to go."

"I'm coming with you, for Lloyd's. And so's he." He pointed to a small figure in a brown suit smoking a cigarette in the lee of the yard office. It was Inspector Nelligan.

The sea was flat as a pancake all the way out to the Teeth. Nobody said much. The engine clanked and spat out black diesel smoke, and Nelligan sat down-wind of the smoke until I pointed out to him that he'd be more comfortable upwind.

"Ta," he said, twitching his little moustache at the diesel. "I'm not much of a sailor." Besides his brown suit, he was wearing shiny leather shoes that the salt would ruin, and a nylon shirt.

"What are you trying to prove out here?"

He looked at me from under the ridge that bore his eyebrows. "Oh, not prove. Just want to be on hand during the recovery of evidence." He turned away to look at the low, blue line of the shore and, as he doubtless intended, I felt disconcerted. If there was evidence of sabotage, Nelligan would assume that I'd done it, to get rid of my brother. If there wasn't, Agutter's rudders were unreliable. Heads I win, tails you lose.

We came up to the Teeth on the last of the flood. The sea under the salvage barge's rusty bow was a shiny green. The only sign of the big humps of rock below was a couple of patches of weed and a line of scum running a quarter of a mile away along the edge of the tide, where three boatloads of holiday makers were feathering for mackerel. Chiefy's hands moved over the worn paint of the wheel and caressed the throttle. The clank of the engine died to a chug, and the blunt nose crept in among the patches of weed. Forsyth nodded to the two wet-suited men sitting alongside him in the cockpit. They got up and began struggling into diving gear.

I pulled my own gear out of the locker. Nelligan looked across sharply and shook his head.

"What?" I said.

"That's evidence down there," said Nelligan. "Not worth sending police divers after, of course. But we wouldn't want you too close to it, would we? I'm sure you'll understand."

I caught Johnny Forsyth's eye. "Little bastard," said Johnny under his breath. I shrugged.

Chiefy said, "Drop the 'ook, Charlie."

As I went forward, my heart was thudding with rage. The anchor plunged into the green gloom, trailing a cloud of bubbles. The barge fell back ten yards and swung to. I stayed forward, hearing the splashes as the divers went down, the tiny cries of tourists hauling mackerel out of the tide a quarter of a mile away, consumed with my powerlessness. Then I leaned on the side, looking at the oily slop of the sea, and making resolutions; whoever had done this, interfered with my rudders and killed my brother and gone tale-bearing to Nelligan, was going to pay dearly.

Forsyth leaned on the rail next to me, tapping his wide, flat fingers on the rusty iron. Finally he said, "This must be pretty horrible for you, Charlie."

"It is not the greatest fun I have ever had," I said.

For a moment, I was going to tell him all about Hegarty and the sabotage. Then I remembered my promises to Hegarty. Gossip is the staple diet of freelancers like Forsyth.

"Put it like this," I said. "I'm getting a new set of engineers' reports before I build another rudder like that."

"Bloody bad luck," said Forsyth. "Bloody bad luck." And we stood and watched our reflections wobbling in the water.

The divers' bubbles moved aimlessly round for ten minutes. Then they converged and combined. A moment later, a black rubber head came up alongside.

"Got her," said the diver. "She's on her port side. Stove in. You sure you want her?"

"Take down the airbags," said Chiefy. They took them, with the slings and the compressor hose. Then we put the crane cable overboard.

The first thing to come up was a twisted tube of aluminium, trailing steel wires. Nobody who did not already know what it was would have been able to identify it as a mast. After the mast was a netful of junk: a spinnaker pole twisted like a corkscrew, three winches still embedded in fragments of white composite deck and a tubular aluminium bunk with pieces of the space frames still attached. It was revolting, like the exhumation of an old corpse.

"Strewth," said Forsyth. "She must be in bits."

I did not answer. Instead I watched the bubbles, feeling sick and numb at the same time. The pile of dripping wreckage in the barge's well grew higher.

When I looked up, Nelligan was watching me, his eyes impersonal above his cigarette. The diver-to-ship telephone squawked.

Forsyth said, "Inflate." Then he waved a hand at the compressor and said, "After you, Charlie." I hit the switch and the sea began to boil.

You raise a wreck by threading slings under the hull and attaching a big rubber bag to each end of each sling. Then you put a couple more bags inside the hull and pump in air. Because of the need to inflate the bags evenly, it is a slow business. The bubbles rose for what seemed like an eternity. The divers came up twice to change tanks. They did not say much, and nobody asked questions. Around us, the tide ebbed hard and great forests of weed waved below the glass-green surface. Chiefy ate a vast tea of ham sandwiches, and offered me some. I refused; my stomach was too tight for eating. The mackerel boats had long since gone home, and a thin evening breeze began to steal across the sea.

At six forty-three, Forsyth's telephone squawked and he said, "Up she comes. Stand by."

And up she came.

The floats came first, huge black bubbles like the heads of nightmare octopuses. They rose in a nest, and in the middle of the nest was *Aesthete*. Not that it looked like *Aesthete*. *Aesthete* had been a knife-edged silver thoroughbred: this thing was a dull bone colour, scoured by wave-borne particles of sand to look like the derelict skull of an old sea monster.

The divers came aboard and crawled out of their suits. I said to one of them, "Is the rudder still there?"

He turned towards me a face with white, exhausted circles under his eyes. "Yeah," he said. "Why?"

"We'll all take a look at the rudder tomorrow," said Nelligan. His shoulders were hunched in his thin brown jacket; he must have been freezing.

"Why not now?" I said.

"Tomorrow'll do," said Nelligan. "It's all arranged. We'll leave it in a locked yard and make our inspection first thing."

"What will you lose by checking now?"

"I don't know anything about boats, Mr. Agutter. I think the inspection should take place in the presence of . . . er . . . qualified parties."

"How about Mr. Barnes? Or Mr. Forsyth?"

He looked down, felt in his pockets, and extracted a

cigarette. Without looking up, he said, "Perhaps you know each other a bit well, Mr. Agutter. They tell me you're a tight little lot, down here in Pulteney."

"What exactly do you mean by that?"

He looked up at me with his soft brown eyes. "What I mean is that we'll look at that boat tomorrow, with a few experts from Plymouth. And when we find nothing wrong with it, we can put it all to bed and I won't have to come out in boats and freeze to death. I hate boats," said Inspector Nelligan. "It'll be left in a locked compound overnight, at Spearman's yard. And if they find nothing wrong with her tomorrow you're off the hook."

Heads I win, tails you lose.

I went to the mast and looked at it, keeping my hands carefully behind my back for Nelligan's benefit. The aluminium was unimaginably battered, but the masthead fittings were still there, the jib halyard with a little scrap of white sailcloth still attached to the shackle. I looked at it, asking it for some sort of clue. I bent to examine it more closely.

The clue was there.

I walked aft to Chiefy, and said, "Come and look at this." He gave the helm to one of the divers and we clambered into the well, Forsyth following. I pointed to the corner of cloth. "What's that?" I said.

"Looks like a corner of a jib." Chiefy stooped to look at the little black number on the cloth. "Number five."

"The number five genoa. Heavy weather. About the size of a pocket handkerchief. Do you think a sailor with Hugo's experience would have taken a knock-down under storm jib?"

"Not likely," said Chiefy. "Not in just force eight."

"So the rudder broke," said Forsyth.

"Or it was sabotaged," I said.

"Strewth," said Chiefy.

* * *

They dropped me off at the quay. I went up the iron ladder and watched the rusty barge chug away into the dusk. The black airbags at its stern pushed a fat wave in front of them, and I listened to the tiny roar of its break against the outside of the quay as Helberrow Point came between me and the barge.

Spearman's was located on the flat between Pulteney and Little Pulteney. They built a good few one-tonners, which are radical boats that incorporate some new and original ideas; so if you build them you do not necessarily want every Tom, Dick and Harry strolling round your lot. Hence the twelve-foot wire fence round the yard.

The barge disappeared into the gathering dusk. The quay was empty. I pulled in the painter of *Squid, Nautilus'* tender, moored with a little fleet of dinghies in the scummy water at the foot of the steps.

Squid was not one of your plywoods or inflatables. She was a sturdy ten-foot carvel rowing-boat and she was heavy enough to be well cursed by those unlucky enough to get the job of dragging her aboard *Nautilus*. On a night like tonight, she was exactly what I needed.

I went down the steps, climbed in, and pulled out to *Nautilus*. She was lying with her nose pointing to the west, in an eddy of the flood tide. I went up under her port side, and tied up to a stanchion out of sight of the shore. Above the harbour, Pulteney rose tier on tier, strings of yellow lights hanging across the face of the cliffs and wobbling in the ripples of the harbour.

I went forward and packed some tools, a flashlight and a camera into a canvas bag. Then I went through to the main cabin, ate a quick corned beef sandwich and washed it down with a slug of Famous Grouse. Finally, I pulled on a heavy oiled jersey and a dark cap with a shiny peak and the badge of the Agutter Line. Then I turned on all the cabin lights and returned on deck.

The sky had deepened from blue to black, and stars

swam among the clouds. There was no moon. A hundred yards away the quay was empty. Lights showed in a French yacht a little to seaward, but there was nobody on deck. Very cautiously, I slipped into *Squid*, laid an oar in the notch of the transom and let go the painter. I gave two figure-of-eight twists to the oar, and the dinghy moved seaward. Anyone watching from the shore would be dazzled by *Nautilus'* lights. Ripples made tiny clocking noises against the planking as I came beyond the shelter of the quay, and the lights of the town wheeled, a mountain of fireflies, as the tide caught the dinghy and began carrying her eastwards.

Once past the end of the quay, I knew I would be invisible against the band of darkness where the sea met the southern horizon. Setting the oars into the rowlocks, I began to row. The tide helped; five minutes later, Helberrow Point had passed to starboard, and I pulled hard with the left to bring her inshore, towards the flat stretch of sediments that the tide has deposited in the eddy behind Helberrow. As I turned, I felt the wind on my cheek. Above, the cirrus was already thickening into a layer of altostratus. Today's calm had been temporary.

It took another ten minutes to pull out of the tide and across to the shore of the flats. The sandy beach shone in the dying starlight, and I strained my eyes to look for the Bastion. The Bastion was a vast slab of concrete left over from the war, and a little past it was the mouth of the lagoon—or rather one of its mouths. The main mouth, artificially deepened, served Spearman's yard. The one by the Bastion served nobody but people like me and Hugo, when we had been young. It was a way of getting into the lagoon without anyone seeing you, which was useful if you wanted surreptitiously to fish for sea trout awaiting entry into the river Poult, which enters the sea here. It is also useful for anyone wishing to approach Spearman's unseen.

The tide swept me briskly through the Bastion channel. A bump on the shallow bottom, and I was into the lagoon. If anyone was watching, this was where they would see me. A puff of wind whistled across the lagoon; I was under the shore now, and it rattled the marram grass at the water's edge with a sound like light, dry bones. I felt acutely alone in the great sweep of beach and sky. I was taking a terrible risk; if Nelligan got to hear about this, he would assume I was a murderer, out to cover my tracks.

I rowed up the shore of the lagoon for perhaps five minutes, keeping low in the boat. Soon, the high wire fence of the yard cut the dark grey sky. I pulled perhaps another sixty strokes; then I found what I was looking for.

People like Nelligan, with shore-based notions of security, seldom appreciate that their standards do not apply by the sea. Wind and waves blow down posts and rust barbed wire. In this particular case, the sand had simply eroded away from the base of a pole, leaving a two-foot gap under the bottom of the wire. I carried *Squid*'s anchor up the beach and dug it well in. Then I shouldered the toolbag and crawled under the wire.

I knew Spearman's like the back of my hand. It consisted of three long corrugated iron sheds set parallel in a large compound of landfill, on which wisps of sand blew to and fro among haphazardly-placed yachts chocked with poles and wedges. The dock was at the far side, facing onto the main channel of the Poult. That was where they kept the crane. That was where they would have hoisted *Aesthete* out of the water.

I crept forward, keeping under the side of one of the long sheds. The wind was getting up now, clattering

115

the halyards against the metal masts. The hulls on their chocks loomed like a field of great beasts sleeping on their feet. A yellow square of light shone from the side of a shed; Harry Howe, the night-watchman. Harry would be watching telly, leaving his light to deter intruders. A car swept down the road inland and stopped in a lay-by favoured by young lovers, and I noticed one of its headlights was out.

I came to the end of the shed, and paused to listen. The only sounds were the slap and ting of the halyards and the distant bubbling yodel of a curlew.

I moved cautiously from the side of the shed to the lee of a chocked yacht, and paused again. Nothing, except that I could suddenly hear my breath roar in my nostrils, and my heartbeat—not particularly quick, but certainly louder than usual—in my chest. Small sounds ·suddenly became significant; the tiny crunch of grit under my feet as I moved down towards the crane, the slop of water against the pilings of the quay.

They had left *Aesthete* in the slings of the crane. I smelt her almost before I saw her, salt and weed, the smell of something that has been underwater for a long time. In the darkness, she had a terrible, lopsided look. As I drew nearer, I could tell even in the blackness the extent of the damage. Her port side was stove clear in for half its length. Underneath, her fin keel was battered and twisted. My eyes travelled aft. The rudder was intact.

I put up my hand and touched it. It was still wet. I increased the pressure. The fin moved. I gave the stock mountings a quick flash of the torch. They were covered in weed. I clawed the weed aside. The torch's beam glittered on stainless steel. The darkness returned, thick and black, when I turned it off and groped in my toolbag for screwdrivers and socket wrenches.

I had not known if I could do the job in the pitch dark, but it was easier than I had feared. The detailed drawings of the rudder came up in my mind as if on a screen, and my fingers navigated surely by touch alone. And because of her broken keel the yacht lay low in the slings, so the work was at a convenient bench level. I put the bolts in my pocket and pulled at the fin. It came away easily. Holding my breath, I pointed the flashlight at the cams and clicked the switch. Then I released my breath in a long, slow sigh.

In place of the titanium bolts specified were two empty holes. Lining the holes were a few crumbs of minced aluminium—all that remained of the aluminium bolts substituted by whoever it was who had meant *Aesthete's* steering to fail. Whoever it was who had murdered Hugo and Henry.

For a few moments, I stood completely absorbed in those little grey flecks of metal, the night-noises of the boatyard entirely shut out. Then I bent down and pulled from the bag the brass chronometer I had brought from *Nautilus*. It was a pretty chronometer, built as a navigational instrument, not a clock. I stuck it on the rudder with a lump of putty, took my camera out of its case, and then draped myself, rudder and camera in folds of the black polythene I had with me and focused as best I could inside my miniature lightproof tent. As I lined up, I thought: right, Nelligan, let's see if I'm still a murder suspect after I've recorded my own sabotage.

My finger tightened on the shutter, and the flash exploded in a sudden glare of white light. Then something twitched violently at the polythene and smashed into the back of my head and the light seemed to rush back into my eyes and mix with a sudden enormous pain at the nape of my neck. It turned from white to red and roared. My hands no longer existed, nor did my legs, which was why my face was grinding into the sand. There were two ideas in my mind. One was that someone had hit me from behind, very hard. The other was that I had been an idiot to leave violence out of my calculations. I could taste oily grit. The last thing I remembered was another big pain, cut off suddenly by black night, no stars.

16

Someone was flicking water into my face. At first, I thought I was at home in bed and that my father had broken out of his wing and was down getting prankish. I said, "Get away," and tried to bat at him with my hand. But my hand seemed oddly heavy, and I could not move it. Also, I was being thrown about and it was playing hell with my co-ordination. In fact, I could not see. It occurred to me that this was because my eyes were shut, so I opened them. This did not help, as there was as much blackness beyond my eyelids as inside them. But it did open the gates for other sensations.

For one thing, I realised that my head contained a terrible, jagged ache, as if it was full of cubes of hot stone. For another, I felt sick. And I was, hideously and agonizingly sick, onto whatever I was lying on, while the stone cubes rattled against the tender lining of my skull. With the nausea came cold. Shuddering violently, I relapsed into coma.

The next time was just as horrible, though it was an improvement in a way. I could move, as I discovered when I managed to put my hand to my forehead. My forehead was wet, as was my hand. In fact, I was lying in six inches of water, which was sloshing violently to and fro, impelled by the heaving of the surface on which I was lying. It was still very dark, but now I could see pale patches overhead.

Muzzily, I came to the conclusion that I was in a small boat. My fingers explored the planking. I knew those planks; I had repaired them myself—*Squid*. How had I got aboard *Squid?* There were no memories. And where was she now? It was a hard struggle to get upright, and not worth it, because on the way back the nausea returned. But this time, the idea of lying down again in the mess was unacceptable, so I achieved a sort of halfway house against the thwart, propped my chin on the edge and tried to persuade the agony in my head to behave like a brain.

There was a wind. I could feel it, and the sea was feeling it, too, because the waves were big. The sprinkling I had felt earlier was spray. In the darkness, the waves were already evil black hills, up whose sides the tender lurched, sometimes broadside-on, sometimes end-on. Now I was propped against the seat, the centre of gravity was higher. I pondered this fact, as *Squid* slithered down the side of a dark wave and up the side of the next. I saw the white water of the crest hang over the gunwale and flung myself towards it to stop her rolling. The sudden movement made me sick again. When I had finished, I groped around on the bottom boards for the oars. If I could keep her head to sea, I would be fine.

There were no oars.

I tried again, groping in the water. It must be the brain that was at fault. *Squid*'s oars lived where all oars should live, under the thwarts unless they were actually in the rowlocks. I searched twice more in the black water. The oars were not there.

I was already shivering, but now I started to shiver in earnest. It dawned on me that these were not inshore seas. Somehow, *Squid,* with me in her, had arrived a long way out in the English Channel in what felt like the run-up to a gale. I was as defenceless as a kitten in a shoebox. I braced myself against the sides, rigid with panic. Another wave sloshed in, half-filling the boat with water that made me gasp as it came up to my waist. But as the water came in, the panic left me. There were things you could do in this situation. The first requirement was to get her head to sea.

Groping forward of the bow thwart, I discovered the painter. I blew a short breath of relief. The painter was thirty feet long. It needed to be, to moor the tender among the gaggle at the quay steps. Then I took off my jersey, ignoring the icy cold of the wind on my wet T-shirt. "Sea anchor," I said to myself. I stripped off the T-shirt and pulled the jersey back over my head. "Wool next the skin," I muttered. "Always wear wool next the skin. Wool warm when wet. Wet when warm. Warm when wet." Babbling foolishly, I tied the T-shirt's arms in a knot, hitched its hem to the end of the painter, and paid it out overboard.

There was a slight—very slight—easing of the dinghy's motion. But she was sluggish still; the water in her made her slow to recover from rolling. So I took off my left shoe and began to bail.

The wind was freshening, to perhaps force six, and there was a lot of water flying about in that black hissing. I bailed a hundred strokes with my left hand, then a hundred with my right, and then changed back again. I changed hands dozens of times. I could feel the sweat running down my back. A hot metal band lay round my forehead and I could hear someone talking. The person was me, I was pretty sure, but I had no time to listen to myself. Instead, I sat on the thwart facing forward and glared into the darkness at the wind that howled over the wavecrests and split itself on the bridge of my nose before it tumbled away into the night astern.

There were two complete certainties in my mind.

The first was that I had to keep bailing, and the other was that I was going to die. After a while, my arms knotted with cramp and I felt a raging thirst. From then on, death seemed preferable to bailing. But I kept bailing anyway, and entered a curious zone.

In this zone, people appeared to me. There were my father and mother first of all, asking me (I was five years old) why I had gone out without oars in an offshore wind. When I told them I did not know, they smiled and wandered off into the darkness. After them came Hugo. Hugo's lips were moving, but no words came out. So he merely shook his head and looked depressed, and left. This upset me, and I wept. Then, very close to my face, there appeared the bronzed visage of Richard Mitchell, my Olympic coach. Richard told me to pull my finger out, and counted the strokes of the bailing shoe at the rate of one a second. After he had done his bit, I was visited by a committee of my clients, requesting a sail-powered ocean liner with an air-powered rudder. I began lecturing them. Sally was there, smiling encouragingly. So were Amy Charlton and Frank Millstone and Archer and Ed Beith and Hector Pollitt and Johnny Forsyth. They all listened for a while, then tiptoed round behind me, keeping step, like Ali Baba's Forty Thieves in a pantomime. Each of them was carrying an enormous titanium bolt. I did not look round because I knew they were going to hit me on the head. I screamed at them not to, and the darkness whirled down again.

I do not know how long it was before I got up again. This time, I was better. Now I knew I had severe concussion. I knew from the alternating dry heat and shivers that I was running a fever. But as I strained my eyes over the stern of the boat, I began to feel a tiny shred of hope. For on what might have been the eastern horizon, a narrow band of paler darkness ran. It must be the dawn. Grinning at that stripe of daylight, I continued to bail. After a while, I could no longer see the daylight and my mind was wandering again. The bailing must have become slower, I suppose. Vaguely, I remember slipping down into water that came all the way up to my neck and laying my face in it gratefully.

This time, I thought I really had gone to Heaven. There was a roaring in my ears, and a sensation of floating, then rising and flying. I tried to open my eyes, but shut them against the brightness. After that, a powerful smell of fish. That was odd; I had never imagined fish in Heaven, somehow, though there must be some in the Glassy Sea. After that, a deep and healing rest, on a surface that yielded and was warm and dry.

When I opened my eyes, I was in a small cabin with a cream-painted ceiling with pipes running across it. I sat up. My head spun. There was a bowl beside the bunk to be sick into. I used it. After a while, I could sit up. My clothes were on the end of the bunk, rough-dried. I pulled them on and stumbled out onto the bridge of a ship. Through the glass, I could see a low, green coast across five miles of dark blue sea. A man with a heavy black moustache turned his head towards me.

"Salut," he said. "Ça va?"

"Ça va," I said, through a mouth that seemed to lack its usual connection with my brain.

He asked me who I was and where I was from, and I told him in halting French made even more dreadful than usual by the motor grinding between my ears. I was on the Breton trawler *Drenec,* he told me. They had found me awash in a dinghy at 0700 hours. I would have sunk pretty soon. I was in luck.

I agreed that I was in luck, and he told me that we would be ashore in an hour, and that I could just walk onto the ferry and I'd be in Plymouth before I knew what. I asked him what port was this, and he told me Roscoff, which is in Brittany. *Drenec* seemed to be a fairly ancient boat, and the time on her chronometer was 1850 hours. I asked him where he had picked me up, and he told me about fifty kilometres southwest of the Isle of Wight.

I went back to the hot little cabin and searched through my pockets. They were empty. "Of course," I said aloud. But I was disappointed. Camera and chronometer and crumbs of aluminium were in the mugger's pocket or at the bottom of the deep blue sea, and would never be seen again. I sat down on the bunk, wincing at the jar of pain at the base of my skull.

When I felt a little better, I went to the bridge and got myself patched through to the telephone system via VHF. I sat down and watched the shearwaters cutting the white wavetops, and the sharp blue horizon waving from side to side, and listened to the hisses and clicks in the receiver. Eventually I heard the voice I wanted: Neville Spearman's.

"Who's there?" he said.

"Charlie Agutter." The long waves of the static rolled between us. "You inspected the yacht's rudder. What did you find?"

"You should have bloody well turned up to the inspection," said Spearman. The hostility in his voice was audible even through the electronic soup.

"I couldn't," I said. "Previous engagement."

"We found two broken titanium bolts," said Spearman. "And before I build any more boats for you, I will want structural engineers' reports and guarantees in blood. The amount of dirt that's flying round here, some of it's going to stick to my yard."

"I'm sorry."

"Me too," said Spearman, and the line went dead.

I shuffled back to the cabin. It was no more than I had expected. I should have felt gloom. What I actually felt was a twinge of pleasure that the sabotage had conformed to pattern. And stronger than that, an urge to lie down and go to sleep for a long time, which I duly did.

I slept off some more of my headache on the night ferry and Sally was at Plymouth to meet me. As I walked down the echoing baggage hall, she was by a pillar at the far end, looking more than ever like an Egyptian temple sculpture. She smiled, but there were black smudges under her happy green eyes. I kissed her on the cheek.

"I'm glad you're back," she said matter-of-factly, as we climbed into the car. "You look bloody awful."

I squinted into the rear-view mirror. The face that squinted back was the usual one, spiky hair, sunken eyes, bat ears and all. But this version looked as if it had been starved for two weeks, then whitewashed and smeared with green paint under the eyes. The eyes themselves had an unhealthy, glassy look.

"Undead," I said.

"Yes." She was driving, threading crisply through the morning traffic along the Hoe. "What happened?"

I was getting good at answering this question now.

I told her. Her white face jerked towards me and the Peugeot swerved violently across the nose of a builder's van.

"But you could have been killed," she said.

"That was the idea," I said. "I'd just discovered that somebody did sabotage *Aesthete*."

I had meant to put it more gently, but my neck hurt and the engine was still buzzing between my ears, and besides, Sally was not the kind of person who appreciated having important things put gently. This time, the Peugeot remained steady in its tracks.

"How?" she said, in a small, cold voice.

I told her.

125

"The same way as *Ae*," she said. "But why?"

"Do you think Amy would sabotage a boat to kill her husband and give Pollitt a clear field?"

"Do what?" She laughed. "Amy couldn't change a lightbulb."

"Well, what about Pollitt, to give himself a clear field with Amy?"

"Not exactly up his alley, is it? That means it would have been him who hit you on the head." She paused. "And it couldn't have been him, because he was off somewhere boozing. Apparently he got himself breathalysed the night before last, down on the coast road."

"Really?" I said, not too interested.

"Three times over the limit. I reckon it's Amy's fault. She doesn't half muck him about. They stopped him for having a headlight out and he fell out onto the road." She turned onto the A303, driving a Morris 1000 into the kerb of a roundabout. "What's wrong with you?"

I was gazing through the windscreen. But I was not seeing the streams of traffic heading down the dual carriageway. Instead, I was back there at Spearman's in the dark, watching a car pull into the lovers' lay-by. A car with only one headlight. Perhaps Pollitt did know something after all.

She tried to take me to see Dr. Allison. But the headache was down to a dull thud now, and the cotton wool wrapping my thoughts was losing its grip. So I asked her to drop me at the office, and she looked across at me and must have seen some convincing reason for not objecting, because she did as she was asked.

I rang the *Yachtsman*. Pollitt wasn't there; they said he was supposed to be in Pulteney, so I asked Chiefy if he'd seen him. Chiefy, who had a special talent for

126

knowing exactly what went on, said Frank Millstone had lent him an office in one of his buildings down by the harbour. Then he asked me what had been happening, and I told him I'd fallen into my tender from the quay steps and come round in mid-Channel. He did not tell me how lucky I was to be alive, because he knew I knew. When Chiefy rang off, I went to see Pollitt.

It was a small room above a yacht-chandlery. As I walked in, Pollitt was typing.

He looked round, rolled his piece out of the platen and placed it smoothly face-down on the desk. Then he smiled broadly and said, "Well, well, Charlie!" He came round the desk, hand outstretched. "You look as if you've been in the wars!"

So did he. His tan looked greenish and I could smell the drink on him when he was ten feet away. His hand was cold and wettish.

"I have," I said. "Bloody stupid thing happened."

"Really?" said Pollitt. "Do tell."

"I fell down the quay steps when I was untying my tender," I said. "Late at night. Offshore breeze. Woke up in the middle of the Channel."

"The middle of the Channel?" His amazement sounded genuine enough. But then it was a pretty amazing story.

I explained to him my subsequent tribulations, searching his face for hints the while. I didn't find any.

"You were lucky," he said, when I had finished. Was there a double meaning there?

"I was. Heard you had a spot of bother the other night."

"Ah," he said. "Yes. The officers got me."

"Bit of a shocker," I said.

"Well, you know how it is. I went out to dinner at the Lobster Pot, and there they were on the way back."

"Was Amy in the car?"

"No. I'd dropped her—" He stopped himself. "How did you know I'd been having dinner with Amy?"

"I guessed."

"Bloody nymphomaniac," said Pollitt. He sat down at his desk and pulled out a half-bottle of whisky and drank from it. When he looked up, his face had turned weaselly. "None of your bloody business, though, Agutter. What do you want, anyway?"

"Social visit," I said.

"How's your deal with Archer?" said Pollitt.

"Fine."

"That's not what I heard."

"You didn't hear anything from Archer."

"Sources close to Archer."

"Like Amy?"

He clamped his hands on the desk and came at me. But he was unfit and half-drunk, so I picked him up and put him back in his chair.

"You're not yourself, Hector," I said. "You finish your nice story and then get some kip."

He subsided. "She doesn't love Archer," he said. "She was drunk at the dance the other night. That's all. And as for you, you just watch it. It's the Captain's Cup soon and the selectors read my column."

"Easy, Hector," I said. And I left him there, in the sleazy little room in his wooden chair, with his typescript of cheap secrets flat on the desk in front of him.

I went back to my office and dialled Sally. "Come on," I said. "We're off for lunch."

"Where?" she said.

"The Lobster Pot. Try out your friend Pat Forsyth's cooking. See you there in twenty minutes."

I got there first. In earlier days, it had been called the Angel, but in the wake of the Millstone invasion the brewery had strung fishnets across the ceilings and nailed dried starfish to the walls, and Pat Forsyth had got the bistro franchise in what had previously been the skittle-alley. The food was medium to bad, but there was nothing they could do to the tomato juice, so I ordered one.

Johnny Forsyth came out of the kitchen with a sandwich in his hand. "Charlie," he said. "Just pinching a snack off the wife. Heard you had an accident."

"Amazing, the way news travels in this town."

He looked slightly wounded. "Just taking an interest," he said.

"Sorry," I said. "Sore head. Have a drink."

He grinned at me. "Nope," he said. "I'm painting a picture for Millstone this afternoon. Got to keep a clear head. Hey, there's Sally." He watched Sally's graceful walk as she came across the room. I felt his eyes on us as we talked, quietly, and ordered potted shrimps from the bar. After a while he said, loudly, "See you, then," and left.

Sally and I sat down at a table. There were a couple of other lunchers, but the place was by no means full. It very seldom was.

"I wonder how they make a profit here," I said.

"I'm not sure they do," said Sally. "They always seem to be just about bankrupt."

"Listen," I said. "Go and have a word with Pat. Ask her if Amy and Pollitt were here all evening the night before last."

Sally looked at me, hard. "Is that why we're out to lunch?"

"Please," I said.

Sally got up. "If you insist," she said, and dived into the kitchen area.

She returned twenty minutes later, with our order of potted shrimps. "Pat says that they were here all evening," she said.

"Pity."

"Except that Pollitt had to go out and telephone

some people. He was gone about three-quarters of an hour. After about nine-ish. Amy sat up at the bar and talked to Pat. Then Pollitt came back and they started eating again."

"Did she notice anything strange about him?"

"He was drunk. He was quarrelling with Amy."

"Nothing strange about that."

"I suppose not," said Sally. "Bloody hell." She paused. "I used to think Pulteney was the most beautiful place in the world. Do you remember the fun we had, Hugo and you and me and Ed Beith? And now it's all gone miserable and ugly, and there are things going on that nobody understands." Her long green eyes were glassy with tears. "And even the potted shrimps here are disgusting." She pushed her plate away, and took a long, juddering breath. "Charlie, I've got to go."

"I'll take you home."

"No," she said. "Don't. I'll be fine."

She got up and left.

I paid the bill. Pat Forsyth smiled at me; an artificial smile. She was an unhappy woman, who liked to give the impression of being the patient victim of malevolent fate, but actually merely seemed to complain a lot about very minor afflictions.

My head hurt. I was tired and fed up. So I took it slowly back up the hill to the house where the aspirins lived.

Evidence or not, I didn't believe Pollitt had left dinner, driven a mile to the marina, whacked me on the head, loaded me into the boat and cast me adrift. He didn't have the strength. And he didn't have the guts.

It was a fine afternoon. The sky was blue, with a light southwesterly breeze herding clouds like sheep. George Evans the postman, late as usual, was ducking under the honeysuckle over my garden gate.

He said it was a nice day, but privately I was

studying his red face and light blue eyes and wondering, was it you who smashed me one at Spearman's?

"Not looking too good," said George.

"Overwork," I lied, and watched him go down the road, whistling. I didn't believe in Pollitt as saboteur and mugger. That left the field wide open; anyone in Pulteney might have Agutter on his mind. It was a nasty, naked feeling.

I went in and called Scotto, telling him to have *Sorcerer* ready for an outing on the afternoon tide. What I really wanted to do was go to bed for a couple of days. But the start-gun waits for no man, and we had six months' practice on *Sorcerer* to cram into three weeks. I could always grab forty winks on a bunk.

Also, I admitted to myself, nobody was banging anyone on the head on *Sorcerer*.

I had ten minutes to spare before I had to leave, so I shaved quickly and then went to see my father. The nurse was reading the *Daily Post* in the kitchen. She put on her large, lipstick smile above her starched apron.

"He's very well today," she said. "The doctor gave him some new pills, and he's had ever so many visitors."

He was under a tartan rug in the armchair by the window. *Lloyd's List* trembled in his bony fingers. He recognized me and laid his newspaper aside. He said, "You've been very quiet for a couple of days. Where've you been?"

"France," I said.

"Oh," he said. "My bloody memory. Archer told me."

"Archer?"

"Everyone in Pulteney knows." He laughed. "Clumsy oaf. Falling down the quay steps into yer own tender. Hee!" His liver-spotted hand spanked mirthfully at the arm of his chair. Then he looked at me sideways, as he did on the rare occasions he wanted to make a confession. "Nice to see yer, though. Sounded nasty."

"It was a bit." If Hector Pollitt was useful for anything, it was as a spreader of rumours.

"Charlie," he said. "Are you in money trouble?"

I was taken aback. We rarely discussed money. "Why do you ask?" I said.

His fingers plucked nervously at his rug. "Frank Millstone came round," he said. "He said you were going broke. That you'd have to sell up. You know he wants to turn this house into a hotel or something. He said he'd make me an offer for my half, a decent offer, so I could be comfortable for the rest of my life." He was grabbing handfuls of the rug, now. "Are you going broke, Charlie?"

I said, "No. There's nothing to worry about." Inwardly, I was furious.

He grabbed my hand and shook it. "Be careful," he said, and in the watery eyes, I read affection and perhaps fear. "Now tell me the gossip."

We chatted for five minutes, then I went out and used the telephone in the hall to call Millstone.

"Frank," I said. "Charlie Agutter. What do you mean by sneaking round here and trying to frighten my father into selling you the house?"

Millstone said coldly, "He's over twenty-one."

"And what do you mean by telling him I'm going broke?"

"What I said," said Millstone. "You're in big trouble, Charlie."

"You may not have heard," I said. "I'm sailing one of my boats for Sir Alec Breen, in the Captain's Cup trials."

Millstone chuckled his ripe, jolly chuckle. "Well, then, you'd better make sure you win," he said.

I rang off.

Nurse Bollom was watching me, her mouth a thin

red line. She had an idea that there was something unhealthy about the house. She would have preferred a bungalow, with me far away.

As I opened the garage doors, I indulged in a little paranoiac fantasy. Why had Frank Millstone chosen yesterday to make another offer to my father? Was it because he knew about my financial state? Or did he have reason to be sure that the obstructive Charlie Agutter was out of his way, for good?

I climbed into the car and my hand went to the ignition key. I drew it back. Climbing out, I looked carefully under the bonnet, then under the car itself, seeking unfamiliar bulges. There was only the usual mixture of rust and oil. As I drove between the banks of yellow gorse flowers to New Pulteney, the feeling of vulnerability returned.

Of course, I thought, as I parked the car in the New Pulteney Marina car park, I could always tell Nelligan. Assuming he believed me, he could launch a full-scale murder investigation.

On either side of the gently bouncing jetty, the racing-boats lay low and sharp. The sight of the boats and the nip of the wind reminded me why I was here: to race. No, I thought. No Nelligan. Just you and me, you murdering bastard, whoever you are.

Sorcerer carried a crew of ten men. Offshore racing is a small world, so I already knew the four who had come with the boat. There was Dike the foredeck man, wearing an obscene T-shirt to which his head seemed connected without benefit of neck. Halyards Joe was reputed to originate near Burnham-on-Crouch, but it was hard to confirm this since few had ever heard him speak. George, known as Walter because he was a winchman, had enormous arms that hung to bare brown knees. These three crouched on the deck next to Scotto and a bearded Henry the Eighth lookalike called Al, who specialised in mastwork. Their appearance made it easy to understand why mastmen, winch-grinders and other classes of essential and highly-skilled deckhands are classed under the general heading of gorillas.

The more intellectual section of the crew included Morrie, a sail-trimmer who had come with the boat and was an authority on the tuning of her mast. Further, there was Doug Mitchell, tactician and navigator, who had sailed himself round the world twice without getting lost; Nick Thwaite, special trimmer, who had been sent down by Capote's the sailmakers to make sure we got the best of any new sails we might chance to order from them; Crispin Hughes-Affrick, winner of the Flying Dutchman Championships the previous year, mainsheet and spare helmsman; and me, helmsman and managing director of the yacht *Sorcerer*, a wholly-owned subsidiary of Breen Holdings.

We exchanged courteous greetings, as befitted gentlemen amateurs. Then we had a serious discussion, as befitted amateurs who were all being heavily subsidised by the boat's owner. Scotto, as full-time boatnigger, was the only one who drew a salary. The rest of them had to put up with free air tickets, lavish living expenses and fast cars on loan. Or, in my case, a potential boost to a very bad reputation.

The Captain's Cup trials are a series of races that begin in early summer. From the contenders, the selectors pick out the three boats that will sail in the English team. Most of the opposition had been working since before Christmas, so by that standard we were a late-come and disunited crew. On our side was the fact that *Sorcerer* was nicely tuned, and that the gorillas knew each other. It was only a matter of fine tuning, brisk routines and luck. Quite a lot of luck.

That day, I started with a violent headache and a fuzzy mind. But the breeze was crisp, and though the routines were a little slack the potential was there.

After three hours, my head was clear and *Sorcerer* was once again an extension of my mind, as she had been when she was on the drawing-board.

There were a couple of things that needed changing: she was wearing a straight keel when she needed an ellipse, and I would have liked to put a cam rudder on her, but for the moment it seemed scarcely politic. So I called my office on the VHF and Ernie the draughtsman pulled *Sorcerer's* original plans out of the chest and began drawing a keel.

We reached home with the big spinnaker, red and gold with the *Sorcerer's* caduceus, ballooning huge against the horizon. Seeing that cloud of sail against the sky, hearing the sharp fizz of the wake, there was a moment when I felt a pang of pleasure in being alive. Then I remembered that someone among the folds of the green cliffs on the port bow wanted to kill me, and the pleasure faded.

As we motored in, I called a crew meeting.

"Out again first thing tomorrow," I said. "Then we'll lift her out and they'll put a new keel on at Spearman's. That'll take two days. Back in the water on Tuesday. Scotto, a word."

After we had tied up and the crew were drifting off towards their Red Stripes, I said to Scotto, "Big favour. Stay with the boat, could you?"

"What did you think I'd be doing?" said Scotto.

"I mean really stay with her. They're taking her into a shed, and they're locking her up. Even so, I want you not to let her out of your sight. Sleep aboard. Okay?"

Scotto stared at me. "Bloody hell," he said. Then he shrugged. "You're the boss. What's happening?"

"Enemy action," I said. "Lock her up and nip over to Spearman's with me."

Neville Spearman was in his office, at the drawingboard with Johnny Forsyth. There was a set of plans in front of them. I saw the name *Crystal* at the top.

"What are you doing to that thing?" I said. "Ed Beith rebuilding her again?"

Forsyth grinned at me, showing widely-separated teeth. He looked particularly pleased with himself. "Ed?" he said. "No. We were just . . . looking into her a bit. You might meet her on the water."

"She's falling apart, I heard," I said. "Hull delaminating."

"Not any more," said Forsyth. "I've fixed her." There was real conviction in his voice. "You want to watch out for her, Charlie."

"Anyway," I said. "A word, Neville?"

Spearman went round to his desk and sat down in front of an array of photographs of boats: fishing-boats and customs launches as well as yachts, all built by Spearman's. The skin around his eyes was dark from overwork. He did not look particularly pleased to see us.

"This is private, I'm afraid, Johnny," I said.

Forsyth stuck his big hands into his pockets and shouldered his way out of the door.

"What's so private?" said Spearman.

"Oh, you know how things get around," I said. Spearman nodded, without much conviction. I could tell that my stock with him had not been improved by my acquisition of *Sorcerer*.

"Your office rang," he said. "Keel's on its way from Wolverhampton in the morning."

We discussed the keel for a quarter of an hour. It was not an enormous job, but Neville was wary. When I told him that Scotto would be sleeping aboard, and that I wanted *Sorcerer* in a locked shed, he looked even more tired.

At the end, I said, "I'm upset about *Aesthete's* rudder. I'm sorry if it's put you in difficulties."

"So am I," said Neville. "And I don't like it."

"They were titanium bolts."

"But they broke. Frankly, Charlie, it looks like you

136

ballsed up the calculations." He drew papers towards him. The subject was closed.

"Bring her in tomorrow," he said. "We'll lift her straight out and get to work." He returned to the papers on his desk and we left, dismissed. Three weeks ago he would have been all over me.

As we left the yard, Scotto said, "I'm minding the boat. Spearman's looking at you like a leper. What's going on?"

He stared at me with his faded blue eyes, hands in the pockets of his jeans, six and a half feet high and three feet wide. I thought for a moment. What the victims of attempted murder need are bodyguards. Well, why not?

"Let's get a drink," I said.

We drove to the Mermaid. Scotto ordered lager, and I had a pint of Bass. Then I told him the truth about what had happened the night before last.

"Ugh," said Scotto, when I had finished. "What did they do that for?"

"Sporting manoeuvre," I said. "When I was in Montreal for the Olympics, some enterprising person put a coat of fresh varnish on my boat very early one morning, so when we dropped her on the gravel before we put her in, we would get a lot of stones and whatnot stuck to the bottom and we would go a bit slower as a result. We were lucky, because we spotted it and wiped it off. You can't always be that lucky. And we are playing for big money, so people are just naturally going to be rougher. Now then, I'm going to Ireland for a couple of days and when I come back I'll need a bit of minding. Meanwhile, you're in charge of *Sorcerer.*"

Scotto sucked at his lager. "Yeah. Shall I get my gun?"

"Gun?" I said.

"I was one of the armed guards on *Australia II* at Newport, 1983. I've got it in me bus."

"Just get a bit of iron bar and keep your eyes open."

Scotto's enormous face took on a disappointed air. Then he cheered up. "Right," he said. "Let's get to it, shall we?"

The following morning it was apparent that he had slept on board. We had a good outing practising sail changes. When we came in, we had a crew meeting and Scotto took her round to the yard for her new keel. I went home, packed a bag, drove to Plymouth and caught the Brymon Airways flight for Cork.

17

After we landed, I picked up a hire car and drove to the Shamrock Hotel in Kinsale. Next morning, I got up early and took my headache down to breakfast. The dining-room was cold and empty, full of the bluish-grey light of the sea. I sat and crumbled the soda bread in the basket, and wondered where to start. Then the holiday breakfasters started to trickle in, fathers heavy-eyed with last night's stout, and the drifts of cigarette smoke drove me out into the telephone box.

I had to start with Hegarty. I was nervous about Hegarty. I had to hope that his regard for the truth was greater than his regard for his own reputation. If this was the case, he would be unique in the world of offshore racing.

I need not have worried.

"Hell, yes," he said, when I asked if I could come down and do some interviewing. "I'll set you up a desk and you can ask who you like what you like, and we'll tell 'em you're going to give us some work, and you're checking us out. You could send us some, come to that."

"Next job that suits," I said, and meant it.

The desk he had promised me was in a small green office. The first man I talked to was Sheehy, the yard foreman. He was small, with twitching hands and shuffling boots; he gave the impression of acute nervousness until you noticed the steady eyes under his sandy brows. Sheehy kept track of all boat movements through the yard.

"Ae," he said. "We had her out of the water. I looked at her keel bolts and the rudder assembly my own self, and they was fine. That would have been Thursday evening, before the weekend when the rudder came off her." He blew smoke at his square, twitching hands.

"Where did she stand the night?"

"Beyond in the yard, on her props," said Sheehy. "We put her in the water the next day."

"What time did you check the rudder?"

"It would have been five in the evening. Tight as a drum, it was." He shook his head, his eyes never leaving mine. "Bloody odd, them bolts going. You'd hold a steam train with one of them."

After he had gone, the whole yard trooped through and I asked them to corroborate Sheehy's story, which they did, and then to add anything of their own. Nobody added anything important. After all, most of them were carpenters or painters or riggers, and they saw hundreds of boats every year.

I was shown over the lofts by the Construction Foreman, a blond Dutchman. Then I saw the paint sheds with White, an old man wrinkled like a walnut and coughing from years of solvent vapours. Last came the rigging sheds, for which my guide was one Dennis, with black hair growing low on his forehead and one finger distorted by what must have been an accident with some kind of power tool. It was a lovely yard, and perfectly secure. But I was not here to admire the view.

My last interview was with Garrett, the watchman,

a tiny brown man in a filthy brown raincoat and enormous boots.

"What time do you come on?" I said.

"Six o'clock in the evening," said Garrett. "But you understand I'm busy part of the time."

"How's that?"

"The Archaeological Association," said Garrett. "We meets in the Marine, nightly." He looked at me, hard. "And we drinks Lucozade, in case you was wonderin'."

"I was," I said. "How d'you make sure nobody gets into the yard?"

"I turns the dog loose," said Garrett.

"He's a fierce dog?"

"He would have the leg off you and still call to the house for his breakfast," said Garrett, matter-of-factly.

"And do you remember him behaving differently, ever?"

"There was only the Saturday night, when that boat of yours come in with the bust rudder."

"Nothing before that?"

"Nothing. He's a very lively dog altogether."

"Oh." It was beginning to look as if my Irish trip had been a waste of time. I decided on one last try. "But before the boat came in with the bust rudder, was he not behaving strangely then?"

"I could not say," said Garrett.

"I see," I said. "Well—"

"And the reason I could not say was because I did not then have the pleasure of the dog's acquaintance." Garrett drew himself up to his full four feet eleven inches. "The reason being that I was then in possession of the previous dog, Brian. Two days before your troubles with the rudder, Brian was found stiff. Poison was suspected. But then he was a bloody man-eater, so I wasn't surprised."

I stared at him. He was eyeing me with triumph, as

if I were the captain of a rival Archaeology Association that he had just worsted in debate.

"He was poisoned on what night?"

Garrett calculated on his fingers. "It would have been the Thursday."

"And you noticed nothing strange in the yard."

"I did not."

"Very well," I said. "Thanks for your help."

"Not a bit. Are ye done?"

"I am."

He turned and marched from the room. So Thursday night was dog-poisoning night in Crosshaven. From my notes, I made a table of the movements of everyone in the yard. Now I would have to go round their houses, twenty-three of them, and check out the husbands' stories with their wives. Any discrepancies might be significant—assuming the saboteur was employed by the yard. It was a big assumption.

As it happened, it didn't work out like that.

At six o'clock, Billy Hegarty put his head round the plywood door and asked me how I was getting on. I told him. He shrugged, and asked me to dinner in Kinsale that evening. I refused, on the grounds that I had to work. I could see that he didn't think I'd get anywhere. At six-thirty, I drove off to the Marine Bar and ate smoked salmon sandwiches and drank a pint of Murphy's, the best stout in Ireland. Then I walked back into the car park, got into the car, and looked at the first address on my list. It was in Crosshaven village, so I started the engine and pulled out onto the road. Something was digging into my back, so I shifted position. The lump did not go away. It dug in harder.

A voice from the back seat said, "Keep drivin' and do as you're told and ye might not get hurt."

My heart gave one leap and seemed to stop. The world became very still. The voice said, "Turn left, after the post-box."

142

I turned left, into a narrow lane that wound up a steep hill, overhung with oak trees. I shifted my eyes to the rear view mirror. The back seat was empty; he must be down on the floor.

"Keep yer eyes ahead of yiz," said the voice. It had a nervous, strangled quality. The accent was Northern Irish, but there was something not quite right about it.

"Who are you?" I said, keeping my voice steady with an effort.

"Ask no questions and ye'll hear no lies. Turn right at the end of the brick wall."

The curtain of oaks had parted a fraction, to reveal the mouth of a cart-track. The track wound through thickets of brambles. There was a distant flash of blue sea, a huge mound of ponticum, covered in mauve flowers. My mouth was dry.

"Turn left," said the voice. We turned away from the sea. Ahead were rhododendrons, and above them pillars and window sockets entwined with brambles— the ruins of a big house. "Don't do nothing stupid, and let me see yer hands."

I got out. The wind sighed in the trees. The air was soft, with that Irish smell of bracken and recent rain.

"Turn around," said the voice. I turned towards the house, but not before I had seen him getting out of the car. A chill came on the air. It was the figure of the bogeyman who follows the coffins in West Belfast. Black balaclava, black woollen gloves; and in the hands the gun. Not an Armalite, though. A sawn-off shotgun, pump action.

I said, "Is this political?"

"Shut yer mathe," he said. Again, there was something wrong with the accent. Carefully, the man lit a cigarette. He put it through the mouth-hole of the balaclava. It looked ridiculous. And the fear went, for a moment, and I began to think clearly. People in England are under the impression that the Provisional IRA spends its leisure time robbing and intimidating

143

in the South. But I had been to Ireland enough times to realise that the Provos had better, or anyway different, things to do than intimidate private citizens for no good reason.

Some smoke had caught in the wool of the balaclava. The man coughed. I smiled.

"What are ye laughing at?" he said.

What I was smiling at was the fact that the accent was a fake, a County Cork approximation of Belfast. The man threw away the cigarette and gestured with the gun. The fear returned. The gun looked real enough; and as long as the gun was real, it didn't really matter much who stood behind it.

"What do you want?" I said.

"Less of you," said the man. "Some of the lads doesn't want you stickin' in your nose where it don't belong."

"What lads?" I asked.

"You don't want to find out," he said. His black-gloved hands shifted nervously on the stock of the gun. I watched him closely. There was something odd about one of the fingers. "This is your first and last warning."

"I see."

"Now," he said. He pulled a metal tool from his pocket and tossed it on the ground at my feet. "Take out the valves from the wheels of the car." Picking it up, I crouched and unscrewed the valve pistons. The tyres subsided with a hiss. "Don't you be bothering us again." He aimed the muzzle of the shotgun at my feet. I watched it, halfway between fear and amusement, thinking: this amateur IRA-man doesn't know what he's doing. He hadn't even asked for his pliers back.

The bang of the shotgun made me jump nearly out of my skin. He fired again, kicking up soil between us. I threw myself behind the car. Pigeons clattered away from their roosts, and a cock pheasant crowed in alarm.

"Stay away, you Brit bastard," he said. I crouched behind the car, shaking. Pathetic he might be, but his gun had been loaded. "You have been warned."

He backed away from me towards a rhododendron bush, the gun still trained. Then he dived into the bush. I watched him from behind the car. My fingers closed on a large stone. He came out of the bush wheeling a moped. He levelled the gun, leaning the moped against his hip.

"Stay where you are," he said. "Don't try nothing." He sounded a little desperate and the Northern accent was slipping badly. He was perhaps twenty-five feet away. I said nothing, waiting. The birds began to sing again. This man was the key. I couldn't let him go.

He began wheeling the moped away sideways, pointing the gun at me one-handed. I hoped it was as awkward as it looked. When he was twenty yards off he straddled the moped, slung the gun, and started pedalling frantically. I began running after him, clutching the stone like a rugby ball. His black and khaki figure was outlined against the bushes. I smelt raw petrol from the moped's exhaust. I was six feet behind him when the engine caught and whirred. Raising the stone in both hands, I flung it at his back.

It hit him between the shoulder blades. His head jerked round in surprise just as the front wheel of the moped lurched into a deep rut in the road, and he went flying over the handlebars. I kept running. The last two paces I covered in mid-air. I saw the whites of his eyes swivel in the holes of the balaclava. Then I landed with both feet on his stomach. The air went out of him with a whoosh and the gun flew into a bramble-bush. I pulled it out and pointed it at him. The moped engine coughed and stopped.

He lay folded like a clasp-knife, retching, as peace

returned to the woods. Pigeons cooed in the canopy of leaves, and flecks of dappled sunlight shifted over his gaping mouth. One of his gloves had been torn off in the crash. The strangely twisted finger was now revealed. Half the nail was gone, as if in an accident with a power tool of some kind. It belonged to Lenny Dennis, who had shown me round the rigging loft at Hegarty's yard that afternoon.

After a while, he rolled onto his back and struggled into a sitting position.

"Take off your hood, Mr. Dennis," I said.

He pulled it off. He was red and puffy, and his eyes shifted left and right like the eyes of a dog in a crate.

"How long have you been a member of a paramilitary organization?" I said.

He swore at me.

"Shall we pop down to the Gardai and tell them what's going on?" I said. "I'd say you'd be safer with them than with the Provos. The Provos can get a bit nasty with freelancers."

He did some more swearing.

"Or you could just tell me why you put on this little play, and I'll decide what to do about you after."

This time he did not swear, but stared at me with eyes that were sullen and angry.

"Are you going to answer?" I said. "Or are we going to walk down the hill and talk to Billy Hegarty?"

"Hegarty?" he said. His forehead was suddenly white and sweaty.

"And then the Gardai. Think about it."

He thought about it. Finally, he said, "And if I tell you?"

"Not a word, if you do what you're told."

His eyes searched my face for guarantees. I don't know if he found what he was looking for, but he began talking. "A fella telephoned and said would I poison that bloody dog," he said.

"Who was he?"

146

"I never heard him before. Some English fella."

"What made him think you'd consider poisoning dogs?"

"He said he knew I needed the money. He said he'd seen me credit rating."

"Your credit rating? How did he get hold of that?"

"God knows. I had a bad year on the horses, and the wife ran berserk with the Access card," he said, pathetically. "Yer man said he'd give me two hundred quid, cash. Anyways, I hated the bloody dog."

"And the other dog?"

"I run out of poison so I give it some of the wife's sleeping pills."

"How did the fella with the English voice pay you?"

"In notes. In the post."

"You're sure you didn't see him? Why should I believe you?"

"For Chrissakes," he said. "I have the envelope here." He pulled a crumpled paper out of his pocket. I looked at his face. It was stupid and desperate.

"Okay," I said. "Now what about all this Provo stuff?"

"You was askin' questions," he said. "I wanted to give yez a scare."

"Your own private idea," I said. "No suggestions on the telephone."

"No." His arms hung limp by his sides and he was staring at his feet. He looked like a man who would back three-legged horses and have a wife who went mad with the Access card.

"Anything else you can tell me?"

He shook his head.

"Because if there's anything you've left out, I'll come for you."

He shook his head again. I smoothed the envelope over the barrel of the gun and glanced down at it. It was typed with Dennis's address, and postmarked Bundoyle, County Longford.

"You can explain to the hire mob about the car," I said. "I'll have the moped. And if your Englishman telephones again, tell him you'll call back, and get his number, and then you bloody well ring me." I jacked the cartridges out of the gun and flung it far into the rhododendrons. "And you'd better pray to God that I find what I'm looking for."

He stared at me for a moment. He was sniffing. His eyes were red and tears were running down his face. "'Tis me brother's gun," he whimpered, and blundered like an animal into the rhododendrons after it.

I got onto the moped and drove away.

18

I rode the moped as far as Cork and left it on St. Patrick's Quay, where a Mr. Flynn was pleased to rent me an accident-damaged Opel Kadett. It was completely dark as I threaded the grim northern suburbs of Cork, and the Opel was barely controllable. But my mood was as bright as the undipped headlights of the oncoming cars. I had another lead. True, it was a slender one. But the envelope had been typed on a word processor and the person who had arranged the dog poisonings had access to credit ratings.

Bundoyle was marked on the map as a town of between one and two thousand inhabitants, which meant that very few industrial establishments within its boundaries would be big enough to own a word processor, or to have access to credit ratings.

Bundoyle, as it turned out, was a few miles northeast of Longford. On the map, it looked like a four-hour drive, but the Kadett and the roads between them made it more like six. I pulled off the road at about two A.M. and caught three hours' fitful sleep in a lay-by.

Eight o'clock saw me driving across a flat green bog in a grey drizzle that limited my field of vision to two hundred yards. A concrete grotto with a concrete Madonna loomed out of the murk, then a double line of grey cement houses, one with a plastic Guinness sign. I was dirty and ravenous. The pub looked nasty and shut tight. But I got stiffly out of the car and hammered on the door.

After a couple of minutes, a fat woman answered, wearing a man's check dressing-gown. Ten minutes later, I was seated in the lounge bar with a large pot of mahogany-coloured tea, eating a toasted sandwich which contrived to contain not only cheese and ham but also mashed potato.

The fat woman came back, tightly corseted now, to clear away the dishes. I showed her the envelope. She said it was nice, but had no idea where it had come from.

"We'll ask Thomas," she said, drawing herself a small glass of stout from the pumps. I was about to ask who Thomas was and when he would be arriving when brakes screeched outside and a head in a peaked cap stuck itself round the door.

"Ye have the phone bill, God help ye," said the postman.

"Come in, Thomas!" cried the fat lady. "We have an English gentleman with a mystery."

I showed him the envelope. He put his head on one side, with a proprietorial air. " 'Tis one of them word processors, right enough. I'd say it was from Curran's."

"Curran Electric," said the landlady. "They sells fridges," she added.

"On the road, a couple of miles out," said the postman.

"Who runs it?"

"Fella name of White."

"What about Mr. Curran?"

"Sure there does be no Mr. Curran. I'd say it's only a name."

150

"Good," I said. "I think I'll pop out and pay them a visit."

"Yer man's not there," said the postman, with authority. "'Tis his daughter's half-term in England."

"Ah," I said, slightly taken aback by the breadth of his knowledge. "Well, I'll go anyway."

"Fine," said the postman.

Curran's was a white concrete-and-metal shoebox in the grey drizzle on the outskirts of town. I parked between the only other two cars in the car park and pushed open the swing door marked RECEPTION. There was a small area with a bench, some magazines and a painting of a lorry among mountains. The receptionist looked up and smiled. She was operating a word processor. I walked over to the desk.

"Is Mr. White in?" I said, allowing my eyes to stray over the letters on her desk. They were all in the same typeface as the envelope.

"Mr. White's in England," said the receptionist. She was pretty, with dark hair, a roman nose and the restless eye of a thoroughbred mare. "What was it in connection with?"

"Oh, business," I said, vaguely. "Credit control."

"Mr. White looks after that," she said.

"Ah. Could you ever tell me where he's gone in England?"

"By all means." Her fingers battered at the keyboard. The printer screamed, and a sheet of paper wound itself out of the slot. "There you are, so," she said.

"Thank you," I said, and took my leave.

The address was in London. But what sent my heart slamming against my ribs, as I sat in the driver's seat of the Opel, was the list of directors at the bottom of the page. The list that began F. Millstone *(Managing)*.

I got home in a state of greasy exhaustion. The only sign of life was a faint smell of dettol drifting through from my father's wing. There was a note on my table in his ancient, spidery handwriting:

Millstone rang up. He says that he is going to keep on trying to buy the house until one of us sells it to him. He is a terrible nuisance, could you have a word with him, he is making me very tired.

My father was not the only one who was tired. After I had swallowed a cup of coffee, I rang the London number on the Curran Electric paper. The voice that answered was Irish.

"Mr. White?" I said.

"Speaking."

"I've just come from Curran Electric," I said. "My name's Charles Agutter. Tell me something, are you interested in sailing?"

"Sailing?" said White. "No. We're an electrical goods company. What do you want?"

"Are any of your staff English?" I asked.

"No. We're all—excuse me, who are you? Why are you asking me all this?"

"Because someone with access to credit ratings has been bribing people to poison dogs and sending the money in Curran Electric envelopes and this person speaks with an English accent. What have you got to say, Mr. White?"

"Is this some class of a joke?" White's voice was full of genuine exasperation and puzzlement. "Who are you and what do you want?"

"This is a murder investigation," I said.

"Murder?" he said.

"Tell me now," I said, injecting my voice full of menace. "Do you remember any unusual transactions in your department this last week?"

"I do not," he said sharply. "We are after having our Board visit, and everything has been most regular and proper."

"I see." I paused. "And was Mr. Millstone there?"

"He was," said White.

152

"I'll send him your regards," I said. "Thank you for your assistance." And I put the telephone down.

I spent the rest of the morning trying to concentrate on the numberless petty chores of getting *Sorcerer* ready, and at half-past twelve I went down to see Scotto and inspect her new keel. Scotto had been doing odd jobs all weekend. There had been no trouble of any description. Having conferred, we went and had some lunch in the Mermaid.

"Find anything?" said Scotto.

"Yes." I told him about Curran Electric.

"What does that mean?" he said.

"I don't know," I said. "Dennis's telephone calls could have come from England and the money could have been despatched by one of the directors at the meeting, namely Frank Millstone."

Scotto placed two crab sandwiches in his mouth at the same time, and frowned. "But why would he fix the rudder? He was on the bloody boat."

"He wouldn't have expected any problems; maybe a sort of dignified rudder failure, but not a crisis. When we were poncing about by the lighthouse there, he said something very interesting. He told me he never thought I'd bring her in that close."

Scotto pondered once again. "So you reckon he did it?"

"Not himself," I said.

"So you reckon he got Pollitt to do it?" He posted in two more sandwiches and washed them down with lager. "Why?"

"No idea," I said. Actually, I was beginning to have various ideas, but none of them was yet strong enough to stand the light of day. "Shall we pop along to Millstone's?"

"Let's go."

I rang him first.

Georgina answered. She was his secretary. I had known her for twenty-five years. "He's in a meeting,

Charlie," she said. "But he wants to see you anyway. He has a call in to you."

"He does?"

"Could you manage ten past two?"

"Yes."

Millstone's house sat on the south side of a hill overlooking Pulteney. It was made of concrete, steel and large expanses of plate glass and it crouched in a six-acre garden surrounded by a high wall. The gates were locked. I spoke into an entry-phone, and we drove between beautifully-mown lawns and onto a tarmac sweep. I had been to the house several times before, on business—I was not part of Frank's social circle. Each time, I had been made vaguely uncomfortable by the blank, eyeless look of the thing.

The man who opened the door was as big as Scotto, and looked hard. We went into an anteroom. Georgina Pearn asked if we wanted coffee.

At precisely 2:10 Frank Millstone came to his office door. His hair was wet, and he was wearing a towelling robe and a large, tough smile. He ignored Scotto, and said, "Come in, Charlie."

I said to Scotto, "I won't be long," and went in.

Frank lowered his huge frame into a chair behind a big desk with four telephones and a Reuters screen.

"We'd better forgive and forget about the Yacht Club party," he said.

I ignored him. I'd already worked out the approach.

"My father tells me you've been pestering him about our house."

"I expressed my intention of pursuing it," said Frank.

"Is that why you were going to ring me?"

"Correct," said Frank.

"Well, it's not for sale. As he told you and I have told you."

"Charlie." He purred the word like a big cat, and

154

his eyes practically chirruped in their nest of wrinkles. "Look here, we don't need bad blood between us. I'm sorry your rudders aren't working out. I'm sorry your contract with Archer isn't going too well. And I'm sorry if anything gives you the idea that I'm not on your side. But I asked you here because I want to help you."

"I didn't know I needed help."

He pulled a sheet of paper towards him. "You've got a big overdraft, Charlie. And a couple of nasty-looking loans to pay, your father to support. And you've got no income."

"Clever of you to find this out," I said. "How do you do it?"

He laughed, and flattened the timber of his desk with his big, hard hands. "We call it credit control," he said.

"Do you really?" I said, mildly.

"So all you've got is Alec Breen taking up your time for the summer with that old boat of his."

"She's a good boat."

He rolled on, still smiling. "So I'm making you a proposition. I want your house for a nice hotel, very select. I'll make a deal with you now. You can have two hundred thousand quid for it, and your dad can stay on for as long as he wants. Okay?"

It was a tempting offer. Two hundred thousand pounds would have solved a lot of problems. The trouble was, most of my problems seemed likely to have been created by Millstone, and I have never enjoyed being blackmailed.

"Not for sale," I said. "In fact, it is even less for sale than it was before, because I don't deal with people who try to frighten my father out of his wits."

Millstone's eyes were earnest. "Listen," he said. "When I came to Pulteney it was a dirty little hole. You could smell the fish miles away. I've changed all that. It's been my life's work. Other men collect

155

paintings. I've tried to turn Pulteney into a place people can enjoy."

"Very noble," I said. "Pity you didn't ask the people who live here, first."

"Be practical," said Millstone.

"I think that's up to me."

"I'm worried that you're going to go broke," said Millstone earnestly. "Then I'll get your house anyway. Couldn't we keep it amicable?"

I was tired and I was edgy. The hypocrisy of the man disgusted me. Anger bubbled up, and I stopped being sensible.

"Do you call arranging for my boats to be sabotaged amicable?" I said.

The smile clicked off. He frowned. His eyes lost their twinkle and became flat and hard, like pebbles. "Your boats weren't sabotaged," he said. "The rudders bust because they were badly designed."

"Not because someone with his eye on my house decided that I needed ruining?"

Millstone rose and leaned forward over his desk. "I think you're under a lot of strain, Charlie. Because if you weren't, you certainly wouldn't be suggesting what I think you're suggesting."

I could feel the hammers of anger beating in my temples. I got up and walked towards the door.

Millstone said, "I want your house, Charlie. But, if I hear any more accusations of sabotage, I'll sue you for your last—" I slammed the door on him.

Georgina showed me and Scotto along the concrete-walled corridor to the front door of the house.

"I hear you've got a boat for the Cup trials," she said. "Congratulations."

I thanked her. Then it occurred to me that a little digging might be in order. "And Frank's buying Ed Beith's, I hear."

Georgina looked around, and put a finger to her

156

lips. "Not so loud," she said. "It's confidential; they're still arguing."

Well, I couldn't help it if she assumed that the person I had heard it from was Millstone himself.

"Nice pool," said Scotto as we went through the hall.

I looked into a plate glass conservatory. Inside were tropical palms and a pool with blue water and white marble dolphins. Beside the pool, reading a book and wearing a minute bikini that showed off her creamy redhead's skin and foxy little breasts, was Amy Charlton.

"Lunchtime swim with Frank, is it, Amy?" I said. "You do get around these days."

She looked up. "Oh, piss off, Agutter."

As we walked towards the car, a blue Mercedes drew up, and Jack Archer got out. He looked neat and dapper as ever, carrying a pigskin briefcase.

"Ah," he said. "Hello, Charlie." His square, brown face was smiling, but I thought he looked a little worried. "I was going to ring you. Sorry to hear about the results of the *Aesthete* inspection the other day. I . . . that is, unless something happens to make me decide to the contrary, I may have to start thinking about putting out some of those design jobs elsewhere. I'm sure you understand. Unless, of course, things go very well for *Sorcerer*."

"Are you sailing?" I said, to cover up the fact that my heart was beating too hard. It was no more than I had expected, but now that it had happened it was very unpleasant.

"With Frank," he said. "If he gets a boat."

"I'm sure he'll do his best," I said, not altogether succeeding in keeping the irony out of my voice.

As we went down the drive, Scotto said, "What was that all about?"

"Millstone wants my house," I said. "Archer wants

me to stop designing boats for him. The bank manager wants my skin. And the only way out is to get into the Captain's Cup team, and win. Is it possible?"

"'Course it is," said Scotto. I wished I shared his confidence.

As we drove, I thought about Amy. I was now good and sure that Amy was mixed up in it somewhere. She had been two-timing Henry with Pollitt, and two-timing Pollitt with Archer. Was she also two-timing Archer with Millstone? And where, if anywhere, did bashing Charlie Agutter fit into her complicated love-life? As we drove back down to the village, I decided that I should go and see Sally. She knew Amy well. Perhaps she'd have some ideas. And then I'd visit Ed Beith. Georgina had mentioned his discussions with Frank. It would be interesting to find out their content.

But first, there was work to do.

With Scotto and a couple of yard hands, I spent the afternoon and early evening re-rigging *Sorcerer*. As it was getting dark I called Sally, but there was no answer. So I thought I might as well go and see Ed first.

I drove out of Pulteney fast. It was dark, and the sky over the whalebacked hills was pricked with stars. Ahead, the lights of a town reddened the sky. I frowned. There should be no town. I forked left where the signpost said Lydiats Manor Only—Private Road. The glow intensified from dirty red to glaring orange. I put my foot on the accelerator and the BMW tyres screamed as I breasted the rise and dived into the deep lane that led down into the valley.

The valley was burning. That was what it looked like at first; but once the eyes had accustomed themselves to the glare, it became apparent that it was not the whole valley. Ed's house stood at the far end of the lake of flame, untouched, its windows yellow with electric light. I drove through the gate, past the burning turkey huts, and came to a halt in the gravel sweep in front of the house. A man ran past with a bucket in each hand, the sweat on his face blazing red in the glare. The heat was fierce. A gust of smoke whirled down the house's front and I choked. It stank of feathers. Then the meaning of that sank in, and I stood quite still for a moment. Above the roaring of the flames, I heard a voice yelling my name, and in the red glow I saw two figures standing at the end of the stone barn. Behind them, a fire-engine was sending a wholly inadequate jet of water into the nearest part of the fire. I went across. It was Ed Beith. He was standing, with his hands in the pockets of his boiler suit, shaking his head. The person next to him was Sally.

Ed said, "Oh, Charlie. How are you?" as if we were at a cocktail party. Sally looked at me, then back at the flames. The red light painted her face with black hollows. I wondered what she was doing here.

"Buckets," I said.

Ed raised his black eyebrows, as if surprised. "Buckets?" he said. "Ah, buckets."

The word set him going. He ran for the stables, and we ran after him and got a dozen buckets. By now, there were several farm-hands there and neighbours who had seen the glow and come down the hill. So we got a bucket chain going from the cowshed tap and as the flames rose and danced and sparks whirled high above the red ruins of Ed's turkeys, we splashed our buckets at the edges.

But the huts had been made of wood and we might as well have tried to bail out the sea with a teacup. Four more fire-engines arrived, and a fireman asked us politely to stand back. The bucket chain faltered and stopped.

Ed thanked its links, and said, "Not much we can do here. Let's go in and have a drink."

We went into the kitchen. It was much tidier than

159

usual. Ed pulled a bottle of champagne out of the fridge, divided it between three tumblers and gave Sally and me one each.

"Let's drink to 'em," he said. "One hundred thousand Christmas dinners, all bloody burnt." He drank deeply. Sally was eyeing him.

"Listen," I said. "Can't we stop it spreading?"

"It's spread," said Ed. He had already been drinking, by the sound of him. "Those little gurks were sitting in dry wood-houses on wood-shavings. They're the only thing that'll burn. House is quite safe." He slapped the kitchen wall. "Stone. Proper job, Lydiats."

"I'm sorry," I said.

Ed shrugged. He sat down with a thump on a wooden chair. "No insurance. Thank God they weren't any older. Poor little gurks."

"No insurance?" I said.

"Ah, well. Hundred thousand quid down the drain. So what?" But the thought seemed to depress him. Sally was standing close to him, drawn and silent. The ticking of the clock was loud in the foreground of the roar and crackle outside. Ed sat and stared bleakly at a silver salt-cellar on the kitchen table.

Then he reached out a large hand, picked up the telephone and dialled.

"Frank Millstone, please," he said. "Frank, hello. D'you still want to buy the yacht *Crystal?*" I started forward.

"Ed!" I shouted. "Wait a minute—"

Sally grabbed my hand. "Sit down and shut up," she said fiercely. "This is nothing to do with you."

A tinny voice muttered on the other end. "Very well," Ed was saying. "You've got her. Sails and all. Send me your contract."

He put down the telephone. His face was grey and hard, and he picked up his tumbler of champagne and drained it. "Well," he said. "Who needs insurance when you've got a boat to sell?"

The kitchen door opened, and a man with a smoke-streaked face said, "Wind's changing. Fire's heading for the barns."

"I'm there," said Ed, and rushed out of the room.

I ran after him, out into the yard. The flames were leaning downwind, clawing hungrily at the range of old stone and clapboard buildings on the side of the hill, where Ed kept his machinery.

"Get a hose!" shouted Ed. "Any hose! Damp down the weather-boarding!"

The smoke was choking, and the heat tightened the skin on my face. I ran for a tap, screwed up the hose, and started soaking the elm boards. A tractor started up inside. Ed roared out, parked it upwind, and ran back to collect another.

Steam drifted from the weather-boarding. It was very hot. When I looked round, Sally was standing next to me, with a scarf wrapped round her face against the smoke.

I said to her, "What's Amy up to?" I had to shout, above the roar of the flames.

"What's what?"

"Amy. Up to. She's all mixed up with this."

Sally said, "No. She can't be."

"She's been screwing Pollitt. And Archer. And she was at Millstone's today, looking like a fixture." A wall collapsed with a roar into the lake of fire.

"A what?"

"Fixture. Concubine."

"I told you," she shouted. "She's got an itch. It doesn't mean anything."

"People are getting killed," I said. "Things are happening, all around her."

"Shut up!" screamed Sally. I stared at her in amazement. The hose's jet strayed onto the ground.

She was saying something, but I couldn't hear. Deep in the burning sheds, something went whoomph. A mat of flame licked across the ground at us. I charged at her and shoved her out of range, into the darkness. Two firemen appeared with a big hose. We lay in the shadow where we had fallen. I could feel her body shaking.

"Are you hurt?" I said.

"No." Her voice was unsteady. "But I've had enough."

"It's all right," I said soothingly.

"No it bloody well isn't." She sounded panicky. "There you are playing bloody boats, taking yourselves so bloody seriously. And you say it's only a game. But it's not a game anymore, Charlie. It's got on top of you. And it's killed my lovely Hugo, and Henry, and someone's trying to kill you now. And Ed's poor turkeys. I suppose someone did that to make him sell his boat, is that it?" She laughed; the sound was unpleasantly shrill. "You're not looking for a saboteur, you're looking for a madman. But don't kid yourself that this madman's any different from you. He's just another brat playing a game that's got out of hand. Well, I'm not a child any more."

"Wait," I said.

"No," she said. "The only sane one's Ed. He's selling his boat and getting out. He does it for fun, and when it stops being fun, that's it. Why don't you leave it to the police?"

"Sally," I said, and tried to take her arm. "You're not making sense."

"Leave me alone!" she cried. "I've had enough! You're all mad!"

There was a cracking roar from the turkey sheds, and the night sky was filled with a blizzard of sparks. Ed Beith's voice shouted, "Come on, Charlie!" He was silhouetted against the flames, struggling with the

162

hitch of a water trailer. I ran down to help him. Halfway, I looked back for Sally.

She was gone.

I ran on into the red glare and the disgusting stink of feathers. I have never felt lonelier in my life.

The night went in the slop of water and the taste of soot. We kept the fire off the barns. By dawn, it was under control and I drove home to bed for a couple of hours. When I woke, I tried to ring Sally. Nobody answered the telephone. I made some coffee and put in extra sugar. Perhaps I was trying to console myself for the fact that the closeness we had felt in Kinsale was gone.

By eight-thirty, I was shuddering in *Sorcerer's* trench as we moved down-channel for the day's practice.

19

___

Slowly, I woke up. The boat was going well with the new keel, and the crew seemed none the worse for a three-day lay-off. We spent a cold, wet day slamming through a short sea to the south of the Teeth. *Sorcerer* had a lighter feel; she was sailing more than ever like a giant dinghy, which was what I wanted of her. It wasn't until we were sliding downhill, homeward bound, that the no-talking rule was relaxed and I got a chance to talk to Scotto.

Crispin, the relief helmsman, had the wheel, and Scotto and I were sitting with our legs under the windward lifelines, gazing down the coast of England towards the murky grey clouds in the general direction of the Isle of Wight.

"Did you hear Millstone's got *Crystal?*" he said.

Scuttlebutt moved at amazing speed. "I heard."

"Not a bad sled, that *Crystal.*"

"We can beat her."

Scotto slapped *Sorcerer's* hull with his vast hand. "'Course we can," he said.

And there we were again, playing the children's game.

I got up from the rail. "Right," I said. "Final exercise."

The windburned faces the crew turned to me were not at all enthusiastic: it had been a long, hard day.

"Channel buoy to harbour light," I said. "We'll try the tri-radial."

The Channel buoy marked the outer extremity of the Pulteney channel. It was a red cage with a bell, a relic of the days when my father's big ships had used the harbour. Now it served as a handy mark for yachts wishing to cut a dash on the way in. Furthermore, it was precisely one sea mile from the light at the end of the quay, so it gave competitors watching from the Yacht Club a rough measure of the way the opposition's boats were travelling.

The buoy came up to starboard. As the huge red-and-gold sail collapsed, its smaller brother blossomed, and *Sorcerer*'s bow came up until the readout by the mainsheet track read 100 degrees off the wind. Nobody spoke as the cockpit tilted and the water began to fly. *Sorcerer* leaned steeply over and the water slithered under her and up from her retroussé transom in the fan of thin spray that meant high speed. The rigging groaned and she heeled a degree or so more; there was a slight shudder and she was up.

The speed of racing-yachts was once limited by their waterline length. A yacht used to send up a bow wave at its nose and a quarter wave at its tail and sailed along in the trough between the two, unable to cross its own bow wave. The theoretical maximum for *Sorcerer*'s forty-three feet of waterline was less than nine knots. But obviously nobody had told *Sorcerer* this, because she skimmed across the water like a flat pebble, with no bow wave and a V of spray at her tail while the log needle went round to fourteen knots.

"Strewth," said Scotto.

It took us dead on five minutes to make the harbour light.

"Sails off," I said.

"Hardly worth putting 'em up," said one of the trimmers, and everyone laughed. It was partly a release of tension, and partly that this was the first time *Sorcerer* had ever got up and gone off the clock like that. Suddenly we weren't just a good crew in an old boat, but a good crew in a boat that could do it.

I raised my glasses and trained them on the balcony of the Pulteney Yacht Club. Despite the overcast sky and the cool wind, there were several people out there. I moved my glasses slightly and found myself looking at another pair, trained on me from above the well-filled blazer of Frank Millstone. I waved. Millstone lowered them quickly and turned to the group at his elbow. I identified Hector Pollitt, Jack Archer and Johnny Forsyth. Johnny said something, presumably about *Sorcerer's* turn of speed, and they laughed and shook their heads. But Millstone did not laugh. Instead he drained his drink and walked quickly in at the French windows. Inside the windows, I saw the figure of a woman, white-faced against the dark interior of the bar. Amy.

As we motored up-channel towards the marina, I called the crew together.

"We've got over two weeks till the first of the trials," I said. "We'll be out every day. Now she's shown what she'll do with the new keel, I want her moving like that all the time. But the boat's only half of it. The rest of you stay off the beer and no picking fights with grizzly bears. Watch yourselves and we'll win."

There was some grinning, and some serious nodding. The word for crews at this level of racing was dedicated. The free air tickets and the living expenses were only icing. The cake was winning. Winning was the only thing they didn't make jokes about, and the will to win was what made them different from other people. Inhuman, some would say. Or mad.

I stayed to talk to Scotto after the rest of them had cleared up and filtered away.

"Watch out," I said.

"What's happened?"

I took a deep breath. "I think someone set fire to Ed's turkey shed to . . . persuade him to sell his boat."

"You mean Millstone did."

I shrugged. "Would he do a thing like that?"

Scotto said, "I dunno."

"He'd be a fool to."

"Who else would?"

There were alternatives. Hector Pollitt, for one. Amy, for another. Anyone who didn't care what they did to get Millstone a boat.

"Get the law in," said Scotto.

"Not yet," I said. "The papers'd get it. Hegarty'd lose most of his customers. And if it got to court, Millstone'd get a million quid's worth of barrister and the case'd be flung out for lack of evidence."

"Strikes me there's loads of evidence," said Scotto.

"Courts want things proved beyond reasonable doubt. What we've got is coincidences."

Scotto shook his massive head.

"So what we want to do is beat him in the trials."

"You're going to wait that long?"

I tried to smile at him, but I could feel my face ugly and stretched. "I have an idea. If we win the first race of the trials, I can get going on it."

"We can but try," said Scotto. "You got a definite plan?"

"Tell you later," I said. The idea was so horrible that I could scarcely even bring myself to think about it.

"Am I still sleeping on board?" he said.

"'Fraid so."

"It's a bloody salt swamp down there."

"You'll survive."

He nodded. "How about if I got Georgia down?"

"Why not? But there's not much room for two in one of those bunks."

"We'll manage." Scotto paused. "She says she's got Red Indian blood. Her ancestors did it in canoes, standing up."

I laughed and jumped onto the jetty. Outside the car park, I turned automatically in the direction of Sally's house. Then I remembered last night, did a three-point turn in the gateway, and drove back towards Pulteney. Children's games, ending in tears.

But not hers this time. Or mine. Millstone's.

20

When I got home, I poured myself a large Famous Grouse, looked at the answering machine and decided not to listen to the messages until I had got the salt off. So I took my glass upstairs and stood under the shower for ten minutes, hot as I could stand it, trying not to listen to the shouting from next door. My father seemed to be having a bad day. My throat was sore from the smoke of Ed's turkey chicks. I was looking forward to a bit of telephoning, dinner and ten hours' kip. I stepped out of the shower and pulled on a pair of O.M. Watts trousers and an *Aesthete* crew shirt, for old times' sake. Then I went down to the living-room, feeling pink, clean and a bit woozy from the hot shower and the whisky.

There were a dozen or so messages, mostly from newspapers. The only important ones were from Breen and Sally. The one from Sally was important because it wasn't there. Breen's secretary wanted me to ring him, and had left a number. I called the number. A woman told me that I was expected to dinner. She then gave me an address between Marlborough and Newbury and put the telephone down. I sat down and held my head in my hands for a couple of minutes. Then I changed into a blazer and my RORC tie, and trudged wearily through to the garage.

Two hours later, I was winding through the manicured lanes of North Hampshire, reflecting that it was only a matter of time before the inhabitants of the area erected a fence around it and posted security guards to spare them the necessity of contact with the outside world. Breen's home was long, low and half-timbered, with an immaculate garden and a lake beside which was sited the helicopter pad.

Breen was waiting in a large, beamed room full of chintz furniture. He was dressed in a khaki safari suit, drinking what looked like Coca-Cola and chewing the inevitable cigar. He looked uneasy in the sea of chintz; at last, I thought, a room he could not dominate. He introduced me to a tall, pale woman in a pair of expensively modified silk pyjamas.

"My wife, Camilla," he said. "Charlie Agutter, who's sailing *Sorcerer* in the Captain's Cup trials."

She had once been beautiful. Now she looked tired of doing nothing. "The Captain's Cup trials?" she said. "What are they?"

"A series of races between boats who want to get into the Cup team," I said. "Half a dozen inshore races and three long offshore races."

"I'm afraid I know absolutely nothing about boats," she said.

Dinner was steak and a bottle of very good burgundy, of which Breen drank none. Lady Breen asked me questions in whose answers she was obviously not interested. I wondered why I had been asked. It was as if by doing Breen violence in Lymington, I had cracked his shell, and he felt I should be admitted to some sort of intimacy. But he was obviously a man not used to intimacy, so the dinner had an aching formality that none of my previous encounters with him had shown. Afterwards, Lady Breen said she had a headache and asked to be excused.

After she had gone, Breen lit another cigar, gestured at the long oak table with its Paul de Lamerie silver, and said, "Shall we adjourn?"

He led the way down a passage to a heavy oak door, which he unlocked. The room behind it was filing-cabinet green and dove-grey, with a big oak desk on which sat a computer terminal and a telephone. It might have been any office in any high-rise block in London. In it, Breen regained the poise that the chintz had upset.

"Right," he said. "Nice dinner. Let's talk."

I told him about the success of the new keel. He seemed gratified. "Anything else?" I told him that a new mainsail would be useful. "More bloody Kevlar, I suppose," he said. "Costs twice as much as Dacron and lasts half as long."

I began to explain.

"I know. They don't stretch, and you might get an extra twenty-fifth of a knot. There again, you might not. Whoever said this game was like tearing up tenners under a cold shower had it right, except he should have said fifties." The eyes above the cigar had a little glint of excitement in them. I was surprised. He was positively talkative, for him. "If you need a mainsail, get it. But you'd better win with it." He leaned back in his black leather swivel chair, blowing a thin stream of smoke. "Now, tell me about the opposition."

I ran down the list of entrants to the Captain's Cup trials, discussing their boats and their crews. As we went on, I began once again to see the qualities that had set Breen apart from the crowd. He had no scruples at all about being boring, and even fewer about being bored. When he got at a subject he picked it up and worried it, and would not leave it alone until he had modified it into a form he could digest.

It took us three hours to discuss the first eleven competitors, and never once were we allowed to stray from the point. When we had finished with the eleventh, he cut the end off a fresh cigar.

"That leaves *Sorcerer* and Millstone," he said. "Tell me, Charlie, why have you been saving Millstone till last?"

"No reason," I said. Well, it was true; there were no conscious reasons.

"I'm going to ask you an insulting question," said Breen. "Are you frightened of Frank Millstone?"

I was; insulted, I mean. I said, "No."

"Badly put. Does he worry you?"

It sounded better that way. "Yes," I said. "He worries me. But not for long."

"How's that?"

"Because I am going to beat the hell out of him, and then I am going to turn him over to the law."

"Charlie," said Breen, "I like you. Also, I like your priorities. But one of the reasons I asked you over here was to remind you that the first of the trials is very soon and that you are my employee. There are thirteen boats in the race, Charlie, not two. Your job is to come in first."

"Yes."

"I like to offer carrots, Charlie. If you win this race, you can design me a 150-foot schooner and name your fee. Also, I will influence Archer to give you your contract back. If you lose it, you don't get the schooner, or any help with the contract, but you keep your legs. But if you start mucking about with Millstone off the water and by so doing prejudice my chance, you can wave your legs goodbye, because I will have sawn off your arse. Understood?" The eyes above the cigar now held no trace of amusement. They seemed to fill the room. "Now then, it's midnight. You're going to need your kip. Get out of here."

I got out, as instructed. I was exhausted, but I had no trouble staying awake.

Whoever was sabotaging boats and burning turkeys

had so far done it to his own timetable. This time, he was going to do it to my timetable and I was going to be ready for him.

Unfortunately, the method used had to be one that would prejudice Breen's chance for the Cup.

Next morning, I went to Portsmouth to put the first part of my plan into operation. As I was leaving Pulteney, I saw a green Cortina in a lay-by, with its bonnet open and a man bending over the engine. The legs were long and lanky. I slowed down, and stopped. It was Johnny Forsyth. His hands were covered in oil and his acne-scarred face sullen.

"Bloody distributor," he said. "Shorting out."

"Where are you heading?" I said.

"Hamble," he said.

"Hop in."

When we were in the car he said, "Saw you coming off the harbour buoy last night. Going nicely."

"Yes. Are you sailing the day after tomorrow?"

"On *Crystal*. I was working on her hull for Ed Beith. I'm staying with her for Millstone."

"What have you been up to?"

"A few bits and pieces." Johnny's face was watching the road, his eyes narrow, his cheek flat and grainy, not giving anything away. "Bit of work on the rig. Cheering up the hull."

"How's it going?"

"She'll be very nice." His narrow eyes moved across at me. "Very fast. A bit of serious competition for you." He laughed, with that lipless stretch of the face. "I'm doing tactics, too."

We left it at that. I dropped him at the Hamble, went on to a security consultant to pick up some brochures and price lists, and collected him on the way back. I dropped him at the marina. He climbed out of the car and said, "Thanks," but I was looking past him. Archer's blue Mercedes was parked two cars down. Archer was in it. So was Amy. They were kissing, long and very, very hard.

Forsyth followed my eyes. His face reddened and his eyes narrowed. He said, "Bitch!"

"What?" I said, taken aback.

He turned back to me with a smile that was visibly false. "Nothing," he said. "Must dash."

I returned to Pulteney quay and the Zodiac which was waiting to take me out to where *Sorcerer* was playing jibing. Chiefy was driving, but we did not talk. I was watching *Sorcerer*'s big orange spinnaker against the blue-green sea, and thinking. Breen wanted me to win the race, and that was the limit of his interest. For me, winning was only the first step to finding out who was trying to wreck my career. And if I had to fly across Breen's bows in the process, it was just too bad.

Just too bad for whom? For me, more than likely.

The next two weeks went well. By dint of tinkering and fine tuning, we got the boat up and onto her running legs again; and each time, it seemed to come easier. The routine took over: up before dawn, running with the crew, sail till dusk or after, then work on equipment modifications far into the night. After ten days, we started some night practice. It was solid, concentrated effort.

On the seventeenth evening, I left Scotto and Georgia to sleep aboard and drove home in a trance of exhaustion. I crawled back to my house, showered, boiled an egg and sat down to eat it. The next thing I knew it was pitch dark and the telephone was ringing, and I was still in the armchair.

"What?" I said into the receiver, gluey-mouthed.

There was the noise of someone forcing money into a callbox.

"Charlie? It's Georgia."

"Georgia?" I said, and looked at my watch. Two A.M.

"You'd better get down here," said Georgia.

"Where are you?" I could remember my own name now. And hers. She sounded out of breath, as if she had been running.

"Marina callbox. I was on *Sorcerer* with Scotto. He's hurt. You'd better come."

I went. Fog lay over the road in grey wisps and the grit of the marine car park was damp with it. Navigating by the tap of halyard against mast, I blundered across to the jetties. Lights shone yellow from a cabin hatch. The fog seemed to be inside my head as well as outside it.

"Who's there?" A small, shapeless figure loomed out of the darkness, crouching.

"Me."

The figure relaxed and said, in Georgia's voice, "Charlie, thank God you're here." As we entered the lamplit circle of fog, I saw that she was wearing three jerseys and carrying a baseball bat.

"Where's Scotto?"

She switched on a flashlight and we climbed aboard *Sorcerer*. The deck rocked a little. Scotto's voice came hoarsely up from the hatch.

"Georgia?" he called, and ended on a grunt of pain. Until I felt the relief wash over me, I did not realise I had been expecting the worst.

He was lying on his back on the cabin floor. It was not a comfortable place to lie—a bit like an oversized fibreglass coffin, stark white under the unshielded bulbs, clammy with the condensation that ran down the walls. He had a sleeping bag over him, and his tan was yellow, not brown.

"What's wrong with you?"

Scotto grinned, a weak approximation to his normal rat-trap. "Fell on my back," he said.

"Let's have a look," I said. "Move your toes."

"Nothing's bust," said Scotto. "Look." He did a straight leg-lift that turned his face from yellow to grey and brought beads of sweat popping out on his forehead. "She made me lie down, that's all."

"Turn over," I said.

"I'm okay," said Scotto, and turned with difficulty onto his face. A broad red weal ran across the huge brown pads of muscle on either side of his spine. I prodded the weal. Scotto said, "Hey!"

"What happened?" I said.

"Someone pushed me down the hatch."

"Oh," I said, as if it happened every day. "You'd better get down to Casualty for an X-ray."

Scotto said, "I heard someone moving about on deck. I went up to the hatch nice and quiet, but the boat must have moved about a bit. First thing I knew, I got a knee in the chest and down I went." Scotto paused. "S'pose I screwed up," he said. "But Georgia went out with the baseball bat."

"Somebody was running down the jetty," said Georgia. "They were running pretty fast, considering."

"Considering what?"

"I got a swing in," said Scotto. "That's why I went down the hatch, because I was hitting the guy with the hand I was meant to be holding on with. I got him smack in the mouth."

"How d'you know, if you couldn't see him?"

"Because I've got his toothmarks in my knuckles."

"Great," I said. "Now all we've got to do is find someone with your knucklemarks in his teeth."

"I thought of that," said Scotto.

"The guy went off in a car," said Georgia. "I heard the engine."

I sighed. I was very tired. "Georgia, I'm going to stay with *Sorcerer*. Can you get him down to the hospital? Take my car."

Georgia sighed back, and sat down. The light threw golden reflections on her warm brown skin. "He's not going to be much good to me here. C'mon, Scotto."

Between us, we managed to get him on his feet and drag him to the car. Then I trudged back down to the jetty and aboard *Sorcerer*. I went below, pulled Scotto's sleeping bag over my clothes, and lay down on the bottom bunk. For a moment, I lay listening to the slap of the ripples echoing in the hollow hull. Then I went to sleep.

I was beginning a very nice dream, in which Sally and I were in a biplane flying over a range of mountains. The engine of the biplane had a knock. The knock got louder and louder. "We'll have to go down," I yelled in the rush of the wind. A landing strip opened below a crack in the clouds, a postage stamp of concrete among grey rocks. But the aeroplane would not go down. The knocking was hideously loud now. I opened my eyes. It was still dark and someone was banging on the hull.

"Arright," I croaked. I felt like death. "Wharrisit?"

"It's me, Georgia!"

"What time is it?"

"About three, I dunno. Listen, come quick."

I lurched out of bed and crawled up the companionway. Georgia dazzled me with a flashlight. "Come to the hospital."

"Something wrong?"

"Scotto's gone berserk."

"Cool him down, then."

"No. He wants you."

"Oh." I started for the jetty. "Hey. No. I've got to stay with the boat."

"I will."

"You bloody won't."

"I will. I've got Scotto's gun."

I fought an urge to sit down on the jetty and weep. "Get back to Scotto."

"I'm staying," said Georgia. "I might scream."

My arms were pig-lead and I still felt weepy. I said, "Don't shoot anybody," and trudged off up the jetty.

The BMW was hot, and smelt of burning clutch-plates. I took it back towards Pulteney, hypnotised by the white lines in the yellow headlamps. I sang, trying to stay awake. Even so, I bounced off the hedge and dented the driver's door. But at least that woke me up. Ten minutes later, I was turning into the car park of Pulteney Cottage Hospital.

The long, white building was dark and quiet. The only sign of life was the cold light burning above the casualty department door. The Cottage Hospital was staffed by a single night nurse. In an emergency, she called a duty doctor, who zigzagged sleepily up from the village. I climbed out of the car and went in.

Tonight—this morning, rather—the duty doctor was a smallish, timid man with large eyebrows, who did not approve of Pulteney's irregularities. But he didn't look at all sleepy. He was standing to attention, with his fists clenched at his sides, saying, "Nurse! I said call the police!"

"No reply from the station," said the nurse, who was called Hilda Hicks, a round, philosophical Pulteney native.

"Can I help?" I said.

"Ah," said the doctor, rounding on me. "Who are you—Mr. Agutter, ah, yes. Nurse, dial 999." But Hilda, not wishing to miss anything, stayed where she was.

I said, "What's the trouble?"

"An Australian with spinal contusions has gone berserk in the sluice room," said the doctor, his eyebrows working. "He weighs about twenty stone, and he has the biggest dorsals I have ever seen."

"New Zealander," I said. "Is he concussed?"

"Not noticeably," said the doctor, wincing.

"But we don't know about the other chap," said Hilda. "Evening, Charlie."

"Evening, Hilda. What other chap?" I said.

"The chap he was chasing. He's got him locked in the sluice now," said Hilda.

"Ah. Perhaps I'd better go and have a look. Don't let's call the police just yet." A dreadful burst of New Zealand shouting came from above.

"That's him," said the doctor.

"I recognise the voice," I said, and started up the stairs. "Scotto!"

"Charlie!" said Scotto's voice from behind a locked door. "About bloody time." The door opened. Scotto had no shirt on. His mighty torso was half-covered with an elastic strapping, which finished in a twisted end, as if he had torn himself away halfway through the operation. His face was greyish-yellow.

"What the hell are you playing at?" I said.

He pointed at the inside door of the sluice-room. "The bastard's in there."

"What bastard?"

"I was getting bandaged up when this bastard came in wanting two of his teeth put back, and I was trying to ask him a few questions when he made a run for it."

"Is he the one you hit?"

"I dunno. But he didn't seem too pleased to see me. Did you, you sneaky little bastid?"

"Easy," I said. Doctor Harris and the nurse were in the room now. I addressed myself to the closed door. "This is Charlie Agutter," I said. "If you come out, we'll just ask you a couple of questions and you can go. If not, I'll call the law and it'll be GBH. Well?"

A high, panicky voice behind the door said, "Piss off, Agutter!" It was a voice I recognized.

"We're coming in."

There was a silence, then the sound of a window opening.

"Look out!" said Scotto. Leaping to his feet, he slammed his shoulder into the door. It burst inwards and he went down after it, groaning in agony. I

179

stepped over him and stuck my head out of the window.

A narrow ledge ran across the plain brick of the Victorian building. Hector Pollitt had made about ten feet, and was hanging on to a drainpipe thirty feet above the tarmac.

"For heaven's sake come back, Hector," I said quietly.

He jerked his head round to look at me. The blood on his chin was black in the reflected light from below. "Get away from me!" he said, in a high, panicky voice.

"Take it easy," I said. "Come back. Nobody's going to hurt you."

"Oh, yeah," he said, sarcastically.

"Scotto won't touch you. I won't touch you. Just come back."

"Ask him what he was doing on *Sorcerer*," yelled Scotto from behind me.

"Come on," I said gently. "Take a couple of steps. We know you haven't done anything. You'll be fine. And you can have the whole story for your magazine."

I could see the whites of his eyes, big as moons. And I could smell the drink on him.

"You're a nice chap, Hector," I lied. "But you've got some nasty friends. That's all over now." I climbed out onto the window sill, and held out my hand. I could see his knees shaking. He stretched out a hand towards me. "It wasn't you who clobbered me at the marina, was it?" I said quietly. "Who was using your car?" Then I cursed myself.

Because Pollitt froze and I saw his eyes flash as they swivelled in the moon. He pulled his hand away and gripped the drainpipe to swing himself onto the continuation of the ledge. As his weight reached its furthest outward point, I heard myself shout, "No!" For the upper section of the drainpipe was bending under the weight. Slowly, horribly slowly, it keeled

180

outwards. I saw Pollitt's bloody mouth, silver and black in the pale, cold light as, still clinging, he lay backwards in space and fell.

At last he yelled. The yell was cut short by a horrible crash. I clung to the window, shaking. In the yellow square of light below was the shadow of my own head, and something else. It was human, but its limbs were sprawled like a starfish's, and no living human head had ever been at that angle to a body. And the eyes looked up at me, wide, wide open, seeing nothing at all. Hector Pollitt of the *Yachtsman* had written his last story.

21

We stood jammed in that window for a long moment, the doctor, Hilda and I. Then the doctor's profession-al reflexes starting working and he dashed down the stairs, closely pursued by Hilda. Scotto was on his hands and knees now. He was still groaning.

"Things are going to start happening," I said. "I'll be back."

"Where the hell are you going?" he said.

"Never mind." I ran out to the car park, turned on the headlights of the BMW, and made the tyres screech as I reversed away.

I was aware that someone behind me was yelling, but I paid no attention. I was entirely awake, now.

The road howled under the car's bonnet, but I was hardly there. I was in the marina again, the night after we had pulled *Aesthete* from the Teeth, creeping among the chocked boats in the dark, watching a car parking in the lay-by. A car with one of its lights out: Pollitt's car, in which he had later been breathalysed. But had Pollitt been driving it? When I asked him five minutes ago, it had frightened him. Frightened him to death.

But I couldn't see Pollitt as a saboteur and a killer. Had somebody else been driving that night? Someone of whom Pollitt was frightened enough to go swinging on drainpipes high above tarmac car parks?

The tyres screamed on the bends, the headlights muddied with grey fog. I saw the marina entrance at the last moment and went through it broadside. *Sorcerer's* lights were still on. I jumped onto her deck and Georgia rose from the cockpit.

"Don't!" I roared. "It's me!" Her hands went down.

"Charlie?" she said. "What is it?"

I took the .38 revolver out of her hand and flung it as far as I could into the fog-shrouded water. "Police'll be here any minute," I said. "Clean it all up. Don't tell anyone anything." Then I ran back to the car and drove back to the hospital, fast.

My watch said I had been away twenty minutes. As I approached, I could see the flashing blue glare in the fog. The car park seemed full of police cars. I climbed out and went to the Emergency door.

The constable inside it said, "Can I help you, sir?"

"I saw what happened."

"What did happen, sir?"

I told him. He said, "If you would care to step this way?" in a voice full of old-world Devonshire charm. We went through into an office with tatty black PVC furniture illuminated by a fluorescent tube. Scotto was there, the colour of a corpse under the greenish light. So was the doctor. So was Detective Inspector Nelligan.

"Well, well, well," said Detective Inspector Nelligan. He paused to extract a John Player Special and light it. "Mr. Charles Agutter. I was just saying I wondered where you had gone. Where had you gone?"

"Back to the boat," I said. "I wanted to tell the person on board what had happened, and that I might be . . . delayed getting back."

"Considerate, and true," said Nelligan. He turned and murmured to a uniformed policeman, who left the room. "Now, are you in a position to tell me what is taking place? I believe you know Mr. Hector Pollitt. Knew, I should say."

"Hasn't Mr. Scott already told you?"

"I haven't told anybody anything," said Scotto.

"Yes," said Nelligan, blowing smoke. "Dead unco-operative. I wonder why."

"Perfectly straightforward," I said. "Mr. Hector Pollitt had been writing things about me I didn't like. I'd told Mr. Scott as much. So when Mr. Scott chanced to bump into Mr. Pollitt, Mr. Scott, er . . . espoused my cause."

"Let's not be flippant," said Nelligan. "There's a dead man here, and Scott was chasing him when he died."

"Correction," I said. "Scott was on the other side of a window when Pollitt fell to his death from a ledge from which I was attempting to rescue him. Dr. Harris and the nurse will tell you so."

Nelligan said, "Mr. Scott was still chasing him. And I'd like to know how he came by those bruises."

"He fell down a hatchway on the boat. Is that illegal, nowadays?"

Nelligan lit a new cigarette from the stub of the old one, and said, "Perhaps Mr. Agutter and I should have a private chat. If you would excuse us?"

After the room had emptied, he poked fussily at a speck of ash on the sleeve of his jacket and said, "Of course, you're right, Mr. Agutter. We could nick your friend for breach of the peace, assault maybe. But is it worth it?" He paused, interrogating a cloud of smoke. "Of course it isn't. Not so much because of wasting magistrate's time, because I don't much care about that. But here we are with a dead body that's written some nasty things about you. And the dead body has two front teeth missing, and there are toothmarks in your mate's hand, and the doctor says they match. And you go belting out into the night as soon as the balloon goes up."

I said, "Was it Pollitt that told you I was having an affair with my brother's wife?"

"The first time I met you, you mean? Yes, it was." He paused again, looking at his lacquered shoes. "I have a terrible prejudice, Mr. Agutter. It is a prejudice against people who take the law into their own hands. If someone is getting across you, why not tell me, and we can apply the sanctions of the law?"

I laughed at his mild, sallow face. "What we're in here is offshore racing," I said. "The law of offshore racing is, if you can get away with it, do it."

"Ah," said Nelligan, vaguely. "Very glorious. Are you telling me that three men have suffered fatal accidents so someone can win a boat race?"

"No," I said.

The vagueness left his face and the brow-ridge came down and it was hard and pugnacious under the lights. "You've got a lot of enemies in this town, Agutter. Powerful ones. Personally, I don't like any of you rich gits in your smart boats. But it's my job to keep the Queen's peace, and that's what I am going to do. So you can settle your quarrels by the law, and I mean of England, not the jungle. Understand?"

It was five in the morning, and I was beginning to judder with exhaustion. This new, hard Nelligan was real enough, but I did not believe in him. He was between me and whoever had sabotaged my rudders and killed my brother; and he was between *Sorcerer* and the Cup. I was going to fix them both, in my own way.

"Can I go now?" I said.

"Oh," said Nelligan, vague again. "By all means, yes."

"And Mr. Scott."

Nelligan spread his hands.

I took Scotto back to *Sorcerer*. It was grey dawn and the last police car was leaving. Georgia's face still wore traces of outrage.

"Body search," she said. "Every sail out of its bag. The lot."

"What did they find?"

"Nothing. What did you expect?"

"Oh, dope. Corpses. Just as well that gun's in the drink."

"How's Scotto?" she said.

"Stiffening up," I said. "Can you stay with the boat? Scotto can have a bath at my place. I'll drop him off, and you can nip over when someone arrives to relieve you."

"And then you might explain."

I laughed.

I took Scotto back to my house, showered and shaved. I groaned at the mirror. My face was about the same colour as the shaving-foam, and the bags under my eyes looked like lumps of slate. For someone who needed his eight hours a night, I was staying awake an awful lot.

Scotto was slumped in the corner of the drawing-room. He stank of embrocation. "You want to go sailing?" I said. "Coffee first."

He shrugged, and winced with pain.

"Pollitt," I said, as I brought in the jug. "Do you think he was coming aboard *Sorcerer* to bend something?"

"Why else?" he said.

"Did you have the lights on?"

"Yeah."

"So what if he wanted to talk?"

"I've got nothing to say to him."

186

"What if he thought it was me?"

Scotto drank his coffee in silence, then said, "Yeah."

"Maybe he wanted to tell me something?"

Scotto nodded his vast head slowly. "So maybe I shouldn't have slapped him."

"Too late now," I said. "Anyway, he might have been trying to bend something, at that. Let's go boating." But privately, I thought: Pollitt had reason to be fed up with Amy. What if he had found out something about one of Amy's lovers, and got drunk enough to tell me what he knew?

As we drove back to the marina, I could not get rid of the picture of his terror-frozen face, black and white under the moon.

By eleven-thirty, the Official Measurer had finished his pre-race inspection and *Sorcerer* was out and propped. The crew were back. Scotto started on her bottom with the pressure hose, making sure no particle of muck remained. The rest of us milled around, scrubbing, oiling and making sure that she wasn't carrying an ounce more weight than she had to. Some of it was useful, and some of it was superstition. But then, in my experience, races are won by ninety per cent sailing, nine per cent luck and one per cent superstition. This may not sound like much, but in an offshore race lasting a hundred hours, a one per cent margin means a commanding lead.

At two o'clock, we had the final crew meeting. I issued last instructions and told everybody to be on the dock at eight. Then I went home.

First, I went to see my father. He was watching sails through his telescope, banging the arm of his wheelchair with his fist and swearing continuously.

I said, "Hello." He wheeled round. "Race day tomorrow," I said. "Trials begin."

"What races?" he said.

"Captain's Cup trials. Olympic Triangles tomorrow and Tuesday in Pulteney Bay. Then the Duke's Bowl, offshore, a week on Tuesday."

"Yes," he said. "Saw you with the glass. Got that boat going well, boy. You'll smash those idiots out there." He gestured at the window with a clawlike arm.

"Yes."

"You look shagged," he said. "Get yer head down. Good luck." He fumbled in the pocket of his dreadful tartan dressing-gown.

The nurse said, "Here, let me."

He said, "Damn your eyes, woman, I'll do it myself." She stepped back, drawing her breath in sharply, and he found what he was looking for. "Here," he said. "Take this. First sovereign I ever earned. Put it on yer watch-chain."

"Thanks," I said.

"And beat that Millstone feller."

"Has he been pestering you?"

"Mr. Millstone called round," said the nurse. "He was ever so nice to us, wasn't he? Captain Agutter—"

"Get out, blast you!" roared my father, with astonishing vigour.

She said, "Well!" and scuffled off.

My father pulled a bottle of whisky from under a draped table. "Bloody Millstone trying to buy the house again. Said it was the last chance." I wondered what he meant by that. "Nerve of the swine. Sent him packing. Decent whisky, this. Chiefy brought it," he said. "Don't bother about glasses."

His liver-spotted hands trembled as he raised it to his lips. He took a shaky gulp and passed it to me. "Here's to Agutters in Pulteney," he said.

"Agutters in Pulteney," I said.

"Now you get along."

I patted him on the shoulder. It was like patting a skeleton. "Goodbye," I said.

Downstairs, I rove a bootlace through the sovereign and hung it round my neck, feeling a bit of an idiot but strangely moved. Then I called Breen's office. It took some time to get through; he was probably in his helicopter.

"Ready to go," I said.

"Splendid." There was a strange, whining hum behind his voice.

"Shall we expect you on board?"

"Not on the Olympic Triangles. But I'll come on the offshore race. The Duke's Bowl."

"Bring your seasick pills."

He laughed. "I was talking to Peregrine Apsley today," he said. "He's on the selection committee. He thinks we're in with a good chance. Mind you, he's about the only one who does."

Peregrine Apsley was an ex-Submariner, tough as old boots and a hideous snob.

"Oh well, we'll try to bring 'em round," I said.

"By the way, I'd like a report on that business last night. Dead bodies. Don't like it. Telex me, would you, by tomorrow at the latest?"

Exhaustion and whisky combined to make me resent this. I said, "Haven't got time. If you want a private detective, hire one. Meanwhile, get stuffed."

Then I put the telephone down and stared at the receiver. Dear, dear, I remember thinking, getting tense before the race, Agutter. This was not the way to speak to an owner. Then I thought, well, compared to the stroke I intended to pull on his boat, slamming the phone down wasn't all that serious.

I poured myself another Famous Grouse and sat staring at the telephone. Outside, the wind huffed petals off the last tulips in the garden and the afternoon life of Pulteney hummed along in its usual calm style. I felt out of it, in a backwater. I should be doing something. There was one thing I wanted to do, more than anything else. But I didn't dare.

"Yellow rat," I said to myself, aloud. Then I lifted the telephone and dialled Sally's number.

The telephone rang and rang, until it began to sound hollow, as if I could hear it in the emptiness of her house. And as it rang, I felt lonelier, less and less equipped to go on the cold sea and out-think the meanest and sharpest sailors in England. There was only one place to go, when you felt like that: bed.

So I went.

Next morning, I got up very early, walked the quiet streets down to the quay and put in an hour's hard work on *Nautilus'* moorings, preparing a little surprise for later in the day. When I got home for breakfast, the kitchen clock said 7:15.

22

The battle flags of the moored Trials boats were
fluttering straight out as I walked down the jetty an
hour later, greeting acquaintances and mentally
checking the competition rocking under the feverish
activity of its crews. There was enough wind to start
the halyards singing, but not to make them scream;
force five westerlies, the early shipping forecast had
said. I could still taste the triple-strength coffee, thick
and black, with the race day breakfast of three eggs,
ham and fried potatoes, two slices of toast with honey
and an orange to follow. I did not want to eat it; the
nerves had shrunk my stomach. But if I didn't, there
was always the possibility of the low-sugar shakes out
there on the course. There were too many imponder-
ables in racing, without the shakes. No sense in risking
any that could be avoided.

I was getting some looks, this morning. The rise and
fall and current shaky resurgence of Charlie Agutter
was a topic of great interest in the fleet and among the
spectators, Press, and other hangers-on who had been
filtering into Pulteney during the past couple of days.
It was not surprising. From the point of view of those
who knew no better, Charlie Agutter had several

weeks ago killed his brother. And now he was going out in an oldish boat to risk everything on winning a boat race. Had I been a journalist, I would probably have thought it quite a good story. As Charlie Agutter, it made me more than somewhat nervous.

Sorcerer was looking businesslike with her red-and-gold caduceus battle flag billowing from the forestay. I was the last aboard; I had timed it that way, because the crew was a good unit and I wanted them to feel at home together before I went aboard. Scotto was there, his bandages invisible under his bulky wet-gear. I said, "How are you?" and he looked at me as if I was mad. If Scotto was not admitting any disabilities, he would not be acting disabled. It was as simple as that. "Okay," I said. "Any problems?"

There were no problems. *Sorcerer* was in as good shape as she would ever be.

"Cast off," I said. "Flags, Scotto."

Scotto went for the locker, plied the halyard, and the two flags went up the backstays—the Royal Ocean Racing Club Class 1 pennant, and below, the C flag flown by all Captain's Cup boats. They snapped and fluttered in the stiff breeze as we motored down the creek, past the ends of the jetties.

The creek widened. I said, "Number two genoa."

Ahead, the sea was grey, with the occasional white horse. The wind blew flat and hard along the coast. Nobody on the boat spoke, except me.

"Up main," I said.

The grinders applied their colossal arms and shoulders to the Lewmar halyard winches, and the ochre-and-white Kevlar sail ran briskly up the mast.

"Up genoa."

The trimmers squinted at the tell-tales, playing the sheets. *Sorcerer* leaned smoothly away from the wind and accelerated for the open grey horizon. Her crew arranged themselves in position; right aft, me at the wheel, and Doug the tactician with his clipboard. In the cockpit, Nick the trimmer, a mastman, a halyardsman and Crispin, the spare helmsman, on the mainsheet. Then there were the gorillas; Scotto in the cockpit and Dike, the foredeck hand. We all sat to weather, on the uphill side of the boat, and sucked glucose tablets. The crew gazed out at the grey sea and the far-off white triangles of sails by the tiny black shapes of the committee boats. It was cold and raw and peaceful. But I could feel the boat alive under the wheel. Doug the tactician flicked buttons on the digital readout by his seat, and peered through his binoculars at the distant white sails, and scribbled in waterproof pencil on his clipboard. The peace was purely temporary. This was the moment of drawing breath, before sailing became war.

We put in a couple of practice tacks, feeling our way through wind and water. At first we were overstrung; Nick the trimmer oversheeted the genoa, and I swore harder than was necessary. But after ten minutes or so, we began to quieten down as everyone found their groove of concentration. I was telling people to do things; adjust the backstays, ease sheets, shift their weight. But if you had asked me afterwards, I wouldn't have known what I was saying. I was part of the equipment.

"Coming up to five-minute gun," said Doug. "We'll take the right-hand end."

The first leg of an Olympic triangle heads into the wind, which makes the pre-start manoeuvres complicated. The basic idea is to cross the line bang on the start-gun, travelling at maximum speed. In theory, it is a good idea to start at one end or the other, since the eyesight of the starters on the committee boat has been known to be unreliable. If you start at the right-hand end, close-hauled on the starboard tack, with the wind blowing over the starboard side of the boat, you have the right of way over other boats. If you start at the left-hand end of the line, away from the committee boat, you tend to have clearer water.

In practice, it is not as easy as that.

We sailed up to within fifty yards of the minesweeper that was doing duty as committee boat, picking our way through the dipping masts and gleaming hulls crowding the start area.

"Five minutes," said Doug. As he spoke, one of the minesweeper's turrets boomed a puff of white smoke and the crowd of yachts bore away. I could see Archer, his close-cropped brown hair fluttering in the breeze at *Crystal*'s helm. He saw me, too; he gave no sign of recognition.

Race rules begin at the five-minute gun. Pre-start manoeuvres are so complicated that they are governed by special right-of-way rules which are stretched to breaking-point at every start. Offensive sailing can leave the opposition miles away from the line at the start-gun, or push them over it before the gun, which is just as bad. So as Doug muttered a string of suggestions in my ear, I steered my way through the tangle of jockeying hulls, reaching away for position from which to make the run-in, watching the digital stopwatch readout, which was counting down in ten-second jumps.

At three minutes and ten seconds, Doug said, "Watch him." I heard the clatter of waves on hull. Just behind my left shoulder, a silver bow was slicing the water. "Can't tack across him," said Doug. "We'd hit."

"Trying to force us off the line," I muttered. "Let's do him. Ready about!" I shouted.

A warning hail came down the wind from astern. I ignored it, pulling the wheel down until the luff of the mainsail shivered. The silver bow came on, shouting.

"Go!" I called. "Go" was one of our codewords. It

meant jibe; turn with the wind passing under the stern of the boat, not her head. The boom swung over. Two minutes, the readout said. We sagged away to starboard. After perhaps thirty seconds, I brought *Sorcerer*'s nose hard on the wind. The start-line on the committee boat's side was bang on the nose; there was clear water between us and it, and it was our right of way. Ahead and to port, the boat which had tried to ease us out had thought better of it, and was going down for the start. But she was going to be early, and too far down the line.

"No protest flag," said Doug. "Yet."

"She didn't have to alter course. We're in the clear."

"Correct. You were lucky, though. Go for it."

The start boat came closer. She was long and grey and high. The wind would do funny things round her hull and upperworks; I didn't want to get too close.

"Look out," said Doug.

I had seen. Down to port, a gaggle of five boats was approaching, close-hauled on the port tack. They were led by a green-and-orange hull that I recognised as *Crystal.* They were on a collision course.

"They'll tack," I said. "Hail."

"Starboard," yelled Scotto. Archer was perhaps a hundred and twenty feet away. He glanced over his right shoulder, then returned his eyes forward. The boats astern of him were tacking.

"Bastard," said Doug. "We'll cut him in half."

As I looked down *Sorcerer*'s deck, I could see green-and-orange hull and ochre Kevlar where there should have been clear water. It was my right of way; Archer knew it. I could hear myself yelling, but I did not alter course. I could see the place where we would hit, felt *Sorcerer* falter as he took the wind momentarily from her sails as he crossed her.

I think it was that little falter that saved him. His transom went past *Sorcerer*'s nose with perhaps two inches to spare. The faces of his crew were round-eyed, except Johnny Forsyth. Johnny was grinning his hard, evil, racing grin.

"Bastards," said Doug.

The green-and-orange hull turned in the water ten feet from the minesweeper's side. Boom and genoa came over. They were level with us and to windward, and we were getting dirty wind from them.

"Wait for it," I said.

And it happened as it had to. The back-draughts from the minesweeper's sides bulged his genoa and main back the wrong way, and for a split second *Crystal* wallowed.

"Zero," said Doug.

Above our heads the start-gun boomed, and we were away, ahead and upwind of the fleet on the starboard tack, with Archer's nose a couple of feet aft of our stern. When I glanced back I could see his foredeck man at the hatch, his crew out on the weather deck and above them, the flicker of back-draughts in his luffs as they in their turn caught the dirty wind deflected by *Sorcerer*'s main. Behind him and to leeward, the rest of the fleet jostled, a chaos of sails and hulls.

"He'll have to tack," said Doug.

"Never mind him," I said. "Let's get to the mark."

The windward mark lay a couple of miles southwest of Beggarman's Head, at the western end of Pulteney Bay. It was slack water, so tide was not a factor until the beginning of the ebb. By that time, we should be round the mark. I could see the buoy, a big orange inflatable against the dark cliffs of the headland. Doug and I knew what we were going to do. I looked to port. The remaining eleven yachts were tightly bunched, masts bristling from the pack. The best of them was ten seconds behind us; two of the last boats had protest flags fluttering on their backstays. *Crystal* was a quarter of a mile away, on the port tack. As I watched, she tacked again onto starboard. We were well clear of her.

"Tack now," said Doug.

We tacked, and tacked again. Now we were on the starboard tack, to starboard of the rhumb line, the direct line between the committee boat and the buoy. *Crystal* lay a hundred yards to leeward. We were still clear of her. The rest of the fleet seemed in no hurry to follow.

"And again," said Doug.

I waited, just to make sure. It was a short tack, this one, and it had to be in the right place. To leeward, there was activity on Archer's foredeck. He was setting his number one genoa. In my humble opinion, Archer was too far to leeward; he had miscalculated. I kept my eye on the windspeed and direction readout. When I saw what I was looking for I said, "Ready about. Helm's a-lee."

I saw Archer look up and across. It was a struggle not to wave at him, because what we had done was sail into a wind-bend, where the westerly was bent southwards by the face of Beggarman's Head, so that instead of making the mark with another tack, we had enough of a lift to make it on this one. The nice thing about wind-bends is that they operate in a small area; this one had not yet affected anyone else in the fleet. Then I saw Archer's bow come up; he had got it too, but his wind was lighter than mine because he was too far over, in the shadow of the distant headland.

We stayed in that narrow corridor of sou'westerly breeze for perhaps five minutes. During those five minutes, the rest of the fleet fell back. Only Archer managed to stay in touch, and he was a good twenty seconds behind now.

We came round the first mark clean as a whistle, and the tri-radial popped up like a balloon. We settled down for the first reaching leg. There wasn't quite enough wind for *Sorcerer* to get out of the water and start tobogganing, but she dragged her old bones through the swell well enough, and I was able to relax a bit—but not too much; the first windward leg is always hard work, and there's a temptation to slacken off on the reach.

I had just checked astern. The fleet was round the mark, with Archer well out in front, but too far away to interfere with us. My eyes ran up to the hard curve of the mainsail with the huge swell of spinnaker beyond it, then caught on something. At first I didn't know what it was; it was merely a hangnail of the mind, something out of place. So I ran my eye back over it. And as so often happens, it chose the moment to do what it was going to do.

What I had seen was high at the masthead; a thread, fluttering where the starboard backstay joined the masthead casting. I had time to say, "Look out," and then there was a bang and the boat lurched heavily. The tri-radial collapsed and the boom whacked across. I had to force myself not to shut my eyes, because if you were to choose the best way of losing your mast overboard, that would probably be it.

We lay head to wind, sail flapping. What had happened was that the starboard backstay had broken. The backstay is there to support the mast from astern, and to put the right degree of bend into it. Scotto stood on the transom, staring at the line trailing in the water.

"Move," I said; he had been there all of two seconds.

"Get some headsail on her," he said.

I yelled for the genoa, praying that he knew what he was doing, because if he didn't the mast was going to be a useful corkscrew. The fleet was on us now. The genoa went up and filled. When I dared look at the backstay, instead of double cables converging on the masthead blocks from the slope of the transom, there was only one. But at its base, the single cable forked, with a tackle leading to each of the chainplates of the original double backstay.

"Tri-radial!" I yelled, and pushed the wheel.

23

She came round like a dinghy, and there was a stiffening of the faces in the cockpit as the strain came on the jury backstay. The wind hit the tri-radial and we waited for the bang. But the bang didn't come. At that point we all stopped worrying about it, because we had a race on our hands.

We were now well down to leeward of the rhumb line. Amazingly, the whole process had only taken about twenty seconds. The bulk of the fleet was still astern, but our lead was gone. Also, we had managed to drift a long way to leeward. We still had a commanding position, though: as the wind struck into the sails again I pointed up, and we roared across the nose of the fleet on the port tack, pummelling the genoa into the rail and bearing off when the sightlines I had scribed on the deck told me we could make the mark on *Sorcerer*'s best point of sailing. There was one boat to windward: *Crystal*. She was screwed down tight and going for the mark like the hammers of hell. I couldn't crank *Sorcerer* that hard, not with one backstay gone.

But I did it anyway.

That reaching leg was more or less a drag race. I stayed as close to *Crystal* as I dared, trying to keep in close contact so I'd be ahead and inside at the mark, and Archer would have to give me room to jibe. But unless *Sorcerer* would get up and run, *Crystal* had the legs of her. *Sorcerer* showed no signs of getting up; *Crystal* edged closer.

At the jibe mark, boats turn with the wind passing across their sterns. A sailful of wind crashing from one side of the boat to the other is not, generally, cruel and unusual punishment. But it is a good idea to have your backstays in working order. I knew I was going to have to take it easy. Scotto was mind-reading.

"They've spotted us," he said.

I glanced across, hearing the wind's roar in my right ear. A couple of hundred feet of grey water, then *Crystal*'s deck; and under her boom, the black circles of a pair of binoculars.

"They're coming up to cover," said Doug. "Two minutes to the mark."

"We won't be able to stay ahead that long."

"Can you luff 'em, then?"

Crystal answered that one. Her hail floated across the water. "Mast abeam!"

"She's right, sod it," said Doug. *Crystal* had now established an overlap, and we could no longer knock her off course by sailing across her bows on a course closer to the wind than hers. "Let's make the buoy."

"Look at her go," I said. A dark shadow of wind was moving across the water at her. Archer took his gust nicely and it brought his stem past my sightlines and forward of the mast.

"Stay inside him," Doug said.

I tried, hoping to get within that magic two lengths of the buoy where Archer would have to give me room to manoeuvre. But he was too far ahead. His jibe was beautifully smooth, and the spray from his quarter splashed over our bow. As we came up to the mark, he was already round. But the rest of the fleet was well behind. All was not lost.

"Cover him," said Doug. "Go on."

The wind shadow of a boat on a broad reach on the port tack extends about a hundred feet onto her starboard bow. We luffed, sailing to the left of the rhumb line, trying to blanket *Crystal.* I saw Forsyth's face under the boom. It was hard and preoccupied. *Crystal's* wake crooked faintly to the left.

"Follow on," said Doug.

We could afford a little boat-for-boat, because the rest of the fleet was between five and twenty seconds astern. I pulled the wheel and the trimmers took up the slack. A shadow was travelling out of the eye of the wind, darkening the grey waves.

"Look out," I said. "We'll do for him."

As the shadow arrived, I pulled the wheel very gently. And for the first time that day, *Sorcerer* shuddered, came up and began to go. Spray fizzed astern and she made ground on *Crystal* fast—so fast that Archer failed to see what was happening until it was too late and his sails were shuddering in our dirty wind. He bore away for the mark, and we bore away with him, alongside.

The crews sat on the uphill rail, with their feet out. Doug and I crouched on the leeward side of the trench, looking across the twenty foot gap that separated us from *Crystal. Crystal* began edging ahead, but as soon as she got into our mucky wind she fell back again, until she was level. I could feel a tight grin trying to stretch my face, but kept it off; I didn't want to provoke the opposition, unless there was a special reason for doing so. Just now, we wanted things as calm as possible, because if Archer blew his cool and did an illegal luff we'd either have a collision, in which case we'd probably both be disqualified, or we'd have to take evasive action and protest. I wanted a clean win, boat-for-boat, not squabbles in the committee-room later. So I concentrated on the sails and the wind and the distant orange tube of the mark, and ignored the lines of eyes at *Crystal*'s weather rail.

Archer's head was only just visible, because of the heel of his boat. The wind was screaming in her rigging; we'd have to shorten sail if it went on freshening. Then I realized that there was another noise. Someone was shouting. It wasn't Archer; but Archer was looking pained, and beside him was Johnny Forsyth, his face congested with blood and his lips moving. I couldn't hear what he was saying; but I saw his eyes glance across at *Sorcerer* and was surprised by the fury in them. Then Archer shook his head again, and Forsyth's hands went up and his head disappeared out of sight behind the boat's side.

Doug's face was stiff as a poker, but his voice was unsteady with suppressed glee. "It looks like the tactician don't agree with the helmsman," he said.

I nodded, not really interested. I had to stay on top till the mark; that was all. "How close?" I said.

"Sorry," said Doug, and began counting down. *Crystal* edged ahead again, and dropped back.

"Five lengths," said Doug.

Crystal started up again, was backwinded and dropped back. She was perhaps five feet away now, creaking and drumming, the wakes quarrelling in the canyon between the shining hulls.

"Two," said Doug. "Water at the mark!"

I pulled the wheel across, and the tri-radial came down as the sheets came in, and the jury backstay tackle groaned as Scotto put his mighty shoulders into the winch, and the needles of the close-hauled dial came to rest at their marks.

"Excellent," said Doug, and I glanced quickly over my shoulder.

Archer had had to bear quickly away at the buoy. He was on port tack, to leeward, but he had lost his overlap.

"Blew him away," said Doug.

"Watch for the protest flag." I settled down, squinting between the luff of the mainsail and the close-hauled indicator.

"Still nothing," said Doug after two minutes. "Fleet's round."

"He's left it too late," I said. "We're clear."

It is one thing being in front: it is another staying there. The difference was not so much on the windward leg as afterwards, on the run home. On the second beat to windward we kept position between the wind and the fleet, covering Archer closely. We slipped round the windward mark, and the running 'chute popped out above the foredeck.

"Coming up to cover," said Doug. "Watch him."

It was calm and still on the deck, with that peculiar stillness that always comes when you are running before the wind. The wind is blowing as hard as ever, but you are travelling at the same speed. It can be very deceptive, which is why things happen so fast and so catastrophically on the run.

What was happening on this run was that *Crystal,* a very fast boat downwind, was catching us again. Slowly, it was true, but catching us, Doug punched the readout, and narrowed his eyes. I waited for the computer between his ears to yield results.

"We'll do it," he said. "Unless the bastard covers us."

"Then we'll have to stop him."

We were both running with the wind on the quarter, rather than dead astern. You go faster that way, even though you travel in a series of jibing zigzags rather than a straight line. The trick is to keep the zigzags shallow, while at the same time preventing the opposition from stealing your wind.

Crystal was a hundred and twenty feet astern. As I watched, the clouds blew off the sun, and a ribbon at her forestay bloomed into a huge pigeon's breast of a running kite, gold and blue with a great cartoon diamond at its centre. She looked hugely beautiful, a tower of sail topping the blade of her green-and-orange bow with the bow-wave glittering below. She dipped like a Victorian dancer.

"On starboard," said Doug, unnecessarily. I had been watching for half a second; few winning helmsmen spend much time admiring the opposition. "Better jibe now."

I said, "Go!" and pulled the wheel a fraction. The boom smacked over. Up on the foredeck, they clipped on the spinnaker boom and the big sail swung smoothly across.

"Them astern," said Doug. "Covering now."

"Go," I said.

The boom went over again, and the spinnaker. Each time the mainsheet man had to retrim, the foredeck hands had to dip the spinnaker pole, and the grinders had to tail and trim the yards of slender spinnaker guys and sheets. A jibe swings an awful lot of wind through an awful lot of sail.

"They've gone again," said Doug.

"Go," I said.

We went. So did *Crystal*. We zigzagged down the final leg like two warplanes dogfighting. The sweat shone on the gorillas' faces. A sort of rhythm began to establish itself. That was what I had been waiting for.

"Go! Go!" I shouted, at the tenth jibe.

The pounding of feet sounded on the foredeck as the sweating hands went to the spinnaker pole. The mainsail boom crashed over. The spinnaker had moved round four feet when Doug said, "Them astern's gone to cover."

"Yes!" I yelled it much louder than was necessary to answer Doug. The spinnaker went back and so did the main boom. For the first time since rounding the mark, *Crystal* and *Sorcerer* were sailing on different tacks.

"That," said Doug with reverence, "is what is known as a dummy jibe."

Down the wind there floated a hard, angry roaring as Johnny Forsyth came to the same conclusion. *Crystal* dipped and jibed, but it was no good. She was right out of touch now; she didn't have a hope.

We got the winner's gun twenty seconds ahead.

"Nice," said Doug. And the whole boat was talking now, not roaring, but quietly satisfied. There were a lot of races to go; there was no point in getting over-excited. Still, it had been a good one.

"Class," said Scotto, handing me a mug of Bovril. "Showed the bastards."

I sipped the Bovril, realising that I was shivering. The hot drink formed a lump of heat in the belly that made the spray seem even colder than it really was.

"Want me to take her in?" he said.

I shook my head. "I'm fine." This was a break with Scotto's personal tradition, and he looked surprised. "How's the back?" I said.

"Great," he said.

"Nice work with the backstay."

He nodded, watching the rest of the fleet coming over the line. "Fixed by tomorrow," he said.

Little do you know, Scotto, I thought. I turned away and looked at the bleak, grey tunnel between clouds and sea, out of which the wind howled with the wail of a hungry ghost, and I spoke to Hugo, very quietly, and told him what I planned to do that evening. We were on the way back, but *Sorcerer* would not be racing tomorrow.

24

It is traditional, when returning from races, to pass by the end of Pulteney Quay. The tradition dates from the days when competitors at Pulteney Regatta kept their boats on moorings in the harbour. Spectators would gather on the quay in the hope of cheering heroes and gloating as the inexperienced missed their moorings. Of course, most of the racing-boats now lived at the marina, and the tougher international boats tended to ignore such courtesies. But I made a point of observing them. For one thing, I liked the old Pulteney a good deal better than the new. For another, the sail-past served today's purposes nicely.

The crowd on the quay head was thick. As the figures grew above pinhead size, I searched with Doug's binoculars. I felt a moment of extreme pleasure. Sally was there and beside her, in his wheelchair, my father, banging the armrest, with behind him Nurse Bollom, her wide face chapped and sullen.

"Some committee," said Scotto, grinning.

I nodded, the pleasure fading at the thought of what I had to do. But it couldn't be helped.

I took *Sorcerer* right in close. The crew were all back

in the trench now, and she was powering along on a beam reach under genoa and main, no spinnaker. The boats in the harbour grew bigger, and then we were among them. Sighting down the deck, I could see *Nautilus'* bottle-green hull and gold stripe to the left of my forestay. I gritted my teeth. The crowd on the quay were waving and cheering. I passed the wheel between my fingers. The wake slapped against the sides of the moored boats. Sorry, folks, I thought, and twitched the wheel.

Sorcerer's bow came across, heading now for a sliver of open water beyond the head of the quay. It was then that I felt it: a steady wrenching of the wheel, plucking it out of my hand, blurring the spokes till they came to rest with a hideous clonk.

"What the hell?" said Scotto.

I pulled at the wheel. It was jammed hard over. Scotto joined me, and Doug and one of the grinders on the twin wheel at the far side of the cockpit. Sailcloth was rattling and booming overhead.

"Hooked a bloody mooring line," I said. "Get her straight."

Above, the mast was bending nastily against the grey clouds. The wheel began to turn. I was shouting orders. Suddenly there was a lurch, and she was free.

"Fouled a hawser," said Scotto.

He was right, of course. I had laid the hawser myself, at an angle to *Nautilus'* regular mooring, early that morning. It had been good helmsmanship to get the keel over the top of it and only hang up the rudder, while making sure the rudder would hit it so its leading edge wouldn't slide over the top.

"She all right?" said Scotto.

We were passing under the quay head. The crowd was cheering and waving again, except my father, who was shaking his head, and his nurse, who looked fed up. Sally was smiling. But it seemed to me that her smile was not so much for me as for the boat, because it had won.

"No," I said to Scotto.

I gave him the wheel, and let him feel the vibration that meant a twisted rudder stock.

"We'll have to take her out," he said. "No bloody race tomorrow. If I find the bastard who hooked us up, I'll kill him."

It was the only way I could get *Sorcerer* out of the water. And I had to have *Sorcerer* out of the water to prove a theory about who was causing all this sudden death around Pulteney. But it did not make me feel very noble.

Round at the marina, we called the crane straight over and pulled her out. Scotto and I went and stood underneath and were dripped on by the hull. Doug, aloft, waggled the wheel. The stock was bent, all right; it was maybe five degrees out of true. We'd never bend it back. It needed a new one, and a new one would take at least twenty-four hours—as I had intended.

So I gave the orders to the yard men. I left Scotto to supervise the removal of the rudder, and went to ring Breen.

"Good," he said, when he answered. "You won."

"Did you hear what happened next?"

"What?" His voice had gone cold.

I told him. I could almost hear him ticking away at the far end: cost, time, disadvantages.

"You miss one race," he said at the end. "Inshore. Not a major disaster. You'll have her ready for the Duke's Bowl?"

"Yes."

"Good enough. Now tell me about the competition."

I resailed the race for his benefit. At the end, he said, "Good." He sounded pleased. "Keep her out of the

209

water for as long as you need. The Bowl is in what, a week?"

"Eight days," I said.

"Do what you have to do. I'll ask around behind the scenes. See how the . . . selectors view it. Bye."

I uncoiled from the telephone box, smiling nervously at the fat woman who was waiting to use it, and went back to the crane. The rudder was already off; the crew was standing in the cold shed, reluctant to go home.

"Let's go to the Mermaid," I said. "Scotto, I'll give you a lift."

"What about the boat?" said Scotto.

"Leave her," I said. We got into the BMW. "She's okay while they're working on her."

He shrugged. Then he looked across at me, looked away again and said, "How come you hit that thing this evening?"

"What thing?"

"The thing you hit. Charlie, did you do it on purpose?"

"Well . . . yes, actually."

"So would you just explain why?"

"Because I want her out of the water. Somebody's sabotaged two of my boats so far this season. They were both contenders. So I reckon someone's going to sabotage this one, and I want to make it easy for them. So we'll have the boat out of the water for a week, and advertise the fact, and they can have their chance."

"Are you crazy?" said Scotto.

"Like a fox," I said.

We were in front of the Mermaid now. "I'll drop you off here. Back in twenty minutes."

When I got back to the marina, a small, red-haired man was waiting by the office. At his feet were two

210

metal boxes, of the kind photographers use to carry their equipment. We shook hands, and went in to Neville Spearman's office.

Neville's manner was perceptibly warmer, though by no means effusive. That was what winning did for you. Agutter might, in his view, be on the way back, though there was still some distance to go. If we could win the trials and then the Cup, he would be so pleased he would hardly be able to stay off his knees—not because of his innate sportsmanship, but because a Captain's Cup winning Agutter would be very good for Agutter's local yard in terms of work and publicity and prices.

"This is Mr. Brewis," I said. "He's a security consultant."

Spearman said, "Pleased to meet you," but his grey-rimmed eyes were watchful and suspicious.

"We'd like to rig up a few bits on *Sorcerer*," he said. "If you wouldn't mind."

"A few bits? We've got security of our own," said Spearman.

"Which didn't stop you getting a yardful of police-men the other night."

"I think you're being a bit . . . over-cautious," said Spearman. "I mean, what would happen if all my clients got the screaming abdabs?"

Mr. Brewis coughed. "That's unlikely," he said. "Mr. Agutter has requested a couple of magic-eye devices, with radio link to a monitoring centre. Fitting and operation will be conducted with maximum discretion."

"He means that we're not going to tell anyone," I said. "I'll bring *Nautilus* round, and we'll do some work on her deck and we'll keep the monitoring equipment below. Can you give me a berth the far side, where we won't be too obvious?"

"Hang on," said Spearman. I could see that Charlie

Agutter was not far enough on the road back to be worth much extra trouble, yet. "I don't know about this—"

"I'm afraid it's necessary," I said. "And I have to ask you not to talk to anyone. Not anyone at all."

There was a silence, while Spearman thought through the pros and cons of cooperating with Agutter. "Of course, if you want it like that," he said at last, sniffily. "But I don't know what things are coming to."

"That's Pulteney for you, nowadays. Bloody awful, isn't it?"

Spearman shook his head. Behind the dark eyesockets, he would be thinking that Pulteney nowadays meant he built big, expensive yachts—not fishing-boats with owners who pared his prices to the bone.

"All right, Mr. Brewis," I said. "I'll join you in a moment." He rose and went outside with his boxes. Alone with Spearman, I said, "I'll be brutally frank, Neville. Besides you and me and Brewis, only Scotto knows about this, and Scotto doesn't talk much. So if anybody else comes to know, it won't be hard to work out who told them."

He looked at me for a long, silent minute. Then he said, "Why shouldn't I toss you off the yard?"

I let him work it out for himself. Then, in case he was coming to unhelpful conclusions, I told him about Breen's offer to commission a 150-foot schooner if we won the Cup. "And you would probably like to build it, if you've got time."

It was like offering fillet steak to a shark, if he had time. "There's a big difference between winning the first Trial race and winning the Cup," he said.

"If you don't cooperate, I've got no chance."

He sighed, and said, "All right. But the first sniff of a problem and we call in the police."

"All right," I said. "How long for the rudder stock?"

"Not before the weekend," he said.

"Fair enough. I also want a modification. I don't like that double backstay. Let's have a single one, please. My office will give you specifications."

And I left to join Mr. Brewis.

25

It was no hardship living on *Nautilus* for a few days. She was a pretty spacious old machine, and I established myself in her after-cabin, with drawing-board, and did some running with *Sorcerer's* crew. Scotto spent the days with his head in *Sorcerer's* electronics, and the nights in the fore-cabin. The alarm signals lived in the saloon.

After two nights, I was beginning to wonder if anything was actually going to happen. It was entirely possible that *Nautilus'* presence in the marina would prevent anything in the way of enemy action.

On the eighth evening, I had wandered up to the callbox to try to ring Sally. As usual, nowadays, there was no reply. I wanted to go after her, but I could not leave the marina. I walked moodily through the dusk, casting a jaundiced eye over the corrugated iron sheds and the rusty iron fence. It was a dull, chilly evening and the marina looked like a prisoner-of-war camp. I felt like a prisoner, too.

Nautilus' cabin lights were on. I walked down the hatch and found Scotto at the mahogany table in the saloon, playing cribbage with Georgia.

Georgia said hello, and we talked. I asked after

214

Sally. Georgia said she was out at Ed Beith's, clearing up the mess. I felt a twinge of something very like jealousy, and poured some drinks, giving myself a larger-than-usual Famous Grouse to dull the ache. They asked me if I wanted to play poker. I refused, and sat on a berth half-reading a book. The whisky infiltrated my bloodstream, and the saloon gave off a mellow glow. I sat and meditated on the foul discomfort of racing-boats compared to *Nautilus'* solid mahogany and cushions. I moved only to throw another shovelful of coal on the stove that glowed in the corner, and sat back again, to watch the fingers of red spread through the black lumps. The sounds of the cribbage-players behind me were lulling, and my eyelids were heavy.

I sneezed. The next breath bore the smell of petrol.

"What's that smell?" I said.

"Petrol," said Scotto.

I was still watching the stove. Something peculiar was happening. The air around it was shimmering, as if tremendously hot. The smell of petrol was suffocating. The cabin turned red, and a great whoomph blew me backwards and onto the card table. I could smell burnt hair, and the skin of my face was tight. The cabin was a sheet of flame. Georgia screamed. I could see a hulking mass of flames reeling across the cabin sole, and I thought: that's Scotto. I yanked the extinguisher off the wall and smashed in the plunger and great white loops of foam began to spurt out and at him, and his flames went out. The extinguisher ran out.

I shouted, "Fore-cabin!" and grabbed Scotto's wrist and dragged him through the door. The flames were everywhere again, but not on Scotto.

I grabbed another extinguisher, said, "Hatch, Georgia!" and opened the door to the saloon again.

The timber was alight now. The extinguisher's white loops plunged into the fire and it retreated for a moment. Then big ugly flames jumped back. I slammed the door. Georgia had the forehatch open — thank God I had left it unbolted. Scotto was making pedalling movements with his legs. I guided them onto a bunk and he crawled on deck, followed by Georgia.

The air was suddenly icy cold. I slammed the hatch. Scotto was saying in a low voice, "What the hell? What the hell?"

I said, "Someone put a plastic bag of petrol down the stove-pipe," as much to myself as him.

Georgia had her knife out, cutting the clothing off him. It was nearly dark now, and the coach-roof windows were full of a jumping red glow.

"Get him ashore!" I yelled. "Get help!" And I ran for the bucket forrard of the mast, scooped up a pailful of harbour water and went for the afterhatch. As I went down the deck, I heard a sound from below. My mind was scarcely working. *Nautilus,* my last solid tie with Hugo, was slipping away. The sound was a foreign one, nothing to do with *Nautilus.* I opened the door. The flames whooshed out at me, and I flung in my bucket of water, and the sound shrieked out at me. The cabin was a furnace. There was no chance. None at all.

And with the realisation that *Nautilus* was doomed came another. The alien sound suddenly took on meaning. It was the siren of *Sorcerer*'s intruder alarm.

I stood still for a moment. The siren cut off abruptly. In the silence, I could hear the roar of the flames, the clatter of Scotto and Georgia stumbling along the jetty, the slap of *Nautilus'* halyards, high and serene above the hull. And I knew what I had to do.

I refilled the bucket with water and tipped it over my head. I went and grabbed an axe from its clips on the bulkhead. Then I returned on deck and dived down the forehatch. The heat was terrible and I felt

216

the skin of my hand stick to the brass handle of the head door. But what was driving me was stronger than pain. The head was like a pitch black oven, but I had installed it myself, so I knew it backwards.

I laid about me with the axe, heard the smash of the lavatory pan, felt the resistance as the blade met copper. And I kept chopping for what felt like an hour as the heat grew. I knew I was trapped in a little box besieged by fire, but I kept hacking, hacking. At last I hit the spot, and felt the jet of seawater from the severed plumbing splash on my legs. If I sank her, I might at least save her hull. Then I burst out into the fore-cabin. The bunks were already burning fiercely and the smoke was terrible. I went through the hatch like a jack-in-the-box and spent a moment on all fours, coughing a cough that tasted of incinerators.

When I looked up, I saw that Scotto and Georgia were only a hundred yards away. To my amazement, I found I could only have been below for a couple of minutes at most. So I got onto my feet and lurched across the deck and onto the jetty.

Suddenly a starter motor whinnied in the car park. I looked up sharply. Besides mine and Scotto's, it was the only one on the lot. It was too far away for me to see anything but a dim outline: a saloon.

"That's who's been on *Sorcerer*," I said to myself, and began to run.

Running was agony. But the anger was stronger than the pain, and I kept my legs pumping even though my throat was raw and my face felt as if it had been skinned. I heard the whinny of the starter motor again; trouble with the engine, you bastard, I thought, as my shoes hit the grit of the car park. Don't start.

But it did start. The sweat was pouring into my eyes, and I saw the dark shape of it slew violently, wheels spinning, and scream away for the gates without lights. I wrenched open the door of the BMW. It started first turn of the key and I put my foot to the floor as the other car turned onto the main road. Turned left.

I was thirty seconds behind it, still too far behind to get my lights on its number plate. I saw the rear lights flick on. Then it was round the bend and into Pulteney. When I glanced in my rear-view mirror, I could see another light. This one was red and smoky, down on the jetties of the marina. I settled grimly in my seat and followed the other car round the bend.

It was fast, the other car. I had my foot flat down and the old BMW was juddering with effort, but I was still making no ground. Two fire-engines flashed by; Georgia had got to a telephone.

Just before Pulteney, the other car turned right after a thatched cottage. I followed, tyres shrieking as I drifted. The lane was narrow, but I knew it well. It twisted and turned like an eel, but I drove it almost unconsciously, thinking of the car ahead that contained whoever had killed Hugo and wrecked *Aesthete* and caused the death of wretched little Hector Pollitt, and had tonight dropped a plastic bag full of petrol down *Nautilus'* stove-pipe to create a diversion while he mangled *Sorcerer*.

The lane turned onto a straight. I went round the corner sideways, banged the bank, and the wheel wrenched at my burned hands. I shouted with pain and let go, and the BMW rammed the verge. Cursing, I wrestled it into reverse, backed off, and stamped on the gas.

At the far end of the straight, slightly uphill, two rear lights vanished abruptly. I drove up to the brow of the hill. The lights of Pulteney were spread below. I knew of old that the lane swept down the side of the hill, in plain view, to join the top of Fore Street. The lights of the car in front made yellow cones down the hill into Pulteney. On Fore Street, I gained a little, but he turned right onto Quay Street, ignoring the "Unsuitable for Motor Vehicles" sign, and I clattered after him. A white-faced man flattened himself in a doorway. My own house flashed by. Then we were at the top of Naylor's Hill, turning left onto the Plymouth road.

As I hit the straight, I glanced down at the petrol gauge. Empty. I had about three miles in the tank. Cursing, I put my foot down again and went past the last petrol station for twenty miles. The car in front drew ahead. I switched off my lights; the moon was out, and I knew the road well enough to navigate by the white line.

After a couple of miles, the car in front slowed down. I thought: he thinks he's lost me. And I hung back as he turned right, down the road to Brundage.

The Brundage road is a dead end. The kind of people who live in Brundage are retired or work on the land, and have very little to do with the kind of people who live in Pulteney—except for one. Amy.

It was a pretty safe bet that Amy and the fire-bomb artist could be left to get on with each other for a bit. I turned around, went back to the petrol station and filled up. The girl at the till looked at me, took in my smoke-blackened clothes and blistered face and looked away. I got in and drove to Brundage.

The lights were on in Amy's house, and there was a car parked in the drive. It was a car I recognized. A Mercedes, blue, gleaming in the hall lamp, except where it was splashed with mud. Archer's car. When I felt the bonnet, it was hot.

I stood by it for a minute. Then I walked softly across the lawn to the front door, which was open.

Inside the door, a woman screamed. I broke into a run, went through the door, and arrived in a parquet-floored hall with a red Bokhara carpet.

I had been wrong about it being safe to leave Amy to get on with the fire-bomber.

She was lying face down on the rug, arms and legs

219

spread out like a starfish. She was wearing a white silk shirt and a black velvet skirt with a deep slit up the side, to show off her good legs. There was blood on the collar of the shirt.

This much I took in as I went through the door. Then I caught a glimpse of something moving out of the corner of my eye and I ducked, too late to avoid something big and heavy that slammed into my shoulders and knocked me flat on the floor beside Amy.

I lay there with a headful of bees and the wool of the Bokhara under my nose. Then I heard the car starting in the drive. I crawled to the door, but all I saw were his tail lights disappearing down the lane. I tottered back to look at Amy.

She was breathing, all right. Some of the blood was coming from a cut in the back of her head. I didn't want to move her. I went to the telephone, dialled 999, and asked for the ambulance.

When I put the receiver down, I went back to see what I could do, and for the first time I looked at her face.

I took a big breath, then another, and said something very ugly under my breath. Amy's face, pretty, foxy Amy's face, looked as if it had been hit by a small truck. She had two black eyes, and her nose was flat. There was blood everywhere, more than I had at first thought. The Bokhara rug was a marsh of it.

I ran to the kitchen and got towels and a bowl of water and ice from the refrigerator. Then I went back and knelt beside her and gently, very gently, began to clean away the blood on her face. When the worst of it was off, I wrapped the ice in a towel and made a cold pad and laid it over the ruins of her nose.

Her lips moved. Blood oozed from the corners of her mouth. She mumbled something between teeth that were probably broken.

"Don't talk," I said.

"He hit me."

"Who hit you?" Her eyes were puffing up and narrowing. "Was it Archer?" I said.

She said, "Sally."

"What about Sally?"

"Gone to Sally." Her head rolled sideways and her eyes closed.

I ran to the telephone and dialled Sally's number. It rang for a long time, with a suspicion of echo, as if in an empty hall. Archer, or whoever was driving his car, would not have had time to get there yet. So Sally must be away from home.

After fifteen rings, I dialled Ed Beith's number. Ed answered quickly.

"Sally?" he said. "She was helping clear up here. She left ten minutes ago."

"Where was she heading?"

"Home," said Ed. As usual, he radiated calm. But then why shouldn't he? He had no idea of what was going on at the other end of the line.

I could hear the distant bray of the ambulance siren. I ran for the door. The marble front doorstep flared white. In the middle, a patch of red caught my eye. Blood. There was blood everywhere tonight, and unless I hurried there would be more. But this blood was different. I stopped in mid-stride. It was a footprint, heading outwards towards the drive.

I put my foot alongside it. My shoes are size nine. This footprint was a good two inches longer. The sole belonged to a Topsider, offshore racing's favourite deck-shoe.

The scream of the ambulance was in the lane now. I ran into the drive and crouched behind a rhododendron as it came through the gate. The attendants jumped down and went into the house. I heard one of them say, "Blimey." Then I sidled out of the gate, got into my car, and drove with squealing tyres up the lane and onto the main road.

In the driver's seat, a wave of exhaustion hit me. The whole of me hurt like hell. I turned off the main road, into the lane that led past Sally's house. My heart started to beat faster; what if she was there already? Would he deal with her the same way as he had dealt with Amy? My foot grew heavier on the accelerator. The tyres screamed round a bend, and I over-corrected.

A pair of tail lights came up ahead. I drew out to overtake and I was halfway past before I realised that the car I was overtaking was Archer's Mercedes. I glanced across the wall and through the wood at her house. Lights were on. He must have been waiting out here, and now he was moving in.

I could not see the driver. But he recognised my car as I had recognised his, because he swerved across the road at me, and I swerved at him, and the cars collided with a crash, flank to flank. We screamed along beside the stand of oaks that sheltered Sally's house. I accelerated. So did he. I twisted the wheel at him. Locked side by side, we careered down the narrow lane.

I saw it coming long before it happened. Sally's gates were flanked by massive granite posts, one on each side. I was heading straight for the right-hand one. I braked hard. Then I tried to power out of it, but the Mercedes held me fast. The gatepost hurtled towards me at fifty miles an hour. I changed down into second, tramped on the accelerator. The pair of us slewed sideways, but the forward movement was too much. Tyres yelling, I slid at thirty miles an hour into the gatepost.

The seatbelt held. The passenger door came in to meet me. There was a smell of spilt petrol. The Merc's engine roared. It reversed into the lane and headed back towards the main road. I turned the BMW's key. Nothing.

The door would not open. Groaning at the pain from my burns, I crawled out of the window. In the drive, the wind soughed in the trees. Sally's Peugeot was there, and lights shone from the kitchen window.

I staggered across the gravel and hammered on the front door.

26

The wind was up. It hissed in the oaks and made them toss their heads like lunatics. My eyes would hardly stay open. When the door opened, I fell inwards and for the second time that night tasted Persian rug. The house seemed to be singing like a mad choir, timbers creaking, windows rattling, doors slamming, pipes ticking. I lay there for a moment, confused by it all. Gradually, I became aware that Sally was calling my name. I got up on my hands and knees.

"Your face," she said.

I sat down in one of the hard hall chairs.

"What have you been doing?" she said.

I focused my eyes on her with difficulty. They felt burnt. My face felt burnt, too, and my hand was in agony and my body was full of aches, with a sharper ache where the fire-raiser had whacked me with a chair, and where I had hit the gatepost in the car.

"Driving," I said.

"Tell me."

"Later. Telephone."

I rang the hospital and got Hilda Hicks.

"Ooh, Mr. Agutter," she said. "We've had that Scotto chap in again, nasty burns."

"How bad?" I said, my brain conjuring up a flayed Scotto, dying.

"He's gone home," said Hilda. "With that nice Georgia."

"Someone said you had Amy Charlton in," I said. "Is she all right?"

"Poorly," said Hilda. "She's asleep. Georgia said if you rang to give you a number." She gave me the number. When I rang, Georgia answered.

"Scotto's okay," she said. "Hard to believe, but he had the clothes burned off him and just about nothing else, except his eyelashes. You might have left me the eyelashes," she said, aggrieved.

"Nautilus?"

"Sunk. Burned out. But you saved the hull. I'm sorry, Charlie."

"So am I," I said. "Can Scotto sail?"

"Ask him," she said.

Scotto came on the line. They must be in bed together. Bed. What a beautiful word.

"Are you hurt?" I said.

"Not a lot," said Scotto.

"Can you sail tomorrow?"

"Of course," said Scotto.

"Can you get down early and go over *Sorcerer* from top to bottom? Get the others out to help."

"Yeah. Dike's sleeping aboard tonight, just in case."

"I'll get down when I can. Scotto, that guy was aboard *Sorcerer* after he torched *Nautilus*. The alarm went."

"It did?" Scotto sounded less than his usual confident self.

If you want to stop a boat, there are a lot of ways of doing it and very few ways of finding out how it has been done, until the boat stops. Which was not what we wished to happen, in a Captain's Cup trial.

"Pardon my asking," said Scotto. "But you left the marina chasing the guy. Did you catch him?"

"He caught me," I said. "And that was the other thing I meant to tell you. Do not have any communication with Frank Millstone, or Archer, or any other *Crystal* crew."

"Okay," said Scotto. "Er . . . nice work with the fire extinguisher."

"Not at all. Sorry if you were . . . er . . . put out." I rang off. Sally was staring at me.

"Children's games," I said.

"Shut up," she said. I was pleased to notice that she remembered our conversation. In my present state, the strangest things were giving me pleasure.

"What happened?" said Sally.

I explained as I dialled another number.

"He was coming here?" she said.

"He was."

"But why?"

"I was hoping you could straighten me out," I said.

The telephone was ringing, and a voice said, "Police."

I got through to Nelligan, and said, "Do you want the bloke who's been fixing all those rudders?"

"Nobody's fixed any rudders that I've seen proved," he said.

"All right. Try arson and attempted murder."

"Oh." He sounded impressed. "Who do I go and see?"

"You could start with Jack Archer. He'll be staying with Frank Millstone. Try asking him who's been driving his car tonight. And you could go and visit Mrs. Charlton in hospital. She's got concussion. Try asking her how she got concussed."

I heard the scrape of a match as he lit a John Player Special. "Millstone and Mrs. Charlton aren't exactly pals of yours, are they, Mr. Agutter? Sure you're not being a little bit mischievous? Tell you what, we'll send a man round to Mr. Millstone in the morning."

I was too tired to argue. "Bit influential, is he?" I said.

"Good night," said Nelligan, and put the telephone down.

Sally helped me into the kitchen, and said, *"Nautilus* is burnt. *Sorcerer* has been interfered with. Amy's been beaten up. Your car's a write-off. What is it, Charlie?" As she spoke, she was dabbing at my face with a wet cloth. The cloth was coming away dirty. "What's going on?"

Her Egyptian face was moving in and out of focus, the long, green eyes serious as she did something painful to my left cheek.

"Someone wants me out of the trials," I said. "What size would you say Archer's feet were?"

She frowned. "No idea. Eight? Nine?"

"Not twelve?"

"Not twelve."

"No." It was getting harder and harder to make my mind work. "What I think is going on is that someone started out to try and get me out of the Cup, and found he enjoyed the work, and now he's a raving psycho."

"Why beat up Amy?"

"He could have been screwing her. Just about everyone else has. Jealous, maybe."

"But why come after me?"

"There," I said, "you have me."

"Millstone?" she said.

"Not impossible," I said. "He's got big feet, all right. And he hates Agutters. But then again . . ."

Suddenly I could not breathe sitting down, so I stood up from the kitchen table. And all the pain, the burns and the aches and the misery of losing a brother and a boat and the worst misery of being this close to whoever had done it all but not being certain, came smashing down on me. And I saw the wooden table

227

and the chairs and the paintings on the walls tilt, shrink and flee. And I fainted.

I was having a bloody awful dream. In the dream, I was back in *Nautilus'* cabin. The flames were pouring over me like lava, and I was struggling with the hatch. But the hatches would not open. The pain was horrible, and I yelled.

I yelled myself awake.

I was lying in a big bed onto which green light poured, filtered by young oak leaves on the trees outside. Sally's bed. My right hand was bandaged with nice white bandages. My face was covered with something greasy.

"Good morning," said Sally. She was sitting at a desk in the window, writing.

"Good morning," I said, and lay there soaking up the light. Everything was very bright and calm. Because, as I lay there in the bed, the facts had sorted themselves and the jigsaw was complete. And I knew what was going on, and why, and who was responsible for it. And now that I knew, I could handle it in a way Hugo would have appreciated.

I tried to sit up. Pain drove away my self-satisfaction.

"Yes," said Sally, watching me coolly. "The doctor said you ought to be in hospital. But I said we'd look after you here."

"What's wrong with me?" I said.

"Burns to face and hands. Bruised ribs. Contusions on neck and shoulders. Possible concussion."

"Great." I sat up, despite the noisy protests of my back muscles. I could still taste *Nautilus'* smoke in my throat. "What's the time?"

"Eleven o'clock. The quack thought you were in a coma, except for the snoring."

"Eleven o'clock." I looked around the room. "Where are my clothes?"

"I threw them away." She grinned at me. "You won't need any for a couple of days."

"I've got a race," I said. "The Duke's Bowl. I've got to go."

"Nobody's indispensable," she said.

"I am. Today I am." I swung my feet onto the floor. Except for a few bandages, I was in a state of nature. "Clothes. Please, Sally. Or I'll have to go like this."

She sighed. The happiness went out of her eyes, and she went into another room and returned with a bundle that she threw on the bed. Then she went back to her chair and watched me as I dressed, taking in my winces and grunts of agony, and making no effort to help.

"I'll make some breakfast," she said at last.

"Could you ring the hospital?" I said. "Find out how Amy is, if she can remember anything?"

She nodded and went downstairs.

It took me five minutes to tie the shoes she gave me. They had been Hugo's. When I tried to walk to the door, it was even worse. I sat on the bed and wondered how the hell I was going to survive a race from Pulteney to Cherbourg and back, starting in four hours. That led me on to Breen, and the fact that he was arriving in an hour and a half. I hooked a chair, and managed to get across the room by hanging on to its back and shoving it in front of me. I got out of the door and to the stairs, where I clung to the banisters and inched downstairs.

By the time I had reached the bottom, my muscles had warmed up to the point where I could shuffle along unsupported. I staggered to the kitchen. She was frying eggs at the Aga.

"How's Amy?" I said.

"Sedated," said Sally. "She came round confused, hysterical, incoherent, and as far as I could gather from Hilda not mentioning names." She put the bacon and eggs and toast in front of me, and I washed it down with the strong coffee. "Hugo used to eat all that stuff before he went off," said Sally. Her eyes were far away. "It's funny, the little things that get you." We both sat in silence for a moment. "Charlie, you are going to catch whoever did this, aren't you?"

"Yes," I said, and I could feel the certainty in my voice. "How's my car?"

"The neighbour towed it into the side with his tractor," she said. "You might as well ring up the scrapper."

I rang the scrapper. Then I made another call, this time to Neville Spearman. We had harsh words, Neville and I. But finally, he told me what I wanted to know.

Then I hobbled back to Sally and said, "Could you possibly give me a lift down?"

As we turned into Fore Street, she said, "What happens if that . . . person comes again?"

I said, with complete certainty, "He won't."

The jetties were lined with yachts. People with trolleys of gear and provisions moved along them like ants on blades of grass, lit by a watery sun. I saw *Sorcerer*'s triple spreaders; and, at one of the outermost berths, *Crystal*'s fractional rig and four spreaders, and her big green-and-orange battle flag on the forestay.

"Are you sure?" she said.

"Quite sure."

A Transit van had drawn up to the end of the jetty. It had *Crystal* painted on its side. Archer and Johnny Forsyth got out and carried a big sailbag down to the jetty between them.

"Good luck," said Sally, and leaned over and kissed me on the mouth. She might have done it to avoid kissing me on the cheek, and getting tannic acid jelly over her face.

Then again, she might not.

Using a walking stick I had scooped from her hall

stand on the way out, I hobbled down the jetty. The wind wailed in the rigging of the moored yachts. I was feeling better; so much better that I could almost walk.

They helped me aboard *Sorcerer* with a certain tenderness.

"Blimey," Scotto said when he saw me. "You look terrible."

"You don't look so good, yourself," I said. He had no eyebrows and his hair was all burned off at the front and he was wearing a long-sleeved sweatshirt, motor-cycle gauntlets, shorts and heavy leg bandages.

He slapped *Sorcerer*'s side with his gauntlet, and winced with pain. "We went over her," he said.

"What did you find?"

"Nothing," he said. "She's just fine."

"So we're going out there and waiting for her to fall to bits."

"The bastard may have left her alone after all," said Scotto.

I tilted my head back and looked up at the taut spider's web of steel and aluminium wailing among the scudding grey clouds. "What if it's something up in the rig?"

"We checked that, too." Scotto looked less happy. "I brought some spares."

I grunted. Short of re-rigging, there was no way of checking. And spares tended not to be much use when you had the stick over the side.

"Good day, gentlemen," said a voice from the jetty.

I turned. It was Breen, small, chubby and business-like, his wavy hair crisp, cigar jutting from his pink face above an immaculately-creased blazer and canvas trousers. He stepped lightly aboard, accepted his seabag from his chauffeur, and went below. I had a nasty moment of déjà vu. Last time I had seen him on a boat had been in Kinsale.

This was not the kind of thinking that won races.

231

Stiffly, I clambered below and climbed into my dry-suit. Breen's cigar was polluting the air. I said, "On deck only, if you wouldn't mind."

Breen looked at me sharply, then took the cigar out of his mouth and pitched it out of the hatch.

"Sorry," I said.

"You're the skipper," he said. "I'll stay out of the way." His hand strayed to the pocket where he kept the cigars, then snatched itself away again. "Have you been in a fight?"

"Protecting your interests," I said, and grinned at him in a way that hurt my face. "Now, if you wouldn't mind, we'd better get a move on. I'll tell you later."

"Certainly," he said. This time he actually had a cigar out before he remembered. I had the feeling that he was out of his element, as he looked around at the stark, white interior, sailbags, space frames, cooking stove, cots and radio.

He scuttled up the companionway. I followed, more laboriously, and began to concentrate on what Doug had on his clipboard. Scotto, moving stiffly because of the bandages inside his coat and gloves, let go the shore lines and stuck *Sorcerer's* nose into the wind that was bowling across the short grey seas from the direction of France.

27

The Duke's Bowl is the first long race of the National Ocean Racing Club's season of offshore races. Yachts of all ratings compete and the results are adjusted according to their ratings, so it has been known for antiques which arrive hours after the leaders to win on corrected time.

We sailed out through a jostling throng of yachts, from wooden pensioners via every shape and size of cruiser-racer, to giant maxis built of state-of-the-art materials, tuned like Stradivariuses and eighty feet overall. Captain's Cup hopefuls were out in force. I waved to a couple of friends. Then the first gun went and the waving stopped, and we started trying, hard.

I saw *Crystal* plugging out beyond the red, white and blue hull of *Flag*, a big American maxi the Sound Yacht Club was entering for the Lancaster Great Circle Race later in the year. There was no denying that she looked extremely businesslike. I watched her tack and come back under *Flag*'s nose, Archer playing his favourite trick. When I brought my eyes back inboard, Breen was watching me.

I knew why. I beckoned him aft, and said, "Did you know that someone on *Crystal* tried to fix your boat?"

The two eyes and the cigar focused right between my eyes. "When?" he said.

"Last night."

He gave no visible sign of emotion. "What did they do?" he said.

"We were going over her all morning. Couldn't find anything. Must be in the rig."

The eyes and the cigar tilted back. As he looked up, I noticed for the first time that under the chubby pink flesh of his face he had a lower jaw like the ram of a battleship. He studied the taut web of the rig for perhaps thirty seconds. Then he said, "So something's going to break."

"One has to assume it's possible."

"What are you proposing to do about it?"

"Start the race, and drive her till she pops, if she's going to."

Breen's eyes were deep and remote. He was still as an Easter Island head against the pale sun which was painting the sea cold blue and giving a hectic glitter to the white wakes of racing-boats.

"Charlie," said Doug, at my elbow.

"Excuse me," I said to Breen, politely.

Then I went into race mode and the world shrank until it was made of the close-hauled indicator and the flutter of the tell-tales, the lift of the deck and the intricate lacework of other boats' tracks, and Doug's steady mutter in my ear as the seconds on the readout clicked down, ten by ten. The five-minute gun went. The horde of white triangles converged on the invisible line between the two committee boats.

A puff of white smoke drifted from the right-hand boat, followed a split second later by the sound of a gun. We ramped over the line in echelon with three other boats, towards the right-hand end. *Crystal* was somewhere in the tangle far down to the left. I did not have much time to think about her, because we were engaged in a ding-dong tacking duel with our costarters all the way down to the western end of the Teeth. We were fifth round the buoy. I eased the wheel with my good hand until the compass settled on 118 degrees. The wind was freshening, and the foredeck men had changed down to the number three genoa. Ahead, grey waves marched out of a cold grey horizon. The wind was cold, but I was sweating with the concentration of the first beat.

"Crispin," I said. "Take over."

All this time, I had been dimly aware that Breen was not behaving like an owner. Normally, owners fall into two types. One is the exaggeratedly helpful, who gets in the way hurling himself after loose sheets. The other is the Big Smiler, who sits as far back as he can, out of the way, and grins like a Cheshire Cat at anyone whose eye he can catch. Breen was sitting still, but he was not smiling.

He pulled me back and said, "Did you re-rig the mast after the last race?"

"No," I said.

"I got a bill for a backstay."

"Yes," I said. "We bust one. So we made a modification, put on a single instead of a double."

Breen said, "Well, if I was going to sabotage a boat, I'd go for some brand-new equipment. How would you sabotage a backstay?"

The bow plunged into a wave, and spray flew aft. It caught Breen full in the face, but he didn't even blink.

"I'd slack it off," I said. "Then I'd put a kink in. Then I'd crank up the purchase till it straightened. That way you'd have a stay about as strong as button-thread. It'd take about five minutes."

"Well?" said Breen.

"Well," I said, tracing with my eye the taut wire that ran from the transom, through the high, rushing air, to the masthead casting seventy feet above us. "And why the hell not?"

I beckoned Scotto. "We need a volunteer," I said.

235

"And some of your spares." Scotto went to fetch. I said to Breen, "It's not necessarily the backstay. Are you sure you don't want to retire?"

"Balls," said Breen, with sudden and terrifying vigour. "This is the first time I've been away from a telephone in five years. Fix that stay, and if we lose the mast we lose the damn mast."

"All right," I said, slightly awed. "You're the owner."

Sorcerer's crew might not have been together long, but they showed no signs of it now. Within three minutes, Dike the foredeck man was walking up the mast like an orang-outang, while Al the mastman applied his gigantic shoulders to the halyard winch.

"If you needed proof that man was descended from apes, you'd have it right here," said Doug. Breen turned and glared at him. Then, surprisingly, he laughed.

It was the first time I had heard Breen laugh. It seemed likely that it was the first time anybody had heard him laugh. It made me like him, a lot; after all, it was his money at risk, and there was even a certain amount of danger about the situation—though the danger was mostly for Dike.

Dike did not, however, seem to mind. He sang noisily as he shackled the jury backstay to the mast-head casting. He yelled insults at Scotto as Scotto effected a temporary junction between jury backstay and chainplate, and took the strain. And he sang again, obscenely, as he lowered the old backstay to the deck. On the way down the mast, *Sorcerer* hit a seventh wave and stopped dead. He looped out into space like a spider on its web, and crashed into the sail. Al the mastman lowered him with a run, and he unclipped and shambled aft on his prehensile Docksiders.

"Nice work," said Breen.

Dike grinned at him, showing more gaps than teeth.

"Let's have a look at the stay," he said. He ran the black coil through his square, calloused hands. Half-way, he stopped. "Oi, oi," he said. "There you are." It was a tiny bump in the cable. Dike looked down at it thoughtfully. "What's it blowing?" he said.

"Force six, gusting seven."

Dike twisted his head on his non-existent neck. "Shit," he said. Then, evidently thinking deeply, he returned forward.

"He was lucky," said Scotto. "Could have gone any time."

"Thank you," I said to Breen.

"Not at all," said Breen. His eyes were glittering with excitement, and I realised that for ten minutes he had not had a cigar in his face. Now he cut off the end of a new one, and lit it, bending down into the trench to shield the flame. When he came up again, his eyes were dull once more.

"Now then," he said. "Maybe you'd better tell me what's going on."

So we went and sat on the weather deck, feet out through the rail, staring at the rest of the fleet reaching out across the growing seas for the far-off coast of France. And I told him everything, omitting nothing. Except the fact that I had twisted *Sorcerer*'s rudder myself.

When I was finished, he said, "So he threatened you with bankruptcy when you wouldn't sell your house. Upon which he intimidated your old and feeble father. And in order to further his own interests he is employing some bloke who you say has been responsible for murder, arson, and intimidation, and grievous bodily harm, and you reckon that Millstone knows it, but as long as this bloke's useful, he's not turning him in. So why the hell haven't you turned him in yourself, Charlie?"

I waited while a wave broke over *Sorcerer*'s bow and the deck swam clear.

"I'll do it after we've won this race," I said. "By fair means. I felt I owed it to my brother, and some other people." Like my father, and Sally, and my old friend Ed Beith, and all the other people in Pulteney who had woken from the sleep of centuries to find Millstone standing on their faces.

"Fair enough," said Breen. "I don't much like vendettas on my time, but as long as you beat them, we'll make an exception, this once."

"Yes," I said.

"Beat who?" said Doug, who had come to sit beside us.

"Crystal."

"She's a fast boat," said Doug. "And it's her kind of breeze."

But that did not stop us trying.

The wind veered westerly soon after dark, and we pulled out the kite. *Sorcerer* began to fly. It was very dangerous sailing, over-canvassed in a confused sea, and Crispin and I had to change often—not only to keep alert, but because of the sheer physical strain of cranking the wheel. *Sorcerer* carved through the waves with her lee rail feet under and the vees of spray whizzing back from her stanchions. She creaked and she groaned and the wind screamed a horrible chord in her drum-tight rigging. It was exciting at first. Then the wet and the cold and the screaming wind blew away the thrill of doing something very fast and very dangerous, leaving only the dogged determination to hang on through the next twenty hours.

This time, there was an extra edge to the determination, and its name was *Crystal.*

We rounded the buoy at four A.M. with a force eight kicking up the sea and Cap de la Hague flashing white to the southeast. The maxis were already round. We were lying third of the Captain's Cup trialists. Ahead were *Ariel,* a Joe Grimaldi boat; and *Crystal. Crystal*

238

had come round the buoy twenty minutes before us.

I handed the helm to Crispin, who had come up from below. "I'm going for a kip," I said. "Sir Alec, why don't you get your head down?"

He had been sitting on the stern, visible only by the glow of his cigar. Now the glow moved left and right, once, precisely, as he shook his head. "I'll stay up," he said. "Don't want to miss the fun."

It had started to rain. Fun, I thought, as I went into the wet cabin and rolled my aching limbs into a wet bunk. That was one way of putting it.

I woke for the early morning shipping forecast. Force seven, gusting eight, they said.

On deck, a dirty grey morning had developed, with horizontal rain from the sou'west. I took the wheel from Crispin, and Crispin went gratefully below.

Sorcerer was giving of her best, under main and triradial. She was flying along the seas on gossamer wings of spray, and the log needle spent most of its time hovering between twelve and fourteen knots.

"Are we catching *Crystal?*" I said to Doug.

"Hard to tell," he said. "Have to wait till we see her."

He was joking, of course, because visibility was down to five hundred yards in the rain. *Sorcerer* might have been on a solo cruise, for all the competition that was visible.

Breen was still crouched on the stern. "Had enough?" I said.

He grinned at me. The cigar was soaking wet. "Catch 'em," he said.

I did my best. The rain stopped, and Dike brought up sausage, beans, eggs and porridge mixed together in tin pint mugs. The wind held. The cloud cover lifted gradually. VHF said that *Ariel* had lost her mast, and had retired. At six minutes to noon, Dike shouted from the foredeck, "There she is!"

A mile away and on the starboard bow was a white sail and a green-and-orange spinnaker. Breen rose to his feet and winced at the pain in his stiff joints.

"Take 'em," he snarled.

"It might not be as easy as that," I muttered.

Through glasses, it was apparent that *Crystal* was going well, with a heavy kite powering her across the water. There were eight figures visible in her cockpit, with Archer, small and stubby, at the helm.

"She's moving," said Breen.

"Yes," I said. The clouds parted, and a long beam of sun lanced across the heaving grey, drawing after it a stripe of turquoise flecked with white. *Crystal* suddenly gleamed, and the wet-gear of her crew was piercing yellow. But I was not looking at her crew. I was looking at the boat's side, abaft the shroud chainplates, where a tiny gleam of silver ticked like a pulse in the sun's brilliance—a jet of water.

"She's pumping," I said.

Doug and Scotto trained their glasses. "She's got two blokes at it down there," said Scotto. "Must be making water."

"Here we go, here we go, here we go," said Doug.

It is hard to describe the fierce up-welling of power that you get when you see the competition after a long time out of view. This time, it was more than ever like champagne in the blood.

Sorcerer seemed to feel it, too. She came up and out of the water and set herself to hurdle the big swells like a steeplechaser, fast up to the crests and then breaking loose into the troughs with that marvellous lift under the feet that was more like flying than sailing, landing between the sheets of water hissing from the flare of her bow. It must have been a noble sight from *Crystal*'s cockpit. Or a terrifying one.

Because yard by yard, we were hauling her down.

After ten minutes, even Breen had noticed. His

thick shock of grey hair was plastered to his head, and the spray streamed down his face, and he was thumping the deck with his fist, and muttering, "Go *on*, go *on*."

"Land," said Doug.

The clouds were clearing, though the wind had not abated; if anything, it was up a knot or two. Across the white-streaked sea lay the low, green land. Between us and it were four sails canted—*Crystal* and three late maxis. And a shimmer of white water that rose like reversed rain, and drifted at the sky.

"The Teeth," said Scotto to Breen, and pointed.

During the next half-hour, we narrowed the distance to half a mile. Through the glasses I could see *Crystal* clearly. They were still pumping. I could see the faces too: Archer at the wheel; next to him, Millstone and Johnny Forsyth. I could see their heads in profile. They were making jerky, emphatic movements. I saw Archer shrug his shoulders, and raise his hands in the air, away from the wheel. And I saw Johnny Forsyth step up and take his place. Then Archer vanished from the picture.

"Go *on*. Go *on*. Go *on*," said Breen behind me, drumming.

Figures scrambled onto *Crystal*'s foredeck. A ribbon of sail went up, and burst into a fat balloon of orange and gold.

"Stone me," said Scotto. "That's his big kite. In force eight?"

It lifted *Crystal* for a moment. The water under her bow made a rainbow in the sun.

"He'll blow it out for sure," said Scotto. "He must be crazy."

A gust hit us, then swept on across the water towards *Crystal*, darkening the waves.

"Either that or he'll go over," said Scotto. "That'll slow him a bit."

Another gust shivered us. The first one had reached *Crystal*. She took it with a heavy roll, came back and rolled far to leeward again.

"Bloody death roll," said Scotto.

But she came back, her mast sweeping across the sky like an inverted pendulum bob.

Then the next gust hit her. I saw Forsyth's face, at the wheel, turn white. The chute rippled and filled tight. The roll, when it came, was slow and leisurely.

But it was all the way over.

A green wave came between us. We stood on tiptoe, shouting with horror, trying to see over the top. When we rose on the next crest, we saw her, or what was left of her.

She was lying well over on her side, with her mast on the water. Scotto said, "She's not righting."

She was not. The mast fought clear a moment, wavering skyward, trailing its wet rags of sails. Then it lay down again, wearily, as if defeated.

Scotto said, "She's sinking."

There was a moment of complete silence. Then I shouted, "Down spinnaker!" and spun the wheel.

Five minutes later, a life raft was bobbing on the starboard bow. There were ten men in, on and around it. We pulled them in one by one. Millstone was streaming water, his face blue-black with stubble, menacingly silent. Johnny Forsyth was very pale, shivering, with greenish shadows under his eyes that spread onto his cratered cheeks. The rest of the crew was subdued and cold and shocked. The only one who was still talking was Archer, who insisted on coming last. I gave him my hand and he stuck his foot in the loop and heaved himself aboard.

"Below," I said. "Warm up."

Archer was white as the foam on the waves and his eyes were scorching with anger.

"Charlie," he said. Breen came up to listen. From below, we could hear Scotto's voice on the radio, reporting the wreck and the rescue. "I want to tell you that that boat just bloody well fell apart."

"We saw," I said.

I looked across the water at *Crystal*. She was far down in the water now. As I watched, she rose on a wave, and the silver wand of her mast came up as if this time she was going to right herself. Then there was an explosion of bubbles, and the mast plunged down, and there was no more yacht.

But Archer gazed at the little patch of flotsam that was all that remained of her. He continued talking, to himself, not us.

"The bloody deck came off the hull. We've been pumping since Cherbourg. Then that bastard Millstone tells me to put up the big 'chute because you're catching us. And I said don't be a silly bastard but he said he was the owner and he pulled the bloody deck right off her. Thank the Lord I had time to get the lads on the pumps up from below and launch the bloody life raft." He laughed, a harsh bark. "I had the life raft out while the sail was going up."

I said, "Easy, Archer. Let's get you warm," and fed him down the companionway. I gave the helm to Crispin, and said to Breen, "Would you mind coming below a minute? It won't take long."

Below decks, *Sorcerer* was like a steam bath with the heating broken. *Crystal*'s crew crouched in survival blankets and shuddered. Dike was handing out coffee.

Sorcerer lurched under my feet, heeled and steadied. The boys on deck had her sailing again. There was the squawk of Scotto reporting to shore by VHF. I waited until he had finished. Then I went forward and sat down on the cabin sole, with my back against the mast.

28

"All right," I said. "This is the end. Nearly two months ago, somebody sabotaged my boat *Aesthete* and killed my brother."

"Oh, for God's sake," said Millstone.

"Shut up," I said quietly. "And listen. There have been two boats wrecked, and one boat burnt, and this boat interfered with before the race." I found Millstone's eye. He was staring at me, his face a blank, furious mask. "There are three men dead who should not be dead: my brother Hugo, Henry Charlton, and poor bloody Hector Pollitt, who went for a ride on a tiger." They were still watching me.

In the faces of the crew there was incomprehension. But Archer knew what I was talking about, and Millstone, and Forsyth.

"Someone has been running a campaign against me and people connected with me," I said. "At first, I thought the idea was to bankrupt me by making everyone think I couldn't design a boat for a boating lake, so Frank Millstone could buy my house. Then I thought that the idea was to stop me competing in the Cup. But finally, after I had been whacked on the head and Amy Charlton had gone to hospital when some-one pushed her face in last night—"

"What?" said Millstone. "Amy?"

"Broken nose," I said. "Flattened. Might have been worse, but I happened to go through her front door at the psychological moment so our man laid off. Any-way, when I saw Amy I knew that the reason all these things had been happening might have started with me and races and my house. But now, whoever was doing it was strictly working for himself, and he had his own reasons. Reasons that nobody understood but him, because he was mad as a hatter—look out!"

Johnny Forsyth was on his feet. "Agutter!" he shouted. "I should have killed you years ago!"

I had a clear impression of his face, green and ivory-white, the lipless mouth stretched back from his teeth in a terrible crescent grin. His arm went back. I dived sideways, but not quite fast enough, because something caught me on the shoulder and I went over onto the cabin sole. There was shouting and a smell of gas. I could see his feet go up the companion ladder and out of the hatch. The galley stove lay at my side, where it had landed.

"Turn the gas off!" I yelled. Archer, who was sitting by the companionway, turned it off at the bottle. By the time he had done it, I was at the companionway. Feet were thundering on deck. I went up the ladder and out.

It was very bright on deck. For a moment I was dazzled. When I could see again I saw Scotto and Forsyth by the lee rail. Scotto was holding Forsyth's coat. As I watched, Forsyth's fist flicked out, into Scotto's stomach. His other hand was held back, tensed like a spring, ready to break Scotto's neck. There was no time to think. I kicked Forsyth as hard as I could, on the inside of his left knee. His face came round, surprised. *Sorcerer* gave a lurch and he staggered backwards. The lifeline caught him in the back of the legs and he did a reverse somersault over the side.

Overhead, sails roared and flogged as Crispin came head to wind. Forsyth's head came up, vanished again. Fifty feet away, the western end of the Teeth mangled the waves. The head came up again, rose on a wave until its eyes were level with mine.

He was staring at me. I could see the whites all the way round the pupils. I could see into his mind as if into clear water. He took one stroke back towards the boat. Then he seemed to change his mind and trod water. Then finally, he shook his head and turned away.

I lost him in a trough. I scrambled to the wheel. My thumb went for the engine start button. A hand grabbed my wrist.

It was Frank Millstone's. "It's better this way," he said.

"Better for whom?" I said, and shoved him out of the way, hard. But Johnny Forsyth's head was a black speck in the waves, now. He was too far away to come back unless we went after him, and I knew now that he wouldn't come back on his own.

Johnny Forsyth was swimming for the Teeth.

As I watched, a wave came under him and he disappeared in the trough on its far side. He rose on the crest, still swimming. At the moment he reached the top, the wave broke. It took him with it. There was one final, spidery cartwheel of arms and legs. Then the wave rose, whitened and collapsed into the black Teeth. The spray of it lifted fifty feet before the wind caught it, and drifted it away until it thinned to a shining fog, and faded from the face of the sea.

They gave us the race. Nelligan sat with the Committee and heard the evidence. Afterwards, they let me go and I wandered, dazed, into the soft evening light that filled the streets of Pulteney. Sally was waiting, and Ed Beith. And Scotto and Georgia, Sir Alec Breen and Archer.

Archer manoeuvred himself alongside me. He said, "Look, Charlie, it goes without saying that your contract's all right again."

"Thanks," I said.

He smiled at me, the public relations smile, full of charm but without remorse. "I'll pop off and write you a letter, then."

"Fine," I said.

He faded away, back into his round of cocktail parties and polite smiles and saying the correct thing to the Press.

We went up to the house, and I brought the Famous Grouse out to the wrought-iron table in the garden. The smoke from Breen's cigar rose in blue coils towards the swallows hawking in the deep blue sky. There was a great sense of peace; a calm, with no impending storm.

"All right," said Sir Alec. "What's been happening?"

I said, "It's quite simple. Johnny Forsyth reckoned that I got too much work, and he got too little. He had it in his head that if he wrecked my reputation, he'd be able to get the contracts I lost."

"Does that follow?" said Breen.

"Nope. But you have to remember he wasn't quite the full shilling. Did you know Archer asked him to submit designs for a cruiser-racer? Perfectly legitimate, of course. Archer wasn't to know. But it encouraged Johnny in his fantasies."

"Begin at the beginning," said Scotto. He drained his glass and poured a new one.

"Me, too," said Georgia, and held out her glass.

"Forsyth switched the bolts in *Aesthete*'s rudder. It

247

killed Hugo and Henry but it also effectively lost me my contracts. When I took you all on our PR trip on *Ae,* he couldn't risk all his good efforts being undone, so he fixed *Ae's* rudder, too."

"How?" said Breen.

"Very devious, that. He'd worked at Hegarty's before, converting a trawler. He knew a bloke called Lenny Dennis, and knew he was an unsuccessful punter. Our Johnny did a lot of jobs for Millstone, as you know. Well, just after the *Aesthete* wreck Millstone went on his annual visit to a company he owns in Ireland, called Curran Electric. Johnny went along to paint a picture for the reception area of the factory. While he was there, he sent Dennis a bribe, with instructions to poison the dog at Hegarty's yard."

"So you have a sleeping dog," said Ed Beith. "Did this Dennis cove do the dirty work with the rudder?"

"Nope," I said. "Forsyth did. Which is where Amy gets tangled up in this. Because Amy was having an affair with Forsyth—"

"Among others," said Sally.

"Among, as you say, others. The weekend we were in Ireland, Amy and Forsyth were there too, staying in a coastguard cottage just down the beach from Crosshaven. Forsyth fixed *Ae's* rudder on the Thursday night. Presumably Amy joined him on the Friday. On the Saturday, Amy had dinner with Hector Pollitt in Kinsale, and while they were dining and doing whatever they did afterwards, Forsyth went back to the yard and switched broken titanium bolts for the broken aluminium bolts."

"And that should have been the end of Charlie Agutter, boat designer," said Ed.

"Quite. But now Frank Millstone was on my case. Frank has never liked me, and he was obsessed with getting this house. Probably still is. He thought my rudders were cracking up because they were badly designed. He put Pollitt, who had been his tame pressman for some time, onto me. At first, I thought it might be Pollitt or Frank who were fixing the rudders. But then I decided it was a bit bold for Pollitt, and a bit basic for Frank, and I knew I had to look further. Then Sir Alec fixed us up with *Sorcerer,* and we pulled up *Aesthete,* and I went looking in Spearman's yard in the middle of the night. But unfortunately, Johnny had heard me talking to Chiefy about sabotage on the barge, and he came looking for me. By this time, I think Pollitt suspected that he was up to no good. But Pollitt was frightened of Forsyth. Johnny was having car trouble, so he made Pollitt wait in the lay-by by the marina while Johnny bopped me and set me adrift."

"He must have been crazy," said Scotto.

"He was," I said. "He had a theory that he was a full-time victim, oppressed by the forces of reaction in Pulteney and me in particular. He hated Sally because she went around with me, and me because I was supposedly stealing work from him, and Ed Beith because he went around with both of us, and Amy because she went around with anybody who wore trousers. Pollitt woke up the next morning, and discovered he was party to attempted murder, which was not at all what he wanted. So he took a little time to get his courage up, and then he came to see me because he thought I was aboard *Sorcerer* at the marina. But Scotto was there instead, and Scotto bopped him, thinking he'd come to nobble the boat. Forsyth must have been delivering some pretty heavy threats, because when I mentioned to Pollitt that I'd seen his car by the marina the night I got hit, he panicked and fell off his drainpipe."

I took a gulp of whisky. I should have been feeling tired. Instead I felt free. Breen looked at the end of his cigar and said, "Go on."

"So by now, Forsyth was overheating badly," I said. "He'd started out with what he thought was going to be a little sabotage but now he'd cracked me on the head and set me adrift, and the principal witness was dead, he must have thought he could get away with just about anything. And at the same time, Millstone is beginning to overheat, because I have told him what I think of his methods of trying to make me sell my house. Forsyth knows he's negotiating for *Crystal*. Forsyth's been working on *Crystal,* and Forsyth sees a chance of showing what a good boat-doctor he is to a man whose objectives coincide with his—viz., to obliterate Agutter from the scheme of things. Also, Forsyth has been sending you some big bills for boat repairs, Ed, and you have been finding difficulty in paying them. Correct?"

"Correct," said Ed. "The little bleeder. He wasn't even doing the boat any good."

"So in order to clinch the thing, Forsyth creeps over and lights your turkey sheds, so you have to sell to Millstone. And Millstone is then racing *Crystal,* and going very nicely, and in fact wanting to win so badly he can taste it. Except that in the first race, we beat her. Which annoys Millstone, and you can imagine what it does to Forsyth. Well, I don't know who suggested it, but they decide to nobble *Sorcerer,* which is out of the water with a twisted rudder stock."

I looked across at Breen, then at Scotto. Scotto's right eyelid drooped in the suspicion of a wink.

"So Forsyth borrows Archer's car and puts a kink in the backstay. But he makes a bad mistake. He has heard from his close associate Spearman that I have got *Sorcerer* wired for sound. So to divert attention, he puts a fire-bomb aboard *Nautilus.* I'm sure Millstone didn't suspect he'd do anything of the kind; after all, he knew Johnny as a general freelancer who'd do anything for a quid, not as a roaring psycho. But now he'd connived with Johnny in fixing *Sorcerer* he couldn't then turn Johnny in, in case Johnny blew the gaff. Realising this, Johnny began to feel somewhat invincible. After all, you can't get much more powerful in Pulteney than having Frank Millstone under your thumb. So he went to Amy, to chastise her for playing fast and loose. And he was proceeding towards Sally, to chastise her for having married an Agutter and being a friend of Agutters, when I bumped into him. The rest we know about."

There was a silence. Then Sally said, in a small, quiet voice, "How did you find all this out?"

"Asking questions. The one who clinched it was Neville Spearman. I was wondering why Forsyth should bother to burn *Nautilus* as well as nobbling *Sorcerer*. After all, he didn't know we had *Sorcerer* wired. The only people who knew were me, Scotto, Neville Spearman and the man who installed the alarms. Well, yesterday morning before the race, I rang Neville. And he admitted that he'd told Johnny. Couldn't see the problem, he said, Johnny was his right hand, good as a partner."

"Was," said Scotto.

Breen blew a cloud of smoke. "It strikes me that you were very lucky," he said. "*Sorcerer*'s rudder getting twisted at such an opportune moment, I mean."

There was a crash. "Sod it," said Scotto. "Whoops, sorry, I seem to have dropped a glass."

"I'll get you a new one," I said, and went into the house.

When I returned, they were talking about Millstone.

"We can't touch him," Sally was saying. "It's infuriating."

"In a way," said Breen. "But I believe there's been a meeting of the Pulteney Yacht Club Committee, today, and I think I know what they're talking about."

"Oh?" said Ed Beith. "How?"

"I arranged it, through some chaps I know," said Breen, his chubby face inscrutable behind the smoke. "I told them I'd seen Millstone prevent Charlie from going after Forsyth to render assistance out there by the rocks. And I gave them some . . . background." He looked at his watch. "Why don't we go for a bit of a walk?"

We walked down Quay Street, through my office and onto the quay. It was a beautiful evening. The clouds over Beggarman's Point were tinged with gold, and gulls shrieked over the boats in the harbour. Breen turned left, towards the squat wooden bulk of the Yacht Club. There were people drinking on the balcony; the breeze had died until there was barely enough to flap the Red Ensign on the mast. High on the cliff, the church clock was striking eight. A red Jaguar rolled along the quay. At its wheel, staring straight ahead, was Frank Millstone.

He parked by the Yacht Club door, and went in. I saw him push the inner glass door, and stand in the hall, talking to someone I couldn't see properly. Then he came out again, and I saw. It was the Club Secretary, looking grim and shaking his head. His voice floated down the quay.

"Out," he was saying. "Or I'll call the police."

Millstone's fists clenched. He raised a hand. Then he dropped it again, and yanked open the Jaguar's door. The tyres screamed, and the car shot past and into Fore Street.

"Hmm," said Breen. "My friends thought something like that might happen. Barred by the Committee."

I sat down on a bollard. Sally looked down at me, the dark hair swinging on either side of her cheekbones, her eyes full of secret amusement. She was

252

holding Ed Beith's hand, which was as it should be. I knew that what she was thinking was the same as what I was thinking. We did not give a monkey's for yacht clubs. Pulteney was home, and that was that.

"Would you like a drink at the Club?" said Breen.

"No, thank you," I said. "Let's go to the Mermaid. The beer's better."

Praise for the Morganville Vampires Series

Feast of Fools

"Rachel Caine brings her brilliant ability to blend witty dialogue, engaging characters, and an intriguing plot."
—*Romance Reviews Today*

"A rousing horror thriller that adds a new dimension to the vampire mythos . . . a heroine the audience will admire and root for. . . . The key to this fine tale is . . . plausible reactions to living in a town run by vampires that make going to college in the Caine universe quite an experience."
—*Midwest Book Review*

"An electrifying, enthralling coming-of-age supernatural tale."
—*The Best Reviews*

Midnight Alley

"A fast-paced, page-turning read packed with wonderful characters and surprising plot twists. Rachel Caine is an engaging writer; readers will be completely absorbed in this chilling story, unable to put it down until the last page. . . . For fans of vampire books, this is one that shouldn't be missed!"
—*Flamingnet*

"Weaves a web of dangerous temptation, dark deceit, and loving friendships. The nonstop vampire action and delightfully sweet relationships will captivate readers and leave them craving more."
—*Darque Reviews*

The Dead Girls' Dance

"It was hard to put this down for even the slightest break. . . . Forget what happens to the kid with the scar and glasses; I want to know what happens next in Morganville. If you love to read about characters with whom you can get deeply involved, Rachel Caine is so far a one hundred percent sure bet to satisfy that need. I love her Weather Warden stories, and her vampires are even better."
—*The Eternal Night*

"Throw in a mix of vamps and ghosts, and it can't get any better than *Dead Girls' Dance*."
—*Dark Angel Reviews*

continued . . .

LORD OF MISRULE

THE MORGANVILLE VAMPIRES, BOOK FIVE

RACHEL CAINE

nal
jam
books

NAL Jam
Published by New American Library, a division of
Penguin Group (USA) Inc., 375 Hudson Street,
New York, New York 10014, USA
Penguin Group (Canada), 90 Eglinton Avenue East, Suite 700, Toronto,
Ontario M4P 2Y3, Canada (a division of Pearson Penguin Canada Inc.)
Penguin Books Ltd., 80 Strand, London WC2R 0RL, England
Penguin Ireland, 25 St. Stephen's Green, Dublin 2,
Ireland (a division of Penguin Books Ltd.)
Penguin Group (Australia), 250 Camberwell Road, Camberwell, Victoria 3124,
Australia (a division of Pearson Australia Group Pty. Ltd.)
Penguin Books India Pvt. Ltd., 11 Community Centre, Panchsheel Park,
New Delhi - 110 017, India
Penguin Group (NZ), 67 Apollo Drive, Rosedale, North Shore 0632,
New Zealand (a division of Pearson New Zealand Ltd.)
Penguin Books (South Africa) (Pty.) Ltd., 24 Sturdee Avenue,
Rosebank, Johannesburg 2196, South Africa

Penguin Books Ltd., Registered Offices:
80 Strand, London WC2R 0RL, England

First published by NAL Jam, an imprint of New American Library,
a division of Penguin Group (USA) Inc.

First Printing, January 2009
10 9 8 7 6 5 4 3 2 1

To Ter Matthies, Anna Korra'ti, and Shaz Flynn—
courageous fighters, each one.

And to Pat Flynn, who never stopped.

ACKNOWLEDGMENTS

This book wouldn't be here without the support of my husband, Cat, my friends Pat, Jackie, and Sharon, and a host of great online supporters and cheerers-on.

Special thank-you recognition to Sharon Sams, Shaz Flynn, and especially to fearless beta readers Karin and Laura for their excellent input.

Thanks always to Lucienne Diver.

THE STORY SO FAR . . .

Claire Danvers was going to Caltech. Or maybe MIT. She had her pick of great schools, but because she's only sixteen, her parents sent her to a supposedly safe place for a year to mature—Texas Prairie University, a small school in Morganville, Texas.

One problem: Morganville isn't what it seems. It's the last safe place for vampires, and that makes it not very safe at all for the humans who venture in for work or school. The vampires rule the town . . . and everyone who lives in it.

Claire's second problem is that she's gathered both human and vampire enemies. Now she lives with housemates Michael Glass (newly made a vampire), Eve Rosser (always been Goth), and Shane Collins (whose absentee dad is a wannabe vampire killer). Claire's the normal one . . . or she would be, except that she's become an employee of the town Founder, Amelie, and befriended one of the most dangerous, yet most vulnerable, vampires of them all—Myrnin, the alchemist.

Now Amelie's vampire father, Bishop, has come to Morganville and destroyed the fragile peace, turning vampires against one another and creating dangerous new alliances and factions in a town that already had too many.

Morganville's turning in on itself, and Claire and her friends have chosen to stand with the Founder, but it could mean working with their enemies . . . and fighting their friends.

1

It was all going wrong, and Morganville was burning—parts of it, anyway.

Claire stood at the windows of the Glass House and watched the flames paint the glass a dull, flickering orange. She could always see the stars out here in the Middle of Nowhere, Texas—but not tonight. Tonight, there was—

"You're thinking it's the end of the world," a cool, quiet voice said behind her.

Claire blinked out of her trance and turned to look. Amelie—the Founder, and the baddest vampire in town, to hear most of the others tell it—looked fragile and pale, even for a vampire. She'd changed out of the costume she'd worn to Bishop's masked ball—not a bad idea, since it had a stake-sized hole in the chest, and she'd bled all over it. If Claire had needed proof that Amelie was tough, she'd certainly gotten it tonight. Surviving an assassination attempt definitely gave you points.

The vampire was wearing gray—a soft gray sweater, and *pants*. Claire had to stare, because Amelie just didn't do pants. Ever. It was beneath her, or something.

Come to think of it, Claire had never seen her in the color gray, either.

Talk about the end of the world.

"I remember when Chicago burned," Amelie said.

"And London. And Rome. The world doesn't end, Claire. In the morning, the survivors start to build again. It's the way of things. The human way."

Claire didn't particularly want a pep talk. She wanted to curl up in her warm bed upstairs, pull pillows over her head, and feel Shane's arms around her.

None of that was going to happen. Her bed was currently occupied by Miranda, a freaked-out teenage psychic with dependency issues, and as for Shane . . .

Shane was about to *leave*.

"Why?" she blurted. "Why are you sending him out there? You know what could happen—"

"I know a great deal about Shane Collins that you don't," Amelie interrupted. "He's not a child, and he has survived much in his young life. He'll survive this. And he wishes to make a difference."

She was sending Shane into the predawn darkness with a few chosen fighters, both vampire and human, to take possession of the Bloodmobile: the last reliably accessible blood storage in Morganville.

And it was the last thing Shane wanted to do. It was the last thing Claire wanted for him.

"Bishop isn't going to want the Bloodmobile for himself," Claire said. "He wants it destroyed. Morganville's full of walking blood banks, as far as he's concerned. But it'll hurt *you* if you lose it, so he'll come after it. Right?"

The severe, thin line of Amelie's mouth made it clear that she didn't like being second-guessed. It definitely couldn't be called a smile. "As long as Shane has the book, Bishop will not dare destroy the vehicle for fear of destroying his great treasure along with it."

Translation: Shane was bait. Because of the *book*. Claire hated that damn book. It had brought her nothing but trouble from the time she'd first heard about it. Amelie and Oliver, the two biggest vamps in town, had both been scrambling to find it, and it had dropped into Claire's hands instead. She wished she had the courage to grab it from Shane right now, run outside, and toss it in the nearest burning house to get rid of it once and for all, because as far as she could tell, it hadn't done anybody any good, ever—including Amelie.

Claire said, "He'll kill Shane to get it."

Amelie shrugged. "I gamble that killing Shane is far more difficult than it would appear."

"Yeah, you are gambling. You're betting his life."

Amelie's ice gray eyes were steady on hers. "Be clear on this: I am, in fact, betting all our lives. So be grateful, child, and also be warned. I could concede this fight at any time. My father would allow me to walk away—only me, alone. Defeated. I stay out of duty to you and the others in this town who are loyal to me." Her eyes narrowed. "Don't make me reconsider that."

Claire hoped she didn't look as mutinous as she felt. She pasted on what was supposed to be an agreeable expression, and nodded. Amelie's eyes narrowed even more.

"Get prepared. We leave in ten minutes."

Shane wasn't the only one with a dirty job to do; they were all assigned things they didn't particularly like. Claire was going with Amelie to try to rescue another vampire—Myrnin. And while Claire liked Myrnin, and admired him in a lot of ways, she also wasn't too excited about facing down—again—the vampire holding him prisoner, the dreadful Mr. Bishop.

Eve was off to the coffee shop, Common Grounds, with the just-about-as-awful Oliver, her former boss. Michael was about to head out to the university with Richard Morrell, the mayor's son. How he was supposed to protect a few thousand clueless college students, Claire had no idea; she took a moment to marvel at the fact that the vampires really could lock down the town when they wanted. She'd have thought keeping students on campus in this situation would be impossible—kids phoning home, jumping in cars, getting the hell out of Dodge.

Except the vampires controlled the phone lines, cell phones, the Internet, the TV, and the radio, and cars either died or wrecked on the outskirts of town if the vampires didn't want you to leave. Only a few people had ever gotten out of Morganville successfully without permission. Shane had been one. And then he'd come *back*.

Claire still had no idea what kind of guts that had taken, knowing what was waiting for him.

"Hey," Claire's housemate Eve said. She paused, arms full of clothes—black and red, so they'd almost certainly come out of Eve's own Goth-heavy closet— and gave Claire a quick once-over. She'd changed to what in Eve's world were practical fighting clothes— a pair of tight black jeans, a tight black shirt with red skull patterns all over it, and stompy, thick-soled boots. And a spiked black leather collar around her throat that almost dared the vampires, *Bite that!*

"Hey," Claire said. "Is this really a good time to start laundry?"

Eve rolled her eyes. "Cute. So, some people didn't want to be caught dead in their stupid ball costumes, if you know what I mean. How about you? Ready to take that thing off?"

Claire looked down at herself. She was honestly surprised to realize that she was still wearing the tight, garish bodysuit of her Harlequin costume. "Oh, yes." She sighed. "Got anything without, you know, skulls?"

"What's wrong with skulls? And that would be a no, by the way." Eve dumped the armload of clothing on the floor and rooted through it, pulling out a plain black shirt and a pair of blue jeans. "The jeans are yours. Sorry, but I sort of raided everybody's stash. Hope you like the underwear you have on; I didn't go through your drawers."

"Afraid it might get you all turned on?" Shane asked from over her shoulder. "Please say yes." He grabbed a pair of his own jeans from the pile. "And please stay out of my closet."

Eve gave him the finger. "If you're worried about

me finding your porn stash, old news, man. Also, you have really boring taste." She grabbed a blanket from the couch and nodded toward the corner. "No privacy anywhere in this house tonight. Go on, we'll fix up a changing room."

The three of them edged past the people and vampires who packed the Glass House. It had become the unofficial campaign center for their side of the war, which meant there were plenty of people tramping around, getting in their stuff, who none of them would have let cross the threshold under normal circumstances.

Take Monica Morrell. The mayor's daughter had shed her elaborate Marie Antoinette costume and was back to the blond, slinky, pretty, slimy girl Claire knew and hated.

"Oh my God." Claire gritted her teeth. "Is she wearing my *blouse*?" It was her only good one. Silk. She'd just bought it last week. Now she'd never be able to put it on again. "Remind me to burn that later." Monica saw her staring, fingered the collar of the shirt, and gave her an evil smile. She mouthed, *Thanks.* "Remind me to burn it *twice.* And stomp on the ashes."

Eve grabbed Claire by the arm and hustled her into the empty corner of the room, where she shook out the blanket and held it at arm's length to provide a temporary shelter.

Claire peeled off her sweat-soaked Harlequin costume with a whimper of relief, and shivered as the cool air hit her flushed skin. She felt awkward and anxious, stripped to her underwear with just a blanket held up between her and a dozen strangers, some of whom probably wanted to eat her.

Shane leaned over the top. "You done?"

She squealed and threw the wadded-up costume at him. He caught it and waggled his eyebrows at her as she stepped into the jeans and quickly buttoned up the shirt.

"Done!" she called.

Eve dropped the blanket and smiled poison-sweet at Shane.

"Your turn, leather boy," she said. "Don't worry. I won't accidentally embarrass you."

No, she'd embarrass him completely on purpose, and Shane knew it, from the glare he threw her. He ducked behind the blanket. Claire wasn't tall enough to check him out over the top—not that she wasn't tempted—but when Eve lowered the blanket, bit by bit, Claire grabbed one corner and pulled it back up.

"You're no fun," Eve said.

"Don't mess with him. Not now. He's going out there alone."

Eve's face went still and tight, and for the first time, Claire realized that the shine in her eyes wasn't really humor. It was a tightly controlled kind of panic. "Yeah," she said. "I know. It's just—we're all splitting up, Claire. I wish we didn't have to do that."

On impulse, Claire hugged her. Eve smelled of powder and some kind of darkly floral perfume, with a light undertone of sweat.

"Hey!" Shane's wounded yell was enough to make them both giggle. The blanket had drooped enough to show him zipping up his pants. Fast. "Seriously, girls, *not cool.* A guy could do serious damage."

He looked more like Shane now. The leather pants had made him unsettlingly hot-model gorgeous. In jeans and his old, faded Marilyn Manson T-shirt, he was somebody down-to-earth, somebody Claire could imagine kissing.

And she did imagine, just like that. It was, as usual, heart-racingly delicious.

"Michael's going out, too," Eve said, and now the tension she'd been hiding made her voice tremble. "I have to tell him—"

"Go on," Claire said. "We're right behind you."

Eve dropped the blanket and pushed through the

crowd, heading for her boyfriend, and the unofficial head of their strange and screwed-up fraternity.

It was easy to spot Michael in any group—he was tall and blond, with a face like an angel. As he caught sight of Eve heading toward him, he smiled, and Claire thought that was maybe the most complicated smile she'd ever seen, full of relief, welcome, love, and worry.

Eve crashed straight into him, hard enough to rock him back on his heels, and their arms went around each other.

Shane held Claire back with a touch on her shoulder. "Give them a minute," he said. "They've got things to say." She turned to look at him. "And so do we."

She swallowed hard and nodded. Shane's hands were on her shoulders, and his eyes had gone still and intense.

"Don't go out there," Shane said.

It was what she'd been intending to say to *him*. She blinked, surprised.

"You stole my paranoia," she said. "*I* was going to say, *Don't go.* But you're going to, no matter what I say, aren't you?"

That threw him off just a little. "Well, yeah, of course I am, but—"

"But nothing. I'll be with Amelie; I'll be okay. You? You're going off with the cast of *WWE Raw* to fight a cage match or something. It's not the same thing."

"Since when do you ever watch wrestling?"

"Shut up. That's not the point, and you know it. Shane, *don't go.*" Claire put everything she had into it.

It wasn't enough.

Shane smoothed her hair and bent down to kiss her. It was the sweetest, gentlest kiss he'd ever given her, and it melted all the tense muscles of her neck, her shoulders, and her back. It was a promise without words, and when he finally pulled back, he passed his thumb across her lips gently, to seal it all in.

"There's something I really ought to tell you," he said. "I was kind of waiting for the right time."

They were in a room full of people, Morganville was in chaos outside, and they probably didn't have a chance of surviving until sunrise, but Claire felt her heart stutter and then race faster. The whole world seemed to go silent around her. *He's going to say it.*

Shane leaned in, so close that she felt his lips brush her ear, and whispered, "My dad's coming back to town."

That *so* wasn't what she was hoping he'd say. Claire jerked back, startled, and Shane put a hand over her mouth. "Don't," he whispered. "Don't say *anything*. We can't talk about this, Claire. I just wanted you to know."

They couldn't talk about it because Shane's father was Morganville's most wanted, public enemy number one, and any conversation they had—at least here—was in danger of being overheard by unfriendly, undead ears.

Not that Claire was a fan of Shane's father; he was a cold, brutal man who'd used and abused Shane, and she couldn't work up a lot of dread for seeing him behind bars . . . only she knew that Amelie and Oliver wouldn't stop at putting him in jail. Shane's father was marked for death if he came back. Death by burning. And while Claire wouldn't necessarily cry any big tears over him, she didn't want to put Shane through that, either.

"We'll talk about it," she said.

Shane snorted. "You mean, you'll yell at me? Trust me, I know what you're going to say. I just wanted you to know, in case—"

In case something happened to him. Claire tried to frame her question in a way that wouldn't tip their hand to any listening ears. "When should I expect him?"

"Next few days, probably. But you know how it is. I'm out of the loop." Shane's smile had a dark, painful edge to it now. He'd defied his dad once, because of Claire, and that meant cutting the ties to his last living family in the world. Claire doubted his dad had forgotten that, or ever would.

"Why now?" she whispered. "The last thing we need is—"

"Help?"

"He's not *help*. He's chaos!"

Shane gestured at the burning town. "Take a good look, Claire. How much worse can it get?"

Lots, she thought. Shane, in some ways, still had a rose-colored view of his father. It had been a while since his dad had blown out of town, and she thought that Shane had probably convinced himself that the guy wasn't all that bad. He was probably thinking now that his dad would come sweeping in to save them.

It wasn't going to happen. Frank Collins was a fanatic, car-bomb variety, and he didn't care who got hurt.

Not even his own son.

"Let's just—" She chewed her lip for a second, staring at him. "Let's just get through the day, okay? Please? Be careful. Call me."

He had his cell phone, and he showed it to her in mute promise. Then he stepped closer, and when his arms closed around her, she felt a sweet, trembling relief.

"Better get ready," he said. "It's going to be a long day."

2

Claire wasn't sure if *get ready* meant put on her game face, brush her teeth, or pack up a lot of weapons, but she followed Shane to say good-bye to Michael first.

Michael was standing in the middle of a bunch of hard-looking types—some were vampires, and many she'd never seen before. They didn't look happy about playing defense, and they had that smelling-something-rotten expression that meant they didn't like hanging out with the human help, either.

The non-vamps with Michael were older, post-college—tough guys with lots of muscles. Even so, the humans mostly looked nervous.

Shane seemed almost small in comparison—not that he let it slow him down as he rushed the defensive line. He pushed a vampire out of his way as he headed for Michael; the vampire flashed fang at him, but Shane didn't even notice.

Michael did. He stepped in the way of the offended vamp as it made a move for Shane's back, and the two of them froze that way, predators facing off. Michael wasn't the one to look down first.

Michael had a strange intensity about him now—something that had always been there, but being a vampire had ramped it up to about eleven, Claire thought. He still looked angelic, but there were moments when his angel was more fallen than flying. But the smile was real, and completely the Michael she knew and loved when he turned it on them.

He held out his hand for a manly kind of shake. Shane batted it aside and hugged him. There were manly backslaps, and if there was a brief flash of red in Michael's eyes, Shane didn't see it.

"You be careful, man," Shane said. "Those college chicks, they're wild. Don't let them drag you into any Jell-O shot parties. Stay strong."

"You too," Michael said. "Be careful."

"Driving around in a big, black, obvious lunch wagon in a town full of starving vampires? Yeah. I'll try to keep it low profile." Shane swallowed. "Seriously—"

"I know. Same here."

They nodded at each other.

Claire and Eve watched them for a moment. The two of them shrugged. "What?" Michael asked.

"That's it? That's your big good-bye?" Eve asked.

"What was wrong with it?"

Claire looked at Eve, mystified. "I think I need guy CliffsNotes."

"Guys aren't deep enough to need CliffsNotes."

"What were you waiting for, flowery poetry?" Shane snorted. "I hugged. I'm done."

Michael's grin didn't last. He looked at Shane, then Claire, and last—and longest—at Eve. "Don't let anything happen to you," he said. "I love you guys."

"Ditto," Shane said, which was, for Shane, positively gushing.

They might have had time to say more, but one of the vampires standing around, looking pissed off and impatient, tapped Michael on the shoulder. His pale lips moved near Michael's ear.

"Time to go," Michael said. He hugged Eve hard, and had to peel her off at the end. "Don't trust Oliver."

"Yeah, like you had to tell me that," Eve said. Her voice was shaking again. "Michael—"

"I love you," he said, and kissed her, fast and hard. "I'll see you soon."

He left in a blur, taking most of the vampires with him. The mayor's son, Richard Morrell—still in his police uniform, although he was looking wrinkled and smoke stained now—led the humans at a more normal pace to follow.

Eve stood there with her kiss-smudged lips parted, looking stunned and astonished. When she regained the power of speech, she said, "Did he just say—?"

"Yes," Claire said, smiling. "Yes, he did."

"Whoa. Guess I'd better stay alive, then."

The crowd of people—fewer now than there had been just a few minutes before—parted around them, and Oliver strode through the gap. The second-most badass vampire in town had shed his costume and was dressed in plain black, with a long, black leather coat. His long graying hair was tied back in a tight knot at the back of his head, and he looked like he was ready to snap the head off anyone, vampire or human, who got in the way.

"You," he snapped at Eve. "Come."

He turned on his heel and walked away. This was not the Oliver they'd known before—certainly not the friendly proprietor of the local coffee shop. Even once he'd been revealed as a vampire, he hadn't been *this* intense.

Clearly, he was done pretending to like people.

Eve watched him go, and the look in her eyes was boiling with resentment. She finally shrugged and took a deep breath. "Yeah," she said. "This'll be *so* much fun. See ya, Claire Bear."

"See you," Claire said. They hugged one last time, just for comfort, and then Eve was leaving, back straight, head high.

She was probably crying, Claire thought. Eve cried at times like these. Claire didn't seem to be able to cry when it counted, like now. It felt like pieces of her were being pulled off, and she felt cold and empty inside. No tears.

And now it was her heart being ripped out, because Shane was being summoned impatiently by yet another hard-looking bunch of vampires and humans near the door. He nodded to them, took her hands, and looked into her eyes.

Say it, she thought.

But he didn't. He just kissed her hands, turned, and walked away, dragging her red, bleeding heart with him—metaphorically, anyway.

"I love you," she whispered. She'd said it before, but he'd hung up the phone before she'd gotten it out. Then she'd said it in the hospital, but he'd been doped up on painkillers. And he didn't hear her now, as he walked away from her.

But at least *she* had the guts to try.

He waved to her from the door, and then he was gone, and she suddenly felt very alone in the world— and very . . . young. Those who were left in the Glass House had jobs of their own, and she was in the way. She found a chair—Michael's armchair, as it turned out—and pulled her feet up under her as humans and vampires moved around, fortifying windows and doors, distributing weapons, talking in low tones.

She might have become a ghost, for all the attention they paid her.

She didn't have to wait long. In just a few minutes, Amelie came sweeping down the stairs. She had a whole scary bunch of vampires behind her, and a few humans, including two in police uniforms.

They were all armed—knives, clubs, swords. Some had stakes, including the policemen; they had them, instead of riot batons, hanging from their utility belts. *Standard-issue equipment for Morganville,* Claire thought, and had to suppress a manic giggle. *Maybe instead of pepper spray, they have garlic spray.*

Amelie handed Claire two things: a thin, silver knife, and a wooden stake. "A wooden stake in the heart will put one of us down," she said. "You must use the silver knife to kill us. No steel, unless you plan to take our heads off with it. The stake alone will not do it, unless you're very lucky or sunlight catches us helpless, and even then, we are slower to die the older we are. Do you understand?"

Claire nodded numbly. *I'm sixteen,* she wanted to say. *I'm not ready for this.*

But she kind of had to be, now.

Amelie's fierce, cold expression seemed to soften, just a touch. "I can't entrust Myrnin to anyone else. When we find him, it will be your responsibility to manage him. He may be—" Amelie paused, as if searching for the right word. "Difficult." That probably wasn't it. "I don't want you to fight, but I need you with us."

Claire lifted the stake and the knife. "Then why did you give me these?"

"Because you might need to defend yourself, or him. If you do, I don't want you to hesitate, child. Defend yourself and Myrnin at all costs. Some of those who come against us may be those you know. Don't let that stop you. We are in this to survive now."

Claire nodded numbly. She'd been pretending that all this was some kind of action/adventure video game, like the zombie-fighting one Shane enjoyed so much, but with every one of her friends leaving, she'd lost some of that distance. Now it was right here in front of her: reality. People were dying.

She might be one of them.

"I'll stay close," she said. Amelie's cold fingers touched her chin, very lightly.

"Do that." Amelie turned her attention to the others around them. "Watch for my father, but don't be drawn off to face him. It's what he wants. He will have his own reinforcements, and will be gathering more. Stay together, and watch each other closely. Protect me, and protect the child."

"Um—could you stop calling me that?" Claire asked. Amelie's icy eyes fixed on her in almost-human puzzlement. "Child, I mean? I'm not a child."

It felt like time stopped for about a hundred years while Amelie stared at her. It probably had been at *least* a hundred years since the last time anybody had dared correct Amelie like that in public.

Amelie's lips curved, very slightly. "No," she agreed. "You are not a child, and in any case, by your age, I was a bride and ruled a kingdom. I should know better."

Claire felt heat build in her face. Great, she was blushing, as everybody's attention focused on her. Amelie's smile widened.

"I stand corrected," she said to the rest of them. "Protect this *young woman*."

She really didn't feel like that, either, but Claire wasn't going to push her luck on that one. The other vampires looked mostly annoyed with the distinction, and the humans looked nervous.

"Come," Amelie said, and turned to face the blank far wall of the living room. It shimmered like an asphalt road in the summer, and Claire felt the connection snap open.

Amelie stepped through what looked like blank wall. After a second or two of surprise, the vampires started to follow her.

"Man, I can't believe we're doing this," one of the policemen behind Claire whispered to the other.

"I can," the other whispered back. "My kids are out there. What else is there to do?"

She gripped the wooden stake tight and stepped through the portal, following Amelie.

Myrnin's lab wasn't any more of a wreck than usual. Claire was kind of surprised by that; somehow she'd

expected Mr. Bishop to tear through here with torches
and clubs, but so far, he'd found better targets.

Or maybe—just maybe—he hadn't been able to get
in. Yet.

Claire anxiously surveyed the room, which was lit
by just a few flickering lamps, both oil and electric.
She'd tried cleaning it up a few times, but Myrnin had
snapped at her that he liked things the way they were,
so she'd left the stacks of leaning books, the piles of
glassware on counters, the disordered piles of curling
paper. There was a broken iron cage in the corner—
broken because Myrnin had decided to escape from it
once, and they'd never gotten around to having it repaired once he'd regained his senses.

The vampires were whispering to one another, in
sibilant little hisses that didn't carry even a hint of
meaning to Claire's ears. They were nervous, too.

Amelie, by contrast, seemed as casual and self-
assured as ever. She snapped her fingers, and two of
the vampires—big, strong, strapping men—stepped up,
towering over her. She glanced up.

"You will guard the stairs," she said. "You two."
She pointed to the uniformed policemen. "I want you
here as well. Guard the interior doors. I doubt anything will come through them, but Mr. Bishop has
already surprised us. I won't have him surprising us
again."

That cut their forces in half. Claire swallowed hard
and looked at the two vampires and one human who
remained with her and Amelie—she knew the two
vampires slightly. They were Amelie's personal bodyguards, and one of them, at least, had treated her kind
of decently before.

The remaining human was a tough-looking African
American woman with a scar across her face, from
her left temple across her nose, and down her right
cheek. She saw Claire watching her, and gave her a
smile. "Hey," she said, and stuck out a big hand.
"Hannah Moses. Moses Garage."

"Hey," Claire said, and shook hands awkwardly. The woman had muscles—not quite Shane-quality biceps, but definitely bigger than most women would have found useful. "You're a mechanic?"

"I'm an everything," Hannah said. "Mechanic included. But I used to be a marine."

"Oh." Claire blinked.

"The garage was my dad's before he passed. I just got back from a couple of tours in Afghanistan—thought I'd take up the quiet life for a while." She shrugged. "Guess trouble's in my blood. Look, if this comes to a fight, stay with me, okay? I'll watch your back."

That was so much of a relief that Claire felt weak enough to melt. "Thanks."

"No problem. You're what, about fifteen?"

"Almost seventeen." Claire thought she needed a T-shirt that said it for her; it would be a great time-saver—that, or some kind of button.

"Huh. So you're about my kid brother's age. His name's Leo. I'll have to introduce you sometime."

Hannah, Claire realized, was talking without really thinking about what she was saying; her eyes were focused on Amelie, who had made her way around piles of books to the doorway on the far wall.

Hannah didn't seem to miss anything.

"Claire," Amelie said. Claire dodged piles of books and came to her side. "Did you lock this door when you left before?"

"No. I thought I'd be coming back this way."

"Interesting. Because someone *has* locked it."

"Myrnin?"

Amelie shook her head. "Bishop has him. He has not returned this way."

Claire decided not to ask how she knew that. "Who else—" And then she knew. "Jason." Eve's brother had known about the doorways that led to different destinations in town—maybe not about how they worked (and Claire wasn't sure she did, either), but he definitely had figured out how to use them. Apart from Claire, Myrnin, and Amelie, only Oliver had the knowledge, and she knew where he'd been since her encounter with Mr. Bishop.

"Yes," Amelie agreed. "The boy is becoming a problem."

"Kind of an understatement, considering he, you know . . ." Claire mimed stabbing with the stake, but not in Amelie's direction—that would be like pointing a loaded gun at Superman. Somebody would get hurt, and it wouldn't be Superman. "Um—I meant to ask, are you—?"

Amelie looked away from her, toward the door. "Am I what?"

"Okay?" Because she'd had a stake in her chest not all that long ago, and besides that, all the vampires in Morganville had a disadvantage, whether they knew it or not: they were sick—really sick—with something Claire could only think of as vampire Alzheimer's.

And it was ultimately fatal.

Most of the town didn't have a clue about that, because Amelie was rightly afraid of what might happen if they did—vampires and humans alike. Amelie had symptoms, but so far they were mild. It took years to progress, so they were safe for a while.

At least, Claire hoped it took years.

"No, I doubt I am all right. Still, this is hardly the time to be coddling myself." Amelie focused on the door. "We will need the key to open it."

That was a problem, because the key wasn't where it was supposed to be. The key ring was gone from where Claire kept it, in a battered, sagging drawer, and the more Claire pawed through debris looking for it, the more alarmed she became. Myrnin kept the weirdest stuff. . . . Books, sure, she loved books; small, deformed dead things in alcohol, not so much. He also kept jars of dirt—at least, she hoped it was dirt. Some of it looked red and flaky, and she was really afraid it might be blood.

The keys were missing. So were a few other things—significant things.

With a sinking feeling, Claire pulled open the half-broken drawer where she'd kept the bag with all the tranquilizer stuff, and Myrnin's drug supplies.

Gone. Only a scrape in the dust to indicate where it had been.

That meant that if—*when*—Myrnin turned violent, she wouldn't have her trusty dart gun to help her. Nor would she have even her trusty injectable pen, so cool, that she'd loaded up for emergencies, because it had been in the bag with the drugs. She'd lost the other supplies she'd had with her.

But even worse, she didn't have any medicine for him, other than the couple of small vials she had with her in her pockets.

In summary: so very screwed.

"Enough," Amelie said, and turned to her bodyguard. "I know this isn't easy, but if you would?"

He gave her a polite sort of nod, stepped forward, and took the lock in his hand.

His hand *burst into flame.*

"Oh my God!" Claire blurted, and clapped her hands over her mouth, because the vampire guy wasn't letting go. His face was contorted with pain, but he held on, somehow, and jerked and twisted the silver-plated lock until, with a scream of metal, it ripped loose. The hasp came with it, right off the door.

He dropped it to the floor. His hand kept burning. Claire grabbed the first thing that came to hand—some kind of ratty old shirt Myrnin had left thrown on the floor—and patted out the fire. The smell of burned flesh made her dry heave, and so did the sight of what was left of his hand. He didn't scream. She almost did it for him.

"A trap," Amelie said. "From my father. Gérard, are you able to continue?"

He nodded as he wrapped the shirt around the ruin of his hand. He was sweating fine pink beads—blood,

Claire realized, as a trickle of it ran down his pale face. She realized that as she was standing there right in front of him, frozen in place, and his eyes flashed red.

"Move," he growled at her. "Stay behind us." And then, after a brief pause, he said, "Thank you."

Hannah took her by the arm and pulled her to the spot in the back, out of vampire-grabbing range. "He needs feeding," she said in an undertone. "Gérard's not a bad guy, but you don't want to make yourself too available for snack attacks. Remember, we're vending machines with legs."

Claire nodded. Amelie put her fingers in the hole left by the broken lock and pulled the door open . . . on darkness.

Hannah said nothing. She didn't let go of Claire's arm.

For a long moment, nothing happened, and then the darkness flickered. Shifted. Things came and went in the shadows, and Claire knew that Amelie was shuffling destinations, trying to find the one she wanted. It seemed to take a very long time, and then Amelie took a sudden step back. "Now," she said, and her two bodyguards charged forward into what looked like complete darkness and were gone. Amelie glanced back at Hannah and Claire, and her black pupils were expanding fast, covering all the gray iris of her eyes, preparing for the dark.

"Don't leave my side," she said. "This will be dangerous."

3

Amelie grabbed Claire's other arm, and before Claire could so much as grab a breath, she was being pulled through the portal. There was a brief wave of chill, and a feeling that was a little like being pushed from all sides, and then she was stumbling into utter, complete blackness. Her other senses went into overdrive. The air smelled stale and heavy, and felt cold and damp, like a cave. Amelie's icy grip on one arm was going to leave bruises, and Hannah Moses's warmer touch on the other seemed light by contrast, although Claire knew it wasn't.

Claire could hear herself and Hannah breathing, but there was no sound at all from the vampires. When Claire tried to speak, Amelie's ice-cold hand covered her mouth. She nodded convulsively, and concentrated on putting one foot in front of the other as Amelie—she hoped it was still Amelie, anyway—pulled her forward into the dark.

The smells changed from time to time—a whiff of nasty, rotten something, then something else that smelled weirdly like grapes? Her imagination conjured up a dead man surrounded by broken bottles of wine, and Claire couldn't stop it there; the dead man was moving, squirming toward her, and any second now he'd touch her and she'd scream. . . .

It's just your imagination; stop it.

She swallowed and tried to tamp down the panic. It

wasn't helping. *Shane wouldn't panic. Shane would*—whatever, Shane wouldn't be caught dead roaming around in the dark with a bunch of vampires like this, and Claire knew it.

It seemed like they went on forever, and then Amelie pulled her to a stop and let go. Losing that support felt as if she were standing on the edge of a cliff, and Claire was really, really grateful for Hannah's grip to tell her there was something else real in the world. *Don't let me fall.*

And then Hannah's hand went away. A fast tightening of her fingers, and she was gone.

Claire was floating in total darkness, disconnected, alone. Her breath sounded loud as a train in her ears, but it was buried under the thunder of her fast heartbeats. *Move,* she told herself. *Do something!*

She whispered, "Hannah?"

Cold hands slapped around her from behind, one pinning her arms to her sides, the other covering her mouth. She was lifted off the ground, and she screamed, a faint buzzing sound like a storm of bees that didn't make it through the muffling gag.

And then she went flying through the air into the darkness . . . and rolled to a stop facedown, on a cold stone floor. There was light here. Faint, but definite, painting the edges of things a pale gray, including the arched mouth of the tunnel at the end of the hall.

She had no idea where she was.

Claire got quickly to her feet and turned to look behind her. Amelie, pale as a pearl, stepped through the portal, and with her came the other two vampires. Gérard had Hannah Moses's arm gripped in his good hand.

Hannah had a bloody gash on her head, and when Gérard let go, she dropped to her knees, breathing hard. Her eyes looked blank and unfocused.

Amelie whirled, something silver in one hand, and stabbed as something came at her from the dark. It screamed, a thin sound that echoed through the tunnel, and a white hand reached out to grab Amelie's shirt.

The invisible portal slammed shut like an iris, and severed the arm just above the elbow.

Amelie plucked the still-grabbing hand from her shirt, dropped the hand to the ground, and kicked it to the side. When she turned back to the others, there was no expression on her face.

Claire felt like throwing up. She couldn't take her eyes away from that wiggling, fish-pale hand.

"It was necessary to come this way," Amelie said. "Dangerous, but necessary."

"Where are we?" Claire asked. Amelie gave her a look and ignored her as she took the lead, heading down the hall. Going through this didn't give her any right to ask questions. Of course. "Hannah? Are you okay?"

Hannah waved her hand vaguely, which really wasn't all that confidence-building. The vampire Gérard answered for her. "She's fine." Sure, he could talk, having one hand burned to the bone. He'd probably classify himself as fine, too. "Take her," Gérard ordered, and pushed Hannah toward Claire as he moved to follow Amelie. The other bodyguard—what was his name?—moved with him, as if they were an old, practiced team.

Hannah was heavy, but she pulled herself back on her own center of gravity after a breath or two. "I'm fine," she said, and gave Claire a reassuring grin. "Damn. That was not a walk in the park."

"You should meet my boyfriend," Claire said. "You two are both masters of understatement."

She thought Hannah wanted to laugh, but instead, she just nodded and patted Claire on the shoulder. "Watch the sides," she said. "We're just starting on this thing."

That was an easy job, because there was nothing to watch on the sides. They were, after all, in a tunnel. Hannah, it appeared, was the rear guard, and she seemed to take it very seriously, although it looked like Amelie had slammed the doorway behind them pretty hard, with prejudice. *I hope we don't have to go back that way,* Claire thought, and shivered at the sight of that pale severed hand behind them. It had finally stopped moving. *I really, really hope we don't have to go back there.*

At the mouth of the tunnel, Amelie seemed to pause for a moment, and then disappeared to the right, around the corner, with her two vampire bodyguards in flying formation behind her. Hannah and Claire hurried to keep up, and emerged into another hallway, this one square instead of arched, and paneled in rich, dark wood. There were paintings on the walls—old ones, Claire thought—of pale people lit by candlelight, dressed in about a thousand pounds of costume and rice white makeup and wigs.

She stopped and backed up, staring at one.

"What?" Hannah growled.

"That's her. Amelie." It definitely was, only instead of the Princess Grace–style clothes she wore now, in the picture she was wearing an elaborate sky blue satin dress, cut way low over her breasts. She was wearing a big white wig, and staring out of the canvas in an eerily familiar way.

"Art appreciation later, Claire. We need to go."

That was true, beyond any argument, but Claire kept throwing glances at the paintings as they passed. One looked like it could have been Oliver, from about four hundred years ago. One more modern one looked almost like Myrnin. *It's the vampire museum,* she realized. *It's their history.* There were glass cases lining the hall ahead, filled with books and papers and jewelry, clothing, and musical instruments. All the fine and fabulous things gathered through their long, long lives.

Ahead, the three vampires came to a sudden, motionless halt, and Hannah grabbed Claire by the arm to pull her out of the way, against the wall. "What's happening?" Claire whispered.

"Sorting credentials."

Claire didn't know what that meant, exactly, but when she risked moving out just a bit to see what was happening, she saw that there were lots of other vampires in here—about a hundred of them, some sitting down and obviously hurt. There were humans, too, mostly standing together and looking nervous, which seemed reasonable.

If these were Bishop's people, their little rescue party was in serious trouble.

Amelie exchanged some quiet words with the vampire who seemed to be in charge, and Gérard and his partner visibly relaxed. That settled the friend-or-foe question, apparently; Amelie turned and nodded to Claire, and she and Hannah edged out from behind the glass cases to join them.

Amelie made a gesture, and immediately several vampires peeled off from the group and joined her in a distant corner.

"What's going on?" Claire asked, and stared around her. Most of the vampires were still dressed in the costumes they'd worn to Bishop's welcome feast, but a few were in more military dress—black, mostly, but some in camouflage.

"It's a rally point," Hannah said. "She's talking strategy, probably. Those would be her captains. Notice there aren't any humans with her?"

Claire did. It wasn't exactly a pleasant sensation, the doubt that boiled up inside.

Whatever orders Amelie delivered, it didn't take long. One by one, the vampires nodded and peeled off from the meeting, gathered up followers—including humans this time—and departed. By the time Amelie had dispatched the last group, there were only about ten people left Claire didn't know, and they were all standing together.

Amelie came back to them, saw the group of humans and vamps, and nodded toward them.

"Claire, this is Theodosius Goldman," Amelie said. "Theo, he prefers to be called. These are his family."

Family? That was a shock, because there were so many of them. Theo seemed to be kind of middle-aged, with graying, curly hair and a face that, except for its vampiric pallor, seemed kind of . . . nice.

"May I present my wife, Patience?" he said with the kind of old manners Claire had only seen on *Masterpiece Theater.* "Our sons, Virgil and Clarence. Their wives, Ida and Minnie." There were more vampires bowing, or in the case of the one guy down on the floor, with his head held in the lap of a female vamp, waving. "And their children."

Evidently the grandkids didn't merit individual introductions. There were four of them, two boys and two girls, all pale like their relatives. They seemed younger than Claire, at least physically; she guessed the littler girl was probably about twelve, the older boy around fifteen.

The older boy and girl glared at her, as if she were personally responsible for the mess they were in, but Claire was too busy imagining how a whole family—down to grandkids—could all be made vampires like this.

Theo, evidently, could see all that in her expression, because he said, "We were made eternal a long time ago, my girl, by"—he cast a quick look at Amelie, who nodded—"by her father, Bishop. It was a joke of his, you see, that we should all be together for all time." He really did have a kind face, Claire thought, and his smile was kind of tragic. "The joke turned on him, though. We refused to let it destroy us. Amelie showed us we did not have to kill to survive, and so we were able to keep our faith as well as our lives."

"Your faith?"

"It's a very old faith," Theo said. "And today is our Sabbath."

Claire blinked. "Oh. You're Jewish?"

He nodded, eyes fixed on her. "We found a refuge here, in Morganville. A place where we could live in peace, both with our nature and our God."

Amelie said, softly, "But will you fight for it now, Theo? This place that gave you refuge?"

He held out his hand. His wife's cool white fingers closed around it. She was a delicate china doll of a woman, with masses of sleek black hair piled on top of her head. "Not today."

"I'm sure God would understand if you broke the Sabbath under these circumstances."

"I'm sure he would. God is forgiving, or we would not still be walking this world. But to be moral is not to need his divine forgiveness, I think." He shook his head again, very regretfully. "We cannot fight, Amelie. Not today. And I would prefer not to fight at all."

"If you think you can stay neutral in this, you're wrong. I will respect your wishes. My father will not."

Theo's face hardened. "If your father threatens my family again, then we *will* fight. But until he comes for us, until he shows us the sword, we will not take up arms against him."

Gérard snorted, which proved what he thought about it; Claire wasn't much surprised. He seemed like a practical sort of guy. Amelie simply nodded. "I can't force you, and I wouldn't. But be careful. I cannot spare anyone to help you. You should be safe enough here, for a time. If any others come through, send them out to guard the power station and the campus." She allowed her gaze to move beyond Theo, to touch the three humans huddled in the far corner of the room, under another painting, a big one. "Are these under your Protection?"

Theo shrugged. "They asked to join us."

"Theo."

"I will defend them if someone tries to harm them." Theo pitched his voice lower. "Also, we may need them, if we can't get supplies."

Claire went cold. For all his kind face and smile,

Theo was talking about using those people as portable blood banks.

"I don't want to do it," Theo continued, "but if things go against us, I have to think of my children. You understand."

"I do," Amelie said. Her face was back to a blank mask that gave away nothing of how she felt about it. "I have never told you what to do, and I will not now. But by the laws of this town, if you place these humans under your Protection, you owe them certain duties. You know that."

Another shrug, and Theo held out his hands to show he was helpless. "Family comes first," he said. "I have always told you so."

"Some of us," Amelie said, "are not so fortunate in our choice of families."

She turned away from Theo without waiting for his response—if he'd been intending to give one—and without so much as a pause, slammed her fist into a glass-fronted wall box labeled EMERGENCY USE ONLY three steps to the right. It shattered in a loud clatter, and Amelie shook shards of glass from her skin.

She reached into the box and took out . . . Claire blinked. "Is that a *paintball* gun?"

Amelie handed it to Hannah, who handled it like a professional. "It fires pellets loaded with silver powder," she said. "Very dangerous to us. Be careful where you aim."

"Always am," Hannah said. "Extra magazines?"

Amelie retrieved them from the case and handed them over. Claire noticed that she protected herself even from a casual touch, with a fold of fabric over her fingers. "There are ten shots per magazine," she said. "There is one already loaded, and six more here."

"Well," Hannah said, "any problem I can't solve with seventy shots is probably going to kill us, anyway."

"Claire," Amelie said, and handed over a small, sealed vial. "Silver powder, packed under pressure. It will explode on impact, so be very careful with it. If you throw it, there is a wide dispersal through the air. It can hurt your friends as much as your enemies."

There were real uses for silver powder, like coating parts in computers; Claire supposed it wasn't exactly restricted, but she was surprised the vampires were progressive enough to lay in a supply. Amelie raised pale eyebrows at her.

"You've been expecting this," Claire said.

"Not in detail. But I've learned through my life that such preparations are never wasted, in the end. Sometime, somewhere, life always comes to a fight, and peace always comes to an end."

Theo said, very quietly, "Amen."

4

They left the museum by way of a side door. It was risky to go out into the night, but since the only other way to exit the museum was to go back into the darkness, nobody argued about the choice.

"Careful," Amelie told them in a very soft voice that hardly reached past the shadows. "I have gathered my forces. My father is doing the same. There will be patrols, especially here."

The flames hadn't reached Founder's Square, which was where they came out—the heart of vamp territory. It didn't look like the calm, orderly place Claire remembered, though; the lights were all out, and the shops and restaurants that bordered it were closed and empty.

It looked afraid.

The only place she could see movement was on the marble steps of the Elders' Council building, where Bishop's welcome feast had been held. Gérard hissed a warning, and they all froze, silent and still in the dark. Hannah's grip on Claire's arm felt like an iron band.

There were three vampires standing there, scanning the area.

Lookouts.

"Go," Amelie said in a whisper so small it was like a ghost. "Move, but be careful."

They reached the edge of the shadows by the corner

of the building, but just as Claire was starting to relax a little, Amelie, Gérard, and the other vampires moved in a blur, scattering in all directions.

This left Claire flat-footed for one horrible second, before Hannah tackled her facedown on the grass. Claire gasped, got a mouthful of crunchy dirt and bitter chlorophyll, and fought to get her breath. Hannah's heavy weight held her down, and the older woman braced her elbows on Claire's back.

She's firing the pistol, Claire thought, and tried to raise her head to see where Hannah was shooting.

"Head down!" Hannah snarled, and shoved Claire down with one hand while she continued to fire with the other. From the screams in the dark, she was hitting something. "Get up! Run!"

Claire wasn't quick enough to suit either the marines or the vampires, and before she knew it, she was being half pulled, half dragged at a dead run through the night. It was all a confusing blur of shadows, dark buildings, pale faces, and the surly orange glow of flames in the distance.

"What is it?" she screamed.

"Patrols." Hannah kept on firing behind them. She wasn't firing wildly, not at all; it seemed like she took a second or two between every shot, choosing her target. Most of the shots seemed to hit, from the shouts and snarls and screams. "Amelie! We need an exit, *now!*"

Amelie looked back at them, a pale flash of face in the dark, and nodded.

They charged up the steps of another building on Founder's Square. Claire didn't have time to get more than a vague impression of it—some kind of official building, with columns in front and big stone lions snarling on the stairs—before their little party came to a halt at the top of the stairs, in front of a closed white door with no knob.

Gérard started to throw himself against it. Amelie stopped him with an outstretched hand. "It will do no good," she said. "It can't be opened by force. Let me."

The other vampire, facing away and down the steps, said, "Don't think we have time for sweet talk, ma'am. What you want us to do?" He had a drawling Texas accent, the first one Claire had heard from any vampire. She'd never heard him speak at all before.

He winked at her, which was even more of a shock. Until that moment, he hadn't even looked at her like a real person.

"A moment," Amelie murmured.

The Texan nodded behind them. "Don't think we've got one, ma'am."

There were shadows converging in the dark at the foot of the steps—the patrol that Hannah had been shooting at. There were at least twenty of them. In the lead was Ysandre, the beautiful vampire Claire hated maybe more than she hated any other vampire in the entire world. She was Bishop's girl through and through—Amelie's vampire sister, if they thought in those kinds of terms.

Claire hated Ysandre for Shane's sake. She was glad the vamp was here, and not attacking Shane's Bloodmobile—one, because she wasn't so sure Shane could resist the evil witch, and two, she wanted to stake Ysandre herself.

Personally.

"No," Hannah said, when Claire took a step out from behind her. "Are you crazy? Get back!"

Hannah fired over her shoulder. It was at the outer extreme of the paintball gun's range, but the pellet hit one of the vampires—not Ysandre, Claire was disappointed to see—right in the chest. Silver dust puffed up in a lethal mist, and the close formation scattered. Ysandre might have had a few burns, but nothing that wouldn't heal.

The vampire Hannah had shot in the chest toppled over and hit the marble stairs, smoking and flailing.

Amelie slammed her palm flat against the door and

closed her eyes, and deep inside the barrier something groaned and shifted with a scrape of metal. "Inside," Amelie murmured, still wicked controlled, and Claire spun and followed the three vampires across the threshold. Hannah backed in after, grabbed the door, and slammed it shut.

"No locks," she said.

Amelie reached over and pushed Hannah's gun hand into an at-rest position at her side. "None necessary. They won't get in." She sounded sure of it, but from the look Hannah continued to give the door—as if she wished she could weld it shut with the force of her stare—she wasn't so certain. "This way. We'll take the stairs."

It was a library, full of books. Some—on this floor—were new, or at least newish, with colorful spines and crisp titles that Claire could read even in the low light. She slowed down a little, blinking. "You guys have *vampire* stories in here?" None of the vampires answered. Amelie veered to the right, through the two-story-tall shelves, and headed for a set of sweeping marble steps at the end. The books got older, the paper more yellow. Claire caught sight of a sign that read FOLKLORE, CA. 1870–1945, ENGLISH, and then another that identified a *German* section. Then *French*. Then script that might have been Chinese.

So many books, and from what she could tell, every single one of them had to do in some way with vampires. Was it history or fiction to them?

Claire didn't really have time to work it out. They were taking the stairs, moving around the curve up to the second level. Claire's legs burned all along the calf muscles, and her breathing was getting raspy from the constant movement and adrenaline. Hannah flashed her a quick, sympathetic smile. "Yeah," she said. "Consider it basic training. Can you keep up?"

Claire gave her a gasping nod.

More books here, old and crumbling, and the air tasted like dry leather and ancient paper. Toward the back of the room, there were things that looked like wine racks, the fancy X-shaped kind people put in cellars, only these held rolls of paper, each neatly tied with ribbon. They were scrolls, probably very old ones. Claire hoped they'd go that direction, but no, Amelie was turning them down another book aisle, toward a blank white wall.

No, not quite blank. It had a small painting on the wall, in a fussy gilt frame. Some bland-looking nature scene . . . and then, as Amelie stared at it, the painting *changed*.

It grew darker, as though clouds had come across the meadow and the drowsy sheep in the picture.

And then it was dark, just a dark canvas, then some pinpricks of light, like candle flames through smoke. . . .

And then Claire saw Myrnin.

He was in chains, silver-colored chains, kneeling on the floor, and his head was down. He was still wearing the blousy white pantaloons of his Pierrot costume, but no shirt. The wet points of his damp hair clung to his face and his marble-pale shoulders.

Amelie nodded sharply, and put a hand against the wall to the left of the picture, pressing what looked like a nail, and part of the wall swung out silently on oiled hinges.

Hidden doors: vampires sure seemed to love them.

There was darkness on the other side. "Oh, *hell* no," Claire heard Hannah mutter. "Not again."

Amelie sent her a glance, and there was a whisper of amusement in the look. "It's a different darkness," she said. "And the dangers are very different, from this point on. Things may change quickly. You will have to adapt."

Then she stepped through, and the vampires followed, and it was just Claire and Hannah.

Claire held out her hand. Hannah took it, still shaking her head, and the dark closed around them like a damp velvet curtain.

There was the hiss of a match dragging, and a flare

of light from the corner. Amelie, her face turned ivory by the licking flame, set the match to a candle and left the light burning as she flicked on a small flashlight and played it around the room. Boxes. It was some kind of storeroom, dusty and disused. "All right," she said. "Gérard, if you please."

He swung another door open a crack, nodded, and widened it enough to slip through.

Another hallway. Claire was getting tired of hallways, and they were all starting to look the same. Where were they now, anyway? It looked like some kind of hotel, with polished heavy doors marked with brass plates, only instead of numbers, each door had one of the vampire markings, like the symbol on Claire's bracelet. Each vampire had one; at least she thought they did. So these would be—what? Rooms? Vaults? Claire thought she heard something behind one of the doors—muffled sounds, thumping, scratching. They didn't stop, though—and she wasn't sure she wanted to know, really.

Amelie brought them to a halt at the T-intersection of the hall. It was deserted in every direction, and disorienting, too; Claire couldn't tell one hallway from another. *Maybe we should drop crumbs,* she thought. *Or M&M's. Or blood.*

"Myrnin is in a room on this hall," Amelie said. "It is quite obviously a trap, and quite obviously meant for me. I will stay behind and ensure your escape route. Claire." Her pale eyes fixed on Claire with merciless intensity. "Whatever else happens, you must bring Myrnin out safely. Do you understand? Do not let Bishop have him."

She meant, *Everybody else is expendable.* That made Claire feel sick, and she couldn't help but look at Hannah, and even at the two vampires. Gérard shrugged, so slightly she thought it might have been her imagination.

"We are soldiers," Gérard said. "Yes?"

Hannah smiled. "Damn straight."

"Excellent. You will follow my orders."

Hannah saluted him, with just a little trace of irony. "Yes sir, squad leader, sir."

Gérard turned his attention to Claire. "You will stay behind us. Do you understand?"

She nodded. She felt cold and hot at the same time, and a little sick, and the wooden stake in her hand didn't seem like a heck of a lot, considering. But she didn't have any time for second thoughts, because Gérard had turned and was already heading down the hall, his wing man flanking him, and Hannah was beckoning Claire to follow.

Amelie's cool fingers brushed her shoulder. "Careful."

Claire nodded and went to rescue a crazy vampire from an evil one.

The door shattered under Gérard's kick. That wasn't an exaggeration; except for the wood around the door hinges, the rest of it broke into hand-sized pieces and splinters. Before that rain of wreckage hit the floor, Gérard was inside, moving to the left while his colleague went right. Hannah stepped in and swept the room from one side to the other, holding her air pistol ready to fire, then nodded sharply to Claire.

Myrnin was just as she'd seen him in the picture— kneeling in the center of the room, anchored by tight-stretched silvery chains. The chains were double-strength, and threaded through massive steel bolts on the stone floor.

He was shaking all over, and where the chains touched him, he had welts and burns.

Gérard swore softly under his breath and fiercely kicked the eyebolts in the floor. They bent, but didn't break.

Myrnin finally raised his head, and beneath the mass of sweaty dark hair, Claire saw wild dark eyes, and a smile that made her stomach twist.

"I knew you'd come," he whispered. "You fools. Where is she? Where's Amelie?"

"Behind us," Claire said.

"Fools."

"Nice way to talk to your rescuers," Hannah said. She was nervous, Claire could see it, though the woman controlled it very well. "Gérard? I don't like this. It's too easy."

"I know." He crouched down and looked at the chains. "Silver coated. I can't break them."

"What about the bolts in the floor?" Claire asked. In answer, Gérard grabbed the edge of the metal plate and twisted. The steel bent like aluminum foil, and, with a ripping shriek, tore free of the stones. Myrnin wavered as part of his restraints fell loose, and Gérard waved his partner to work on the other two plates while he focused on the second in front.

"Too easy, too easy," Hannah kept on muttering. "What's the point of doing this if Bishop is just going to let him go?"

The eyebolts were all ripped loose, and Gérard grabbed Myrnin's arm and helped him to his feet.

Myrnin's eyes sheeted over with blazing ruby, and he shook Gérard off and went straight for Hannah.

Hannah saw him coming and put the gun between them, but before she could fire, Gérard's partner knocked her hand out of line, and the shot went wild, impacting on the stone at the other side of the room. Silver flakes drifted on the air, igniting tiny burns where they landed on the vampires' skin. The two body-guards backed off.

Myrnin grabbed Hannah by the neck.

"No!" Claire screamed, and ducked under Gérard's restraining hand. She raised her wooden stake.

Myrnin turned his head and grinned at her with wicked vampire fangs flashing. "I thought you were here to save me, Claire, not kill me," he purred, and whipped back toward his prey. Hannah was fumbling with her gun, trying to get it back into position. He stripped it away from her with contemptuous ease.

"I *am* here to save you," Claire said, and before she could think what she was doing, she buried the stake in Myrnin's back, on the left side, right where she thought his heart would be.

He made a surprised sound, like a cough, and pitched forward into Hannah. His hand slid away from her throat, clutching blindly at her clothes, and then he fell limply to the floor.

Dead, apparently.

Gérard and his partner looked at Claire as if they'd never seen her before, and then Gérard roared, "What do you think you're—"

"Pick him up," Claire said. "We can take the stake out later. He's old. He'll survive."

That sounded cold, and scary, and she hoped it was true. Amelie had survived, after all, and she knew Myrnin was as old, or maybe even older. From the look he gave her, Gérard was reassessing everything he'd thought about the cute, fragile little human he'd been nurse-maiding. Too bad. Claire thought one of her strengths was that everybody always underestimated her.

She was cool on the outside, shaking on the inside, because although it *was* the only way to keep Myrnin calm right now without tranquilizers, or without letting him rip Hannah's throat out, she'd just killed her boss.

That didn't seem like a really good career move.

Amelie will help, she thought a bit desperately, and Gérard slung Myrnin over his shoulder in a fireman's carry, and then they were running, moving fast again back down the hall to where Amelie had stayed to secure their escape.

Gérard came to a fast halt, and Hannah and Claire almost skidded into him. "What?" Hannah whispered, and looked past the two vampires in the lead.

Amelie was at the corner ahead of them, but ten feet past her was Mr. Bishop.

They were standing motionless, facing each other.

Amelie looked fragile and delicate, compared to her father in his bishop's robes. He looked ancient and angry, and the fire in his eyes was like something out of the story of Joan of Arc.

Neither of them moved. There was some struggle going on, but Claire couldn't tell what it was, or what it meant.

Gérard reached out and grabbed her arm, and Hannah's, and held them in place. "No," he said sharply. "Don't go near them."

"Problem, sir, that's the way out," Hannah said. "And the dude's alone."

Gérard and the Texan sent her a wild look, almost identical in their disbelief. "You think so?" the Texan said. "Humans."

Amelie took a step backward, just a small one, but a shudder went through her body, and Claire knew—just *knew*—it was a bad sign. Really bad.

Whatever confrontation had been going on, it broke.

Amelie whirled to them and screamed, "Go!" There was fury and fear in her voice, and Gérard let go of both girls and dumped Myrnin off his shoulder, into their arms, and he and the Texan pelted not for the exit, but to Amelie's side.

They got there just in time to stop Bishop from ripping out her throat. They slammed the old man up against the wall, but then there were others coming out into the hall. Bishop's troops, Claire guessed.

There were a lot of them.

Amelie intercepted the first of Bishop's vampires to run in her direction. Claire recognized him, vaguely—one of the Morganville vamps, but he'd obviously switched sides, and he came for Amelie, fangs out.

She put him down on the floor with one twisting move, fast as a snake, and looked back at Hannah and Claire, with Myrnin's body sagging between them. "Get him *out*!" she shouted. "I'll hold the way!"

"Come on," Hannah said, and shouldered the bulk of Myrnin's limp weight. "We're leaving."

Myrnin felt cold and heavy, like the dead man he was, and Claire swallowed a surge of nausea as she struggled to support his limp weight. Claire gritted her teeth and helped Hannah half carry, half drag Myrnin's staked body down the corridor. Behind them, the sounds of fighting continued—mainly bodies hitting the floor. No screaming, no shouting.

Vampires fought in silence.

"Right," Hannah gasped. "We're on our own."

That really wasn't good news—two humans stuck God knew where, with a crazy vampire with a stake in his heart in the middle of a war zone.

"Let's get back to the door," Claire said.

"How are we going to get through it?"

"I can do it."

Hannah threw her a look. "You?"

It was no time to get annoyed; hadn't she just been thinking that being underestimated was a gift? Yeah, not so much, sometimes. "Yes, really. I can do it. But we'd better hurry." The odds weren't in Amelie's favor. She might be able to hang on and cover their retreat, but Claire didn't think she could win.

She and Hannah dragged Myrnin past the symbol-marked doorways. Hannah counted off, and nodded to the one where they'd entered.

Not too surprisingly, it was marked with the Founder's Symbol, the same one Claire wore on the bracelet on her wrist.

Hannah tried to open it. "Dammit! Locked."

Not when Claire tried the knob. It opened at a twist, and the single candle in the corner illuminated very little. Claire caught her breath and rested her trembling muscles for a few seconds as Hannah checked the room and pronounced it safe before they entered.

Claire let Myrnin slide in a heap to the floor. "I'm sorry," she whispered to him. "It was the only way. I hope it doesn't hurt too much."

She had no idea if he could hear her when he was like this. She wanted to grab the stake and pull it out, but she remembered that with Amelie, and with Sam, it had been the other vampires who'd done it. Maybe they knew things she didn't. Besides, the disease weakened them—even Myrnin.

She couldn't take the risk. And besides, having him wake up wounded and crazy would be even worse, now that they didn't have any vampires who could help control him.

Hannah returned to her side. "So," she said, as she checked the clip on her paintball gun, frowned, and exchanged it for a new one, "how do we do this? We got to go back to that museum first, right?"

Did they? Claire wasn't sure. She stepped up to the door, which currently featured nothing but darkness, and concentrated hard on Myrnin's lab, with all its clutter and debris. Light swam, flickered, shivered, and snapped into focus.

No problem at all.

"Guess it's only roundabout getting here," Claire said. "Maybe that's on purpose, to keep people out who shouldn't be here. But it makes sense that once Amelie got here, she'd want to take the express out." She turned back. "Shouldn't we wait?"

Hannah opened the door and looked out into the hall. Whatever she saw, it couldn't have been good news. She shook her head. "We bug out, right now."

With a grunt of effort, Hannah braced Myrnin's deadweight on one side and dragged him forward. Claire took his other arm.

"Did he just twitch?" Hannah asked. " 'Cause if he twitches, I'm going to shoot him."

"No! No, he didn't; he's fine," Claire said, practically tripping over the words. "Ready? One, two . . ."

And *three*, they were in Myrnin's lab. Claire twisted out from under Myrnin's cold body, slammed the door shut, and stared wildly at the broken lock. "I need to fix that," she said. But what about Amelie? No, she'd know all the exits. She didn't have to come here.

"Girl, you need to get us the hell out of here, is

what you need to do," Hannah said. "You dial up the nearest Fort Knox or something on that thing. Damn, how'd you learn this, anyway?"

"I had a good teacher." Claire didn't look at Myrnin. She couldn't. For all intents and purposes, she'd just killed him, after all. "This way."

There were two ways out of Myrnin's lab, besides the usually-secured dimensional doorway: steps leading up to street level, which were probably the absolute worst idea ever right now, and a second, an even more hidden dimensional portal in a small room off to the side. That was the one Amelie had used to get them in.

But the problem was, Claire couldn't get it to work. She had the memories clear in her head—the Glass House, the portal to the university, the hospital, even the museum they'd visited on the way here. But nothing *worked.*

It just felt . . . dead, as if the whole system had been cut off.

They were lucky to have made it this far.

Amelie's trapped, Claire realized. *Back there. With Bishop. And she's outnumbered.*

Claire double-checked the other door, too, the one she'd blocked.

Nothing. It wasn't just a malfunctioning portal; the whole network was down.

"Well?" Hannah asked.

Claire couldn't worry about Amelie right now. She had a job to do—get Myrnin to safety. And that meant getting him to the only vampire she knew offhand who could help him: Oliver. "I think we're walking," she said.

"The hell we are," Hannah said. "I'm not hauling a dead vampire through the streets of Morganville. We'll get ourselves killed by just about *everybody.*"

"We can't leave him!"

"We can't take him, either!"

Claire felt her jaw lock into stubborn position.

"Well, fine, you go ahead. Because I'm not leaving him. I can't."

She could tell that Hannah wanted to grab her by the hair and yank her out of there, but finally, the older woman nodded and stepped back. "Third option," she said. "Call in the cavalry."

5

It wasn't quite the Third Armored Division, but after about a dozen phone calls, they did manage to get a ride.

"I'm turning on the street—nobody in sight so far," Eve's voice said from the speaker of Claire's cell phone. She'd been giving Claire a turn-by-turn description of her drive, and Claire had to admit, it sounded pretty frightening. "Yeah, I can see the Day House. You're in the alley next to it?"

"We're on our way," Claire said breathlessly. She was drenched with sweat, aching all over, from the effort of helping drag Myrnin out of the lab, up the steps, and down the narrow, seemingly endless dark alley. Next door, the Founder House belonging to Katherine Day and her granddaughter—a virtual copy of the house where Claire and her friends lived—was dark and closed, but Claire saw curtains moving at the upstairs windows.

"That's my great-aunt's house, Great-Aunt Kathy," Hannah panted. "Everybody calls her Gramma, though. Always have, as far back as I can remember."

Claire could see how Hannah was related to the Days; partly her features, but her attitude for sure. That was a family full of tough, smart, get-it-done women.

Eve's big, black car was idling at the end of the alley, and the back door kicked open as the two of them—three? Did Myrnin still count?—approached. Eve took a look at Myrnin, and the stake in his back, sent Claire a you've-got-to-be-kidding-me look, and reached out to drag him inside, facedown, on the backseat. "Hurry!" she said, and slammed the back door on the way to the driver's side. "Damn, he'd better not bleed all over the place. Claire, I thought you were supposed to—"

"I know," Claire said, and climbed into the middle of the big, front bench seat. Hannah crammed in on the outside. "Don't remind me. I was supposed to keep him safe."

Eve put the car in gear and did a ponderous tank-heavy turn. "So, who staked him?"

"I did."

Eve blinked. "Okay, that's an interesting interpretation of *safe.* Weren't you with Amelie?" Eve actually did a quick check of the backseat, as if she were afraid Amelie might have magically popped in back there, seated like a barbarian queen on top of Myrnin's prone body.

"Yeah. We were," Hannah said.

"Do I have to ask? No, wait, do I *want* to ask?"

"We left her," Claire said, miserable. "Bishop set a trap. She was fighting when we had to go."

"What about the other guys? I thought you went with a whole entourage!"

"We left most of them. . . ." Her brain caught up with her, and she looked at Hannah, who looked back with the same thought in her expression. "Oh, crap. The other guys. They were in Myrnin's lab, but not when we came back. . . ."

"Gone," Hannah said. "Taken out."

"Super. So, we're winning, then." Eve's tone was wicked cynical, but her dark eyes looked scared. "I talked to Michael. He's okay. They're at the university. Things are quiet there so far."

"And Shane?" Claire realized, with a pure bolt of guilt, that she hadn't called him. If he'd called her, she wouldn't have known; she'd turned off the ringer, afraid of the noise when creeping around on a rescue mission.

But as she dug out her phone, she saw that she hadn't missed any calls after all.

"Yeah, he's okay," Eve said, and steered the car at semihigh speed around a corner. The town was dark, very dark, with a few houses lit up by lanterns or candles or flashlights. Most people were waiting in the dark, scared to death. "They had some vamps try to board the bus, probably looking for a snack, but it wasn't even a real fight. So far they're cruising without too much trouble. He's fine, Claire." She reached over and took Claire's hand to squeeze it. "You, not so much. You look awful."

"Thanks. I think I earned it."

Eve took back her hand to haul the big wheel of the car around for a turn. Headlights swept over a group on the sidewalk—unnaturally pale. Unnaturally still. "Oh, crap, we've got bogeys. Hang on, I'm going to floor it."

That was, Claire thought, a pretty fantastic idea, because the vampires on the curb were now in the street, and following. There was a kind of manic glee to how they pursued the car, but not even a vamp could keep up with Eve's driving for long; they fell back into the dark, one by one. The last one was the fastest, and he nearly caught hold of the back bumper before he stumbled and was left behind in a black cloud of exhaust.

"Damn freaks," Eve said, trying to sound tough but not quite making it. "Hey, Hannah. How's business?"

"Right now?" Hannah laughed softly. "Not so fantastic, but I'm not bothered about it. Let's see if we can make it to the morning. Then I'll worry about making ends meet at the shop."

"Oh, we'll make it," Eve said, with a confidence Claire personally didn't feel. "Look, it's already four a.m. Another couple of hours, and we're fine."

Claire didn't say, *In a couple of hours, we could all be dead*, but she was thinking it. What about Amelie? What were they going to do to rescue her?

If she's even still alive.

Claire's head hurt, her eyes felt grainy from lack of sleep, and she just wanted to curl up in a warm bed, pull the pillow over her head, and not be *so responsible.*

Fat chance.

She wasn't paying attention to where Eve was going, and anyway, it was so dark and strange outside she wasn't sure she'd recognize things, anyway. Eve pulled to a halt at the curb, in front of a row of plate glass windows lit by candles and lanterns inside.

Just like that, they were at Common Grounds.

Eve jumped out of the driver's side, opened the back door, and grabbed Myrnin under the arms, all the while muttering, "Ick, ick, ick!" Claire slid out to join her, and Hannah grabbed Myrnin's feet when they hit the pavement, and the three of them carried him into the coffee shop.

Claire found herself shoved immediately out of the way by two vampires: Oliver and some woman she didn't know. Oliver looked grim, but then, that wasn't new, either. "Put him down," Oliver said. "No, not there, idiots, over there, on the sofa. You. Off." That last was directed at the frightened humans who were seated on the indicated couch, and they scattered like quail. Eve continued her *ick* mantra as she and Hannah hauled Myrnin's deadweight over and settled him facedown on the couch cushions. He was about the color of a fluorescent lightbulb now, blue-white and cold.

Oliver crouched next to him, looking at the stake in Myrnin's back. He steepled his fingers for a moment, and then looked up at Claire. "What happened?"

She supposed he could tell, somehow, that it was *her* stake. Wonderful. "I didn't have a choice. He came after us." The *us* part might have been an exaggeration; he'd come after Hannah, really. But eventually he would have come after Claire, too; she knew that.

Oliver gave her a moment to squirm while he stared at her, and then looked back at Myrnin's still, very corpselike body. The area where the stake had gone in looked even paler than the surrounding tissue, like the edge of a whirlpool draining all the color out of him. "Do you have any of the drugs you have been giving him?" Oliver asked. Claire nodded, and fumbled in her pocket. She had some of the powder form of the drug, and some of the liquid, but she hadn't felt confident at all that she'd be able to get it into Myrnin's mouth without a fight she was bound to lose. When Myrnin was like this, you were going to lose fingers, at the very least, if you got anywhere near his mouth.

Not so much an issue now, she supposed. She handed over the vials to Oliver, who turned them over in his fingers, considering, and then handed back the powder. "The liquid absorbs into the body more quickly, I expect."

"Yes." It also had some unpredictable side effects, but this probably wasn't the time to worry about that.

"And Amelie?" Oliver continued turning the bottle over and over in his fingers.

"She's—we had to leave her. She was fighting Bishop. I don't know where she is now."

A deep silence filled the room, and Claire saw the vampires all look at one another—all except Oliver, who continued to stare down at Myrnin, no change in his expression at all. "All right, then. Helen, Karl, watch the windows and doors. I doubt Bishop's patrols will try storming the place, but they might, while I'm distracted. The rest of you"—he looked at the humans and shook his head—"try to stay out of our way."

He thumbed the top off the vial of clear liquid and

held it in his right hand. "Get ready to turn him faceup," he said to Hannah and Claire. Claire took hold of Myrnin's shoulders, and Hannah his feet.

Oliver took the stake in his left hand and, in one smooth motion, pulled it out. It clattered to the floor, and he nodded sharply. "Now."

Once Myrnin was lying on his back, Oliver motioned her away and pried open Myrnin's bloodless lips. He poured the liquid into the other vampire's mouth, shut it, and placed a hand on his high forehead.

Myrnin's dark eyes were open. Wide-open. Claire shuddered, because they looked completely dead— like windows into a dark, dark room . . . and then he blinked.

He sucked in a very deep breath, and his back arched in silent agony. Oliver held his hand steady on Myrnin's forehead. His eyes were squeezed shut in concentration, and Myrnin writhed weakly, trying without much success to twist free. He collapsed limply back on the cushions, chest rising and falling. His skin still looked like polished marble, veined with cold blue, but his eyes were alive again.

And crazy. And hungry.

He swallowed, coughed, swallowed again, and gradually, the insane pilot light in his eyes went out. He looked tired and confused and in pain.

Oliver let out a long, moaning sigh, and tried to stand up. He couldn't. He made it about halfway up, then wavered and fell to his knees, one hand braced on the arm of the couch for support. His head went down, and his shoulders heaved, almost as if he were gasping or crying. Claire couldn't imagine Oliver— *Oliver*—doing either one of those things, really.

Nobody moved. Nobody touched him, although some of the other vampires exchanged unreadable glances.

He's sick, Claire thought. It was the disease. It made it harder and harder for them to concentrate, to do the things they'd always taken for granted, like make other vampires. Or revive them. Even Oliver, who hadn't believed anything about the sickness . . . even he was starting to fail.

And he knew it.

"Help me up," Oliver finally whispered. His voice sounded faint and tattered. Claire grabbed his arm and helped him climb slowly, painfully up; he moved as if he were a thousand years old, and felt every year of it. One of the other vampires silently provided a chair, and Claire helped him into it.

Oliver braced his elbows on his thighs and hid his pale face in his hands. When she started to speak, he said, softly, "Leave me."

It didn't seem a good idea to argue. Claire backed off and returned to where Myrnin was, on the couch.

He blinked, still staring at the ceiling. He folded his hands slowly across his stomach, but didn't otherwise move.

"Myrnin?"

"Present," he said, from what seemed like a very great distance away. He chuckled very softly, then winced. "Hurts when I laugh."

"Yeah, um—I'm sorry."

"Sorry?" A very slight frown worked its way between Myrnin's eyebrows, made a slow V, and then went on its way. "Ah. Staked me."

"I . . . uh . . . yeah." She knew what Oliver's reaction would have been, if she'd done that kind of thing to him, and the outcome wouldn't have been pretty. She wasn't sure what Myrnin might do. Just to be sure, she stayed out of easy-grabbing distance.

Myrnin simply closed his eyes for a moment and nodded. He looked old now, exhausted, like Oliver. "I'm sure it was for the best," he said. "Perhaps you should have left the wood in place. Better for everyone, in the end. I would have just—faded away. It's not very painful, not comparatively."

"No!" She took a step closer, then another. He just looked so—defeated. "Myrnin, don't. We need you."

He didn't open his eyes, but there was a tiny, tired smile curving his lips. "I'm sure you think you do, but you have what you need now. I found the cure for you, Claire. Bishop's blood. It's time to let me go. It's too late for me to get better."

"I don't believe that."

This time, his great dark eyes opened and studied her with cool intensity. "I see you don't," he said. "Whether or not that assumption is reasonable, that's another question entirely. Where is she?"

He was asking about Amelie. Claire glanced at Oliver, still hunched over, clearly in pain. No help. She bent closer to Myrnin. No way she wouldn't be overheard by the other vampires, though, she knew that. "She's—I don't know. We got separated. The last I saw, she and Bishop were fighting it out."

Myrnin sat up. It wasn't the kind of smooth, controlled motion vampires usually had, as though they'd been practicing it for three or four human lifetimes; he had to pull himself up, slowly and painfully, and it hurt Claire to watch. She put her hand against his shoulder blade to brace him. His skin still felt marble-cold, but not *dead*. It was hard to figure out what the difference was—maybe it was the muscles, underneath, tensed and alive again.

"We have to find her," he said. "Bishop will stop at nothing to get her, if he hasn't already. Once you were safely away, she'd have retreated. Amelie is a guerrilla fighter. It's not like her to fight in the open, not against her father."

"We're not going anywhere," Oliver said, without taking his head out of his hands. "And neither are you, Myrnin."

"You owe her your fealty."

"I owe nothing to the dead," Oliver said. "And until I see proof of her survival, I will not sacrifice my life, or anyone else's, in a futile attempt at rescue."

Myrnin's face twisted in contempt. "You haven't changed," he said.

"Neither have you, fool," Oliver murmured. "Now shut up. My head aches."

Eve was pulling shots behind the counter, wearing a formal black apron that went below her knees. Claire slid wearily onto a barstool on the other side. "Wow," she said. "Flashback to the good times, huh?"

Eve made a sour face as she thumped a mocha down in front of her friend. "Yeah, don't remind me," she said. "Although I have to say, I missed the Monster."

"The Monster?"

Eve patted the giant, shiny espresso machine beside her affectionately. "Monster, meet Claire. Claire, meet the Monster. He's a sweetie, really, but you have to know his moods."

Claire reached out and patted the machine, too. "Nice to meet you, Monster."

"Hey." Eve caught her wrist when she tried to pull back. "Bruises? What gives?"

Amelie's grip on her really had raised a crop of faint blue smudges on her upper arm, like a primitive tattoo. "Don't freak. I don't have any bite marks or anything."

"I'll freak if I wanna. As long as Michael isn't here, I'm kind of—"

"What, my mom?" Claire snapped, and was instantly sorry. And guilty, for an entirely different reason. "I didn't mean—"

Eve waved it away. "Hey, if you can't spark a 'tude on a day like this, when can you? Your mother's okay, by the way, because I know that's your next question. So far, Bishop's freaks haven't managed to shut down the cell network, so I've been keeping in touch, since nothing's happening here except for some serious caffeine production. Landlines are dead, though. So is the Internet. Radio and TV are both off the air, too."

Claire looked at the clock. Five a.m. Two hours until

dawn, more or less—probably less. It felt like an eternity.

"What are we going to do in the morning?" she asked.

"Good question." Eve wiped down the counter. Claire sipped the sweet, chocolatey comfort of the mocha. "When you think of something, let us know, because right now, I don't think anybody's got a clue."

"You'd be wrong, thankfully," Oliver said. He seemed to come out of nowhere—*God*, didn't Claire hate that!—as he settled on the stool next to her. He seemed almost back to normal now, but very tired. There was a shadow in his eyes that Claire didn't remember seeing before. "There is a plan in place. Amelie's removal from the field of battle is a blow, but not a defeat. We continue as she would want."

"Yeah? You want to tell us?" Eve asked. That earned her a cool stare. "Yeah, I didn't think so. Vampires really aren't all about the sharing, unless it benefits them first."

"I will tell you what you need to know, when you need to know it," Oliver said. "Get me one of the bags from the walk-in refrigerator."

Eve looked down at the top of her apron. "Oh, I'm sorry, where does it say *servant* on here? Because I'm so very not."

For a second, Claire held her breath, because the expression on Oliver's face was murderous, and she saw a red light, like the embers of a banked fire, glowing in the back of his eyes.

Then he blinked and said, simply, "Please, Eve."

Eve hadn't been expecting that. She blinked, stared back at him for a second, then silently nodded and walked away, behind a curtained doorway.

"You're wondering if that hurt," Oliver said, not looking at Claire at all, but staring after Eve. "It did, most assuredly."

"Good," she said. "I hear suffering's good for the soul, or something."

"Then we shall all be right with our God by morning." Oliver swiveled on the stool to look her full in the face. "I should kill you for what you did."

"Staking Myrnin?" She sighed. "I know. I didn't think I had a choice. He'd have bitten my hand off if I'd tried to give him the medicine, and by the time it took effect, me and Hannah would have been dog food, anyway. It seemed like the quickest, quietest way to get him out."

"Even so," Oliver said, his voice low in his throat, "as an Elder, I have the power to sentence you, right now, to death, for attempted murder of a vampire. You do understand?"

Claire held up her hand and pointed to the gold bracelet on her wrist—the symbol of the Founder. Amelie's symbol. "What about this?"

"I would pay reparations," he said. "I imagine I could afford it. Amelie would be tolerably upset with me, for a while, always assuming she is still alive. We'd reach an accommodation. We always do."

Claire didn't say anything else in her defense, just waited. And after a moment, he nodded. "All right," he said. "You were right to take the action you did. You have been right about a good deal that I was unwilling to admit, including the fact that some of us are"—he cast a quick look around, and dropped his voice so low she could make out the word only from the shape his lips gave it—"unwell."

Unwell. Yeah, that was one way to put it. She resisted an urge to roll her eyes. *How about dying? Ever heard the word* pandemic?

Oliver continued without waiting for her response. "Myrnin's mind was . . . very disordered," he said. "I didn't think I could get him back. I wouldn't have, without that dose of medication."

"Does that mean you believe us now?" She meant, *about the vampire disease,* but she couldn't say that out loud. Even the roundabout way they were speaking was dangerous; too many vampire ears with too little to do, and once they knew about the sickness, there was no predicting what they might do. Run, probably. Go off to rampage through the human world, sicken, and die alone, very slowly. It'd take years, maybe decades, but eventually, they'd all fall, one by one. Oliver's case was less advanced than many of the others, but age seemed to slow down the disease's progress; he might last for a long time, losing himself slowly.

Becoming nothing more than a hungry shell.

Oliver said, "It means what it means," and he said it with an impatient edge to it, but Claire wondered if he really did know. "I am talking about Myrnin. Your drugs may not be enough to hold him for long, and that means we will need to take precautions."

Eve emerged from the curtain carrying a plastic blood bag, filled with dark cherry syrup. That was what Claire told herself, anyway. Dark cherry syrup. Eve looked shaken, and she dumped the bag on the counter in front of Oliver like a dead rat. "You've been planning this," she said. "Planning for a siege."

Oliver smiled slowly. "Have I?"

"You've got enough blood in there to feed half the vampires in town for a month, *and* enough of those heat-and-eat meals campers use to feed the rest of us even longer. Medicines, too. Pretty much anything we'd need to hold out here, including generators, batteries, bottled water. . . ."

"Let's say I am cautious," he said. "It's a trait many of us have picked up during our travels." He took the blood bag and motioned for a cup; when Eve set it in front of him, he punctured the bag with a fingernail, very neatly, and squeezed part of the contents into the cup. "Save the rest," he said, and handed it back to Eve, who looked even queasier than before. "Don't look so disgusted. Blood in bags means none taken unwillingly from your veins, after all."

Eve held it at arm's length, opened the smaller refrigerator behind the bar, and put it in an empty spot on the door rack inside. "Ugh," she said. "Why am I behind the bar again?"

"Because you put on the apron."

"Oh, you're just *loving* this, aren't you?"

"Guys," Claire said, drawing both of their stares. "Myrnin. Where are we going to put him?"

Before Oliver could answer, Myrnin pushed through the crowd in the table-and-chairs area of Common Grounds and walked toward them. He *seemed* normal again, or as normal as Myrnin ever got, anyway. He'd begged, borrowed, or outright stolen a long, black velvet coat, and under it he was still wearing the poofy white Pierrot pants from his costume, dark boots, and no shirt. Long, black, glossy hair and decadently shining eyes.

Oliver took in the outfit, and raised a brow. "You look like you escaped from a Victorian brothel," he said. "One that . . . specialized."

In answer, Myrnin skinned up the sleeves of the coat. The wound in his back might have healed—or might be healing, anyway—but the burns on his wrists and hands were still livid red, with an unhealthy silver tint to them. "Not the sort of brothel I'd normally frequent, by choice," he said, "though of course you might be more adventurous, Oliver." Their gazes locked, and Claire resisted the urge to take a step back. She thought, just for a second, that they were going to bare fangs at each other . . . and then Myrnin smiled. "I suppose I should say thank you."

"It would be customary," Oliver agreed.

Myrnin turned to Claire. "Thank you."

Somehow, she guessed that wasn't what Oliver had expected; she certainly hadn't. It was the kind of snub that got most people hurt in Morganville, but then again, she guessed Myrnin wasn't most people, even to Oliver.

Oliver didn't react. If there was a small red glow in the depths of his eyes, it could have been a reflection from the lights.

"Um—for what?" Claire asked.

"I remember what you did." Myrnin shrugged. "It was the right choice at the moment. I couldn't control myself. The pain . . . the pain was extremely difficult to contain."

She cast a nervous glance at his wrists. "How is it now?"

"Tolerable." His tone dismissed any further discussion. "We need to get to a portal and locate Amelie. The closest is at the university. We will need a car, I suppose, and a driver. Some sturdy escorts wouldn't go amiss." Myrnin sounded casual, but utterly certain that his slightest wish would be obeyed, and again, she felt that flare of tension between him and Oliver.

"Perhaps you've missed the announcement," Oliver said. "You're no longer a king, or a prince, or whatever you were before you disappeared into your filthy hole. You're Amelie's exotic pet alchemist, and you don't give me orders. Not in *my* town."

"Your town," Myrnin repeated, staring at him intently. His face had set into pleasant, rigid lines, but those eyes—not pleasant at all. Claire moved herself prudently out of the way. "What a surprise! I thought it was the Founder's town."

Oliver looked around. "Oddly, she seems unavailable, and that makes it my town, little man. So go and sit down. You're not going anywhere. If she's in trouble—which I do not yet believe—and if there's rescuing to be done, we will consider all the risks."

"And the benefits of not acting at all?" Myrnin asked. His voice was wound as tight as a clock spring. "Tell me, Old Ironsides, how you plan to win this campaign. I do hope you don't plan to reenact Drogheda."

Claire had no idea what that meant, but it meant something to Oliver, something bitter and deep, and his whole face twisted for a moment.

"We're not fighting the Irish campaigns, and whatever errors I made once, I'll not be making them again," Oliver said. "And I don't need advice from a blue-faced hedge witch."

"There's the old Puritan spirit!"

Eve slapped the bar hard. "Hey! Whatever musty old prejudices the two of you have rattling around in your heads, *stop*. We're here, twenty-first century, USA, and we've got problems that don't include your ancient history!"

Myrnin blinked, looked at Eve, and smiled. It was his seductive smile, and it came with a lowering of his thick eyelashes. "Sweet lady," he said, "could you get me one of those delicious drinks you prepared for my friend, here?" He gracefully indicated Oliver, who remembered the cup of blood still sitting in front of him, and angrily choked it down. "Perhaps warm the bag a bit in hot water first? It's a bit disgusting, cold."

"Yeah, sure," Eve sighed. "Want a shot of espresso with that?"

Myrnin seemed to be honestly considering it. Claire urgently shook her head *no*. The last thing she—any of them—needed just now was Myrnin on caffeine.

As Eve walked away to prepare Myrnin's drink, Oliver shook himself out of his anger with a physical twitch, took a deep breath, and said, "It's less than two hours to dawn. Even if something has happened to Amelie—which again, I dispute—it's too risky to launch a search just now. If Bishop has Amelie, he'll have her some place that'll hold against an assault in any case. Two hours isn't enough time, and I won't risk our people in the dawn."

Myrnin flicked a glance toward Claire. "Some of those here aren't affected by the dawn."

"Some of them are also highly vulnerable," Oliver said. "I wouldn't send a human out after Bishop. I wouldn't send a human *army* out after Bishop, unless you're planning to deduce his location from the corpses he leaves behind."

For a horrified second, Myrnin actually mulled that over, and then he shook his head. "He'd hide the bodies," he said regretfully. "A useful suggestion, though."

Claire couldn't tell if he was mocking Oliver, or if he really meant it. Oliver couldn't tell, either, from the long, considering look he gave him.

Oliver turned his attention to her. "Tell me everything."

6

In an hour, the blush of dawn was already on the horizon, bringing an eerie blue glow to the night world. Somewhere out there, vampires all over town would be getting ready for it, finding secure places to stay the day—whatever side they were fighting on.

The ones in Common Grounds seemed content to stay on, which made sense; it was kind of a secured location anyway, from what Oliver and Amelie had said before—one of the key places in town to hold if they intended to keep control of Morganville.

But Claire wasn't entirely happy with the way some of those vampires—strangers, mostly, though all from Morganville, according to Eve—seemed to be whispering in the corners. "How do we know they're on our side?" she asked Eve, in a whisper she hoped would escape vampire notice.

No such luck. "You don't," Oliver said, from several feet away. "Nor is that your concern, but I will reassure you in any case. They are all loyal to me, and through me, to Amelie. If any of them 'turn coats,' you may be assured that they'll regret it." He said it in a normal tone of voice, to carry to all parts of the room.

The vampires stopped whispering.

"All right," Oliver said to Claire and Eve. The light of dawn was creeping up like a warning outside the windows. "You understand what I want you to do?"

Eve nodded and gave him a sloppy, insolent kind of salute. "Sir, yes *sir*, General sir!"

"Eve." His patience, what little there was, was worn to the bone. "Repeat my instructions."

Eve didn't like taking orders under the best of circumstances, which these weren't. Claire quickly said, "We take these walkie-talkies to each of the Founder Houses, to the university, and to anybody else on the list. We tell them all strategic orders come through these, not through cell phone or police band."

"Be sure to give them the code," he said. Each one of the tiny little radios had a keypad, like a cell phone, but the difference was that you had to enter the code into it to access the emergency communication channel he'd established. Pretty high tech, but then, Oliver didn't really seem the type to lag much behind on the latest cool stuff. "All right. I'm sending Hannah with you as your escort. I'd send one of my own, but—"

"Dawn, yeah, I know," Eve said. She offered a high five to Hannah, who took it. "Damn, girl, love the Rambo look."

"Rambo was a Green Beret," Hannah said. "Please. We eat those army boys for breakfast."

Which was maybe not such a comfortable thing to say in a room full of maybe-hungry vampires. Claire cleared her throat. "We should—"

Hannah nodded, picked up the backpack (Claire's, now filled with handheld radios instead of books), and handed it to her. "I need both hands free," she said. "Eve's driving. You're the supply master. There's a checklist inside, so you can mark off deliveries as we go."

Myrnin was sitting off to the side, ominously quiet. His eyes still looked sane, but Claire had warned Oliver in the strongest possible terms that he couldn't trust him. Not really.

As if I would, Oliver had said with a snort. *I've known the man for many human lifetimes, and I've never trusted him yet.*

The vampires in the coffee shop had mostly retreated out of the big, front area, into the better-protected, light-proofed interior. Outside of the plate glass windows, there was little to be seen. The fires had gone out, or been extinguished. They'd seen some cars speeding about, mostly official police or fire, but the few figures they'd spotted had been quick and kept to the shadows.

"What are they doing?" Claire asked as she hitched her backpack to a more comfortable position on her shoulder. She didn't really expect Oliver to reply; he wasn't much on the sharing.

He surprised her. "They're consolidating positions," he said. "This is not a war that will be fought in daylight, Claire. Or in the open. We have our positions; they have theirs. They may send patrols of humans they've recruited, but they won't come themselves. Not after dawn."

"Recruited," Hannah repeated. "Don't you mean strong-armed? Most folks just want to be left alone."

"Not necessarily. Morganville is full of humans who don't love us, or the system under which they labor," Oliver replied. "Some will believe Bishop is the answer. Some will act out of fear, to protect their loved ones. He will know how to appeal to them, and how to pressure. He'll find his human cannon fodder."

"Like you've found yours," Hannah said.

They locked stares for a few seconds, and then Oliver inclined his head just a bit. "If you like."

"I don't," she said, "but I'm used to the front lines. You got to know, others won't be."

Claire couldn't tell anything from Oliver's expression. "Perhaps not," he said. "But for now, we can count on our enemies regrouping. We should do the same."

Hannah nodded. "I'm out first, then you, Eve. Have your keys in your hand. Don't hesitate, run like hell for the car, and get it unlocked. I'll get Claire to the passenger side."

Eve nodded, clearly jittery. She took the car keys out of her pocket and held them in her hand, sorting through until she had the right key pointing out.

"One more thing," Hannah said. "You got a flashlight?"

Eve fumbled in her other pocket and came up with a tiny little penlight. When she twisted it, it gave a surprisingly bright glow.

"Good." Hannah nodded. "Before you get in the car, you shine that in the front and backseats. Make sure you can see all the way down to the carpet. I'll cover you from the door."

The three of them moved to the exit, and Hannah put her left hand on the knob.

"Be careful," Oliver said from the back of the room, which was kind of warmly surprising. He spoiled it by continuing, "We need those radios delivered."

Should have known it wasn't personal. Claire resisted the urge to flip him off.

Eve didn't bother to resist hers.

Then Hannah was swinging open the door and stepping outside. She didn't do it like in the movies; no drama, she just stepped right out, turned in a slow half circle as she scanned the street with the paintball gun held at rest. She finally motioned for Eve. Eve darted out and headed around the hood of the big, black car. Claire saw the glow of her penlight as she checked the inside, and then Eve was in the driver's seat and the car growled to a start, and Hannah pushed her toward the passenger door.

Behind them, the Common Grounds door slammed shut and locked. When she looked back, Claire saw that they were pulling down some kind of steel shutters inside the glass.

Locking up for dawn.

Claire and Hannah made it to the car without any problems. Even so, Claire was breathing hard, her heart racing.

"You okay?" Eve asked her. Claire nodded, still gasping. "Yeah, I know. Terror Aerobics. Just wait until they get it at the gym. It'll be bigger than Pilates."

Claire choked on her fear, laughed, and felt better.

"That's my girl. Locks," Eve said. "Also, seat belts, please. We may be making some sudden stops along the way. Don't want anybody saying hello to Mr. Windshield at speed."

The drive through predawn Morganville was eerie. It was very . . . quiet. They'd mapped out a route, planning to avoid the most dangerous areas, but they almost had to divert immediately, because of a couple of cars parked in the middle of the street.

The doors were hanging open, interior lights were still shining.

Eve slowed down and crawled past on the right side, two wheels up on the curb. "See anything?" she asked anxiously. "Any bodies or anything?"

The cars were completely empty. They were still running, and the keys were in the ignition. One strange thing nagged at Claire, but she couldn't think what it was. . . .

"Those are vampire cars," Hannah said. "Why would they leave them here like that?" Oh. That was the odd thing. The tinting on the windows.

"They needed to pee?" Eve asked. "When you've gotta go . . ."

Hannah said nothing. She was watching out the windows with even more focus than before.

"Yeah, that is weird," Eve said more quietly. "Maybe they went to help somebody." Or hunt somebody. Claire shivered.

They made their first radio delivery to one of the Founder Houses; Claire didn't know the people who answered the door, but Eve did, of course. She quickly explained about the radio and the code, and they were back in the car and rolling in about two minutes flat. "Outstanding," Hannah said. "You girls could give some of my buddies in the marines a run for their money."

"Hey, you know how it is, Hannah: living in Morganville really is combat training." Eve and Hannah awkwardly slapped palms—awkwardly, because Eve kept facing front, and Hannah didn't turn away from her post at the car's back window. She had the window rolled down halfway, and the paintball gun at the ready, but so far she hadn't fired a single shot.

"More cars," Claire said softly. "You see?"

It wasn't just a couple of cars, it was a bunch of them, scattered on both sides of the street now, engines running, lights on, doors open.

Empty.

They cruised past slowly, and Claire took note of the heavy tinting on the windows. They were all the same type of car, the same type Michael had been issued on his official conversion to vampire.

"What the hell is going on?" Eve asked. She sounded tense and anxious, and Claire couldn't blame her. She felt pretty tense herself. "This close to dawn, they wouldn't be doing this. They shouldn't even be outside. He said both sides would regroup, but this looks like some kind of full-on panic."

Claire had to agree, but she also had no explanation. She dug one of the radios out of her backpack, typed in the code that Oliver had given her, and pressed the TALK button. "Oliver? Come in."

After a short delay, his voice came back. "Go."

"Something strange is happening. We're seeing lots of vampire cars, but they're all abandoned. Empty. Still running." Static on the other end. "Oliver?"

"Keep me informed," he finally said. "Count the number of cars. Make a list of license numbers, if you can."

"Er—anything else? Should we come back?"

"No. Deliver the radios."

That was it. Claire tried again, but he'd shut off or he was ignoring her. She pressed the RESET button to scramble the code, and looked at Eve, who shrugged. They pulled to a halt in front of the second Founder House. "Let's just get it done," Eve said. "Let the vamps worry about the vamps."

It seemed reasonable, but Claire was afraid that somehow . . . it wasn't.

Three of the Founder Houses were piles of smoking wood and ash, and the Morganville Fire Department was still pouring water on one of them. Eve cruised by, but didn't stop. The horizon was getting lighter and lighter, and they still had a couple of stops to make.

"You okay back there?" Eve asked Hannah, as they turned another corner, heading into an area Claire actually recognized.

"Fine," Hannah said. "We going to the Day House?"

"Yeah, next on my list."

"Good. I want to talk to Cousin Lisa."

Eve pulled up outside of the big Founder House; it was lit up in every window, a stark contrast to its dark, shuttered neighboring residences. As she put the car in park, the front door opened and spilled a wedge of lemon-colored light across the immaculately kept front porch. Gramma Day's rocker was empty, nodding in the slight wind.

The person at the door was Lisa Day—tall, strong, with more than a slight resemblance to Hannah. She watched them get out of the car. Upstairs windows opened, and gun barrels came out.

"They're all right," she called, but she didn't step outside. "Claire, right? And Eve? Hey, Hannah."

"Hey." Hannah nodded. "Let's get in. I don't like this quiet out here."

As soon as they were in the front door, in a familiar-looking hallway, Lisa slammed down locks and bolts, including a recently installed iron bar that slotted into place on either side of the frame. Hannah watched this with bemused approval. "You knew this was coming?" she asked.

"I figured it'd come sooner or later," Lisa said. "Had the hardware in the basement. All we had to do was put it in. Gramma didn't like it, but I did it, anyway. She keeps yelling about me putting holes in the wood."

"Yeah, that's Gramma." Hannah grinned. "God forbid we should mess up her house while the war's going on."

"Speaking of that," Lisa said, "y'all need to stay here, if you want to stay safe."

Eve exchanged a quick glance with Claire. "Yeah, well, we can't, really. But thanks."

"You sure?" Lisa's eyes were very bright, very focused. "Because we're thinking maybe these vamps will kill each other off this time, and maybe we should all stick together. All the humans. Never mind the bracelets and the contracts."

Eve blinked. "Seriously? Just let them fight it out on their own?"

"Why not? What's it to us, anyway, who wins?" Lisa's smile was bitter and brief. "We get screwed no matter what. Maybe it's time to put a human in charge of this town, and let the vampires find someplace else to live."

Dangerous, Claire thought. Really dangerous. Hannah stared at her cousin, her expression tight and controlled, and then nodded. "Okay," she said. "You do what you want, Lisa, but you be careful, all right?"

"We're being real damn careful," Lisa said. "You'll see."

They came to the end of the hallway, where the area opened up into the big living room, and Eve and Claire both stopped cold.

"Oh, *shit*," Eve muttered.

The humans were all armed—guns, knives, stakes, blunt objects. The vampires who'd been assigned to

guard the house were all sitting tied to chairs with so
many turns of rope it reminded Claire of hangman's
loops. She supposed if you were going to restrain
vamps, it made sense, but—

"What the hell are you doing?" Eve blurted. At
least some of the vampires sitting there, tied and
gagged, were ones who'd been at Michael's house, or
who'd fought on Amelie's side at the banquet. Some
of them were struggling, but most seemed quiet.

Some looked *unconscious*.

"They're not hurt," Lisa said. "I just want 'em out
of the way, in case things go bad."

"You're making one hell of a move, Lisa," Hannah
said. "I hope you know what the hell you're about."

"I'm about protecting my own. You ought to be,
too."

Hannah nodded slowly. "Let's go," she said to
Claire and Eve.

"What about—"

"No," Hannah said. "No radio. Not here."

Lisa moved into their path, a shotgun cradled in her
arms. "Going so soon?"

Claire forgot to breathe. There was a feeling here,
a darkness in the air. The vampires, those who were
still awake, were staring at them. Expecting rescue,
maybe?

"You don't want to do this," Hannah said. "We're
not your enemies."

"You're standing with the vamps, aren't you?"

There it was, out in the open. Claire swallowed hard.
"We're trying to get everybody out of this alive," she
said. "Humans and vampires."

Lisa didn't look away from her cousin's face. "Not
going to happen," she said. "So you'd better pick a
side."

Hannah stepped right up into her face. After a cold
second, Lisa moved aside. "Already have," Hannah
said. She jerked her head at Claire and Eve. "Let's
move."

Outside in the car, they all sat in silence for a few seconds. Hannah's face was grim and closed off, not inviting any conversation.

Eve finally said, "You'd better tell Oliver. He needs to know about this."

Claire plugged in the code and tried. "Oliver, come in. Oliver, it's Claire. I have an update. Oliver!"

Static hissed. There was no response.

"Maybe he's ignoring you," Eve said. "He seemed pretty annoyed before."

"You try." Claire handed it over, but it was no use. Oliver wasn't responding. They tried calling for anyone at Common Grounds instead, and got another voice, one Claire didn't recognize.

"Hello?"

Eve squeezed her eyes shut in relief. "Excellent. Who's this?"

"Quentin Barnes."

"Tin-Tin! Hey man, how are you?"

"Ah—good, I guess." Tin-Tin, whoever he was, sounded nervous. "Oliver's kind of busy right now. He's trying to keep some people from taking off."

"Taking off?" Eve's eyes widened. "What do you mean?"

"Some of the vamps, they're just trying to leave. It's too close to dawn. He's had to lock some of them up."

Things were getting weird all over. Eve keyed the mike and said, "There's trouble at the Day House. Lisa's tied up the vamps. She's going to sit this thing out. I think—I think maybe she's working with some other people, trying to put together a third side. All humans."

"Dude," Tin-Tin sighed, "that's just what we need, getting the vampire slayers all in the mix. Okay, I'll tell Oliver. Anything else?"

"More empty vampire cars. You think they're like those guys who were trying to leave? Maybe, I don't know, getting drawn off somewhere?"

"Probably. Look, just watch yourself, okay?"

"Will do. Eve out."

Hannah stirred in the back. "Let's move out to the next location."

"I'm sorry," Claire said. "I know they're your family and all."

"Lisa always was preaching about how we could take the town if we stuck together. Maybe she's thinking it's the right time to make a move." Hannah shook her head. "She's an idiot. All she's going to do is get people killed."

Claire was no general, but she knew that fighting a war on two fronts and dividing their forces wasn't a great idea. "We have to find Amelie."

"Wherever she's gotten herself off to," Eve snorted. "If she's even still—"

"Don't," Claire whispered. She restlessly rubbed the gold bracelet on her wrist until it dug into her skin. "We need her."

More than ever, she was guessing.

By the time they'd dropped off the next to last radio, at their own home, which was currently inhabited by a bunch of freaked-out humans and a few vampires who hadn't yet felt whatever was pulling some of them off, the dawn was starting to really set in. The horizon was Caribbean blue, with touches of gold and red just flaring up like footlights at a show. Claire delivered the radio, the code, and a warning to the humans and vampires alike. "You have to watch the vamps," she pleaded. "Don't let them leave. Not in the daylight."

Monica Morrell, who was clutching the walkie-talkie in her red-taloned fingers, frowned at her. "How are we supposed to do that, freak? Give them a written warning and scold them really hard? Come on!"

"If you let them go, they may not get wherever it is they're being called before sunrise," Hannah said. She shrugged, a fluid flow that emphasized her muscles, and smiled. "Hey, no skin off my nose or anything, but we may need 'em later. And you could get blamed for not stepping up."

Monica kept on frowning, but she didn't seem inclined to argue with Hannah. Nobody did, Claire noticed. The former marine had an air about her, a confidence that somehow didn't come off at all like arrogance.

"Great," Monica finally said. "Wonderful. Like I needed another problem. By the way, Claire, your house really sucks ass. I hate it here."

It was Claire's turn to smile this time. "It probably hates you right back. I'm sure you'll figure it out," she said. "You're a natural leader, right?"

"Oh, bite it. Someday, your boyfriend won't be around to—" Monica widened her eyes. "Oh, snap! He's *isn't* around, is he? Won't be back, ever. Remind me to send flowers for the funeral."

Eve grabbed the back of Claire's shirt. "Whoa, Mini-Me, chill out. We've got to get moving. Much as I'd like to see the cage match, we're kind of on a schedule."

The hot crimson haze disappeared from Claire's eyes, and she took in a breath and nodded. Her muscles were aching. She realized she'd managed to clench just about every muscle, iron-hard, and tried to relax. Her hands twinged when she stretched them out of fists.

"See you soon," Monica said, and shut the door on them. "Wait, probably not, loser. And your clothes are pathetic, by the way!"

That last part came muffled, but clear—as clear as the sound of the locks snapping into place.

"Let's go," Hannah said, and herded them off the porch and down the walk toward the white picket fence.

Walking on the street, heading vaguely north, was a vampire. "Oh, crap," Eve said, alarmed, but the vamp didn't seem to care about them, or even know they were there. He was wearing a police uniform, and Claire remembered him; he'd been riding with Richard Morrell, from time to time. Didn't seem like a bad guy, apart from the whole vampire thing. "That's Officer O'Malley. Hey! Hey, Officer! Wait up!"

He ignored them and kept walking.

Claire looked east. The sun's golden glow was heating up the sky, fast. It wasn't over the horizon yet, but it would be in a matter of seconds, minutes at most. "We've got to get him," she said. "Get him inside somewhere."

"And do what, babysit him the rest of the day? O'Malley's not like Myrnin," Eve said. "You can't stake him. He's not that old. Seventy, eighty, something like that. He's only a little older than Sam."

"We could run him over," Hannah said. "It wouldn't kill him."

Eve sent her a wide-eyed look. "Excuse me? With my *car*?"

"You're asking for something nonlethal. That's all I've got right now. The three of us aren't any kind of match for a vampire who wants to get somewhere, if he fights us."

Claire took off running toward the vampire, ignoring their shouts. She looked back. Hannah was after her, and gaining.

She still got to Officer O'Malley first, and skidded into his path.

He paused for a second, his green eyes focusing on her, and then he reached out and moved her aside. Gently, but firmly.

And he kept on walking.

"You have to get inside!" Claire yelled, and got in front of him again. "Sir, you have to! Right now! Please!"

He moved her again, this time without as much care. He didn't say a word.

"Oh, God," Hannah said. "Too late."

The sun came up in a fiery burst, and the first rays

of sunlight hit the parked cars, Eve's standing figure, the houses . . . and Officer O'Malley's back.

"Get a blanket!" Claire screamed. She could see the smoke curling off him, like morning mist. "Do something!"

Eve ran to get something from the car. Hannah grabbed Claire and pulled her out of his way.

Officer O'Malley kept walking. The sun kept rising, brighter and brighter, and within three or four steps, the smoke rising up from him turned to flames.

In ten more steps, he fell down.

Eve ran up breathlessly, a blanket clutched in both hands. "Help me get it over him!"

They threw the fabric over Officer O'Malley, but instead of smothering the flames, it just caught fire, too.

Hannah pulled Claire back as she tried to pat out the flames. "Don't," she said. "It's too late."

Claire turned toward Hannah in a raw fury, struggling to get free. "We can still—"

"No, we can't," Hannah said. "There's not a damn thing we can do for him. He's dying, Claire. You tried your best, but he's dying. And he's not going to take our help. Look, he's still trying to crawl. He's not stopping."

She was right, but it hurt, and in the end, Claire wrapped her arms around Hannah for comfort and turned away.

When she finally looked back, Officer O'Malley was a pile of ash and smoke and burned blanket.

"Michael," Claire whispered. She looked at the sun. "We have to find Michael!"

Hannah went very still for a second, and then nodded. "Let's go."

7

The gates of the university were shut, locked, and there were paramilitary-style men posted at the gates, all in black. Armed. Eve coasted the big car slowly up to them and rolled down the window.

"Delivery for Michael Glass," she called. "Or Richard Morrell."

The guard who leaned in was huge, tough, and intimidating—until he saw Hannah in the backseat, and then he grinned like a kid with a new puppy. "Hannah Montana!"

She looked deeply pained. "Don't *ever* call me that again, Jessup, or I *will* gut you."

"Get out and make me stop, Smiley. Yeah, I heard you were back. How were the marines?"

"Better than the damn rangers."

"Don't you just wish?" He lost the smile and got serious again. "Sorry, H, orders are orders. Who sent you? Who's with you?"

"Oliver sent me. You probably know Eve Rosser—that's Claire Danvers."

"Really? Huh. Thought she'd be bigger. Hey, Eve. Sorry, didn't recognize you right off. Long time, no see." Jessup nodded to the other guard, who slung his rifle and pressed in a key code at the panel on the stone fence. The big iron gates slowly parted. "You be careful, Hannah. This town's the Af-Pak border all over again right now."

Inside, except for the guards patrolling the fence, Texas Prairie University seemed eerily normal. The birds sang to the rising sun, and there were students out—*students!*—heading to class as if there were nothing wrong at all. They were chatting, laughing, running to make the cross-campus early-morning bell.

"What the *hell*?" Eve said. Claire was glad she wasn't the only one freaked out by it. "I know they had orders to keep things low profile, but damn, this is ridiculous. Where's the dean's office?"

Claire pointed. Eve steered the car around the winding curves, past dorms and lecture halls, and pulled it to a stop on the nearly deserted lot in front of the Administration Building. There were two police cruisers there, and a bunch of black Jeeps. Not a lot of civilian cars in the lot.

As they walked up the steps to the building, Claire realized there were two more guards outside of the main door. Hannah didn't know these guys, but she repeated their names and credentials, and after a brief, impersonal search, they were allowed inside.

The last time Claire had been here she'd been adding and dropping classes, and the building had been full of grumpy bureaucrats and anxious students, all moving at a hectic pace. Now it was very quiet. A few people were at their desks, but there were no students Claire could see, and the TPU employees looked either bored or nervous. Most of the activity seemed centered down the carpeted hall, which was hung with formal portraits of the former university deans and notables.

One or two of the former deans, Claire was just now realizing, might have been vampires, from the pallor of their skins. Or maybe they were just old white guys. Hard to say.

At the end of the hallway they found not a guard, but a secretary—just as tough as any of the armed men outside, though. She sat behind an expensive-looking antique desk that had not a speck of dust on it, and nothing else except a piece of paper centered exactly in the middle, a pen at right angles to it, and a fancy, black multiline telephone. No computer that Claire could spot—no, there it was, hidden away in a roll-out credenza to the side.

The room was lushly carpeted, so much so that Claire's feet sank into the depth at least an inch; it was like walking on foam. Solid, dark wood paneling. Paintings and dim lights. The windows were covered with fancy velvet curtains, and there was music playing—classical, of course. Claire couldn't imagine anybody would ever switch the station to rock. Not here.

"I'm Ms. Nance," the woman said, and stood to offer her hand to each of them in turn; she didn't even hesitate with Eve, who intimidated most people. She was a tall, thin, gray woman dressed in a tailored gray suit with a lighter gray blouse under the jacket. Gray hair curled into exact waves. Claire couldn't see her shoes, but she bet they were fashionable, gray, and yet somehow sensible. "I'm the secretary to Dean Wallace. Do you have an appointment?"

Eve said, "I need to see Michael."

"I'm sorry? I don't think I know that person."

Eve's expression froze, and Claire could see the horrible dread in her eyes.

Hannah, seeing it too, said, "Let's cut the crap, Ms. Nance. Where's Michael Glass?"

Ms. Nance's eyes narrowed. They were pale blue, not as pale as Amelie's, but kind of faded, like jeans left in the sun. "Mr. Glass is in conference with the dean," she said. "I'm afraid you'll have to—"

The door at the far end of her office opened, and Michael came out. Claire's heart practically melted with relief. *He's okay. Michael's okay.*

Except that he closed the door and walked straight past them, a man on a mission.

He walked right past Eve, who stood there flat-footed, mouth open, fear dawning in her expression.

"Michael!" Claire yelped. He didn't even pause. "We have to stop him!"

"Great," Hannah said, and the three of them took off in pursuit.

It helped that Michael wasn't actually *running*, just moving with a purpose. Claire and Eve edged by him in the hall and blocked his path.

His blue eyes were wide-open, but he just didn't *see* them. He sensed an obstacle, at least, and paused.

"Michael," Claire said. *Dammit, why couldn't I have tranquilizers? Why?* "Michael, you can't go out there. It's already morning. You'll die."

"He's not listening," Hannah said. And she was right; he wasn't. He tried to push between them, but Eve put a hand in the center of his chest and held him back.

"Michael? It's me. You know me, don't you? Please?"

He stared at her with utterly blank eyes, and then shoved her out of his way. Hard.

Hannah sent Claire a quick, commanding look. "Get help. *Now*. I'll try to hold him."

Claire hesitated, but Hannah was without any doubt better equipped to handle a potentially hostile Michael than she was. She turned and ran, past startled desk jockeys and coffee-bearing civil servants, and slid to a stop in front of one of the black-uniformed soldiers. "Richard Morrell," she blurted. "I need him. Right *now*."

The soldier didn't hesitate. He grabbed the radio clipped to his shoulder and said, "Admin to Morrell."

"Morrell, go."

The soldier unclipped the radio and silently offered it to Claire. She took it—it was heavier than the walkie-talkies—and pressed the button to talk. "Richard? It's Claire. We have a big problem. We need to stop Michael and anybody else . . ." How could she say *vampire* without actually saying it? "Anybody else with a sun allergy from going outside."

"Why the hell would they be—"

"I don't know! They just *are*!" The image of Officer O'Malley on fire leaped into her mind, and she caught her breath on a sob. "Help us. They're going out in the sun."

"Give the radio back," he ordered. She handed it to the black-uniformed man. "I need you to go with this girl and help her. No questions."

"Yes sir." He clicked off the radio and looked down at Claire. "After you."

She led the way back toward the hallway. As they reached it, there was a crash of glass, and Hannah came flying out to land flat on her back, blinking.

Michael walked over her. Eve was hauling on his arm, trying to hold him back, but he shook her off.

"We can't let him get outside!" Claire said. She tried to grab him, but it was like grabbing a freight train. She'd forgotten how strong he was now.

"Out of the way," the soldier said, and pulled a handgun from a holster at his side.

"No, don't—"

The bureaucrats scattered, hiding under their desks, dropping their coffee to hug the carpet.

The soldier sighted on Michael's chest, and fired three times in quick succession. Instead of the loud bangs Claire had been expecting, there were soft compressed-air coughs.

And three darts feathered Michael's chest, clustered above his heart.

He *still* took three steps toward the soldier before collapsing in slow motion to his knees, and then onto his face.

"All clear," the soldier said. He took hold of Michael, turned him over, and yanked out the darts. "He'll be under for about an hour, probably no longer than that. Let's get him to the dean's office."

Hannah wiped a trickle of blood from her mouth, coughed, and rolled to her feet. She and Eve helped Claire grab Michael's shoulders and feet, and they carried him down the hallway, past paintings that were going to need some major repair and reframing, past splintered panels and broken glass, into Ms. Nance's office.

Ms. Nance took one look at them and moved smartly to the door marked with a discreet brass plaque that said DEAN WALLACE. She rapped and opened the door for them to carry Michael through.

Dean Wallace was a woman, which was kind of a surprise to Claire. She'd been expecting a pudgy, middle-aged man; *this* Dean Wallace was tall, graceful, thin, and a whole lot younger than Claire would have imagined. She had straight brown hair worn long around her shoulders, and a simple black suit that was almost the negative image of Ms. Nance's, only somehow less formal. It looked . . . lived in.

Dean Wallace's lips parted, but she didn't ask a question. She checked herself, then nodded at the leather couch on the far side of the room, across from her massive desk. "Right, put him there." She had a British accent, too. Definitely not a Texas girl. "What happened?"

"Whatever it is, it's happening all over," Hannah said as they arranged Michael's unconscious body on the sofa. "They're just taking off. It's like they don't even know or care the sun's up. Some kind of homing signal just gets switched on."

Dean Wallace thought for a second, then pressed a button on her desk. "Ms. Nance? I need a bulletin to go out through the emergency communication system. All vampires on campus should be immediately restrained or tranquilized. No exceptions. This is priority one." She frowned as she got the acknowledgment, and looked up at their little group. "Michael seemed very rational, and there was no warning this would happen. I just thought he had somewhere to go. He didn't seem odd, at least at first."

"How many other vampires on campus?" Hannah asked.

"Some professors of course, but they're mostly not here at the moment, since they teach at night. No students, obviously. Apart from the ones Michael and Richard brought in, we have perhaps five in total on the grounds. More were here earlier, but they headed for shelter before sunrise, off campus." Dean Wallace seemed calm, even in the face of all this. "You're Claire Danvers?"

"Yes ma'am," she said, and shook the hand Dean Wallace offered her.

"I had a talk with your Patron recently regarding your progress. Despite your—challenges, you have done excellent course work."

It was stupid to feel pleased about that, but Claire couldn't help it. She felt herself blush, and shook her head. "I don't think that matters very much right now."

"On the contrary, it matters a great deal, I believe."

Eve settled herself down next to the sofa, holding Michael's limp hand. She looked shattered. Hannah leaned against the wall and nodded to the soldier as he exited the office. "So," she said, "want to explain to me how you can have half the U.S. Army walking the perimeter and not have massive student panic?"

"We've told all students and their parents that the university is cooperating in a government emergency drill, and of course that all weapons are nonlethal. Which is quite true, so far as it goes. The issue of keeping students on campus is a bit trickier, but we've managed so far by linking it to the emergency drills. Can't go on for long, though. The local kids are already well informed, and it's only a matter of time before the out-of-town students begin to realize that we're having them on when they can't get word out to their friends and relatives. We're filtering all Internet and phone access, of course." Dean Wallace shook her head. "But that's my problem, not yours, and yours is much more pressing. We can't knock out every vampire in town, and we can't *keep* them knocked out in any case."

"Not enough happy juice in the world," Hannah agreed. "We need to either stop this at its source, or get the heck out of their way."

There was a soft knock on the door, and Ms. Nance stepped in. "Richard Morrell," she announced, and moved aside for him.

Claire stared. Monica's brother looked like about fifty miles of bad road—exhausted, red-eyed, pale, running on caffeine and adrenaline. Just like the rest of them, she supposed. As Ms. Nance quietly closed the door behind him, Richard strode forward, staring at Michael's limp body. "Is he out?" His voice sounded rough, too, as if he'd been yelling. A *lot*.

"Sleeping the sleep of the just," Hannah said. "Or the just drugged, anyway. Claire. Radio."

Oh. She'd forgotten about the backpack still slung over her shoulder. She quickly took out the last radio and handed it over, explaining what it was for. Richard nodded.

"I think this calls for a strategy meeting," he said, and pulled up a chair next to the couch. Hannah and Claire took seats as well, but Eve stayed where she was, by Michael, as if she didn't want to leave him even for a moment.

Dean Wallace sat behind her desk, fingers steepled, watching with interested calm.

"I put in the code, right?" He was already doing it, so Claire just nodded. A signal bleeped to show he was logged on the network. "Richard Morrell, University, checking in."

After a few seconds, a voice answered. "Check, Richard, you're the last station to report. Stand by for a bulletin."

There were a few clicks, and then another voice came over the radio.

This is Oliver. I am broadcasting to all on the network with emergency orders. Restrain every vampire allied to us that you can find, by whatever means necessary. Locked rooms, chains, tranquilizers, cells, use what you have. Until we know how and why this is happening, we must take every precaution during the day. It seems that some of us have resistance to the call, and others have immunity, but this could change at any time. Be on your guard. From this point forward, we will conduct hourly calls, and each location will report status. University station, report.

Richard clicked the TALK button. "Michael Glass and all the other vampires in our group are being restrained. We've got student containment here, but it won't last. We'll have to open the gates no later than tomorrow morning, if we can keep it together until then. Even with the phone and Internet blackout, somebody's going to get word out."

"We're following the plan," Oliver said. "We're taking the cell towers down in ten minutes, until further notice. Phone lines are already cut. The only communication from this point forward will be strategic, using the radios. What else do you need?"

"Whip and a chair? Nothing. We're fine here for now. I don't think anybody will try a daylight assault, not with as many guards as we have here." Richard hesitated, then keyed the mike again. "Oliver, I've been hearing things. I think there are some factions out there forming. Human factions. Could complicate things."

Oliver was silent for a moment, then said, "Yes, I understand. We'll deal with that as it arises."

Oliver moved on to the next station on his list, which was the Glass House. Monica reported in, which was annoying. Claire resisted the urge to grind her teeth. It was a quick summary, at least, and as more Founder Houses reported in, the situation seemed the same: some vampires were responding to the homing signal, and some weren't. At least, not yet.

Richard Morrell was staring thoughtfully into the distance, and finally, when all the reports were finished, he clicked the button again. "Oliver, it's Richard. What happens if *you* start going zombie on us?"

"I won't," Oliver said.

"If you do. Humor me. Who takes over?"

Oliver obviously didn't want to think about this, and Claire could hear the barely suppressed fury in his voice when he replied. "You do," he said. "I don't care how you organize it. If we have to hand the defense of Morganville over to mere humans, we've already lost. Oliver signing out. Next check-in, one hour from now."

The walkie-talkie clicked off.

"That went well," Dean Wallace observed. "He's named you heir apparent to the Apocalypse. Congratulations."

"Yeah, it's one hell of a field promotion." Richard stood up. "Let's find a place for Michael."

"We have some storage areas in the basement—steel doors, no windows. That's where they'll take the others."

"That'll do for now. I want to move him to the jail as soon as we can, centralize the containment."

Claire looked at Eve, and then at Michael's sleeping face, and thought about him alone in a cell—because what else could you call it? Locked away like Myrnin.

Myrnin. She wondered if he'd felt this weird pull, too, and if he had, whether or not they'd been able to stop him from taking off. Probably not, if he'd been determined to go running off. Myrnin was one of those unstoppable forces, and unless he met an immovable object . . .

She sighed and helped carry Michael down the hall, past the stunned bureaucrats, to his temporary holding cell.

Life went on, weirdly enough—human life, anyway. People began to venture out, clean up the streets, retrieve things from burned and trashed houses. The police began to establish order again.

But there were things happening. People gathering in groups on street corners. Talking. Arguing.

Claire didn't like what she saw, and she could tell that Hannah and Eve didn't, either.

Hours passed. They cruised around for a while, and passed bulletins back to Oliver on the groups they saw. The largest one was almost a hundred people, forming up in the park. Some guy Claire didn't know had a loudspeaker.

"Sal Manetti," Hannah said. "Always was a trouble-maker. I think he was one of Captain Obvious's guys for a while, but they had a falling-out. Sal wanted a lot more killing and a lot less talking."

That wasn't good. It really wasn't good how many people were out there listening to him.

Eve went back to Common Grounds to report in, and that was just when things started to go wrong.

Hannah was driving Claire back home, after dropping off a trunk full of blood bags from the university storage vaults, when the radio Claire had in her pocket began to chime for attention. She logged in with the code. As soon as she did, a blast of noise tumbled out of the speaker.

She thought she heard something about Oliver, but she wasn't sure. Her shouted questions weren't answered. It was as if someone had pressed the button by accident, in the middle of a fight, and everybody was too busy to answer.

Then the broadcast went dead.

Claire exchanged a look with Hannah. "Better—"

"Go to Common Grounds? Yeah. Copy that."

When they arrived, the first thing Claire saw was the broken glass. The shutters were up, and two front windows had been shattered out, not in; there were sprays of broken pieces all the way to the curb.

It seemed very, very quiet.

"Eve?" Claire blurted, and bailed before Hannah could tell her to stay put. She hit the front door of the coffee shop at a run, but it didn't open, and she banged into it hard enough to bruise.

Locked.

"Will you *wait*?" Hannah snapped, and grabbed her arm as she tried to duck in through one of the broken windows. "You're going to get yourself cut. Hang on."

She used the paintball gun she carried to break out some of the hanging sharp edges, and before Claire could dart ahead, she blocked the path and stepped over the low wooden sill. Claire followed. Hannah didn't try to stop her, probably because she knew better.

"Oh man," Hannah said. As Claire climbed in after her, she saw that most of the tables and chairs were overturned or shoved out of place. Broken crockery littered the floor.

And people were down, lying motionless among the wreckage. Hannah went from one to the other, quickly assessing their conditions. There were five down that Claire could see. Two of them made Hannah shake her head in regret; the other three were still alive, though wounded.

There were no vampires in the coffee bar, and there was no sign of Eve.

Claire ducked behind the curtain. More signs of a struggle. Nobody left behind, alive or dead. She sucked in a deep breath and opened up the giant commercial refrigerator.

It was full of blood bags, but no bodies.

"Anything?" Hannah asked at the curtain.

"Nobody here," Claire said. "They left the blood, though."

"Huh. Weird. You'd think they'd need that more than anything. Why attack the place if you're not taking the good stuff?" Hannah stared out into the coffee shop, her expression blank and distant. "Glass is broken out, not in. No sign anybody got in the doors, either front or back. I don't think anybody attacked from the outside, Claire."

With a black, heavy feeling gathering in her stomach, Claire swung the refrigerator door shut. "You think the vampires fought to get *out.*"

"Yeah. Yeah, I do."

"Oliver, too."

"Oliver, Myrnin, all of them. Whatever bat signal was calling them got turned up to eleven, I think."

"Then where's Eve?" Claire asked.

Hannah shook her head. "We don't know anything. It's all guesswork. Let's get some boots on the ground and figure this thing out." She continued to stare outside. "If they went out there, most of them could make it for a while in the sun, but they'd be hurt. Some couldn't make it far at all."

Some, like the policeman Claire had seen burn up in front of her, would already be gone. "You think it's Mr. Bishop?" she asked, in a very small voice.

"I hope so."

Claire blinked. "Why?"

"Because if it's not, that's got to be a whole lot worse."

8

Three hours later, they didn't know much more, except that nothing they tried to do to keep the vampires from leaving seemed to work, apart from tranquilizing them and locking them up in sturdy cells. Tracking those who did leave wasn't much good, either. Claire and Hannah ended up at the Glass House, which seemed like the best place to gather—central to most things, and close to City Hall in an emergency.

Richard Morrell arrived, along with a few others, and set up shop in the kitchen. Claire was trying to figure out what to do to feed everybody, when there was another knock at the door.

It was Gramma Day. The old woman, straight-backed and proud, leaned on her cane and stared at Claire from age-faded eyes. "I ain't staying with my daughter," she said. "I don't want any part of that."

Claire quickly moved aside to let her in, and the old lady shuffled inside. As Claire locked the door behind her, she asked, "How did you get here?"

"Walked," Gramma said. "I know how to use my feet just fine. Nobody bothered me." Nobody would dare, Claire thought. "Young Mr. Richard! Are you in here?"

"Ma'am?" Richard Morrell came out of the kitchen, looking very much younger than Claire had ever seen him. Gramma Day had that effect on people. "What are you doing here?"

"My fool daughter's off her head," Gramma said. "I'm not having any of it. Move out of the way, boy. I'm making you some lunch." And she tapped her cane right past him, into the kitchen, and clucked and fretted over the state of the kitchen while Claire stood by, caught between giggles and horror. She was just a pair of hands, getting ordered around, but at the end of it there was a plate full of sandwiches and a big jug of iced tea, and everybody was seated around the kitchen table, except for Gramma, who'd gone off into the other room to rest. Claire had hesitantly taken a chair, at Richard's nod. Detectives Joe Hess and Travis Lowe were also present, and they were gratefully scarfing down food and drink. Claire felt exhausted, but they looked a whole lot worse. Tall, thin Joe Hess had his left arm in a sling—broken, apparently, from the brace on it—and both he and his rounder, heavier partner had cuts and bruises to prove they'd been in a fight or two.

"So," Hess said, "any word on where the vampires are heading when they take off?"

"Not so far," Richard said. "Once we started tracking them, we could keep up only for a while, and then they lost us."

"Aren't they hurt by the sun?" Claire asked. "I mean—"

"They start smoking, not in the Marlboro way, and then they start crisping," Travis Lowe said around a mouthful of turkey and Swiss. "The older ones, they can handle it okay, and anyway, they're not just charging out there anymore. They're putting on hats and coats and blankets. I saw one wrapped up in a Sponge-Bob rug from some kid's bedroom, if you can believe that. It's the younger vamps that are in trouble. Some of them won't make it to the shade if they're not careful."

Claire thought about Michael, and her stomach lurched. Before she even formed the question, Richard saw her expression and shook his head. "Michael's okay," he said. "Saw to it myself. He's got himself a nice, secure jail cell, along with the other vampires we could catch before it was too late. He's not as strong as some of the others. He can't bend steel with his bare hands. Yet, anyway."

"Any word on—" Claire was wearing out the question, and Richard didn't even let her finish it.

"No sign of Eve," he said. "No word from her. I'd try to put a GPS track on her phone, but we'd have to bring the cell network up, and that's too dangerous right now. I've asked the guys on the street to keep an eye out for her, but we've got a lot of things going on, Claire."

"I know. But—" She couldn't put it into words, exactly. She just knew that somewhere, somehow, Eve was in trouble, and they needed to find her.

"So," Joe Hess said, and stood up to look at a blown-up map of Morganville taped to the wall. "This still accurate?" The map was covered in colored dots: blue for locations held by those loyal to Amelie; red for those loyal to Bishop; black for those burned or otherwise put out of commission, which accounted for three Founder Houses, the hospital, and the blood bank.

"Pretty much," Richard said. "We don't know if the vampires are leaving Bishop's locations, but we know they're digging in, just like Amelie's folks. We can verify locations only where Amelie's people were supposed to be, and they're gone from just about every location we've got up in blue."

"Where were they last seen?"

Richard consulted notes, and began to add yellow dots to the map. Claire saw the pattern almost immediately. "It's the portals," she said. "Myrnin got the portals working again, somehow. That's what they're using."

Hess and Lowe looked blank, but Richard nodded. "Yeah, I know about that. Makes sense. But where are they *going*?"

She shrugged helplessly. "Could be anywhere. I don't know all the places the portals go; maybe Myrnin and Amelie do, but I don't think anybody else does." But she felt unreasonably cheered by the idea that the vampires weren't out wandering out in the daylight, spontaneously combusting all over the place. She didn't want to see that happen to them . . . not even to Oliver.

Well, maybe to Oliver, sometimes. But not today.

The three men stared at her for a few seconds, then went back to studying the map, talking about perimeters and strategies for patrols, all kinds of things that Claire didn't figure really involved her. She finished her sandwich and walked into the living room, where tiny, wizened little Gramma Day was sitting in an overstuffed wing chair with her feet up, talking to Hannah. "Hey, little girl," Gramma Day said. "Sit yourself."

Claire perched, looking around the room. Most of the vampires were gone, either confined to cells or locked away for safety; some, they hadn't been able to stop. She couldn't seem to stop anxiously rubbing her hands together. *Shane.* Shane was supposed to be here. Richard Morrell had said that they'd arranged for the Bloodmobile to switch drivers, and that meant Shane would be coming soon for his rest period.

She needed him right now.

Gramma Day was looking at her with distant sympathy in her faded eyes. "You worried?" she asked, and smiled. "You got cause, I expect."

"I do?" Claire was surprised. Most adults tried to pretend it was all going to be okay.

"Sure thing, sugar. Morganville's been ruled by the vampires a long time, and they ain't always been the gentlest of folks. Been people hurt, people killed without reason. Builds up some resentment." Gramma nodded toward the bookcase. "Fetch me that red book right there, the one that starts with *N*."

It was an encyclopedia. Claire got it and set it in

her lap. Gramma's weathered, sinewy fingers opened it and flipped pages, then handed it back. The heading said, *New York Draft Riots, 1863.*

The pictures showed chaos—mobs, buildings on fire. And worse things. Much, much worse.

"People forget," Gramma said. "They forget what can happen, if anger builds up. Those New York folks, they were angry because their men were being drafted to fight the Civil War. Who you think they took it out on? Mostly black folks, of all things. Folks who couldn't fight back. They even burned up an orphanage, and they'd have killed every one of those children if they'd caught them." She shook her head, clicking her tongue in disgust. "Same thing happened in Tulsa in 1921. Called it the Greenwood Riot, said black folks were taking away their business and jobs. Back in France, they had a revolution where they took all those fancy aristocrat folks and cut their heads off. Maybe it was their fault, and maybe not. It's all the same thing: you get angry, you blame it on some folks, and you make them pay, guilty or not. Happens all the time."

Claire felt a chill. "What do you mean?"

"I mean, you think about France, girl. Vampires been holding us all down a long time, just like those aristocrats, or that's how people around here think of it. Now, you think about all those folks out there with generations of grudges, and nobody really in charge right now. You think it won't go bad on us?"

There weren't enough shudders in the world. Claire remembered Shane's father, the fanatical light in his eyes. He'd be one of those leading a riot, she thought. One of those pulling people out of their houses as collaborators and turncoats and hanging them up from lampposts.

Hannah patted the shotgun in her lap. She'd put the paintball gun aside—honestly, it wasn't much use now, with the vampires missing in action. "They're not getting in here, Gramma. We won't be having any Greenwood in Morganville."

"I ain't so much worried about you and me," Gramma said. "But I'd be worried for the Morrells. They're gonna be coming for them, sooner or later. That family's the poster children for the old guard."

Claire wondered if Richard knew that. She thought about Monica, too. Not that she liked Monica—God, no—but still.

She thanked Gramma Day and walked back into the kitchen, where the policemen were still talking. "Gramma Day thinks there's going to be trouble," she said. "Not the vampires. Regular people, like those people in the park. Maybe Lisa Day, too. And she thinks you ought to look after your family, Richard."

Richard nodded. "Already done," he said. "My mom and dad are at City Hall. Monica's headed there, too." He paused, thinking about it. "You're right. I should make sure she gets there all right, before she becomes another statistic." His face had tightened, and there was a look in his eyes that didn't match the way he said it. He was worried.

Given what Claire had just heard from Gramma Day, she thought he probably ought to be. Joe Hess and Travis Lowe sent each other looks, too, and she thought they were probably thinking the same thing. *She deserves it,* Claire told herself. *Whatever happens to Monica Morrell, she earned it.*

Except the pictures from Gramma Day's book kept coming back to haunt her.

The front door banged shut, and she heard Hannah's voice—not an alarm, just a welcome. She spun around and went to the door of the kitchen . . . and ran directly into Shane, who grabbed her and folded his arms around her.

"You're here," he said, and hugged her so tightly that she felt ribs creak. "Man, you don't make it easy, Claire. I've been freaking out all damn day. First I hear you're off in the middle of Vamptown; then you're running around like bait with Eve—"

"You're one to talk about bait," Claire said, and pushed back to look up into his face. "You okay?"

"Not a scratch," he said, and grinned. "Ironic, because I'm usually the one with the battle scars, right? The worst thing that happened to me was that I had to pull over and let a bunch of vampires off the bus, or they'd have ripped right through the walls. You'd be proud. I even let them off in the shade." His smile faded, but not the warmth in his eyes. "You look tired."

"Yeah, you think?" She caught herself on a yawn. "Sorry."

"We should get you home and catch some rest while we can." He looked around. "Where's Eve?"

Nobody had told him. Claire opened her mouth and found her throat clenching tight around the words. Her eyes filled with tears. *She's gone,* she wanted to say. *She's missing. Nobody knows where she is.*

But saying it out loud, saying it to Shane, that would make it real, somehow.

"Hey," he said, and smoothed her hair. "Hey, what's wrong? Where is she?"

"She was at Common Grounds," Claire finally choked out. "She—"

His hands went still, and his eyes widened.

"She's missing," Claire finally said, and a wave of utter misery broke over her. "She's out there somewhere. That's all I know."

"Her car's outside."

"We drove it here." Claire nodded at Hannah, who'd come in behind Shane and was silently watching. He acknowledged her with a glance; that was all.

"Okay," Shane said. "Michael's safe, you're safe, I'm safe. Now we're going to go find Eve."

Richard Morrell stirred. "That's not a good idea."

Shane spun on him, and the look on his face was hard enough to scare a vampire. "Want to try and stop me, *Dick*?"

Richard stared at him for a moment, then turned

back to the map. "You want to go, go. We've got things to do. There's a whole town of people out there to serve and protect. Eve's one girl."

"Yeah, well, she's our girl," Shane said. He took Claire's hand. "Let's go."

Hannah leaned against the wall. "Mind if I call shotgun?"

"Since you're carrying one? Feel free."

Outside, things were odd—quiet, but with a suppressed feeling of excitement in the air. People were still outside, talking in groups on the streets. The stores were shut down, for the most part, but Claire noticed with a stir of unease that the bars were open, and so was Morganville's gun shop.

Not good.

The gates of the university had opened, and they were issuing some kind of passes to people to leave— still sticking to the emergency drill story, Claire assumed.

"Oh, man," Shane muttered, as they turned down one of the streets that led to the heart of town, and Founder's Square—Vamptown. There were more people here, more groups. "I don't like this. There's Sal Manetti up there. He was one of my dad's drinking buddies, back in the day."

"The cops don't like it much, either," Hannah said, and pointed at the police cars ahead. They were blocking off access at the end of the street, and when Claire squinted, she could see they were out of their cruisers and arranged in a line, ready for anything. "This could turn bad, any time. All they need is somebody to strike a match out there, and we're all on fire."

Claire thought about Shane saying his father was coming to town, and she knew he was thinking about that, too. He shook his head. "We've got to figure out where Eve might be. Ideas?"

"Maybe she left us some clues," Claire said. "Back at Common Grounds. We should probably start there."

Common Grounds, however, was deserted, and the steel shutters were down. The front door was locked. They drove around back, to the alley. Nothing was there but trash cans, and—

"What the hell is that?" Shane asked. He hit the brakes and put the car in park, then jumped out and picked up something small on the ground. He got back in and showed it to Claire.

It was a small white candy in the shape of a skull. Claire blinked at it, then looked down the alley. "She left a trail of breath mints?"

"Looks like. We'll have to go on foot to follow it."

Hannah didn't seem to like that idea much, but Shane wasn't taking votes. They parked and locked Eve's car in the alley behind Common Grounds and began hunting for skull candies.

"Over here!" Hannah yelled, at the end of the alley. "Looks like she's dropping them when she makes a turn. Smart. She went this way."

After that, they went faster. The skull candies were in plain sight, easy to spot. Claire noticed that they were mostly in the shadows, which would have made sense, if Eve was with Myrnin or the other vampires. *Why didn't she stay?* Maybe she hadn't had a choice.

They ran out of candy trail after a few blocks. It led them into an area where Claire hadn't really been before—abandoned old buildings, mostly, falling to pieces under the relentless pressure of years and sun. It looked and felt deserted.

"Where now?" Claire asked, looking around. She didn't see anything obvious, but then she spotted something shiny, tucked in behind a tipped-over rusty trash can. She reached behind and came up with a black leather collar, studded with silver spikes.

The same collar Eve had been wearing. She word-lessly showed it to Shane, who turned in a slow circle, looking at the blank buildings. "Come on, Eve," he said. "Give us something. Anything." He froze. "You hear that?"

Hannah cocked her head. She was standing at the end of the alley, shotgun held in her arms in a way that was both casual and scarily competent. "What?"

"You don't hear it?"

Claire did. Somebody's phone was ringing. A cell phone, with an ultrasonic ringtone—she'd heard that older people couldn't hear those frequencies, and kids in school had used them all the time to sneak phone calls and texts in class. It was faint, but it was definitely there. "I thought the networks were down," she said, and pulled her own phone out.

Nope. The network was back up. She wondered if Richard had done it, or they'd lost control of the cell phone towers. Either one was possible.

They found the phone before the ringing stopped. It was Eve's—a red phone, with silver skull cell phone charms on it—discarded in the shadow of a broken, leaning doorway. "Who was calling?" Claire asked, and Shane paged through the menu.

"Richard," he said. "I guess he really was looking for her after all."

Claire's phone buzzed—just once. A text message. She opened it and checked.

It was from Eve, and it had been sent hours ago; the backlog of messages was just now being deliv-ered, apparently.

It read, 911 @ GERMANS. Claire showed it to Shane. "What is this?"

"Nine one one. Emergency message. German's—" He looked over at Hannah, who pushed away from the wall and came toward them.

"German's Tire Plant," she said. "Damn, I don't like that; it's the size of a couple of football fields, at least."

"We should let Richard know," Claire said. She dialed, but the network was busy, and then the bars failed again.

"I'm not waiting," Shane said. "Let's get the car."

9

The tire plant was near the old hospital, which made Claire shudder; she remembered the deserted building way too well. It had been incredibly creepy, and then of course it had also nearly gotten her and Shane killed, too, so again, not fond.

She was mildly shocked to see the hulking old edifice still standing, as Shane turned the car down the street.

"Didn't they tear that place down?" It had been scheduled for demolition, and boy, if any place had ever needed it . . .

"I heard it was delayed," Shane said. He didn't seem any happier about it than Claire was. "Something about historic preservation. Although anybody wanting to preserve that thing has never been inside it running for their life, I'll bet."

Claire stared out the window. On her side of the car was the brooding monstrosity of a hospital. The cracked stones and tilted columns in front made it look like something straight out of one of Shane's favorite zombie-killing video games. "Don't be hiding in there," she whispered. "Please don't be hiding in there." Because if Eve and Myrnin *had* taken refuge there, she wasn't sure she'd have the courage to go charging in after them.

"There's German's," Hannah said, and nodded toward

the other side of the street. Claire hadn't really noticed it the last time she'd been out here—preoccupied with the whole not-dying issue—but there it was, a four-story square building in that faded tan color that everybody had used back in the sixties. Even the windows—those that weren't broken out—were painted over. It was plain, big, and blocky, and there was absolutely nothing special about it except its size—it covered at least three city blocks, all blind windows and blank concrete.

"You ever been inside there?" Shane asked Hannah, who was studying the building carefully.

"Not for a whole lot of years," she said. "Yeah, we used to hide up in there sometimes, when we cut class or something. I guess everybody did, once in a while. It's a mess in there, a real junkyard. Stuff everywhere, walls falling apart, ceilings none too stable, either. If you go up to the second level, you watch yourself. Make sure you don't trust the floors, and watch those iron stairs. They were shaky even back then."

"Are we going in there?" Claire asked.

"No," Shane said. "*You're* not going anywhere. You're staying here and getting Richard on the phone and telling him where we are. Me and Hannah will check it out."

There didn't seem to be much room for argument, because Shane didn't give her time; he and Hannah bailed out of the car, made lock-the-door motions, and sprinted toward a gap in the rusted, sagging fence.

Claire watched until they disappeared around the corner of the building, and realized her fingers were going numb from clutching her cell phone. She took a deep breath and flipped it open to try Richard Morrell again.

Nothing. No signal again. The network was going up and down like a yo-yo.

The walkie-talkie signal was low, but she tried it anyway. There was some kind of response, but it was swallowed by static. She gave their position, on the off chance that someone on the network would be able to hear her over the noise.

She screamed and dropped the device when the light at the car window was suddenly blocked out, and someone battered frantically on the glass.

Claire recognized the silk shirt—*her* silk shirt— before she recognized Monica Morrell, because Monica definitely didn't look like herself. She was out of breath, sweating, her hair was tangled, and what makeup she had on was smeared and running.

She'd been crying. There was a cut on her right cheek, and a forming bruise, and dirt on the silk blouse as well as bloodstains. She was holding her left arm as though it was hurt.

"Open the door!" she screamed, and pounded on the glass again. "Let me in!"

Claire looked behind the car.

There was a mob coming down the street: thirty, forty people, some running, some following at a walk. Some were waving baseball bats, boards, pipes.

They saw Monica and let out a yell. Claire gasped, because that sound didn't seem human at all—more the roar of a beast, something mindless and hungry.

Monica's expression was, for the first time, absolutely open and vulnerable. She put her palm flat against the window glass. "Please help me," she said.

But even as Claire clawed at the lock to open it, Monica flinched, turned, and ran on, limping.

Claire slid over the front seat and dropped into the driver's seat. Shane had left the keys in the ignition. She started it up and put the big car in gear, gave it too much gas, and nearly wrecked it on the curb before she straightened the wheel. She rapidly gained on Monica. She passed her, squealed to a stop, and reached over to throw open the passenger door.

"Get in!" she yelled. Monica slid inside and banged the door shut, and Claire hit the gas as something impacted loudly against the back of the car—a brick, maybe. A hail of smaller stones hit a second later. Claire swerved wildly again, then straightened the wheel and got the car moving more smoothly. Her heart pounded hard, and her hands felt sweaty on the steering wheel. "You all right?"

Monica was panting, and she threw Claire a filthy look. "No, of *course* I'm not all right!" she snapped, and tried to fix her hair with trembling hands. "Unbelievable. What a stupid question. I guess I shouldn't expect much more from someone like you, though—"

Claire stopped the car and stared at her.

Monica shut up.

"Here's how this is going to go," Claire said. "You're going to act like an actual human being for a change, or else you're on your own. Clear?"

Monica glanced behind them. "They're coming!"

"Yes, they are. So, are we clear?"

"Okay, okay, yes! Fine, whatever!" Monica cast a clearly terrified look at the approaching mob. More stones peppered the paint job, and one hit the back glass with enough force to make Claire wince. "Get me out of here! Please!"

"Hold on, I'm not a very good driver."

That was kind of an understatement. Eve's car was huge and heavy and had a mind of its own, and Claire hadn't taken the time to readjust the bench seat to make it possible for her to reach the pedals easily. The only good thing about her driving, as they pulled away from the mob and the falling bricks, was that it was approximately straight, and pretty fast.

She scraped the curb only twice.

Once the fittest of their pursuers had fallen behind, obviously discouraged, Claire finally remembered to breathe, and pulled the car around the next right turn. This section of town seemed deserted, but then, so had the other street, before Monica and her fan club had shown up. The big, imposing hulk of the tire plant glided by on the passenger side—it seemed like miles of featureless brick and blank windows.

Claire braked the car on the other side of the street, in front of a deserted, rusting warehouse complex. "Come on," she said.

"What?" Monica watched her get out of the car and take the keys with uncomprehending shock. "Where are you going? We have to get out of here! They were going to *kill* me!"

"They probably still are," Claire said. "So you should probably get out of the car now, unless you want to wait around for them."

Monica said something Claire pretended not to hear—it wasn't exactly complimentary—and limped her way out of the passenger side. Claire locked the car. She hoped it wouldn't get banged up, but that mob had looked pretty excitable, and just the fact that Monica *had* been in it might be enough to ensure its destruction.

With any luck, though, they'd assume the girls had run into the warehouse complex, which was what Claire wanted.

Claire led them in the opposite direction, to the fence around German's Tire. There was a split in the wire by one of the posts, an ancient curling gap half hidden by a tangle of tumbleweeds. She pushed through and held the steel aside for Monica. "Coming?" she asked when Monica hesitated. "Because, you know what? Don't really care all that much. Just so you know."

Monica came through without any comment. The fence snapped back into place. Unless someone was looking for an entrance, it ought to do.

The plant threw a large, black shadow on the weed-choked parking lot. There were a few rusted-out trucks still parked here and there; Claire used them for cover from the street as they approached the main building, though she didn't think the mob was close enough to really spot them at this point. Monica seemed to get the point without much in the way of instruction; Claire supposed that running for her life had humbled her a little. Maybe.

"Wait," Monica said, as Claire prepared to bolt for a broken-out bottom-floor window into the tire plant. "What are you doing?"

"Looking for my friends," she said. "They're inside."

"Well, *I'm* not going in there," Monica declared, and tried to look haughty. It would have been more effective if she hadn't been so frazzled and sweaty. "I was on my way to City Hall, but those losers got in my way. They slashed my tires. I need to get to my parents.'" She said it as though she expected Claire to salute and hop like a toad.

Claire raised her eyebrows. "Better start walking, I guess. It's kind of a long way."

"But—but—"

Claire didn't wait for the sputtering to die; she turned and ran for the building. The window opened into total darkness, as far as she could tell, but at least it was accessible. She pulled herself up on the sash and started to swing her legs inside.

"Wait!" Monica dashed across to join her. "You can't leave me here alone! You saw those jerks out there!"

"Absolutely."

"Oh, you're just loving this, aren't you?"

"Kinda." Claire hopped down inside the building, and her shoes slapped bare concrete floor. It was bare except for a layer of dirt, anyway—undisturbed for as far as the light penetrated, which wasn't very far. "Coming?"

Monica stared through the window at her, just boiling with fury; Claire smiled at her and started to walk into the dark.

Monica, cursing, climbed inside.

"I'm not a bad person," Monica was saying—whining, actually. Claire wished she could find a two-by-four to whack her with, but the tire plant, although full of wreckage and trash, didn't seem to be big on wooden planks. Some nice pipes, though. She might use one of those.

Except she really didn't want to hit anybody, deep down. Claire supposed that was a character flaw, or something.

"Yes, you really are a bad person," she told Monica, and ducked underneath a low-hanging loop of wire that looked horror-movie ready, the sort of thing that dropped around your neck and hauled you up to be dispatched by the psycho-killer villain. Speaking of which, this whole place was decorated in Early Psycho-Killer Villain, from the vast soaring darkness overhead to the lumpy, skeletal shapes of rusting equipment and abandoned junk. The spray painting—decades of it, in layered styles from Early Tagger to cutting-edge gang sign—gleamed in the random shafts of light like blood. Some particularly unpleasant spray-paint artist had done an enormous, terrifying clown face, with windows for the eyes and a giant, open doorway for a mouth. *Yeah, really not going in there,* Claire thought. Although the way these things went, she probably would have to.

"Why do you say that?"

"Say what?" Claire asked absently. She was listening for any sound of movement, but this place was enormous and confusing—just as Hannah had warned.

"Say that I'm a bad person!"

"Oh, I don't know—you tried to kill me? *And* get me raped at a party? Not to mention—"

"That was payback," Monica said. "And I didn't mean it or anything."

"Which makes it all so much better. Look, can we not bond? I'm busy. Seriously. *Shhhh.*" That last was to forestall Monica from blurting out yet another injured defense of her character. Claire squeezed past a barricade of piled-up boxes and metal, into another shaft of light that arrowed down from a high-up broken window. The clown painting felt like it was watching her, which was beyond creepy. She tried not to look too closely at what was on the floor. Some of it was animal carcasses, birds, and things that had gotten inside and died over the years. Some of it was old cans, plastic wrappers, all kinds of junk left behind by adventurous kids looking for a hideout. She didn't imagine any of them stayed for long.

This place just felt . . . haunted.

Monica's hand grabbed her arm, just on the bruise that Amelie's grip had given her earlier. Claire winced.

"Did you hear that?" Monica's whisper was fierce and hushed. She needed mouthwash, and she smelled like sweat more than powder and perfume. "Oh my *God*. Something's in here with us!"

"Could be a vampire," Claire said. Monica sniffed.

"Not afraid of those," she said, and dangled her fancy, silver Protection bracelet in front of Claire's face. "Nobody's going to cross Oliver."

"You want to tell that to the mob of people chasing you back there? I don't think they got the memo or something."

"I mean, no vampire would. I'm Protected." Monica said it like there was simply no possibility anything else could be true. The earth was round, the sun was hot, and a vampire would never hurt her because she'd sold herself to Oliver, body and soul.

Yeah, right.

"News flash," Claire whispered. "Oliver's missing in action from Common Grounds. Amelie's disappeared. In fact, most of the vampires all over town have dropped out of sight, which makes these bracelets cute fashion accessories, but not exactly bulletproof vests or anything."

Monica started to speak, but Claire frowned angrily at her and pointed off into the darkness, where she'd heard the noise. It had sounded odd—kind of a sigh, echoing from the steel and concrete, bouncing and amplifying.

It sounded as if it had come out of the clown's dark mouth.

Of course.

Claire reached into her pocket. She still had the vial of silver powder that Amelie had given her, but she was well aware that it might not do her any good. If her friend-vampires were mixed in with enemy-vamps, she was out of luck. Likewise, if what was waiting for her out there was trouble of a human variety, instead of bloodsuckers . . .

Shane and Hannah were in here. Somewhere. And so—hopefully—was Eve.

Claire eased around a tattered sofa that smelled like old cats and mold, and sidestepped a truly impressive rat that didn't bother to move out of her way. It sat there watching her with weird, alert eyes.

Monica looked down, saw it, and shrieked, stumbling backward. She fell into a stack of ancient cartons that collapsed on her, raining down random junk. Claire grabbed her and pulled her to her feet, but Monica kept on whimpering and squirming, slapping at her hair and upper body.

"Oh my *God*, are they on me? Spiders? Are there spiders?"

If there were, Claire hoped they bit her. "No," she said shortly. Well, there were, but they were little ones. She brushed them off Monica's back. "Shut *up* already!"

"Are you kidding me? Did you see that rat? It was the size of freaking Godzilla!"

That was it, Claire decided. Monica could just wander around on her own, screaming about rats and spiders, until someone came and ate her. What. *Ever.*

She got only about ten feet away when Monica's very small whisper stopped her dead in her tracks.

"Please don't leave me." That didn't sound like Monica, not at all. It sounded scared, and very young. "Claire, please."

It was probably too late for being quiet, anyway,

and if there were vampires hiding in German's Tire Plant, they all knew exactly where they were, and for that matter, could tell what blood type they were. So stealth didn't seem a priority.

Claire cupped her hands over her mouth and yelled, very loudly, "Shane! Eve! Hannah! Anybody!"

The echoes woke invisible birds or bats high overhead, which flapped madly around; her voice rang from every flat surface, mocking Claire with her own ghost.

In the whispering silence afterward, Monica murmured, "Wow, I thought we were being subtle or something. My mistake."

Claire was about to hiss something really unpleasant at her, but froze as another voice came bouncing through the vast room—Shane's voice. "Claire?"

"Here!"

"Stay there! And shut up!"

He sounded frantic enough to make Claire wish she'd stuck with the whole quiet-time policy, and then Monica stopped breathing and went very, very still next to her. Her hands closed around Claire's arm, squeezing bruises again.

Claire froze, too, because something was coming out of the mouth of that painted clown—something white, ghostly, drifting like smoke. . . .

It had a face. Several faces, because it was a group of what looked like vampires, all very pale, all very quiet, all heading their way.

Staying put was not such a great plan, Claire decided. She was going to go with *run away*.

Which, grabbing Monica's wrist, she did.

The vampires did make sounds then, as their quarry started to flee—little whispering laughs, strange hisses, all kinds of creepy noises that made the skin on the back of Claire's neck tighten up. She held the glass vial in one hand, running faster, leaping over junk when she could see it coming and stumbling across it when she couldn't. Monica kept up, somehow, although

Claire could hear the tortured, steady moaning of her breath. Whatever she'd done to her right leg must have hurt pretty badly.

Something pale landed ahead of her, with a silent leap like a spider pouncing. Claire had a wild impression of a white face, red eyes, a wide-open mouth, and gleaming fangs. She drew back to throw the vial . . . and realized it was Myrnin facing her.

The hesitation cost her. Something hit her from the back, sending her stumbling forward across a fallen iron beam. She dropped the vial as she fell, trying to catch herself, and heard the glass break on the edge of the girder. Silver dust puffed out. Monica shrieked, a wild cry that made the birds panic again high up in heaven; Claire saw her stumble away, trying to put distance between herself and Myrnin.

Myrnin was just outside of the range of the drifting silver powder, but it wasn't Myrnin who was the problem. The other vampires, the ones who'd come out of the clown's mouth, leaped over stacks of trash, running for the smell of fresh, flowing blood.

They were coming up behind them, fast.

Claire raked her hand across the ground and came up with a palm full of silver powder and glass shards as she rolled up to her knees. She turned and threw the powder into the air between her, Monica, and the rest of the vampires. It dispersed into a fine, glittering mist, and when the vampires hit it, every tiny grain of silver caught fire.

It was beautiful, and horrible, and Claire flinched at the sound of their cries. There was so much silver, and it clung to their skin, eating in. Claire didn't know if it would kill them, but it definitely stopped them cold.

She grabbed Monica's arm and pulled her close.

Myrnin was still in front of them, crouched on top of a stack of wooden pallets. He didn't look at all human, not at *all*.

And then he blinked, and the red light went out in

his eyes. His fangs folded neatly backward, and he ran his tongue over pale lips before he said, puzzled, "Claire?"

She felt a sense of relief so strong it was like falling. "Yeah, it's me."

"Oh." He slithered down off the stacked wood, and she realized he was still dressed the way she'd seen him back at Common Grounds—a long, black velvet coat, no shirt, white pantaloons left over from his costume. He should have looked ridiculous, but somehow, he looked . . . right. "You shouldn't be here, Claire. It's very dangerous."

"I know—"

Something cold brushed the back of her neck, and she heard Monica make a muffled sound like a choked cry. Claire whirled and found herself face-to-face with a red-eyed, angry vampire with part of his skin still smoking from the silver she'd thrown.

Myrnin let out a roar that ripped the air, full of menace and fury, and the vampire stumbled backward, clearly shocked.

Then the five who'd chased them silently withdrew into the darkness.

Claire turned to face Myrnin. He was staring thoughtfully at the departing vamps.

"Thanks," she said. He shrugged.

"I was raised to believe in the concept of noblesse oblige," he said. "And I do owe you, you know. Do you have any more of my medication?"

She handed him her last dose of the drug that kept him sane—mostly sane, anyway. It was the older version, red crystals rather than clear liquid, and he poured out a dollop into his palm and licked the crystals up, then sighed in deep satisfaction.

"Much better," he said, and pocketed the rest of the bottle. "Now. Why are you here?"

Claire licked her lips. She could hear Shane—or someone—coming toward them through the darkness, and she saw someone in the shadows behind Myrnin.

Not vampires, she thought, so it was probably Hannah, flanking Shane. "We're looking for my friend Eve. You remember her, right?"

"Eve," Myrnin repeated, and slowly smiled. "Ah. The girl who followed me. Yes, of course."

Claire felt a flush of excitement, quickly damped by dread. "What happened to her?"

"Nothing. She's asleep," he said. "It was too dangerous out here for her. I put her in a safe place, for now."

Shane pushed through the last of the barriers and stepped into a shaft of light about fifty feet away. He paused at the sight of Myrnin, but he didn't look alarmed.

"This is your friend as well," Myrnin said, glancing back at Shane. "The one you care so much for." She'd never discussed Shane with Myrnin—not in detail, anyway. The question must have shown in her face, because his smile broadened. "You carry his scent on your clothes," he said. "And he carries yours."

"Ewww," Monica sighed.

Myrnin's eyes focused in on her like laser sights. "And who is this lovely child?"

Claire almost rolled her eyes. "Monica. The mayor's daughter."

"Monica Morrell." She offered her hand, which Myrnin accepted and bent over in an old-fashioned way. Claire assumed he was also inspecting the bracelet on her wrist.

"Oliver's," he said, straightening. "I see. I am charmed, my dear, simply charmed." He hadn't let go of her hand. "I don't suppose you would be willing to donate a pint for a poor, starving stranger?"

Monica's smile froze in place. "I—well, I—"

He pulled her into his arms with one quick jerk. Monica yelped and tried to pull away, but for all his relatively small size, Myrnin had strength to burn.

Claire pulled in a deep breath. "Myrnin. Please."

He looked annoyed. "Please *what*?"

"She's not free range or anything. You can't just munch her. Let go." He didn't look convinced. "Seriously. *Let go.*"

"Fine." He opened his arms, and Monica retreated as she clapped both hands around her neck. She sat down on a nearby girder, breathing hard. "You know, in my youth, women lined up to grant me their favors. I believe I'm a bit offended."

"It's a strange day for everybody," Claire said. "Shane, Hannah, this is Myrnin. He's sort of my boss."

Shane moved closer, but his expression stayed cool and distant. "Yeah? This the guy who took you to the ball? The one who dumped you and left you to die?"

"Well . . . uh . . . yes."

"Thought so."

Shane punched him right in the face. Myrnin, surprised, stumbled back against the tower of crates, and snarled; Shane took a stake from his back pocket and held it at the ready.

"No!" Claire jumped between them, waving her hands. "No, honest, it's not like that. Calm down, everybody, please."

"Yes," Myrnin said. "I've been staked quite enough today, thank you. I respect your need to avenge her, boy, but Claire remains quite capable of defending her own honor."

"Couldn't have said it better myself," she said. "Please, Shane. Don't. We need him."

"Yeah? Why?"

"Because he may know what's going on with the vampires."

"Oh, that," Myrnin said, in a tone that implied they were all idiots for not knowing already. "They're being called. It's a signal that draws all vampires who have sworn allegiance to you with a blood exchange—it's the way wars were fought, once upon a time. It's how you gather your army."

"Oh," Claire said. "So . . . why not you? Or the rest of the vampires here?"

"It seems as though your serum offers me some portion of immunity against it. Oh, I feel the draw, most certainly, but in an entirely academic way. Rather curious. I remember how it felt before, like an overwhelming panic. As for those others, well. They're not of the blood."

"They're not?"

"No. Lesser creatures. Failed experiments, if you will." He looked away, and Claire had a horrible suspicion.

"Are they *people*? I mean, regular humans?"

"A failed experiment," he repeated. "You're a scientist, Claire. Not all experiments work the way they're intended."

Myrnin had done this to them, in his search for the cure to the vampire disease. He had turned them into something that wasn't vampire, wasn't human, wasn't—well, wasn't anything, exactly. They didn't fit in either society.

No wonder they were hiding here.

"Don't look at me that way," Myrnin said. "It's not my fault the process was imperfect, you know. I'm not a monster."

Claire shook her head.

"Sometimes, you really are."

Eve was fine—tired, shaking, and tear streaked, but okay. "He didn't, you know," she said, and made two-finger pointy motions toward her throat. "He's kind of sweet, actually, once you get past all the crazy. Although there's a lot of the crazy."

There was, as Claire well knew, no way of getting past the crazy. Not really. But she had to admit that at least Myrnin had behaved more like a gentleman than expected.

Noblesse oblige. Maybe he'd felt obligated.

The place he'd kept Eve had once been some kind of storage locker within the plant, all solid walls and a single door that he'd locked off with a bent pipe. Shane hadn't been all that happy about it. "What if something had happened to you?" he'd asked, as Myrnin untwisted the metal as though it were solder instead of iron. "She'd have been locked in there, all alone, no way out. She'd have starved."

"Actually," Myrnin had answered, "that's not very likely. Thirst would have killed her within four days, I imagine. She'd never have had a chance to starve." Claire stared at him. He raised his eyebrows. "What?"

She just shook her head. "I think you missed the point."

Monica tagged along with Claire, which was annoying; she kept casting Shane nervous glances, and she was now outright terrified of Myrnin, which was probably how it should have been, really. At the very least, she'd shut up, and even the sight of another rat, this one big and kind of albino, hadn't set off her screams this time.

Eve, however, was less than thrilled to see Monica. "You're kidding," she said flatly, staring first at her, then at Shane. "You're okay with this?"

"Okay would be a stretch. Resigned, that's closer," Shane said. Hannah, standing next to him with her shotgun at port arms, snorted out a laugh. "As long as she doesn't talk, I can pretend she isn't here."

"Yeah? Well *I* can't," Eve said. She glared at Monica, who glared right back. "Claire, you have to stop picking up strays. You don't know where they've been."

"You're one to talk about diseases," Monica shot back, "seeing as how you're one big, walking social one."

"That's not pot, kettle—that's more like cauldron, kettle. Witch."

"Whore!"

"You want to go play with your new friends back there?" Shane snapped. "The really pale ones with the taste for plasma? Because believe me, I'll drop your skanky butt right in their nest if you don't shut up, Monica."

"You don't scare me, Collins!"

Hannah rolled her eyes and racked her shotgun. "How about me?"

That ended the entire argument.

Myrnin, leaning against the wall with his arms folded over his chest, watched the proceedings with great interest. "Your friends," he said to Claire. "They're quite . . . colorful. So full of energy."

"Hands off my friends." Not that that statement exactly included Monica, but whatever.

"Oh, absolutely. I would never." Hand to his heart, Myrnin managed to look angelic, which was a bit of a trick considering his Lord-Byron-on-a-bender outfit. "I've just been away from normal human society for so long. Tell me, is it usually this . . . spirited?"

"Not usually," she sighed. "Monica's special." Yeah, in the short-bus sense, because Monica was a head case. Not that Claire had time or inclination to explain all the dynamics of the Monica-Shane-Eve relationship to Myrnin right now. "When you said that someone was calling the vampires together for some kind of fight—was that Bishop?"

"Bishop?" Myrnin looked startled. "No, of course not. It's Amelie. Amelie is sending the call. She's consolidating her forces, putting up lines of defense. Things are rapidly moving toward a confrontation, I believe."

That was exactly what Claire was afraid he was going to say. "Do you know who answered?"

"Anyone in Morganville with a blood tie to her," he said. "Except me, of course. But that would include almost every vampire in town, save those who were sworn through Oliver. Even then, Oliver's tie would bind them in some sense, because he swore fealty to her when he came to live here. They might feel the pull less strongly, but they would still feel it."

"Then how is Bishop getting an army? Isn't everybody in town, you know, Amelie's?"

"He bit those he wished to keep on his side." Myrnin shrugged. "Claimed them from her, in a sense. Some of them went willingly, some not, but all owe him allegiance now. All those he was able to turn, which is a considerable number, I believe." He looked sharply at her. "The call continued in the daytime. Michael?"

"Michael's fine. They put him in a cell."

"And Sam?"

Claire shook her head in response. Next to Michael, his grandfather Sam was the youngest vampire in town, and Claire hadn't seen him at all, not since he'd left the Glass House, well before any of the other vamps. He'd gone off on some mission for Amelie; she trusted him more than most of the others, even those she'd known for hundreds of years. That was, Claire thought, because Amelie knew how Sam felt about her. It was the storybook kind of love, the kind that ignored things like practicality and danger, and never changed or died.

She found herself looking at Shane. He turned his head and smiled back.

The storybook kind of love.

She was probably too young to have that, but this felt so strong, so real. . . .

And Shane wouldn't even man up and tell her he loved her.

She took a deep breath and forced her mind off that. "What do we do now?" Claire asked. "Myrnin?"

He was silent for a long moment, then moved to one of the painted-over first-floor windows and pulled it open. The sun was setting again. It would be down completely soon.

"You should get home," he said. "The humans are

in charge for now, at least, but there are factions out there. There will be power struggles tonight, and not just between the two vampire sides."

Shane glanced at Monica—whose bruises were living proof that trouble was already under way—and then back at Myrnin. "What are you going to do?"

"Stay here," Myrnin said. "With my friends."

"*Friends?* Who, the—uh—failed experiments?"

"Exactly so." Myrnin shrugged. "They look upon me as a kind of father figure. Besides, their blood is as good as anyone else's, in a pinch."

"So much more than I wanted to know," Shane said, and nodded to Hannah. "Let's go."

"Got your back, Shane."

"Watch Claire's and Eve's. I'll take the lead."

"What about me?" Monica whined.

"Do you really want to know?" Shane gave her a glare that should have scorched her hair off. "Be grateful I'm not leaving you as an after-dinner mint on his pillow."

Myrnin leaned close to Claire's ear and said, "I think I like your young man." When she reacted in pure confusion, he held up his hands, smiling. "Not in that way, my dear. He just seems quite trustworthy."

She swallowed and put all that aside. "Are you going to be okay here? Really?"

"Really?" He locked gazes with her. "For now, yes. But we have work to do, Claire. Much work, and very little time. I can't hide for long. You do realize that stress accelerates the disease, and this is a great deal of stress for us all. More will fall ill, become confused. It's vital we begin work on the serum as quickly as possible."

"I'll try to get you back to the lab tomorrow."

They left him standing in a fading shaft of sunlight, next to a giant rusting crane that lifted its head three stories into the dark, with pale birds flitting and diving overhead.

And wounded, angry failed experiments lurking in

the shadows, maybe waiting to attack their vampire creator.

Claire felt sorry for them, if they did.

The mobs were gone, but they'd given Eve's car a good battering while they were at it. She choked when she saw the dents and cracked glass, but at least it was still on all four tires, and the damage was cosmetic. The engine started right up.

"Poor baby," Eve said, and patted the big steering wheel affectionately as she settled into the driver's seat. "We'll get you all fixed up. Right, Hannah?"

"And here I was wondering what I was going to do tomorrow," Hannah said, taking—of course—the shotgun seat. "Guess now I know. I'll be hammering dents out of the Queen Mary and putting in new safety glass."

In the backseat, Claire was the human equivalent of Switzerland between the warring nations of Shane and Monica, who sat next to the windows. It was tense, but nobody spoke.

The sun was going down in a blaze of glory in the west, which normally would have made Morganville a vampire-friendly place. Not so much tonight, as became evident when Eve left the dilapidated warehouse district and cruised closer to Vamptown.

There were people out on the streets, *at sunset.*

And they were angry, too.

"Shouty," Eve said, as they passed a big group clustered around a guy standing on a wooden box, yelling at the crowd. He had a pile of wooden stakes, and people were picking them up. "Okay, this is looking less than great."

"You think?" Monica slumped down in her seat, trying not to be noticed. "They tried to kill me! And I'm not even a vampire!"

"Yeah, but you're you, so there's that explained." Eve slowed down. "Traffic."

Traffic? In Morganville? Claire leaned forward and

saw that there were about six cars in the street ahead. The first one was turned sideways, blocking the second—a big van, which was trying to back up but was handicapped by the third car.

The trapped passenger van was vampire-dark. The two cars blocking it in were old, battered sedans, the kind humans drove.

"That's Lex Perry's car, the one turned sideways," Hannah said. "I think that's the Nunally brothers in the third one. They're drinking buddies with Sal Manetti."

"Sal, as in, the guy out there rabble-rousing?"

"You got it."

And now people were closing in around the van, pushing against it, rocking it on its tires.

Nobody in their car spoke a word.

The van rocked harder. The tires spun, trying to pull away, but it tipped and slammed over on its side, helpless. With a roar, the crowd climbed on top of it and started battering the windows.

"We should do something," Claire finally said.

"Yeah?" Hannah's voice was very soft. "What, exactly?"

"Call the police?" Only the police were already here. There were two cars of them, and they couldn't stop what was happening. In fact, they didn't even look inclined to try.

"Let's go," Shane said quietly. "There's nothing we can do here."

Eve silently put the car in reverse and burned rubber backing up.

Claire broke out of her trance. "What are you doing? We can't just leave—"

"Take a good look," Eve said grimly. "If anybody out there sees Princess Morrell in this car, we've all had it. We're all collaborators if we're protecting her, and *you're* wearing the Founder bracelet. We can't risk it."

Claire sank back in her seat as Eve shifted gears

again and turned the wheel. They took a different street, this one unblocked so far.

"What's happening?" Monica asked. "What's happening to our town?"

"France," Claire said, thinking about Gramma Day. "Welcome to the revolution."

Eve drove through a maze of streets. Lights were flickering on in houses, and the few streetlamps were coming on as well. Cars—and there were a lot of them out now—turned on their headlights and honked, as if the local high school had just won a big football game.

As if it were one big, loud party.

"I want to go home," Monica said. Her voice sounded muffled. "Please."

Eve looked at her in the rearview mirror, and finally nodded.

But when they turned down the street where the Morrell family home was located, Eve slammed on the brakes and put the car into reverse, instantly.

The Morrell home looked like the site of another of Monica's infamous, unsupervised parties . . . only this one really was unsupervised, and those uninvited guests, they weren't just there for the free booze.

"What are they doing?" Monica asked, and let out a strangled yell as a couple of guys carried a big plasma television out the front door. "They're stealing it! They're stealing our stuff!"

Pretty much everything was being looted—mattresses, furniture, art. Claire even saw people upstairs tossing linens and clothing out the windows to people waiting on the ground.

And then, somebody ran up with a bottle full of liquid, stuffed with a burning rag, and threw it into the front window.

The flames flickered, caught, and gained strength.

"No!" Monica panted and clawed at the door handle, but Eve had locked it up. Claire grabbed Monica's arms and held them down.

"Get us out of here!" she yelled.

"My parents could be in there!"

"No, they're not. Richard told me they're at City Hall."

Monica kept fighting, even as Eve steered the car away from the burning house, and then suddenly just . . . stopped.

Claire heard her crying. She wanted to think, *Good, you deserve it,* but somehow she just couldn't force herself to be that cold.

Shane, however, could. "Hey, look on the bright side," he said. "At least your little sister isn't inside."

Monica caught her breath, then kept crying.

By the time they'd turned on Lot Street, Monica seemed to be pulling herself together, wiping her face with trembling hands and asking for a tissue, which Eve provided out of the glove box in the front.

"What do you think?" Eve asked Shane. Their street seemed quiet. Most of the houses had lights on, including the Glass House, and although there were some folks outside, talking, it didn't look like mobs were forming. Not here, anyway.

"Looks good. Let's get inside."

They agreed that Monica needed to go in the middle, covered by Hannah. Eve went first, racing up the walk to the front door and using her keys to open it up.

They made it in without attracting too much attention or anybody pointing fingers at Monica—but then, Claire thought, Monica definitely didn't look much like herself right now. More like a bad Monica impersonator. Maybe even one who was a guy.

Shane would laugh himself sick over that if she mentioned it. After seeing the puffy redness around Monica's eyes, and the shattered expression, Claire kept it to herself.

As Shane slammed, locked, and dead bolted the front door, Claire felt the house come alive around them, almost tingling with warmth and welcome. She heard people in the living room exclaim at the same time, so it wasn't just her; the house really had re-acted, and reacted strongly, to three out of four of its residents coming home.

Claire stretched out against the wall and kissed it. "Glad to see you, too," she whispered, and pressed her cheek against the smooth surface.

It almost felt like it hugged her back.

"Dude, it's a *house*," Shane said from behind her. "Hug somebody who cares."

She did, throwing herself into his arms. It felt like he'd never let her go, not even for a second, and he lifted her completely off the ground and rested his head on her shoulder for a long, precious moment before setting her gently back on her feet.

"Better see who's here," he said, and kissed her very lightly. "Down payment for later, okay?"

Claire let go, but held his hand as they walked down the hallway and into the living room of the Glass House, which was filled with people.

Not vampires.

Just people.

Some of them were familiar, at least by sight—people from town: the owner of the music store where Michael worked; a couple of nurses she'd seen at the hospital, who still wore brightly colored medical scrubs and comfortable shoes. The rest, Claire barely knew at all, but they had one thing in common—they were all scared.

An older, hard-looking woman grabbed Claire by the shoulders. "Thank God you're home," she said, and hugged her. Claire, rigid with surprise, cast Shane a what-the-hell look, and he shrugged helplessly. "This damn house won't do *anything* for us. The lights keep going out, the doors won't open, food goes bad in the fridge—it's as if it doesn't want us here!"

And it probably didn't. The house could have ejected them at any time, but obviously it had been a bit uncertain about exactly what its residents might want, so it had just made life uncomfortable for the intruders instead.

Claire could now feel the air-conditioning switching on to cool the overheated air, hear doors swinging open upstairs, see lights coming on in darkened areas.

"Hey, Celia," Shane said, as the woman let go of Claire at last. "So, what brings you here? I figured the Barfly would be doing good business tonight."

"Well, it would be, except that some jerks came in and said that because I was wearing a bracelet I had to serve them for free, on account of being some kind of sympathizer. What kind of sympathizer, I said, and one of them tried to hit me."

Shane lifted his eyebrows. Celia wasn't a young woman. "What did you do?"

"Used the Regulator." Celia lifted a baseball bat propped against the wall. It was old hardwood, lovingly polished. "Got myself a couple of home runs, too. But I decided maybe I wouldn't stay for the extra innings, if you know what I mean. I figure they're drinking me dry over there right now. Makes me want to rip my bracelet off, I'll tell ya. Where are the damn vampires when you need them, after all that?"

"You didn't take your bracelet off? Even when they gave you the chance?" Shane seemed surprised. Celia gave him a glare.

"No, I didn't. I ain't breaking my word, not unless I have to. Right now, I don't have to."

"If you take it off now, you may never need to put it on again."

Celia leveled a wrinkled finger at him. "Look, Collins, I know all about you and your dad. I don't hold with any of that. Morganville's an all-right place. You follow the rules and stay out of trouble—about like anyplace, I guess. You people wanted chaos. Well, this is what it looks like—people getting beaten, shops looted, houses burned. Sure, it'll settle down sometime, but into what? Maybe no place I'd want to live."

She turned away from him, shouldered her baseball

bat, and marched away to talk with a group of adults her own age.

Shane caught Claire looking at him, and shrugged. "Yeah," he sighed. "I know. She's got a point. But how do we know it won't be better if the vamps just—"

"Just what, Shane? *Die?* What about Michael, have you thought about him? Or Sam?" She stomped off.

"Where are you going?"

"To get a Coke!"

"Would you—"

"No!"

She twisted the cap off the Coke she'd retrieved from the fridge—which was stocked up again, although she knew it hadn't been when they'd left. Another favor from the house, she guessed, although how it went shopping on its own she had no idea.

The cold syrupy goodness hit her like a brick wall, but instead of energizing her, it made her feel weak and a little sick. Claire sank down in a chair at the kitchen table and put her head in her hands, suddenly overwhelmed.

It was all falling apart.

Amelie was calling the vampires, probably going to fight Bishop to the death. Morganville was ripping itself in pieces. And there was nothing she could *do*.

Well, there was one thing.

She retrieved and opened four more bottles of Coke, and delivered them to Hannah, Eve, Shane, and—because it felt mean to leave her out at a time like this—Monica.

Monica stared at the sweating bottle as if she suspected Claire had put rat poison in it. "What's this?"

"What does it look like? Take or don't, I don't really care." Claire put it down on the table next to where Monica sat, and went to curl up on the couch next to Shane. She checked her cell phone. The network was back up again, at least for the moment, and she had a ton of voice mails. Most were from Shane, so she saved them to listen to later; two more were from Eve, which she deleted, since they were instructions on where to find her.

The last one was from her mother. Claire caught her breath, tears pricking in her eyes at the sound of Mom's voice. Her mother sounded calm, at least—mostly, anyway.

Claire, sweetie, I know I shouldn't be worrying but I am. Honey, call us. I've been hearing some terrible things about what's happening out there. Some of the people with us here are talking about fights and looting. If I don't hear from you soon—well, I don't know what we'll do, but your father's going crazy. So please, call us. We love you, honey. Bye.

Claire got her breathing back under control, mainly by sternly telling herself that she needed to sound together and completely in control to keep her parents from charging out there into the craziness. She had it more or less managed by the time the phone rang on the other end, and when her mother picked it up, she was able to say, "Hi, Mom," without making it sound like she was about to burst into tears. "I got your message. Is everything okay there?"

"Here? Claire, don't you be worrying about us! We're just fine! Oh, honey, are you okay? Really?"

"Honestly, yes, I'm okay. Everything's—" She couldn't say that everything was okay, because of course it wasn't. It was, at best, kind of temporarily stable. "It's quiet here. Shane's here, and Eve." Claire remembered that Mom had liked Monica Morrell, and rolled her eyes. Anything to calm her fears. "That girl from the dorm, Monica, she's here, too."

"Oh, yes, Monica. I liked her." It really did seem to help, which was not exactly an endorsement of Mom's character-judging ability. "Her brother came by here to check on us about an hour ago. He's a nice boy."

Claire couldn't quite imagine referring to Richard Morrell as a *boy*, but she let it go. "He's kind of in charge of the town right now," she said. "You have the radio, right? The one we dropped off earlier?"

"Yes. We've been doing everything they say, of course. But honey, I'd really like it if you could come here. We want to have you home, with us."

"I know. I know, Mom. But I think I'd better stay here. It's important. I'll try to come by tomorrow, okay?"

They talked a little more, about nothing much, just chatter to make life seem kind of normal for a change. Mom was holding it together, but only barely; Claire could hear the manic quaver in her voice, could almost see the bright tears in her eyes. She was going on about how they'd had to move most of the boxes into the basement to make room for all the company— *company?*—and how she was afraid that Claire's stuff would get damp, and then she talked about all the toys in the boxes and how much Claire had enjoyed them when she was younger.

Normal Mom stuff.

Claire didn't interrupt, except to make soothing noises and acknowledgments when Mom paused. It helped, hearing Mom's voice, and she knew it was helping her to talk. But finally, when her mother ran down like a spring-wound clock, Claire agreed to all the parental requirements to be careful and watch out and wear warm clothes.

Good-bye seemed very final, and once Claire hung up, she sat in silence for a few minutes, staring at the screen of her cell phone.

On impulse, she tried to call Amelie. It rang and rang. No voice mail.

In the living room, Shane was organizing some kind of sentry duty. A lot of people had already crashed out in piles of pillows, blankets, sometimes just on a spare rug. Claire edged around the prone bodies and motioned to Shane that she was going upstairs. He nodded and kept talking to the two guys he was with, but his gaze followed her all the way.

Eve was in her bedroom, and there was a note on the door that said DO NOT KNOCK OR I WILL KILL YOU. THIS MEANS YOU, SHANE. Claire considered knocking, but she was too tired to run away.

Her bedroom was dark. When she'd left in the morning, Eve's kind-of-friend Miranda had been sleeping here, but she was gone, and the bed was neatly made again. Claire sat down on the edge, staring out the windows, and then pulled out clean underwear and her last pair of blue jeans from the closet, plus a tight black shirt Eve had lent her last week.

The shower felt like heaven. There was even enough hot water for a change. Claire dried off, fussed with her hair a bit, and got dressed. When she came out, she listened at the stairs, but didn't hear Shane talking anymore. Either he was being quiet, or he'd gone to bed. She paused next to his door, wishing she had the guts to knock, but she went on to her own room instead.

Shane was inside, sitting on her bed. He looked up when she opened the door, and his lips parted, but he was silent for a long few seconds.

"I should go," he finally said, but he didn't get up.

Claire settled in next to him. It was all perfectly correct, the two of them sitting fully dressed like this, but somehow she felt like they were on the edge of a cliff, both in danger of falling off.

It was exciting, and terrifying, and all kinds of wrong.

"So what happened to you today?" she asked. "In the Bloodmobile, I mean?"

"Nothing really. We drove to the edge of town and parked outside the border, where we'd be able to see anybody coming. A couple of vamps showed, trying to make a withdrawal, but we sent them packing.

Bishop never made an appearance. Once we lost contact with the vampires, we figured we'd cruise around and see what was going on. We nearly got boxed in by a bunch of drunk idiots in pickup trucks, and then the vampires in the Bloodmobile went nuts—that call thing going off, I guess. I dropped them at the grain elevator—that was the biggest, darkest place I could find, and it casts a lot of shadows. I handed off the driving to Cesar Mercado. He's supposed to drive it all the way to Midland tonight, provided the barriers are down. Best we can do."

"What about the book? Did you leave it on board?"

In answer, Shane reached into his waistband and pulled out the small leather-bound volume. Amelie had added a lock on it, like a diary lock. Claire tried pressing the small, metal catch. It didn't open, of course.

"You think you should be fooling with that thing?" Shane asked.

"Probably not." She tried prying a couple of pages apart to peek at the script. All she could tell was that it was handwritten, and the paper looked relatively old. Oddly, when she sniffed it, the paper smelled like chemicals.

"What are you doing?" Shane looked like he couldn't decide whether to be repulsed or fascinated.

"I think somebody restored the paper," she said. "Like they do with really expensive old books and stuff. Comics, sometimes. They put chemicals on the paper to slow down the aging process, make the paper whiter again."

"Fascinating," Shane lied. "Gimme." He plucked the book from her hands and put it aside, on the other side of the bed. When she grabbed for it, he got in her way; they tangled, and somehow, he was lying prone on the bed and she was stretched awkwardly on top of him. His hands steadied her when she started to slide off.

"Oh," she murmured. "We shouldn't—"

"Definitely not."

"Then you should—"

"Yeah, I should."

But he didn't move, and neither did she. They just looked at each other, and then, very slowly, she lowered her lips to his.

It was a warm, sweet, wonderful kiss, and it seemed to go on forever. It also felt like it didn't last nearly long enough. Shane's hands skimmed up her sides, up her back, and cupped her damp hair as he kissed her more deeply. There were promises in that kiss.

"Okay, red flag," he said. He hadn't let her go, but there was about a half an inch of air between their lips. Claire's whole body felt alive and tingling, pulse pounding in her wrists and temples, warmth pooling like light in the center of her body.

"It's okay," she said. "I swear. Trust me."

"Hey, isn't that my line?"

"Not now."

Kissing Shane was the reward for surviving a long, hard, terrifying day. Being enfolded in his warmth felt like going to heaven on moonbeams. She kicked off her shoes, and, still fully dressed, crawled under the blankets. Shane hesitated.

"Trust me," she said again. "And you can keep your clothes on if you don't."

They'd done this before, but somehow it hadn't felt so . . . intimate. Claire pressed against him, back to front under the covers, and his arms went around her. Instant heat.

She swallowed and tried to remember all those good intentions she'd had as she felt Shane's breath whisper on the back of her neck, and then his lips brushed her skin. "So wrong," he murmured. "You're killing me, you know."

"Am not."

"On this, you'll have to trust *me*." His sigh made her shiver all the way to her bones. "I can't believe you brought Monica back here."

"Oh, come on. You wouldn't have left her out there, all alone. I know you better than that, Shane. Even as bad as she is—"

"The satanic incarnation of evil?"

"Maybe so, but I can't see you letting them get her and . . . hurt her." Claire turned around to face him, a squirming motion that made them wrestle for the covers. "What's going to happen? Do you know?"

"What am I, Miranda the teen screwed-up psychic? No, I don't know. All I know is that when we get up tomorrow, either the vampires will be back, or they won't. And then we'll have to make a choice about how we're going to go forward."

"Maybe we don't go forward. Maybe we wait."

"One thing I do know, Claire: you can't stay in the same place, not even for a day. You keep on moving. Maybe it's the right direction, maybe not, but you still move. Every second things change, like it or not."

She studied his face intently. "Is your dad here? Now?"

He grimaced. "Truthfully? No idea. I wouldn't be surprised. He'd know that it was time to move in and take command, if he could. And Manetti's a running buddy from way back. This kind of feels like Dad's behind it."

"But if he does take over, what happens to Michael? To Myrnin? To any other vampire out there?"

"Do you really need me to tell you?"

Claire shook her head. "He'll tell people they have to kill all the vampires, and then, he'll come after the Morrells, and anybody else he thinks is responsible for what happened to your family. Right?"

"Probably," Shane sighed.

"And you're going to let all that happen."

"I didn't say that."

"You didn't say you weren't, either. Don't tell me it's complicated, because it isn't. Either you stand up for something, or you lie down for it. You said that to me one time, and you were right." Claire burrowed closer into his arms. "Shane, you were *right* then. Be right now."

He touched her face. His fingers traced down her cheek, across her lips, and his eyes—she'd never seen that look in his eyes. In anyone's, really.

"In this whole screwed-up town, you're the only thing that's always been right to me," he whispered. "I love you, Claire." She saw something that might have been just a flash of panic go across his expression, but then he steadied again. "I can't believe I'm saying this, but I do. I love you."

He said something else, but the world had narrowed around her. Shane's lips kept moving, but all she heard were the same words echoing over and over inside her head like the tolling of a giant brass bell: *I love you.*

He sounded like it had taken him completely by surprise—not in a bad way, but more as if he hadn't really understood what he was feeling until that instant.

She blinked. It was as if she'd never really seen him before, and he was *beautiful.* More beautiful than any man she'd ever seen in her entire life, ever.

Whatever he was saying, she stopped it by kissing him. A lot. And for a very long time. When he finally backed up, he didn't go far, and this look in his eyes, this intense and overwhelming *need*—that was new, too.

And she liked it.

"I love you," he said, and kissed her so hard he took her breath away. There was more to it than before—more passion, more urgency, more . . . everything. It was as if she were caught in a tide, carried away, and she thought that if she never touched the shore again, it would be good to drown like this, just swim forever in all this richness.

Red flag, some part of her screamed, *come on, red flag. What are you doing?*

She wished it would just shut up.

"I love you, too," she whispered to him. Her voice

was shaking, and so were her hands where they rested on his chest. Under the soft T-shirt, his muscles were tensed, and she could feel every deep breath he took. "I'd do anything for you."

She meant it to be an invitation, but that was the thing that shocked sense back into him. He blinked. "Anything," he repeated, and squeezed his eyes shut. "Yeah. I'm getting that. Bad idea, Claire. Very, very bad."

"Today?" She laughed a little wildly. "Everything's crazy today. Why can't we be? Just once?"

"Because I made promises," he said. He wrapped his arms around her and pulled her close, and she felt a groan shake his whole body. "To your parents, to myself, to Michael. To you, Claire. I can't break my word. It's pretty much all I've got these days."

"But . . . what if—"

"Don't," he whispered in her ear. "Please don't. This is tough enough already."

He kissed her again, long and sweetly, and somehow, it tasted like tears this time. Like some kind of good-bye.

"I really do love you," he said, and smoothed away the damp streaks on her cheeks. "But I can't do this. Not now."

Before she could stop him, he slid out of bed, put on his shoes, and walked quickly to the door. She sat up, holding the covers close as if she were naked underneath, instead of fully clothed, and he hesitated there, one hand gripping the doorknob.

"Please stay," she said. "Shane—"

He shook his head. "If I stay, things are going to happen. You know it, and I know it, and we just can't do this. I know things are falling apart, but—" He hitched in a deep, painful breath. "No."

The sound of the door softly closing behind him went through her like a knife.

Claire rolled over, wretchedly hugging the pillow that smelled of his hair, sharing the warm place in the bed where his body had been, and thought about crying herself to sleep.

And then she thought of the dawning wonder in his eyes when he'd said, *I love you.*

No. It was no time to be crying.

When she did finally sleep, she felt safe.

10

The next day, there was no sign of the vampires, none at all. Claire checked the portal networks, but as far as she could tell, they were down. With nothing concrete to do, she helped around the house—cleaning, straightening, running errands. Richard Morrell came around to check on them. He looked a little better for having slept, which didn't mean he looked good, exactly.

When Eve wandered down, she looked almost as bad. She hadn't bothered with her Goth makeup, and her black hair was down in a lank, uncombed mess. She poured Richard some coffee from the ever-brewing pot, handed it over, and said, "How's Michael?"

Richard blew on the hot surface in the cup without looking at her. "He's at City Hall. We moved all the vampires we still had into the jail, for safekeeping."

Eve's face crumpled in anguish. Shane put a hand on her shoulder, and she pulled in a damp breath and got control of herself.

"Right," she said. "That's probably for the best, you're right." She sipped from her own battered coffee mug. "What's it like out there?" *Out there* meant beyond Lot Street, which remained eerily quiet.

"Not so good," Richard said. His voice sounded hoarse and dull, as if he'd yelled all the edges off it. "About half the stores are shut down, and some of those are burned or looted. We don't have enough police and volunteers to be everywhere. Some of the store owners armed up and are guarding their own places—I don't like it, but it's probably the best option until everybody settles down and sobers up. The problem isn't everybody, but it's a good portion of the town who's been down and angry a long time. You heard they raided the Barfly?"

"Yeah, we heard," Shane said.

"Well, that was just the beginning. Dolores Thompson's place got broken into, and then they went to the warehouses and found the bonded liquor storage. Those who were inclined to deal with all this by getting drunk and mean have had a real holiday."

"We saw the mobs," Eve said, and glanced at Claire. "Um, about your sister—"

"Yeah, thanks for taking care of her. Trust my idiot sister to go running around in her red convertible during a riot. She's damn lucky they didn't kill her."

They would have, Claire was certain of that. "I guess you're taking her with you . . . ?"

Richard gave her a thin smile. "Not the greatest houseguest?"

Actually, Monica had been very quiet. Claire had found her curled up on the couch, wrapped in a blanket, sound asleep. She'd looked pale and tired and bruised, and much younger than Claire had ever seen her. "She's been okay." She shrugged. "But I'll bet she'd rather be with her family."

"Her *family's* under protective custody downtown. My dad nearly got dragged off by a bunch of yahoos yelling about taxes or something. My mom—" Richard shook his head, as if he wanted to drive the pictures right out of his mind. "Anyway. Unless she likes four walls and a locked door, I don't think she's going to be very happy. And you know Monica: if she's not happy—"

"Nobody is," Shane finished for him. "Well, I want her out of our house. Sorry, man, but we did our duty and all. Past this point, she'd have to be a friend to keep crashing here. Which, you know, she isn't. Ever."

"Then I'll take her off your hands." Richard set the cup down and stood. "Thanks for the coffee. Seems like that's all that's keeping me going right now."

"Richard . . ." Eve rose, too. "Seriously, what's it like out there? What's going to happen?"

"With any luck, the drunks will sober up or pass out, and those who've been running around looking for people to punish will get sore feet and aching muscles and go home to get some sleep."

"Not like we've had a lot of luck so far, though," Shane said.

"No," Richard agreed. "That we haven't. But I have to say, we can't keep things locked down. People have to work, the schools have to open, and for that, we need something like normal life around here. So we're working on that. Power and water's on, phone lines are back up. TV and radio are broadcasting. I'm hoping that calms people down. We've got police patrols overlapping all through town, and we can be anywhere in under two minutes. One thing, though: we're getting word that there's bad weather in the forecast. Some kind of real big front heading toward us tonight. I'm not too happy about that, but maybe it'll keep the crazies off the streets for a while. Even riots don't like rain."

"What about the university?" Claire asked. "Are they open?"

"Open and classes are running, believe it or not. We passed off some of the disturbances as role-playing in the disaster drill, and said that the looting and burning was part of the exercise. Some of them believed us."

"But . . . no word about the vampires?"

Richard was silent for a moment, and then he said, "No. Not exactly."

"Then what?"

"We found some bodies, before dawn," he said.

"All vamps. All killed with silver or decapitation. Some of them—I knew some of them. Thing is, I don't think they were killed by Bishop. From the looks of things, they were caught by a mob."

Claire caught her breath. Eve covered her mouth. "Who—?"

"Bernard Temple, Sally Christien, Tien Ma, and Charles Effords."

Eve lowered her hand to say, "Charles Effords? Like, Miranda's Charles? Her Protector?"

"Yeah. From the state of the bodies, I'd guess he was the primary target. Nobody loves a pedophile."

"Nobody except Miranda," Eve said. "She's going to be really scared now."

"Yeah, about that . . ." Richard hesitated, then plunged forward. "Miranda's gone."

"Gone?"

"Disappeared. We've been looking for her. Her parents reported her missing early last night. I'm hoping she wasn't with Charles when the mob caught up to him. You see her, you call me, okay?"

Eve's lips shaped the agreement, but no sound came out.

Richard checked his watch. "Got to go," he said. "Usual drill: lock the doors, check IDs on anybody you're not expecting who shows up. If you hear from any vampire, or hear anything *about* the vampires, you call immediately. Use the coded radios, not the phone lines. And be careful."

Eve swallowed hard, and nodded. "Can I see Michael?"

He paused, as if that hadn't occurred to him, then shrugged. "Come on."

"We're all going," Shane said.

It was an uncomfortable ride to City Hall, where the jail was located, mainly because although the police cruiser was large, it wasn't big enough to have Richard, Monica, Eve, Shane, and Claire all sharing the ride. Monica had taken the front seat, sliding close to her brother, and Claire had squeezed in with her friends in the back.

They didn't talk, not even when they cruised past burned-out, broken hulks of homes and stores. There weren't any fires today, or any mobs that Claire spotted. It all seemed quiet.

Richard drove past a police barricade around City Hall and parked in the underground garage. "I'm taking Monica to my parents'," he said. "You guys go on down to the cells. I'll be there in a minute."

It took a lot more than a minute for them to gain access to Michael; the vampires—all five of those the humans still had in custody—were housed in a special section, away from daylight and in reinforced cells. It reminded Claire, with an unpleasant lurch, of the vampires in the cells where Myrnin was usually locked up, for his own protection. Had anyone fed them? Had anyone even tried?

She didn't know three of the vampires, but she knew the last two. "Sam!" she blurted, and rushed to the bars. Michael's grandfather was lying on the bunk, one pale hand over his eyes, but he sat up when she called his name. Claire could definitely see the resemblance between Michael and Sam—the same basic bone structure, only Michael's hair was a bright gold, and Sam's was red.

"Get me out," Sam said, and lunged for the door. He rattled the cage with unexpected violence. Claire fell back, openmouthed. "Open the door and get me out, Claire! *Now!*"

"Don't listen to him," Michael said. He was standing at the bars of his own cell, leaning against them, and he looked tired. "Hey, guys. Did you bring me a lockpick in a cupcake or something?"

"I had the cupcake, but I ate it. Hard times, man." Shane extended his hand. Michael reached through the bars and took it, shook solemnly, and then Eve threw herself against the metal to try to hug him. It

was awkward, but Claire saw the relief spread over
Michael, no matter how odd it was with the bars between the two of them. He kissed Eve, and Claire had
to look away from that, because it seemed like such
a private kind of moment.

Sam rattled his cage again. "Claire, open the door!
I need to get to Amelie!"

The policeman who'd escorted them down to the
cells pushed off from the wall and said, "Calm down,
Mr. Glass. You're not going anywhere; you know
that." He shifted his attention to Shane and Claire.
"He's been like that since the beginning. We had to
trank him twice; he was hurting himself trying to get
out. He's worse than all the others. They seem to have
calmed down. Not him."

No, Sam definitely hadn't calmed down. As Claire
watched, he tensed his muscles and tried to force the
lock, but subsided in panting frustration and stumbled
back to his bunk. "I have to go," he muttered. "Please,
I need to go. She needs me. Amelie—"

Claire looked at Michael, who didn't seem to be
nearly as distressed. "Um . . . sorry to ask, but . . .
are you feeling like that? Like Sam?"

"No," Michael said. His eyes were still closed. "For
a while there was this . . . call, but it stopped about
three hours ago."

"Then why is Sam—"

"It's not the call," Michael said. "It's Sam. It's killing him, knowing she's out there in trouble and he
can't help her."

Sam put his head in his hands, the picture of misery.
Claire exchanged a look with Shane. "Sam," she said.
"What's happening? Do you know?"

"People are dying, that's what's happening," he
said. "Amelie's in trouble. I need to go to her. I can't
just sit here!"

He threw himself at the bars again, kicking hard
enough to make the metal ring like a bell.

"Well, that's where you're going to stay," the policeman said, not exactly unsympathetically. "The way you're acting, you'd go running out into the sunlight, and that wouldn't do her or you a bit of good, now, would it?"

"I could have gone hours ago before sunrise," Sam snapped. *"Hours ago."*

"And now you have to wait for dark."

That earned the policeman a full-out vicious snarl, and Sam's eyes flared into bright crimson. Everybody stayed back, and when Sam subsided this time, it seemed to be for good. He withdrew to his bunk, lay down, and turned his back to them.

"Man," Shane breathed softly. "He's a little intense, huh?"

From what the policeman told them—and Richard, when he rejoined them—all the captured vampires had been at about the same level of violence, at first. Now it was just Sam, and as Michael said, it didn't seem to be Amelie's summons that was driving him. . . . It was fear for Amelie herself.

It was love.

"Step back, please," the policeman said to Eve. She looked over her shoulder at him, then at Michael. He kissed her, and let go.

She did take a step back, but it was a tiny one. "So—are you okay? Really?"

"Sure. It's not exactly the Ritz, but it's not bad. They're not keeping us here to hurt us, I know that." Michael stretched out a finger and touched her lips. "I'll be back soon."

"Better be," Eve said. She mock-bit at his finger. "I could totally date somebody else, you know."

"And I could rent out your room."

"And I could put your game console on eBay."

"Hey," Shane protested. "Now you're just being mean."

"See what I mean? You need to come home, or it's

total chaos. Dogs and cats, living together." Eve's voice dropped, but not quite to a whisper. "And I miss you. I miss seeing you. I miss you all the time."

"I miss you, too," Michael murmured, then blinked and looked at Claire and Shane. "I mean, I miss all of you."

"Sure you do," Shane agreed. "But not in that way, I hope."

"Shut up, dude. Don't make me come out there."

Shane turned to the policeman. "See? He's fine."

"I was more worried about you guys," Michael confessed. "Everything okay at the house?"

"I have to burn a blouse Monica borrowed," Claire said. "Otherwise, we're good."

They tried to talk a while longer, but somehow, Sam's silent, rigid back turned toward them made conversation seem more desperate than fun. He was really hurting, and Claire didn't know—short of letting him go for a jog in the noontime sun—how to make it any better. She didn't know where Amelie was, and with the portals shut, she doubted she could even know where to start looking.

Amelie had gathered up an army—whatever Bishop hadn't grabbed first—but what she was doing with it was anybody's guess. Claire didn't have a clue.

So in the end, she hugged Michael and told Sam it would all be okay, and they left.

"If they stay calm through the day, I'll let them out tonight," Richard said. "But I'm worried about letting them roam around on their own. What happened to Charles and the others could keep on happening. Captain Obvious used to be our biggest threat, but now we don't know who's out there, or what they're planning. And we can't count on the vampires to be able to protect themselves right now."

"My dad would say that it's about time the tables turned," Shane said.

Richard fixed him with a long stare. "Is that what you say, too?"

Shane looked at Michael, and at Sam. "No," he said. "Not anymore."

The day went on quietly. Claire got out her books and spent part of the day trying to study, but she couldn't get her brain to stop spinning. Every few minutes, she checked her e-mail and her phone, hoping for something, anything, from Amelie. *You can't just leave us like this. We don't know what to do.*

Except keep moving forward. Like Shane had said, they couldn't stay still. The world kept on turning.

Eve drove Claire to her parents' house in the afternoon, where she had cake and iced tea and listened to her mother's frantic flow of good cheer. Her dad looked sallow and unwell, and she worried about his heart, as always. But he seemed okay when he told her he loved her, and that he worried, and that he wanted her to move back home.

Just when she thought they'd gotten past that . . .

Claire exchanged a quick look with Eve. "Maybe we should talk about that when things get back to normal?" As if they ever were normal in Morganville. "Next week?"

Dad nodded. "Fine, but I'm not going to change my mind, Claire. You're better off here, at home." Whatever spell Mr. Bishop had cast over her father, it was still working great; he was single-minded about wanting her out of the Glass House. And maybe it hadn't been a spell at all; maybe it was just normal parental instinct.

Claire crammed her mouth with cake and pretended not to hear, and asked her mom about the new curtains. That filled another twenty minutes, and then Eve was able to make excuses about needing to get home, and then they were in the car.

"Wow," Eve said, and started the engine. "So. Are you going to do it? Move in with them?"

Claire shrugged helplessly. "I don't know. I don't know if we're going to get through the day! It's kind

of hard to make plans." She wasn't going to say anything, truly, she wasn't, but the words had been boiling
and bubbling inside her all day, and as Eve put the
car in drive, Claire said, "Shane said he loved me."

Eve hit the brakes, hard enough to make their seat
belts click in place. "Shane *what*? Said *what*?"

"Shane said he loved me."

"Okay, first impressions—fantastic, good, that's what
I was hoping you'd said." Eve took a deep breath and
let up on the brake, steering out into the deserted
street. "Second impressions, well, I hope that you
two . . . um . . . how can I put this? Watch yourselves?"

"You mean, don't have sex? We won't." Claire said
it with a little bit of an edge. "Even if we wanted to.
I mean, he promised, and he's not going to break that
promise, not even if I say it's okay."

"Oh. *Oh.*" Eve stared at her, wide-eyed, for way
too long for road safety. "You're kidding! Wait,
you're not. He said he loved you, and then he said—"

"No," Claire said. "He said no."

"Oh." Funny, how many meanings that word could
have. This time it was full of sympathy. "You know,
that makes him—"

"Great? Superbly awesome? Yeah, I know. I just—"
Claire threw up her hands. "I just *want* him, okay?"

"He'll still be there in a couple of months, Claire.
At seventeen, you're not a kid, at least in Texas."

"You've put some thought into this."

"Not me," Eve said, and gave her an apologetic
look.

"*Shane?* You mean—you mean you talked about
this? With Shane?"

"He needed some girl guidance. I mean, he's taking
this really seriously—a lot more seriously than I expected. He wants to do the right thing. That's cool,
right? I think that's cool. Most guys, it's just, whatever."

Claire clenched her jaw so hard she felt her teeth grinding. "I can't believe he talked to you about it!"

"Well, you're talking to me about it."

"He's a guy!"

"Guys occasionally talk, believe it or not. Something more than *pass the beer* or *where's the porn?*" Eve turned the corner, and they cruised past a couple of slow blocks of houses, some people out walking, an elementary school with a TEMPORARILY CLOSED sign out front. "You didn't exactly ask for advice, but I'm going to give it: don't rush this. You may think you're good to go, but give it some time. It's not like you have a sell-by date or anything."

Despite her annoyance, Claire had to laugh. "Feels like it right now."

"Well, duh. Hormones!"

"So how old were you when—"

"Too young. I speak from experience, grasshopper." Eve's expression went distant for a second. "I wish I'd waited for Michael."

That was, for some reason, kind of a shock, and Claire blinked. She remembered some things, and felt deeply uncomfortable. "Uh . . . did Brandon . . . ?" Because Brandon had been her family's Protector vampire, and he'd been a complete creep. She couldn't imagine much worse than having Brandon be your first.

"No. Not that he didn't want to, but no, it wasn't Brandon."

"Who?"

"Sorry. Off-limits."

Claire blinked. There wasn't much Eve considered off-limits. "Really?"

"Really." Eve pulled the car up to the curb. "Bottom line? If Shane says he loves you, he does, full stop. He wouldn't say it if he didn't mean it, all the way. He's not the kind of guy to tell you what you want to hear. That makes you really, really lucky. You should remember that."

Claire was trying, really, but from time to time that moment came back to her, that blinding, searing moment when he'd looked into her face and said those words, and she'd seen that amazing light in his eyes. She'd wanted to see it again, over and over. Instead, she'd seen him walk away.

It felt romantic. It also felt frustrating, on some level she didn't even remember feeling before. And now there was something new: doubt. *Maybe that was my fault. Maybe I was supposed to do something I didn't do. Some signal I didn't give him.*

Eve read her expression just fine. "You'll be okay," she said, and laughed just a little. "Give the guy a break. He's the second actual gentleman I've ever met. It doesn't mean he doesn't want to throw you on the bed and go. Just means he won't, right now. Which you have to admit: kinda hot."

Put in those terms, it kind of was.

As it got closer to nightfall, Richard called to say he was letting Michael go. For the second time, the three of them piled into the car and went racing to City Hall. The barricades had mostly come down. According to the radio and television, it had been a very quiet day, with no reports of violence. Store owners—the human ones, anyway—were planning on reopening in the morning. Schools would be in session.

Life was going on, and Mayor Morrell was expected to come out with some kind of a speech. Not that anybody would listen.

"Are they letting Sam out, too?" Claire asked, as Eve parked in the underground lot.

"Apparently. Richard doesn't think he can really keep anybody much longer. Some kind of town ordinance, which means law and order really is back in fashion. Plus, I think he's really afraid Sam's going to hurt himself if this goes on. And also, maybe he thinks he can follow Sam to find Amelie." Eve scanned the dark structure—there were a few dark-tinted cars in the lot, but then, there always were. The rest of the vehicles looked like they were human owned. "You guys see anything?"

"Like what? A big sign saying This Is a Trap?" Shane opened his door and got out, taking Claire's hand to help her. He didn't drop it once she was standing beside him. "Not that I wouldn't put it past some of our finer citizens. But no, I don't see anything."

Michael was being let out of his cell when they arrived, and there were hugs and handshakes. The other vampires didn't have anyone to help them, and looked a little confused about what they were supposed to do. Not Sam.

"Sam, wait!" Michael grabbed his arm on the way past, dragging his grandfather to a stop. Looking at them standing together, Claire was struck again by how alike they were. And always would be, she supposed, given that neither one of them was going to age any more. "You can't go charging off by yourself. You don't even know where she is. Running around town on your white horse will get you really, truly killed."

"Doing nothing will get *her* killed. I can't have that, Michael. None of this means anything to me if she dies." Sam shook Michael's hand away. "I'm not asking you to come with me. I'm just telling you not to get in my way."

"Grandpa—"

"Exactly. Do as you're told." Sam could move vampire-quick when he wanted to, and he was gone almost before the words hit Claire's ears—a blur, heading for the exit.

"So much for trying to figure out where she is from where he goes," Shane said. "Unless you've got light speed under the hood of that car, Eve."

Michael looked after him with a strange expression on his face—anger, regret, sorrow. Then he hugged Eve closer and kissed the top of her head.

"Well, I guess my family's no more screwed up than anybody else's," he said.

Eve nodded. "Let's recap. My dad was an abusive jerk—"

"Mine, too." Shane raised his hand.

"Thank you. My brother's a psycho backstabber—"

Shane said, "You don't even want to talk about my dad."

"Point. So, in short, Michael, your family is *awesome* by comparison. Bloodsucking, maybe. But kind of awesome."

Michael sighed. "Doesn't really feel like it at the moment."

"It will." Eve was suddenly very serious. "But Shane and I don't have that to look forward to, you know. You're our only real family now."

"I know," Michael said. "Let's go home."

11

Home was theirs again. The refugees were all out now, leaving a house that badly needed picking up and cleaning—not that anybody had gone out of their way to trash the place, but with that many people coming and going, things happened. Claire grabbed a trash bag and began clearing away paper plates, old Styrofoam cups half full of stale coffee, crumpled wrappers, and papers. Shane fired up the video game, apparently back in the mood to kill zombies. Michael took his guitar out of its case and tuned it, but he kept getting up to stare out the windows, restless and worried.

"What?" Eve asked. She'd heated up leftover spaghetti out of the refrigerator, and tried to hand Michael a plate first. "Do you see something?"

"Nothing," he said, and gave her a quick, strained smile as he waved away the food. "Not really hungry, though. Sorry."

"More for me," Shane said, and grabbed the plate. He propped it on his lap and forked spaghetti into his mouth. "Seriously. You all right? Because you never turn down food."

Michael didn't answer. He stared out into the dark.

"You're worried," Eve said. "About Sam?"

"Sam and everybody else. This is nuts. What's going on here—" Michael checked the locks on the window, but as a kind of automatic motion, as though his mind wasn't really on it. "Why hasn't Bishop taken over?

What's he *doing* out there? Why aren't we seeing the fight?"

"Maybe Amelie's kicking his ass out there in the shadows somewhere." Shane shoveled in more spaghetti.

"No. She's not. I can feel that. I think—I think she's in hiding. With the rest of her followers, the vampires, anyway."

Shane stopped chewing. "You know where they are?"

"Not really. I just feel—" Michael shook his head. "It's gone. Sorry. But I feel like things are changing. Coming to a head."

Claire had just taken a plate of warm pasta when they all heard the thump of footsteps overhead. They looked up, and then at each other, in silence. Michael pointed to himself and the stairs, and they all nodded. Eve opened a drawer in the end table and took out three sharpened stakes; she tossed one to Shane, one to Claire, and kept one in a white-knuckled grip.

Michael ascended the stairs without a sound, and disappeared.

He didn't come back down. Instead, there was a swirl of black coat and stained white balloon pants tucked into black boots; then Myrnin leaned over the railing to say, "Upstairs, all of you. I need you."

"Um . . ." Eve looked at Shane. Shane looked at Claire.

Claire followed Myrnin. "Trust me," she said. "It won't do any good to say no."

Michael was waiting in the hallway, next to the open, secret door. He led the way up.

Whatever Claire had been expecting to see, it wasn't a *crowd*, but that was what was waiting upstairs in the hidden room on the third floor. She stared in confusion at the room full of people, then moved out of the way for Shane and Eve to join her and Michael.

Myrnin came last. "Claire, I believe you know Theo Goldman and his family."

The faces came into focus. She *had* met them—in that museum thing, when they'd been on the way to rescue Myrnin. Theo Goldman had spoken to Amelie. He'd said they wouldn't fight.

But it looked to Claire like they'd been in a fight anyway. Vampires didn't bruise, exactly, but she could see torn clothes and smears of blood, and they all looked exhausted and somehow—hollow. Theo was worst of all. His kind face seemed made of nothing but lines and wrinkles now, as if he'd aged a hundred years in a couple of days.

"I'm sorry," he said, "but we had no other place to go. Amelie—I hoped that she was here, that she would give us refuge. We've been everywhere else."

Claire remembered there being more of them, some-how—yes, there were at least two people missing. One human, one vampire. "What happened? I thought you were safe where you were!"

"We were," Theo said. "Then we weren't. That's what wars are like. The safe places don't stay safe. Someone knew where we were, or suspected. Around dawn yesterday, a mob broke in the doors looking for us. Jochen—" He looked at his wife, and she bowed her head. "Our son Jochen, he gave his life to delay them. So did our human friend William. We've been hiding, moving from place to place, trying not to be driven out in the sun."

"How did you get here?" Michael asked. He seemed wary. Claire didn't blame him.

"I brought them," Myrnin said. "I've been trying to find those who are left." He crouched down next to one of the young vampire girls and stroked her hair. She smiled at him, but it was a fragile, frightened smile. "They can stay here for now. This room isn't common knowledge. I've left open the portal in the attic in case they have to flee, but it's one way only, leading out. It's a last resort."

"Are there others? Out there?" Claire asked.

"Very few on their own. Most are either with

Bishop, with Amelie, or"—Myrnin spread his hands—
"gone."

"What are they doing? Amelie and Bishop?"

"Moving their forces. They're trying to find an advantage, pick the most favorable ground. It won't last."
Myrnin shrugged. "Sooner or later, sometime tonight,
they'll clash, and then they'll fight. Someone will win,
and someone will lose. And in the morning, Morganville will know its fate."

That was creepy. *Really* creepy. Claire shivered and
looked at the others, but nobody seemed to have anything to say.

"Claire. Attend me," Myrnin said, and walked with
her to one corner of the room. "Have you spoken
with your doctor friend?"

"I tried. I couldn't get through to him. Myrnin, are
you . . . okay?"

"Not for much longer," he said, in that clinical way
he had right before the drugs wore off. "I won't be
safe to be around without another dose of some sort.
Can you get it for me?"

"There's none in your lab—"

"I've been there. Bishop got there first. I shall need
a good bit of glassware, and a completely new library." He said it lightly, but Claire could see the
tension in his face and the shadow in his dark, gleaming eyes. "He tried to destroy the portals, cut off
Amelie's movements. I managed to patch things together, but I shall need to instruct you in how it's
done. Soon. In case—"

He didn't need to finish. Claire nodded slowly.
"You should go," she said. "Is the prison safe? The
one where you keep the sickest ones?"

"Bishop finds nothing to interest him there, so yes.
He will ignore it awhile longer. I'll lock myself in for
a while, until you come with the drug." Myrnin bent
over her, suddenly very focused and very intent. "We
must refine the serum, Claire. We *must* distribute it.

The stress, the fighting—it's accelerating the disease. I've seen signs of it in Theo, even in Sam. If we don't act soon, I'm afraid we may begin to lose more to confusion and fear. They won't even be able to defend themselves."

Claire swallowed. "I'll get on it."

He took her hand and kissed it lightly. His lips felt dry as dust, but it still left a tingle in her fingers. "I know you will, my girl. Now, let's rejoin your friends."

"How long do they need to be here?" Eve asked, as they moved closer. She asked not unkindly, but she seemed nervous, too. There were, Claire thought, an awful lot of near-stranger vampire guests. "I mean, we don't have a lot of blood in the house. . . ."

Theo smiled. Claire remembered, with a sharp feeling of alarm, what he'd said to Amelie back at the museum, and she didn't like that smile at all, not even when he said, "We won't require much. We can provide for ourselves."

"He means, they can munch on their human friends, like takeout," Claire said. "No. Not in our house."

Myrnin frowned. "This is hardly the time to be—"

"This is *exactly* the time, and you know it. Did anybody ask *them* if they wanted to be snack packs?" The two remaining humans, both women, looked horrified. "I didn't think so."

Theo's expression didn't change. "What we do is our own affair. We won't hurt them, you know."

"Unless you're getting your plasma by osmosis, I don't really know how you can promise that."

Theo's eyes flared with banked fire. "What do you want us to do? Starve? Even the youngest of us?"

Eve cleared her throat. "Actually, I know where there's a big supply of blood. If somebody will go with me to get it."

"Oh, hell no," Shane said. "Not out in the dark. Besides, the place is locked up."

Eve reached in her pocket and took out her key

ring. She flipped until she found one key in particular, and held it up. "I never turned in my key," she said. "I used to open and close, you know."

Myrnin gazed at her thoughtfully. "There's no portal to Common Grounds. It's off the network. That means any vampire in it will be trapped in daylight."

"No. There's underground access to the tunnels; I've seen it. Oliver sent some people out using it while I was there." Eve gave him a bright, brittle smile. "I say we move your friends there. Also, there's coffee. You guys like coffee, right? Everybody likes coffee."

Theo ignored her, and looked to Myrnin for an answer. "Is it better?"

"It's more defensible," Myrnin said. "Steel shutters. If there's underground access—yes. It would make a good base of operations." He turned to Eve. "We'll require your services to drive."

He said it as if Eve were the help, and Claire felt her face flame hot. "Excuse me? How about a *please* in there somewhere, since you're asking for a favor?"

Myrnin's eyes turned dark and very cold. "You seem to have forgotten that I employ you, Claire. That I *own* you, in some sense. I am not required to say please and thank you to you, your friends, or *any* human walking the streets." He blinked, and was back to the Myrnin she normally saw. "However, I do take your point. Yes. *Please* drive us to Common Grounds, dear lady. I would be extravagantly, embarrassingly grateful."

He did all but kiss her hand. Eve, not surprisingly, could say nothing but yes.

Claire settled for an eye roll big enough to make her head hurt. "You can't all fit," she pointed out. "In Eve's car, I mean."

"And she's not taking you alone, anyway," Michael said. "My car's in the garage. I can take the rest of you. Shane, Claire—"

"Staying here, since you'll need the space," Shane said. "Sounds like a plan. Look, if there are people looking for them, you ought to get them moving. I'll call Richard. He can assign a couple of cops to guard Common Grounds."

"No," Myrnin said. "No police. We can't trust them."

"We can't?"

"Some of them have been working with Bishop, and with the human mobs. I have proof of that. We can't take the risk."

"But Richard—," Claire said, and subsided when she got Myrnin's glare. "Right. Okay. On your own, got it."

Eve didn't want to be dragged into it, but she went without much of a protest—the number of fangs in the room might have had something to do with it. As the Goldmans and Myrnin, Eve and Michael walked downstairs, Shane held Claire back to say, "We've got to figure out how to lock this place up. In case."

"You mean, against—" She gestured vaguely at the vampires. He nodded. "But if Michael lives here, and we live here, the house can't just bar a whole group of people from entry. It has to be done one at a time—at least that's what I understood. And no, before you ask me, I don't know how it works. Or how to fool it. I think only Amelie has the keys to that."

He looked disappointed. "How about closing off these weird doors Myrnin and Amelie are popping through?"

"I can work them. That doesn't mean I can turn them on and off."

"Great." He looked around the room, then took a seat on the old Victorian couch. "So we're like Undead Grand Central Station. Not really loving that so much. Can Bishop come through?"

It was a question that Claire had been thinking about, and it creeped her out to have to say, "I don't know. Maybe. But from what Myrnin said, he set the doorway to exit-only. So maybe we just . . . wait."

Robbed of doing anything heroic, or for that matter even useful, she warmed up the spaghetti again, and she and Shane ate it and watched some mindless TV show while jumping at every noise and creak, with weapons handy. When the kitchen door banged open nearly an hour later, Claire almost needed a heart transplant—until she heard Eve yell, "We're home! Oooooh, spaghetti. I'm starved." Eve came in holding a plate and shoveling pasta into her mouth as she walked. Michael was right behind her.

"No problems?" Shane asked. Eve shook her head, chewing a mouthful of spaghetti.

"They should be fine there. Nobody saw us get them inside, and until Oliver turns up, nobody is going to need to get in there for a while."

"What about Myrnin?"

Eve swallowed, almost choked, and Michael patted her kindly on the back. She beamed at him. "Myrnin? Oh yeah. He did a Batman and took off into the night. What is *with* that guy, Claire? If he was a superhero, he'd be Bipolar Man."

The drugs were the problem. Claire needed to get more, and she needed to work on that cure Myrnin had found. That was just as important as anything else . . . providing there were any vampires left, anyway.

They had dinner, and at least it was the four of them again, sitting around the table, talking as if the world were normal, even if all of them knew it wasn't. Shane seemed especially jumpy, which wasn't like him at all.

For her part, Claire was just tired to the bone of being scared, and when she went upstairs, she was asleep the minute she crawled between the covers.

But sleep didn't mean it was restful, or peaceful.

She dreamed that somewhere, Amelie was playing chess, moving her pieces at lightning speed across a black-and-white board. Bishop sat across from her, grinning with too many teeth, and when he took her rook, it turned into a miniature version of Claire, and suddenly both the vampires were huge and she was so small, so small, stranded out in the open.

Bishop picked her up and squeezed her in his white

hand, and blood drops fell onto the white squares of the chessboard.

Amelie frowned, watching Bishop squeeze her, and put out a delicate fingertip to touch the drops of blood. Claire struggled and screamed.

Amelie tasted her blood, and smiled.

Claire woke up with a convulsive shudder, huddled in her blankets. It was still dark outside the windows, though the sky was getting lighter, and the house was very, very quiet.

Her phone was buzzing in vibrate mode on the bedside table. She picked it up and found a text message from the university's alert system.

CLASSES RETURN TO NORMAL SCHEDULE EFFECTIVE 7 A.M. TODAY.

School seemed like a million miles away, another world that didn't mean anything to her anymore, but it would get her on campus, and there were things she needed there. Claire scrolled down her phone list and found Dr. Robert Mills, but there was no immediate answer on his cell. She checked the clock, winced at the early hour, but slid out of bed and began grabbing things out of drawers. That didn't take a lot of time. She was down to the last of everything. Laundry was starting to be a genuine priority.

She dialed his phone again after she'd dressed.

"Hello?" Dr. Mills sounded as if she'd dragged him out of a deep, probably happy sleep. *He* probably hadn't been dreaming about being squeezed dry by Mr. Bishop.

"It's Claire," she said. "I'm sorry to call so early—"

"Is it early? Oh. Been up all night, just fell asleep." He yawned. "Glad you're all right, Claire."

"Are you at the hospital?"

"No. The hospital's going to need a lot of work before it's even halfway ready for the kind of work I need to do." Another jaw-cracking yawn. "Sorry. I'm on campus, in the Life Sciences Building. Lab Seventeen. We have some roll-away beds here."

"We?"

"My wife and kids are with me. I didn't want to leave them on their own out there."

Claire didn't blame him. "I've got something for you to do, and I need some of the drug," she said. "It could be really important. I'll be at school in about twenty minutes, okay?"

"Okay. Don't come here. My kids are asleep right now. Let's meet somewhere else."

"The on-campus coffee bar," she said. "It's in the University Center."

"Trust me, I know where it is. Twenty minutes."

She was already heading for the door.

With no sounds coming from any of the other rooms, Claire figured her housemates were all crashed out, exhausted. She didn't know why she wasn't, except for a suppressed, vibrating fear inside her that if she slept any more, something bad was going to happen.

Showered, dressed in her last not-very-good clothes, she grabbed up her backpack and repacked it. Her dart gun was out of darts anyway, so she left it behind. The samples Myrnin had prepared of Bishop's blood went into a sturdy padded box, and on impulse, she added a couple of stakes and the silver knife Amelie had given her.

And books.

It was the first time Claire had been on foot in Morganville since the rioting had started, and it was eerie. The town was quiet again, but stores had broken windows, some boarded over; there were some buildings reduced to burned-out hulks, with blind, open doorways. Broken bottles were on the sidewalks and spots of what looked like blood on the concrete—and, in places, dark splashes.

Claire hurried past it all, even past Common Grounds, where the steel shutters were down inside the windows. There was no sign of anyone within. She imagined Theo Goldman standing there watching her from cover, and waved a little, just a waggle of fingers.

She didn't really expect a response.

The gates of the university were open, and the guards were gone. Claire jogged along the sidewalk, going up the hill and around the curve, and began to see students up and moving, even so early in the morning. As she got closer to the central cluster of buildings, the foot traffic intensified, and here and there she saw alert campus police walking in pairs, watching for trouble.

The students didn't seem to notice anything at all. Not for the first time, Claire wondered if Amelie's semipsychic network that cut Morganville off from the world also kept people on campus clueless.

She didn't like to think they were just naturally that stupid. Then again, she'd been to some of the parties.

The University Center had opened its doors only a few minutes before, and the coffee barista was just taking the chairs down from the tables. Usually it would have been Eve on duty, but instead, it was one of the university staffers, on loan from the food service most likely. He didn't exactly look happy to be there. Claire tried to be nice, and finally got a smile from him as he handed her a mocha and took her cash.

"I wouldn't be here," he confessed, "except that they're paying us triple to be here the rest of the week."

"Really? Wow. I'll tell Eve. She could use the money."

"Yeah, get her in here. I'm not good at this coffee stuff. Give me the plain stuff. Water, beans—can't really screw that up. This espresso is hard."

Claire decided, after tasting the mocha, that he was right. He really wasn't cut out for it. She sipped it anyway, and took a seat where she could watch the majority of the UC entrances for Dr. Mills.

She almost didn't recognize him. He'd shed his white

doctor's coat, of course, but somehow she'd never expected to see someone like him wearing a zip-up hoodie, sweatpants, and sneakers. He was more the suit-
and-tie type. He ordered plain coffee—good choice—
and came to join her at the table.

Dr. Mills was medium everything, and he blended
in at the university just as easily as he had at the
hospital. He'd have made a good spy, Claire thought.
He had one of those faces—young from one angle,
older from another, with nothing you could really remember later about it.

But he had a nice, comforting smile. She supposed
that would be a real asset in a doctor.

"Morning," he said, and gulped coffee. His eyes
were bloodshot and red rimmed. "I'm going back to
the hospital later today. Damage assessments, and
we've already reopened the trauma units and CCU.
I'm going to catch some sleep as soon as we're done,
in case any crash cases come in. Nothing worse than
an exhausted trauma surgeon."

She felt even more guilty about waking him up. "I'll
make this quick," she promised. Claire opened her
backpack, took out the padded box, and slid it across
the table to him. "Blood samples, from Myrnin."

Mills frowned. "I've already got a hundred blood
samples from Myrnin. Why—"

"These are different," Claire said. "Trust me. There's
one labeled *B* that's important."

"Important, how?"

"I don't want to say. I'd rather you took a look
first." In science, Claire knew, it was better to come
to an analysis cold, without too many expectations.
Dr. Mills knew that, too, and he nodded as he took
possession of the samples. "Um—if you want to sleep,
maybe you shouldn't drink that stuff."

Dr. Mills smiled and threw back the rest of his coffee. "You get to be a doctor by developing immunity
to all kinds of things, including caffeine," he said.

"Trust me. The second my head touches the pillow, I'm asleep, even if I've got a coffee IV drip."

"I know people who'd pay good money for that. The IV drip, I mean."

He shook his head, grinning, but then got serious. "You seem okay. I was worried about you. You're just so . . . young, to be involved in all this stuff."

"I'm all right. And I'm really—"

"Not that young. Yes, I know. But still. Let an old man fret a little. I've got two daughters." He tossed his coffee cup at the trash—two points—and stood. "Here's all I could get together of the drug. Sorry, it's not a lot, but I've got a new batch in the works. It'll take a couple of days to finish."

He handed her a bag that clinked with small glass bottles. She peeked inside. "This should be plenty." Unless, of course, she had to start dosing all over Morganville, in which case, they were done, anyway.

"Sorry to make this a gulp-and-run, but . . ."

"You should go," Claire agreed. "Thanks, Dr. Mills." She offered her hand. He shook it gravely.

Around his wrist, there was a silver bracelet, with Amelie's symbol on it. He looked down at it, then at her gold one, and shrugged.

"I don't think it's time to take it off," he said. "Not yet."

At least yours does come off, Claire thought, but didn't say. Dr. Mills had signed agreements, contracts, and those things were binding in Morganville, but the contract she'd signed had made her Amelie's property, body and soul. And her bracelet didn't have a catch on it, which made it more like a slave collar. From time to time, that still creeped her out.

It was getting close to time for her first class, and as Claire hefted her backpack, she wondered how many people would show up. Lots, probably. Knowing most of the professors, they'd think today was a good day for a quiz.

She wasn't disappointed. She also wasn't panicked, unlike some of her classmates during her first class, and her third. Claire didn't panic on tests, not unless it was in a dream where she also had to clog dance and twirl batons to get a good grade. And the quizzes weren't so hard anyway, not even the physics tests.

One thing she noticed, more and more, as she went around campus: fewer people had on bracelets. Morganville natives got used to wearing them twenty-four/ seven, so she could clearly see the tan lines where the bracelets had been . . . and weren't anymore. It was almost like a reverse tattoo.

Around noon, she saw Monica Morrell, Gina, and Jennifer.

The three girls were walking fast, heads down, books in their arms. There was a whole lot different about them; Claire was used to seeing those three stalking the campus like tigers, confident and cruel. They'd stare down anyone, and whether you liked them or not, they were wicked fashion queens, always showing themselves off to best advantage.

Not today.

Monica, who usually was the centerpiece, looked awful. Her shiny, flirty hair was dull and fuzzy, as if she had barely bothered to brush it, much less condition or curl. What little Claire could see of her face looked makeup free. She was wearing a shapeless sweater in an unflatteringly ugly pattern, and sloppy blue jeans, the kind Claire imagined she might keep around to clean house in, if Monica ever did that kind of thing.

Gina and Jennifer didn't look much better, and they all looked defeated.

Claire still felt a little, tiny, unworthy tingle of satisfaction . . . until she saw the looks they were getting. Morganville natives who'd taken off their bracelets were outright glaring at Monica and her entourage, and a few of them did worse than just give them dirty looks. As Claire watched, a big, tough jock wearing a TPU jacket bumped into Jennifer and sent her books flying. She didn't look at him. She just bent over to pick them up.

"Hey, you clumsy whore, what the hell?" He shoved her onto her butt as she tried to get up, but she wasn't his real target; she was just standing between him and Monica. "Hey. Morrell. How's your daddy?"

"Fine," Monica said, and looked him in the eyes. "I'd ask about yours, but since you don't know who he was—"

The jock stepped very close to her. She didn't flinch, but Claire could tell that she wanted to. There were tight lines around her eyes and mouth, and her knuckles were white where she gripped her books.

"You've been Princess Queen Bitch your whole life," he said. "You remember Annie? Annie McFarlane? You used to call her a fat cow. You laughed at her in school. You took pictures of her in the bathroom and posted them on the Internet. Remember?"

Monica didn't answer.

The jock smiled. "Yeah, you remember Annie. She was a good kid, and I liked her."

"You didn't like her enough to stand up for her," Monica said. "Right, Clark? You wanted to get in my pants more than you wanted me to be kind to your little fat friend. Not my fault she ended up wrecking that stupid car at the town border. Maybe it's your fault, though. Maybe she couldn't stand being in town with you anymore after you dumped her."

Clark knocked the books out of her hand and shoved her up against a nearby tree trunk. Hard.

"I've got something for you, bitch." He dug in his pocket and came up with something square, about four inches across. It was a sticky label like a name tag, only with a picture on it of an awkward but sweet-looking teenage girl trying bravely to smile for the camera.

Clark slapped it on Monica's chest and rubbed it so it stuck to the sweater.

"You wear that," he said. "You wear Annie's picture. If I see you take it off today, I swear, what you did to Annie back in high school's going to seem like a Cancún vacation."

Under Annie's picture were the words KILLED BY MONICA MORRELL.

Monica looked down at it, swallowed, and turned bright red, then pale. She jerked her chin up again, sharply, and stared at Clark. "Are you done?"

"So far. Remember, you take it off—"

"Yeah, Clark, you weren't exactly subtle. I get it. You think I care?"

Clark's grin widened. "No, you don't. Not yet. Have a nice day, Queenie."

He walked away and did a high five with two other guys.

As Monica stared down at the label on her chest in utter disgust, another girl approached—another Morganville native who'd taken off the bracelet. Monica didn't notice her until the girl was right in her face.

This one didn't talk. She just ripped the backing off another label and stuck it on Monica's chest next to Annie McFarlane's photo.

This one just said KILLER in big red letters.

She kept on walking.

Monica started to rip it off, but Clark was watching her.

"Suits you," he said, and pointed to his eyes, then to her. "We'll be watching you all day. There are a lot more labels coming."

Clark was right. It was going to be a really long, bad day to be Monica Morrell. Even Gina and Jennifer were fading back now, heading out in a different direction and leaving her to face the music.

Monica's gaze fell on Claire. There was a flash of fear in her eyes, and shame, and genuine pain.

And then she armored up and snapped, "What are you looking at, freak?"

Claire shrugged. "Justice, I guess." She frowned. "How come you didn't stay with your parents?"

"None of your business." Monica's fierce stare wavered. "Dad wanted us all to go back to normal. So people could see we're not afraid."

"How's that going?"

Monica took a step toward her, then hugged her books to her chest to cover up most of the labels, and hurried on.

She hadn't gotten ten feet before a stranger ran up and slapped a label across her back that had a picture of a slender young girl and an older boy of maybe fifteen on it. The words beneath said KILLER OF ALYSSA.

With a shock, Claire realized that the boy in that picture was *Shane*. And that was his sister, Alyssa, the one who'd died in the fire that Monica had set.

"Justice," Claire repeated softly. She felt a little sick, actually. Justice wasn't the same thing as mercy.

Her phone rang as she was trying to decide what to do. "Better come home," Michael Glass said. "We've got an emergency signal from Richard at City Hall."

12

The signal had come over the coded strategy network, which Claire had just assumed was dead, considering that Oliver had been the one running it. But Richard had found a use for it, and as she burst in the front door, breathless, she heard Michael and Eve talking in the living room. Claire closed and locked the door, dumped her backpack, and hurried to join them.

"What did I miss?"

"Shhh," they both said. Michael, Eve, and Shane were all seated at the table, staring intently at the small walkie-talkie sitting upright in the middle. Michael pulled out a chair for Claire, and she sat, trying to be as quiet as possible.

Richard was talking.

—No telling whether or not this storm will hit us full on, but right now, the Weather Service shows the radar track going right over the top of us. It'll be here in the next few hours, probably right around dark. It's late in the year for tornado activity, but they're telling us there's a strong possibility of some real trouble. On top of all the other things we have going on, this isn't good news. I'm putting all emergency services and citizen patrols on full alert. If we get a tornado, get to your designated shelters.

Designated shelters? Claire mouthed to Michael, who shrugged.

> If you're closer to City Hall, come here; we've got a shelter in the basement. Those of you who are Civil Defense wardens, go door-to-door in your area, tell people we've got a storm coming and what to do. We're putting it on TV and radio, and the university's going to get ready as well.

"Richard, this is Hector," said a new voice. "Miller House. You got any news about this takeover people are talking about?"

"We've got rumors, but nothing concrete," Richard said. "We hear there's a lot of talk going around town about taking back City Hall, but we've got no specific word about when these people are meeting, or where, or even who they are. All I can tell you is that we've fortified the building, and the barricades remain up around Founder's Square, for all the good that does. I need everybody in a security-designated location to be on the alert today and tonight. Report in if you see any sign of an attack, any sign at all. We'll try to get to you in support."

Michael exchanged a look with the rest of them, and then picked up the radio. He pressed the button. "Michael Glass. You think Bishop's behind this?"

"I think Bishop's willing to let humans do his dirty work for him, and then sweep in to make himself lord and master on the ashes," Richard said. "Seems like his style. Put Shane on."

Michael held out the radio. Shane looked at it like it might bite, then took it and pressed TALK. "Yeah, this is Shane."

"I have two unconfirmed sightings of your father in town. I know this isn't easy for you, but I need to know: is Frank Collins back in Morganville?"

Shane looked into Claire's eyes and said, "If he is, he hasn't talked to me about it."

He *lied.* Claire's lips parted, and she almost blurted something out, but she just couldn't think what to say. "Shane," she whispered. He shook his head.

"Tell you what, Richard, you catch my dad, you've got my personal endorsement for tossing him in the deepest pit you've got around here," Shane said. "If he's in Morganville, he's got a plan, but he won't be working for or with the vamps. Not that he knows, anyway."

"Fair enough. You hear from him—"

"You're on speed dial. Got it." Shane set the radio back in the center of the table. Claire kept staring at him, willing him to speak, to say *something*, but he didn't.

"Don't do this," she said. "Don't put me in the middle."

"I'm not," Shane said. "Nothing I said was a lie. My dad told me he was coming, not that he's here. I haven't seen him, and I don't want to. I meant what I said. If he's here, Dick and his brownshirts are welcome to him. I've got nothing to do with him, not anymore."

Claire wasn't sure she believed that, but she didn't think he was intentionally lying now. He probably did mean it. She just thought that no matter how much he thought he was done with his dad, all it would take would be a snap of Frank Collins's fingers to bring him running.

Not good.

Richard was answering questions from others on the radio, but Michael was no longer listening. He was fixed on Shane. "You knew? You knew he was coming back here, and you didn't warn me?"

Shane stirred uneasily. "Look—"

"No, *you* look. I'm the one who got knifed and decapitated and buried in the *backyard*, among other things! Good thing I was a ghost!"

Shane looked down. "Who was I supposed to tell? The vamps? Come on."

"You could have told me!"

"You're a vamp," Shane said. "In case you haven't checked the mirror lately."

Michael stood up. His chair slid about two feet across the floor and skidded to an uneven stop; he leaned his hands on the table and loomed over Shane. "Oh, I do," he said. "I check it every day. How about you? You taken a good look recently, Shane? Because I'm not so sure I know you anymore."

Shane looked up at that, and there was a flash of pain in his face. "I didn't mean—"

"I could be just about the last vampire around here," Michael interrupted. "Maybe the others are dead. Maybe they will be soon. Between the mobs out there willing to rip our heads off and Bishop waiting to take over, having your dad stalking me is all I need."

"He wouldn't—"

"He killed me once, or tried to. He'd do it again in a second, and he wouldn't blink, and you know that, Shane. You know it! He thinks I'm some kind of a traitor to the human race. He'll come after me in particular."

Shane didn't say anything this time. Michael retrieved the radio from the table and clipped it to the pocket of his jeans. He shone, all blazing gold and hard, white angles, and Shane couldn't meet his stare.

"You decide you want to help your dad kill some vampires, Shane, you know where to find me."

Michael went upstairs. It was as if the room had lost all its air, and Claire found herself breathing very hard, trying not to tremble.

Eve's dark eyes were very wide, and fixed on Shane as well. She slowly got up from the table.

"Eve—" he said, and reached out toward her. She stepped out of reach.

"I can't believe you," she said. "You see me running over to suck up to my mom? No. And she's not even a murderer."

"Morganville needs to change."

"Wake up, Shane, it *has*! It started months ago. It's been changing right in front of you! Vampires and humans working together. Trusting one another. They're *trying*. Sure, it's hard, but they've got reason to be afraid of us, good reason. And now you want to throw all that away and help your dad set up a guillotine in Founder's Square or something?" Eve's eyes turned bitter black. "Screw you."

"I didn't—"

She clomped away toward the stairs, leaving Shane and Claire together.

Shane swallowed, then tried to make it a joke. "That could have gone better." Claire slipped out of her chair. "Claire? Oh, come on, not you, too. Don't go. Please."

"You should have told him. I can't believe you didn't. He's your friend, or at least I thought he was."

"Where are you going?"

She pulled in a deep breath. "I'm packing. I've decided to move in with my parents."

She didn't pack, though. She went upstairs, closed the door to her room, and pulled out her pitifully few possessions. Most of it was dirty laundry. She sat there on the bed, staring at it, feeling lost and alone and a little sick, and wondered if she was making a point or just running like a little girl. She felt pretty stupid now that she had everything piled on the floor.

It looked utterly pathetic.

When the knock came on her door, she didn't immediately answer it. She knew it was Shane, even though he didn't speak. *Go away,* she thought at him, but he still wasn't much of a mind reader. He knocked again.

"It's not locked," she said.

"It's also not open," Shane said quietly, through the wood. "I'm not a complete ass."

"Yes, you are."

"Okay, sometimes I am." He hesitated, and she heard the floor creak as he shifted his weight. "Claire."

"Come in."

He froze when he saw the stuff piled in front of her, waiting to be put in bags and her one suitcase. "You're serious."

"Yes."

"You're just going to pick up and leave."

"You know my parents want me to come home."

He didn't say anything for a long moment, then reached into his back pocket and took out a black case, about the size of his hand. "Here, then. I was going to give it to you later, but I guess I'd better do it now, before you take off on us."

His voice sounded offhand and normal, but his fingers felt cold when she touched them in taking the case, and there was an expression on his face she didn't know—fear, maybe; bracing himself for something painful.

It was a hard, leather-wrapped case, on spring hinges. She hesitated for a breath, then pried up one end. It snapped open.

Oh.

The cross was beautiful—delicate silver, traceries of leaves wrapped around it. It was on a silver chain so thin it looked like a breath would melt it. When Claire picked up the necklace, it felt like air in her hand.

"I—" She had no idea what to say, what to feel. Her whole body seemed to have gone into shock. "It's beautiful."

"I know it doesn't work against the vamps," Shane said. "Okay, well, I didn't know that when I got it for you. But it's still silver, and silver works, so I hope that's okay."

This wasn't a small present. Shane didn't have a lot

of money; he picked up odd jobs here and there, and spent very little. This wasn't some cheap costume jewelry; it was real silver, and really beautiful.

"I can't—it's too expensive." Claire's heart was pounding again, and she wished she could *think*. She wished she knew what she was supposed to feel, supposed to do. On impulse, she put the necklace back in the box and snapped it shut, and held it out to him. "Shane, I can't."

He gave her a broken sort of smile. "It's not a ring or anything. Keep it. Besides, it doesn't match my eyes."

He stuck his hands in his pockets, rounded his shoulders, and walked out of the room.

Claire clutched the leather box in one sweaty hand, eyes wide, and then opened it again. The cross gleamed on black velvet, clean and beautiful and shining, and it blurred as her eyes filled with tears.

Now she felt something, something big and overwhelming and far too much to fit inside her small, fragile body.

"Oh," she whispered. "Oh *God*." This hadn't been just any gift. He'd put a lot of time and effort into getting it. There was love in it, real love.

She took the cross, put it around her neck, and fastened the clasp with shaking fingers. It took her two tries. Then she went down the hall and, without knocking, opened Shane's door. He was standing at the window, staring outside. He looked different to her. Older. Sadder.

He turned toward her, and his gaze fixed on the silver cross in the hollow of her throat.

"You're an idiot," Claire said.

Shane considered that, and nodded. "I really am, mostly."

"And then you have to go and do these awesome things—"

"I know. I did say I was *mostly* an idiot."

"You kind of have your good moments."

He didn't quite smile. "So you like it?"

She put her hand up to stroke the cross's warm silver lines. "I'm wearing it, aren't I?"

"Not that it means we're—"

"You said you loved me," Claire said. "You did say that."

He shut his mouth and studied her, then nodded. There was a flush building high in his cheeks.

"Well, I love you, too, and you're still an idiot. Mostly."

"No argument." He folded his arms across his chest, and she tried not to notice the way his muscles tensed, or the vulnerable light in his eyes. "So, you moving out?"

"I should," she said softly. "The other night—"

"Claire. Please be straight with me. Are you moving out?"

She was holding the cross now, cradling it, and it felt warm as the sun against her fingers. "I can't," she said. "I have to do laundry first, and that might take a month. You saw the pile."

He laughed, and it was as if all the strength went out of him. He sat down on his unmade bed, hard, and after a moment, she walked around the end and sat next to him. He put his arm around her.

"Life is a work in progress," Shane said. "My mom used to say that. I'm kind of a fixer-upper. I know that."

Claire sighed and allowed herself to relax against his warmth. "Good thing I like high-maintenance guys."

He was about to kiss her—finally—when they both heard a sound from overhead.

Only there was nothing overhead. Nothing but the attic.

"Did you hear that?" Shane asked.

"Yeah. It sounded like footsteps."

"Oh, well, that's fantastic. I thought it was supposed to be exit-only or something." Shane reached under his bed and came up with a stake. "Go get Michael and Eve. Here." He handed her another stake. This one had a silver tip. "It's the Cadillac of vampire killers. Don't dent it."

"You are so weird." But she took it, and then dashed to her room to grab the thin silver knife Amelie had given her. No place to put it, but she poked a hole in the pocket of her jeans just big enough for the blade. The jeans were tight enough to keep the blade in place against her leg, but not so much it looked obvious, and besides, it was pretty flexible.

She hurried down the hall, listening for any other movement. Eve's room was empty, but when she knocked on Michael's door, she heard a startled yelp that sounded very Eve-like. "What?" Michael asked.

"Trouble," Claire said. "Um, maybe? Attic. Now."

Michael didn't sound any happier about it than Shane had been. "Great. Be there in a second."

Muffled conversation, and the sound of fabric moving. Claire wondered if he was getting dressed, and quickly tried to reject that image, not because it wasn't awesomely hot, but because, well, it was *Michael*, and besides, there were other things to think about.

Such as what was upstairs in the attic.

Or who.

The door banged open, and Eve rushed out, flushed and mussed and still buttoning her shirt. "It's not what you think," she said. "It was just—oh, okay, whatever, it was exactly what you think. Now, *what*?"

Something dropped and rolled across the attic floor directly above their heads. Claire silently pointed up, and Eve followed the motion, staring as if she could see through the wood and plaster. She jumped when Michael, who'd thrown on an unbuttoned shirt, put a hand on her shoulder. He put a finger to his lips.

Shane stepped out of his room, holding a stake in either hand. He pitched one underhand to Michael.

Where's mine? Eve mouthed.

Get your own, Shane mouthed back. Eve rolled her eyes and dashed into her own room, coming back with a black bag slung across her chest, bandolier-style. It was, Claire assumed, full of weapons. Eve fished around in it and came up with a stake of her very own. It even had her initials carved in it.

"Shop class," she whispered. "See? I *did* learn something in school."

Michael pressed the button to release the hidden door, and it opened without a sound. There were no lights upstairs that Claire could see. The stairs were pitch-black.

Michael, by common consent, went first, vampire eyes, and all. Shane followed, then Eve; Claire brought up the rear, and tried to move as silently as possible, although not really all that silently, because the stairs creaked beneath the weight of four people. At the top, Claire ran into Eve's back, and whispered, "What?"

Eve, in answer, reached back to grip her hand. "Michael smells blood," she whispered. "Hush."

Michael flicked on a light at the other end of the small, silent room. There was nothing unusual, just the furniture that was always here. There were no signs anybody had been here since the Goldmans and Myrnin had departed.

"How do we get into the attic?" Shane asked. Michael pressed hidden studs, and another door, barely visible at that end of the room, clicked open. Claire remembered it well; Myrnin had shown it to her, when they'd been getting stuff together to go to Bishop's welcome feast.

"Stay here," Michael said, and stepped through into the dim, open space.

"Yeah, sure," Shane said, and followed. He popped his head back in to say, "No, not you two. Stay here."

"Does he just not get how unfair and sexist that is?" Eve asked. "Men."

"You really want to go first?"

"Of course not. But I'd like the chance to *refuse* to go first."

They waited tensely, listening for any sign of trouble. Claire heard Shane's footsteps moving through the attic, but nothing else for a long time.

Then she heard him say, "Michael. Oh man . . . over here." There was tension in his voice, but it didn't sound like he was about to jump into hand-to-hand combat.

Eve and Claire exchanged looks, and Eve said, "Oh, screw it," and dived into the attic after them.

Claire followed, gripping the Cadillac of stakes and hoping she wasn't going to be forced to try to use it.

Shane was crouched down behind some stacked, dusty suitcases, and Michael was there, too. Eve pulled in a sharp breath when she saw what it was they were bending over, and put out a hand to stop Claire in her tracks.

Not that Claire stopped, until she saw who was lying on the wooden floor. She hardly recognized him, really. If it hadn't been for the gray ponytail and the leather coat . . .

"It's Oliver," she whispered. Eve was biting her lip until it was almost white, staring at her former boss. "What *happened*?"

"Silver," Michael said. "Lots of it. It eats vampire skin like acid, but he shouldn't be this bad. Not unless—" He stopped as the pale, burned eyelids fluttered. "He's still alive."

"Vampires are hard to kill," Oliver whispered. His voice was barely a creak of sound, and it broke at the end on what sounded almost like a sob. "*Jesu.* Hurts."

Michael exchanged a look with Shane, then said, "Let's get him downstairs. Claire. Go get some blood from the fridge. There should be some."

"No," Oliver grated, and sat up. There was blood leaking through his white shirt, as if all his skin were gone underneath. "No time. Attack on City Hall, coming tonight—Bishop. Using it as a—diversion—to—" His eyes opened wider, and went blank, then rolled up into his head.

He collapsed. Michael caught him under the shoulders.

He and Shane carried Oliver out to the couch, while Eve anxiously followed along, making little shooing motions.

Claire started to follow, then heard something scrape across the wood behind her, in the shadows.

Oliver hadn't come here alone.

A black shadow lunged out, grabbed her, and something hard hit her head.

She must have made some sound, knocked something over, because she heard Shane call her name sharply, and saw his shadow in the doorway before darkness took all of it away.

Then she was falling away.

Then she was gone.

13

Claire came awake feeling sick, wretched, and cold. Someone was pounding on the back of her head with a croquet mallet, or at least that was how it felt, and when she tried to move, the whole world spun around.

"Shut up and stop moaning," somebody said from a few feet away. "Don't you dare throw up or I'll make you eat it."

It sounded like Jason Rosser, Eve's crazy brother. Claire swallowed hard and squinted, trying to make out the shadow next to her. Yeah, it looked like Jason—skanky, greasy, and insane. She tried to squirm away from him, but ran into a wall at her back. It felt like wood, but she didn't think it was the Glass House attic.

He'd taken her somewhere, probably using the portal. And now none of her friends could follow, because none of them knew how.

Her hands and feet were tied. Claire blinked, trying to clear her head. That was a little unfortunate, because with clarity came the awareness of just how bad this was. Jason Rosser really *was* crazy. He'd stalked Eve. He'd—at least allegedly—killed girls in town. He'd definitely stabbed Shane, and he'd staked Amelie at the feast when she'd tried to help him.

And none of her friends back at the Glass House

would know how to find her. To their eyes, she would have just . . . vanished.

"What do you want?" she asked. Her voice sounded rusty and scared. Jason reached out and moved hair back from her face, which creeped her out. She didn't like him touching her.

"Relax, shortcake, you're not my type," he said. "I do what I'm told, that's all. You were wanted. So I brought you."

"Wanted?"

A low, silky laugh floated on the silence, dark as smoke, and Jason looked over his shoulder as the hidden observer rose and stepped into what little light there was.

Ysandre, Bishop's pale little girlfriend. Beautiful, sure. Delicate as jasmine flowers, with big, liquid eyes and a sweetly rounded face.

She was poison in a pretty bottle.

"Well," she said, and crouched down next to Claire. "Look at what the cat dragged in. Meeow." Her sharp nail dragged over Claire's cheek, and judging from the sting, it drew blood. "Where's your pretty boyfriend, Miss Claire? I really wasn't done with him, you know. I hadn't even properly *started.*"

Claire felt an ugly lurch of anger mix with the fear already churning her stomach. "He's probably not done with you, either," she said, and managed to smile. She hoped it was a cold kind of smile, the sort that Amelie used—or Oliver. "Maybe you should go looking. I'll bet he'd be *so* happy to see you."

"I'll show that boy a real good time, when we do meet up again," Ysandre purred, and put her face very close to Claire's. "Now, then, let's talk, just us girls. Won't that be fun?"

Not. Claire was struggling against the ropes, but Jason had done his job pretty well; she was hurting herself more than accomplishing anything else. Ysandre grabbed Claire's shoulder and wrenched her upright against the wooden wall, hard enough to bang Claire's injured head. For a dazed second, it looked like Ysandre's ripe, red smile floated in midair, like some undead Cheshire cat.

"Now," Ysandre said, "ain't this nice, sweetie? It's too bad we couldn't get Mr. Shane to join us, but my little helper here, he's a bit worried about tackling Shane. Bad blood and all." She laughed softly. "Well, we'll make do. Amelie likes you, I hear, and you've got on that pretty little gold bracelet. So you'll do just fine."

"For what?"

"I ain't telling you, sweetie." Ysandre's smile was truly scary. "This town's going to have a wild night, though. Real wild. And you're going to get to see the whole thing, up close. You must be all atingle."

Eve would have had a quip at the ready. Claire just glared, and wished her head would stop aching and spinning. What had he hit her with? It felt like the front end of a bus. She hadn't thought Jason could hit that hard, truthfully.

Don't try to find me, Shane. Don't. The last thing she wanted was Shane racing to the rescue and taking on a guy who'd stabbed him, and a vampire who'd led him around by a leash.

No, she had to find her own way out of this.

Step one: figure out where she was. Claire let Ysandre ramble on, describing all kinds of lurid things that Claire thought it was better not to imagine, considering they were things Ysandre was thinking of doing to *her*. Instead, she tried to identify her surroundings. It didn't look familiar, but that was no help; she was still relatively new to Morganville. Plenty of places she'd never been.

Wait.

Claire focused on the crate that Jason was sitting on. There was stenciling on it. It was hard to make it out in the dim light, but she thought it said BRICKS

BULK COFFEE. And now that she thought about it, it smelled like coffee in here, too. A warm, morning kind of smell, floating over dust and damp wood.

And she remembered Eve laughing about how Oliver bought his coffee from a place called Bricks. *As in, tastes like ground-up bricks,* Eve had said. *If you order flavored, they add in the mortar.*

There were only two coffee shops in town: Oliver's place, and the University Center coffee bar. This didn't look like the UC, which wasn't that old and was mostly built of concrete, not wood.

That meant . . . she was at Common Grounds? But Common Grounds didn't make any sense; there wasn't any kind of portal leading to it.

Maybe Oliver has a warehouse. That sounded right, because the vampires seemed to own a lot of the warehouse district that bordered Founder's Square. Brandon, Oliver's second-in-vampire-command, had been found dead in a warehouse.

Maybe she was close to Founder's Square.

Ysandre's cold fingers closed around Claire's chin and jerked it up. "Are you listening, honey?"

"Truthfully, no," Claire said. "You're kind of boring."

Jason actually laughed, and turned it into a fake cough. "I'm going outside," he said. "Since this is going to get all personal now." Claire wanted to yell to him not to go, but she bit her tongue and turned it into a subsonic whine in the back of her throat as she watched him walk away. His footsteps receded into the dark, and then finally a small square of light opened a long way off.

It was a door, too far for her to reach—way too far.

"I thought he'd never leave," Ysandre said, and put her cold, cold lips on Claire's neck, then yelled in shock and pulled away, covering her mouth with one pale hand. "You *bitch*!"

Ysandre hadn't seen the silver chain Claire was

wearing in the dim light, as whisper-thin as it was. Now there were welts forming on the vampire's full lips—forming, breaking, and bleeding.

Fury sparked in Ysandre's eyes. Playtime was over.

As Claire squirmed away, the vampire followed at a lazy stroll. She wiped her burned lips and looked at the thin, leaking blood in distaste. "Tastes like silver. Disgusting. You've just ruined my good mood, little girl."

As she rolled, Claire felt something sharp dig into her leg. *The knife.* They'd found the stake, but she guessed their search hadn't exactly been thorough; Jason was too crazy, and Ysandre too careless and arrogant.

But the knife wasn't going to do her any good at all where it was, unless . . .

Ysandre lunged for her, a blur of white in the darkness, and Claire twisted and jammed her hip down at an awkward angle.

The knife slipped and tore through the fabric of her jeans—not much of it, just a couple of inches, but enough to slice open Ysandre's hand and arm as it reached for her, all the way to the bone.

Ysandre shrieked in real pain, and spun away. She didn't look so pretty now, and when she turned toward Claire again, from a respectful distance this time, she hissed at her with full cobra fangs extended. Her eyes were wild and bloodred, glowing like rubies.

Claire twisted, nearly yanking her elbow out of its joint, and managed to get the ropes around her wrist against the knife. She didn't have long; the shock wouldn't keep Ysandre at bay for more than a few seconds.

But getting a silver knife to cut through synthetic rope? That was going to take a while—a while she didn't have.

Claire sawed desperately, and got a little bit of give on the bonds—enough to *almost* get her hand into her pocket.

But not.

Ysandre grabbed her by the hair. "I'm going to destroy you for that."

The pain in her head was blinding. It felt like her scalp was being ripped off, and on top of that, the massive headache roared back to a new, sickening pulse.

Claire loosened the rope enough to plunge her aching hand into her pocket and grab the handle of the knife. She yanked it out of the tangle of fabric and held it at a trembling, handicapped *en garde*—still tied up, but whatever, she wasn't going to stop fighting, not *ever*.

Ysandre shrieked and let her go, which made no sense to Claire's confused, pain-shocked mind. *I didn't stab her yet. Did I?* Not that she wanted to stab anybody, even Ysandre. She just wanted—

What was going on?

Ysandre's body slammed down hard on the wooden floor, and Claire gasped and flinched away . . . but the vampire had fallen facedown, limp, and weirdly broken.

A small woman dressed in gray, her pale hair falling wild around her shoulders, dropped silently from overhead and put one impeccably lovely gray pump in the center of Ysandre's back, holding her down as she tried to move.

"Claire?" The woman's face turned toward her, and Claire blinked twice before she realized whom she was looking at.

Amelie. But not Amelie. Not the cool, remote Founder—this woman had a wild, furious energy to her that Claire had never seen before. And she looked *young*.

"I'm okay," she said faintly, and tried to decide whether this version of Amelie was really here, or a function of her smacked-around brain. She decided it would be a good idea to get her hands and feet untied before figuring anything else out.

That took long minutes, during which Amelie

(really?) dragged Ysandre, whimpering, into the corner and fastened her wrists to a massive crossbeam with chains. The chains, Claire registered, had been there all along. Lovely. This was some kind of vamp playpen/storage locker—probably Oliver's. And she felt sick again, thinking about it. Claire sawed grimly at the ropes binding her and finally parted one complete twist around her hands. As she struggled out of the loops of rope, she saw deep white imprints in her skin, and realized that her hands were red and swollen. She could still feel them, at least, and the burn of circulation returning felt as if she were holding them over an open flame.

She focused on slicing the increasingly dulled knife through the rope on her feet, but it was no use.

"Here," Amelie said, and bent down to snap the rope with one twist of her fingers. It was *so* frustrating, after all that hard work, to see just how easy it was for her. Claire stripped the ties away and sat for a moment breathing hard, starting to feel every cut, bump, and bruise on her body.

Amelie's cool fingers cupped Claire's chin and forced her head up, and the vampire's gray eyes searched hers. "You have a head injury," Amelie said. "I don't think it's too serious. A headache and some dizziness, perhaps." She let go. "I expected to find you. I did not expect to find you *here*, I confess."

Amelie looked *fine.* Not a prisoner. Not a scratch on her, in fact. Claire had lots more damage, and she hadn't been dragged off as Bishop's prisoner. . . .

Wait. "You—we thought Bishop might have gotten you. But he didn't, did he?"

Amelie cocked an eyebrow at her. "Apparently not."

"Then where did you go?" Claire felt a completely useless urge to lash out at her, crack that extreme cool. "Why did you *do this*? You left us alone! And you called the vampires out of hiding—" Her voice failed her for a second as she thought about Officer

O'Malley, and the others she'd heard about. "You got some of them killed."

Amelie didn't respond to that. She simply stared back, as calm as an ice sculpture—calmer, because she wasn't melting.

"Tell me why," Claire said. "Tell me why you did that."

"Because plans change," Amelie replied. "As Bishop changes his moves, I must change mine. The stakes are too high now, Claire. I've lost half the vampires of Morganville to him. He's taking away my advantage, and I needed to draw them to me, for their own safety."

"You got *vampires* killed, not just humans. I know humans don't mean anything to you. But I thought the whole point of this was to save *your* people!"

"And so it is," Amelie said. "As many as can be saved. As for the call, there is a thing in chess known as a blitz attack, you see—a distraction, to cover the movement of more important pieces. You retrieved Myrnin and set him in play again; this was most important. I need my most powerful pieces on the board."

"Like Oliver?" Claire rubbed her hands together, trying to get the annoying tingle out of them. "He's hurt, you know. Maybe dying."

"He's served his purpose." Amelie turned her attention toward Ysandre, who was starting to stir. "It's time to take Bishop's rook, I believe."

Claire clutched the silver knife hard in her fist. "Is that all I am, too? Some kind of sacrifice pawn?"

That got Amelie's attention again. "No," she said in surprise. "Not entirely. I do care, Claire. But in war, you can't care too much. It paralyzes your ability to act." Those luminous eyes turned toward Ysandre again. "It's time for you to go, because I doubt you would enjoy seeing this. You won't be able to return here. I'm closing down nodes on the network. When I'm finished, there will be only two destinations: to me, or to Bishop."

"Where is he?"

"You don't know?" Amelie raised her eyebrows again. "He is where it is most secure, of course. At City Hall. And at nightfall, I will come against him. That's why I came looking for you, Claire. I need you to tell Richard. Tell him to get all those who can't fight for me out of the building."

"But—he *can't*. It's a storm shelter. There are supposed to be tornadoes coming."

"Claire," Amelie said. "Listen to me. If innocents take refuge in that building, they will be killed, because I can't protect them anymore. We're at endgame now. There's no room for mercy." She looked again at Ysandre, who had gone very still, listening.

"Y'all wouldn't be saying this in front of me if I was going to walk out of here, would you?" Ysandre asked. She sounded calm now. Very still.

"No," Amelie said. "Very perceptive. I wouldn't." She took Claire by the arm and helped her to her feet. "I am relying on you, Claire. Go now. Tell Richard these are my orders."

Before Claire could utter another word, she felt the air shimmer in front of her, in the middle of the big warehouse room, and she fell . . . out over the dusty trunk in the Glass House attic, where Oliver had been. She sprawled ungracefully on top of it, then rolled off and got to her feet with a thump.

When she waved her hand through the air, looking for that strange heat shimmer of an open portal, she felt nothing at all.

I'm closing the portals, Amelie had said.

She'd closed this one, for sure.

"Claire?" Shane's voice came from the far end of the attic. He shoved aside boxes and jumped over jumbled furniture to reach her. "What happened to you? Where did you go?"

"I'll tell you later," she said, and realized she was still holding the bloody silver knife. She carefully put it back in her pocket, in the makeshift holster against her leg. It was so dull she didn't think it would cut anything again, but it made her feel better. "Oliver?"

"Bad." Shane put his hands around her head and tilted it up, looking her over. "Is everything okay?"

"Define *everything*. No, define *okay*." She shook her head in frustration. "I need to get the radio. I have to talk to Richard."

Richard wasn't on the radio. "He's meeting with the mayor," said the man who answered. Sullivan, Claire thought his name was, but she hadn't really paid attention. "You got a problem there?"

"No, Officer, you've got a problem *there*," she said. "I need to talk to Richard. It's really important!"

"Everybody needs to talk to Richard," Sullivan said. "He'll get back to you. He's busy right now. If it's not an emergency response—"

"Yes, okay! It's an emergency!"

"Then I'll send units out to you. Glass House, right?"

"No, it's not—" Claire wanted to slam the radio down in frustration. "It's not an emergency *here*. Look, just tell Richard that he needs to clear everybody out of City Hall, as soon as possible."

"Can't do that," Sullivan said. "It's our center of operations. It's the main storm shelter, and we've got one heck of a storm coming tonight. You're going to have to give me a reason, miss."

"All right, it's because—"

Michael took the radio away from her and shut it off. Claire gaped, stuttered, and finally demanded, "Why?"

"Because if Amelie says Bishop's got himself installed in City Hall, somebody there has to know. We don't know who's on his team," Michael said. "I don't know Sullivan that well, but I know he never was happy with the way things ran in town. I wouldn't put it past him to be buying Bishop's crap about giving the city back to the people, home rule, all that stuff.

Same goes for anybody else there, except maybe Joe Hess and Travis Lowe. We have to know who we're talking to before we say anything else."

Shane nodded. "I'm thinking that Sullivan's keeping Richard out of the loop for a reason."

They were downstairs, the four of them. Eve, Shane, and Claire were at the kitchen table, and Michael was pacing the floor and casting looks at the couch, where Oliver was. The older vampire was asleep, Claire guessed, or unconscious; they'd done what they could, washed him off and wrapped him in clean blankets. He was healing, according to Michael, but he wasn't doing it very fast.

When he'd woken up, he'd seemed distant. Confused.

Afraid.

Claire had given him one of the doses she'd gotten from Dr. Mills, and so far, it seemed to be helping, but if Oliver was sick, Myrnin's fears were becoming real.

Soon, it'd be Amelie, too. And then where would they be?

"So what do we do?" Claire asked. "Amelie said we have to tell Richard. We have to get noncombatants out of City Hall, as soon as possible."

"Problem is, you heard him giving instructions to the Civil Defense guys earlier—they're out telling everybody in town to *go* to City Hall if they can't make it to another shelter. Radio and TV, too. Hell, half the town is probably there already."

"Maybe she won't do it," Eve said. "I mean, she wouldn't kill *everybody* in there, would she? Not even if she thinks they're working for Bishop."

"I think it's gone past that," Claire said. "I don't know if she has any choice."

"There's always a choice."

"Not in chess," Claire replied. "Unless your choice is to lie down and die."

*   *   *

In the end, the only way to be sure they got to the right person was to get in the car and drive there. Claire was a little shocked at the color of the sky outside—a solid gray, with clouds moving so fast it was like time-lapse on the Weather Channel. The edges looked faintly green, and in this part of the country, that was never a good sign.

The only good thing about it was that Michael didn't have to worry about getting scorched by sunlight. He brought a hoodie and a blanket to throw over his head, just in case, but it was dark outside, and getting darker fast. Premature sunset.

Drops of rain were smacking the sidewalk, the size of half-dollars. Where they hit Claire's skin, they felt like paintball pellets. As she looked up at the clouds, a horizontal flash of lightning peeled the sky in half, and thunder rumbled so loudly she felt it through the soles of her shoes.

"Come on!" Eve yelled, and started the car. Claire ran to open the backseat door and piled in beside Shane. Eve was already accelerating before she could fasten her seat belt. "Michael, get the radio."

He turned it on. Static. As he scanned stations, they got ghosts of signals from other towns, but nothing came through clearly in Morganville—probably because the vampires jammed it.

Then one came in, loud and clear, broadcasting on a loop.

Attention Morganville residents: this is an urgent public service announcement. The National Weather Service has identified an extremely dangerous storm tracking toward Morganville, which will reach our borders at six twenty-seven this evening at its present speed. This storm has already been responsible for devastation in several areas in its path, and there has been significant loss of life due to tornadic activity. Morganville and the surrounding areas are on tornado watch through ten p.m. this

evening. If you hear an alert siren, go immediately to a designated Safe Shelter location, or
to the safest area of your home if you cannot
reach a Safe Shelter. Attention Morganville
residents—

Michael clicked it off. There was no point in lis-
tening to the repeat; it wasn't going to get any better.
"How many Safe Shelters are there?" Shane asked.
"University dorms have them, the UC—"
"Founder's Square has two," Michael said, "but no-
body can get to them right now. They're locked up."
"Library."
"And the church. Father Joe would open up the
basements, so that'll fit a couple of hundred people."
Everybody else would head to City Hall, if they didn't
stay in their houses.
The rain started to fall in earnest, slapping the wind-
shield at first, and then pounding it in fierce waves.
The ancient windshield wipers really weren't up to it,
even at high speed. Claire was glad she wasn't trying
to drive. Even in clear visibility she wasn't very good,
and she had no idea how Eve was seeing a thing.
If she was, of course. Maybe this was faith-based
driving.
Other cars were on the road, and most of them were
heading the same way they were. Claire looked at the
clock on her cell phone.
Five thirty p.m.
The storm was less than an hour away.
"Uh-oh," Eve said, and braked as they turned the
last corner. It was a sea of red taillights. Over the
roll of thunder and pounding rain, Claire heard horns
honking. Traffic moved, but slowly, one car at a time
inching forward. "They're checking cars at the barricade. I can't believe—"
Something happened up there, and the brake lights
began flicking off in steady rows. Cars moved. Eve fell

into line, and the big, black sedan rolled past two police cars still flashing their lights. In the red/blue/red
glow, Claire saw that they'd moved the barricades aside
and were just waving everyone through.

"This is crazy," she said. "We can't get people out.
Not fast enough! We'd have to stop everybody from
coming in first, and then give them somewhere to
go. . . ."

"I'm getting out of the car here," Michael said. "I
can run faster than you can drive in this. I'll get to
Richard. They won't dare stop me."

That was probably true, but Eve still said, "Michael,
don't—"

Not that it stopped him from bailing out into the
rain. A flash of lightning streaked by overhead and
showed him splashing through thick puddles, weaving
around cars.

He was right; he was faster.

Eve muttered something about "Stupid, stubborn,
bloodsucking boyfriends," and followed the traffic toward
City Hall.

Out of nowhere, a truck pulled out in front of them
from a side street and stopped directly in their path.
Eve yelled and hit the brakes, but they were mushy
and wet, and not great at the best of times, and Claire
felt the car slip and then slide, gathering speed as
it went.

Glad I put on my seat belt, she thought, which was
a weird thing to think, as Eve's car hydroplaned right
into the truck. Shane stretched out his arm to hold
her in place, anyway—instinct, Claire guessed—and
then they all got thrown forward hard as physics took
over.

Physics hurt.

Claire rested her aching head against the cool
window—it was cracked, but still intact—and tried to
shake it off. Shane was unhooking himself from the
seat belt and asking her if she was okay. She made

some kind of gesture and mumbled something, which
she hoped would be good enough. She wasn't up to
real reassurances at the moment.

Eve's door opened, and she got dragged out of the
car.

"Hey!" Shane yelled, and threw himself out his own
door. Claire fumbled at the latch, but hers seemed
stuck; she navigated the push button on her seat belt
and opted for Shane's side of the car instead.

As she stumbled out into the shockingly warm rain,
she knew they were really in trouble now, because the
man holding a knife to Eve's throat was Frank Collins,
Shane's father and all-around badass, crazy vampire
hater. He looked exactly like she remembered—tough,
biker-hard, dressed in leather and tattoos.

He was yelling something at Eve, something Claire
couldn't hear over the crash of thunder. Shane threw
himself into a slide over the trunk of the car and
grabbed at his dad's knife hand.

Dad elbowed him in the face and sent him staggering. Claire grabbed for the silver knife in her jeans,
but it was gone—she'd dropped it somewhere. Before
she could look for it, Shane was back in the fight,
struggling with his dad. He moved the knife enough
that Eve slid free and ran to grab on to Claire.

Frank shoved his son down on the hood of the car
and raised the knife. He froze there, with rain pouring
from his chin like a thin silver beard, and off the point
of the knife.

"No!" Claire screamed, "No, don't hurt him!"

"Where's the vampire?" Frank yelled back. "Where
is Michael Glass?"

"Gone," Shane said. He coughed away pounding
rain. "Dad, he's gone. He's not here. *Dad.*"

Frank seemed to focus on his son for the first
time. "Shane?"

"Yeah, Dad, it's me. Let me up, okay?" Shane was
careful to keep his hands up, palms out in surrender.
"Peace."

It worked. Frank stepped back and lowered the knife. "Good," he said. "I've been looking for you, boy." And then he hugged him. Shane still had his hands up, and froze in place without touching his father. Claire shivered at the look on his face.

"Yeah, good to see you, too," he said. "Back off, man. We're not close, in case you forgot."

"You're still my son. Blood is blood." Frank pushed him toward the truck, only lightly crushed where Eve's car had smacked it. "Get in."

"Why?"

"Because I said so!" Frank shouted. Shane just looked at him. "Dammit, boy, for once in your life, do what I tell you!"

"I spent most of my life doing what you told me," Shane said. "Including selling out my friends. Not happening anymore."

Frank's lips parted, temporarily amazed. He laughed.

"Done drunk the suicide cola, didn't you?" When he shook his head, drops flew in all directions, and were immediately lost in the silver downpour. "Just get in. I'm trying to save your life. You don't want to be where you're trying to go."

Strangely enough, Frank Collins was making sense. Probably for all the wrong reasons, though.

"We have to get through," Claire shouted over the pounding rain. She was shivering, soaked through every layer of clothing. "It's important. People could die if we don't!"

"People are going to die," Collins agreed. "Omelets and eggs. You know the old saying."

Or chess, Claire thought. Though she didn't know whose side Frank Collins was playing on, or even if he knew he was being manipulated at all.

"There's a plan," Frank was saying to his son. "In all this crap, nobody's checking faces. Metal detectors are off. We seize control of the building and make things right. We shuffle these bastards off, once and for all. We can *do it!*"

"Dad," Shane said, "everybody in that building tonight is going to be killed. We have to get people *out*,
not get them *in*. If you care anything about those idiots who buy your revolutionary crap, you'll call this
off."

"Call it off?" Frank repeated, as uncomprehending
as if Shane were speaking another language. "When
we're this close? When we can *win*? Dammit, Shane,
you used to believe in this. You used to—"

"Yeah. Used to. Look it up!" Shane shoved his father away from him, and walked over to Eve and
Claire. "I've warned you, Dad. Don't do this. Not
today. I won't turn you in, but I'm telling you, if you
don't back off, you're dead."

"I don't take threats," Frank said. "Not from you."

"You're an idiot," Shane said. "And I tried."

He got back in the car, on the passenger-side front
seat where Michael had been. Eve scrambled behind
the wheel, and Claire in the back.

Eve reversed.

Frank stepped out into the road ahead of them, a
scary-looking man in black leather with his straggling
hair plastered around his face. Add in the big hunting
knife, and cue the scary music.

Eve let up on the gas. "No," Shane said, and moved
his left foot over to jam it on top of hers. "Go. He
wants you to stop."

"Don't! I can't miss him, no—"

But it was too late. Frank was staring into the headlights, squarely in the center of the hood, and he was
getting closer and closer.

Frank Collins threw himself out of the way at the
last possible second, Eve swerved wildly in the opposite direction to miss him, and somehow, they didn't
kill Shane's dad.

"What the hell are you *doing*?" Eve yelled at
Shane. She was shaking all over. So was Shane. "You
want to run him over, do it on your own time! *God!*"

"Look behind you," Shane whispered.

There were people coming after them. A *lot* of people. They'd been hiding in the alley, Claire guessed. They had guns, and now they opened fire. The car shuddered, and the back window exploded into cracks, then fell with a crash all over Claire's neck.

"Get up here!" Shane said, and grabbed her hands to haul her into the front seat. "Keep your head down!"

Eve had sunk down on the driver's side, barely keeping her eyes above the dashboard. She was panting hoarsely, panicked, and more gunshots were rattling the back of the car. Something hit the front window, too, adding more cracks and a round, backward splash of a hole.

"Faster!" Shane yelled. Eve hit the gas hard, and whipped around a slower-moving van. The firing ceased, at least for now. "You see why I didn't want you to stop?"

"Okay, your father is officially *off my Christmas list*!" Eve yelled. "Oh my God, look at my car!"

Shane barked out a laugh. "Yeah," he agreed. "That's what's important."

"It's better than thinking about what would have happened," Eve said. "If Michael had been with us—"

Claire thought about the mobs Richard had talked about, and the dead vampires, and felt sick. "They'd have dragged him off," she said. "They'd have killed him."

Michael had been right about Shane's dad, but then, Claire had never really doubted it. Neither had Shane, from the sick certainty on his face. He wiped his eyes with his forearm, which really didn't help much; they were all dripping wet, from head to toe.

"Let's just get to the building," Shane said. "We can't do much until we find Richard."

Only it wasn't that simple, even getting in. The underground parking was crammed full of cars, parked haphazardly at every angle. As Eve inched through the shadows, looking for any place to go, she shook her head. "If we do manage to get people to leave, they won't be able to take their cars. Everybody's blocked in," she said. "This is massively screwed up." Claire, for her part, thought some of it seemed deliberate, not just panic. "Okay, I'm going to pull it against the wall and hope we can get out if we need to."

The elevator was already locked down, the doors open but the lights off and buttons unresponsive. They took the stairs at a run.

The first-floor door seemed to be locked, until Shane pushed on it harder, and then it creaked open against a flood of protests.

The vestibule was full of people.

Morganville's City Hall wasn't all that large, at least not here in the lobby area. There was a big, sweeping staircase leading up, all grand marble and polished wood, and glass display cases taking up part of one wall. The License Bureau was off to the right: six old-time bank windows, with bars, all closed. Next to each window was a brass plaque that read what the windows were supposed to deliver: RESIDENTIAL LICENSING, CAR REGISTRATION, ZONING CHANGE REQUESTS, SPECIAL PERMITS, TRAFFIC VIOLATIONS, FINE PAYMENTS, TAXES, CITY SERVICES.

But not today.

The lobby was jammed with people. Families, mostly—mothers and fathers with kids, some as young as infants. Claire didn't see a single vampire in the crowd, not even Michael. At the far end, a yellow Civil Defense sign indicated that the door led to a Safe Shelter, with a tornado graphic next to it. A policeman with a bullhorn was yelling for order, not that he was getting any; people were pushing, shoving, and shouting at one another. "The shelter is now at maximum capacity! Please be calm!"

"Not good," Shane said. There was no sign of Richard, although there were at least ten uniformed police officers trying to manage the crowd. "Upstairs?"

"Upstairs," Eve agreed, and they squeezed back into the fire stairs and ran up to the next level. The sign in the stairwell said that this floor contained the mayor's office, sheriff's office, city council chambers, and something called, vaguely, Records.

The door was locked. Shane rattled it and banged for entrance, but nobody came to the rescue.

"Guess we go up," he said.

The third floor had no signs in the stairwell at all, but there was a symbol—the Founder's glyph, like the one on Claire's bracelet. Shane turned the knob, but again, the door didn't open. "I didn't think they could do that to fire stairs," Eve said.

"Yeah, call a cop." Shane looked up the steps. "One more floor, and then it's just the roof, and I'm thinking that's not a good idea, the roof."

"Wait." Claire studied the Founder's glyph for a few seconds, then shrugged and reached out to turn the knob.

Something clicked, and it turned. The door opened. "How did you . . . ?"

Claire held up her wrist, and the gold bracelet. "It was worth a shot. I thought, maybe with a gold bracelet—"

"Genius. Go on, get inside," Shane said, and hustled them in. The door clicked shut behind them, and locked with a snap of metal. The hallway seemed dark, after the fluorescent lights in the stairs, and that was because the lights were dimmed way down, the carpet was dark, and so was the wood paneling.

It reminded Claire eerily of the hallway where they'd rescued Myrnin, only there weren't as many doors opening off it. Shane took the lead—of course—but the doors they could open were just simple offices, nothing fancy about them at all.

And then there was a door at the end of the hall with the Founder's Symbol etched on the polished brass doorknob. Shane tried it, shook his head, and motioned for Claire.

It opened easily at her touch.

Inside were—apartments. Chambers? Claire didn't know what else to call them; there was an entire complex of rooms leading from one central area.

It was like stepping into a whole different world, and Claire could tell that it had once been beautiful: a fairytale room, of rich satin on the walls, Persian rugs, delicate white and gold furniture.

"Michael? Mayor Morrell? Richard?"

It was a queen's room, and somebody had completely wrecked it. Most of the furniture was overturned, some kicked to pieces. Mirrors smashed. Fabrics ripped.

Claire froze.

Lying on the remaining long, delicate sofa was François, Bishop's other loyal vampire buddy, who'd come to Morganville along with Ysandre as his entourage. The vampire looked completely at ease—legs crossed at the ankles, head propped on a plump satin pillow. A big crystal glass of something in dark red rested on his chest.

He giggled and saluted them with the blood. "Hello, little friends," he said. "We weren't expecting you, but you'll do. We're almost out of refreshments."

"Out," Shane said, and shoved Eve toward the door.

It slammed shut before she could reach it, and there stood Mr. Bishop, still dressed in his long purple cassock from the feast. It was still torn on the side, where Myrnin had slashed at him with the knife.

There was something so ancient about him, so completely uncaring, that Claire felt her mouth go dry. "Where is she?" Bishop asked. "I know you've seen my daughter. I can smell her on you."

"Ewww," Eve said, very faintly. "So much more than I needed to know."

Bishop didn't look away from Claire's face, just pointed at Eve. "Silence, or be silenced. When I want to know your opinion, I'll consult your entrails."

Eve shut up. François swung his legs over the edge

of the sofa and sat up in one smooth motion. He downed the rest of his glass of blood and let the glass fall, shedding crimson drops all over the pale carpet. He'd gotten some on his fingers. He licked them, then smeared the rest all over the satin wall.

"Please," he said, and batted his long-lashed eyes at Eve. "Please, say something. I love entrails."

She shrank back against the wall. Even Shane stayed quiet, though Claire could tell he was itching to pull her to safety. *You can't protect me,* she thought fiercely. *Don't try.*

"You don't know where Amelie is?" Claire asked Bishop directly. "How's that master plan going, then?"

"Oh, it's going just fine," Bishop said. "Oliver is dead by now. Myrnin—well, we both know that Myrnin is insane, at best, and homicidal at his even better. I'm rather hoping he'll come charging to your rescue and forget who you are once he arrives. That would be amusing, and very typical of him, I'm afraid." Bishop's eyes bored into hers, and Claire felt the net closing around her. "Where is Amelie?"

"Where you'll never find her."

"Fine. Let her lurk in the shadows with her creations, until hunger or the humans destroy them. This doesn't have to be a battle, you know. It can be a war of attrition just as easily. I have the high ground." He gestured around the ruined apartment with one lazy hand. "And of course, I have everyone here, whether they know it or not."

She didn't hear him move, but flinched as François trailed cold fingers across the back of her neck, then gripped her tightly.

"Just like that," Bishop said. "Just precisely like that." He nodded to François. "If you want her, take her. I'm no longer interested in Amelie's pets. Take these others, too, unless you wish to save them for later."

Claire heard Shane whisper, "No," and heard the complete despair in his voice just as Bishop's follower wrenched her head over to the side, baring her neck.

She felt his lips touch her skin. They burned like ice.

"Ah!" François jerked his head back. "You little peasant." He used a fold of her shirt to take hold of the silver chain around her neck, and broke it with a sharp twist.

Claire caught the cross in her hand as it fell.

"May it comfort you," Bishop said, and smiled. "My child."

And then François bit her.

"Claire?" Somewhere, a long way off, Eve was crying. "Oh my God, Claire? Can you hear me? Come on, please, *please* come back. Are you sure she's got a pulse?"

"Yes, she's got a pulse." Claire knew that voice. Richard Morrell. But why was he here? Who called the police? She remembered the accident with the truck—no, that was before.

Bishop.

Claire slowly opened her eyes. The world felt very far away, and safely muffled for the moment. She heard Eve let out a gasp and a flood of words, but Claire didn't try to identify the meaning.

I have a pulse.

That seemed important.

My neck hurts.

Because a vampire had bitten her.

Claire raised her left hand slowly to touch her neck, and found a huge wad of what felt like somebody's shirt pressed against her neck.

"No," Richard said, and forced her hand back down. "Don't touch it. It's still closing up. You shouldn't move for another hour or so. Let the wounds close."

"Bit," Claire murmured. "He bit me." That came in a blinding flash, like a red knife cutting through the fog. "Don't let me turn into one."

"You won't," Eve said. She was upside down—no,

Claire's head was in her lap, and Eve was leaning over her. Claire felt the warm drip of Eve's tears on her face. "Oh, sweetie. You're going to be okay. Right?" Even upside down, Eve's look was panicked as she appealed to Richard, who sat on her right.

"You'll be all right," he said. He didn't look much better than Claire felt. "I have to see to my father. Here." He moved out of the way, and someone else sat in his place.

Shane. His warm fingers closed over hers, and she shivered when she realized how cold she felt. Eve tucked an expensive velvet blanket over and around her, fussing nervously.

Shane didn't say anything. He was so *quiet*.

"My cross," Claire said. It had been in her hand. She didn't know where it was now. "He broke the chain. I'm sorry—"

Shane opened her fingers and tipped the cross and chain into her hand. "I picked it up," he said. "Figured you might want it." There was something he wasn't saying. Claire looked at Eve to find out what it was, but she wasn't talking, for a change. "Anyway, you're going to be okay. We're lucky this time. François wasn't that hungry." He closed her fingers around the cross and held on.

His hands were shaking. "Shane?"

"I'm sorry," he whispered. "I couldn't move. I just *stood there.*"

"No, he didn't," Eve said. "He knocked Franny clear across the room and he would have staked him with a chair leg, except Bishop stepped in."

That sounded like Shane. "You're not hurt?" Claire asked.

"Not much."

Eve frowned. "Well—"

"Not much," Shane repeated. "I'm okay, Claire."

She kind of had to take that at face value, at least right now. "What time—"

"Six fifteen," Richard said, from the far corner of

the small room. This, Claire guessed, had been some kind of dressing area for Amelie. She saw a long closet to the side. Most of the clothes were shredded and scattered in piles on the floor. The dressing table was a ruin, and every mirror was broken.

François had had his fun in here, too.

"The storm's heading for us," Eve said. "Michael never got to Richard, but he got to Joe Hess, apparently. They evacuated the shelters. Bishop was pretty mad about that. He wanted a lot of hostages between him and Amelie."

"So all that's left is us?"

"Us. And Bishop's people, who didn't leave. And Fabulous Frank Collins and his Wild Bunch, who rolled into the lobby and now think they've won some kind of battle or something." Eve rolled her eyes, and for an instant was back to her old self. "Just us and the bad guys."

Did that make Richard—no. Claire couldn't believe that. If anyone in Morganville had honestly tried to do the right thing, it was Richard Morrell.

Eve followed Claire's look. "Oh. Yeah, his dad got hurt trying to stop Bishop from taking over downstairs. Richard's been trying to take care of him, and his mom. We were right about Sullivan, by the way. Total backstabber. Yay for premonitions. Wish I had one right now that could help get us out of this."

"No way out," Claire said.

"Not even a window," Eve said. "We're locked in here. No idea where Bishop and his little sock monkey got off to. Looking for Amelie, I guess. I wish they'd just kill each other already."

Eve didn't mean it, not really, but Claire understood how she felt. Distantly. In a detached, shocked kind of way.

"What's happening outside?"

"Not a clue. No radios in here. They took our cell phones. We're"—the lights blinked and failed, putting the room into pitch darkness—"screwed," Eve finished. "Oh man, I should not have said that, should I?"

"Power's gone out to the building, I think," Richard said. "It's probably the storm."

Or the vampires screwing with them, just because they could. Claire didn't say it out loud, but she thought it pretty hard.

Shane's hand kept holding hers. "Shane?"

"Right here," he said. "Stay still."

"I'm sorry. I'm really, really sorry."

"What for?"

"I shouldn't have gotten angry with you, before, about your dad. . . ."

"Not important," he said very softly. "It's okay, Claire. Just rest."

Rest? She couldn't rest. Reality was pushing back in, reminding her of pain, of fear, and most important, of time.

There was an eerie, ghostly sound now, wailing, and getting louder.

"What is that?" Eve asked, and then, before anybody could answer, did so herself. "Tornado sirens. There's one on the roof."

The rising, falling wail got louder, but with it came something else—a sound like water rushing, or—

"We need to get to cover," Richard said. A flashlight snapped on, and played over Eve's pallid face, then Shane's and Claire's. "You guys, get her over here. This is the strongest interior corner. That side faces out toward the street."

Claire tried to get up, but Shane scooped her in his arms and carried her. He set her down with her back against a wall, then got under the blanket next to her with Eve on his other side. The flashlight turned away from them, and in its sweep, Claire caught sight of Mayor Morrell. He was a fat man, with a politician's smooth face and smile, but he didn't look anything like she remembered now. He seemed older, shrunken inside his suit, and very ill.

"What's wrong with him?" Claire whispered.

Shane's answer stirred the damp hair around her face. "Heart attack," he said. "At least, that's Richard's best guess. Looks bad."

It really did. The mayor was propped against the wall a few feet from them, and he was gasping for breath as his wife (Claire had never seen her before, except in pictures) patted his arm and murmured in his ear. His face was ash gray, his lips turning blue, and there was real panic in his eyes.

Richard returned, dragging another thick blanket and some pillows. "Everybody cover up," he said. "Keep your heads down." He covered his mother and father and crouched next to them as he wrapped himself in another blanket.

The wind outside was building to a howl. Claire could hear things hitting the walls—dull thudding sounds, like baseballs. It got louder. "Debris," Richard said. He focused the light on the carpet between their small group. "Maybe hail. Could be anything."

The siren cut off abruptly, but that didn't mean the noise subsided; if anything, it got louder, ratcheting up from a howl to a scream—and then it took on a deeper tone.

"Sounds like a train," Eve said shakily. "Damn, I was really hoping that wasn't true, the train thing—"

"Heads down!" Richard yelled, as the whole building started to shake. Claire could feel the boards vibrating underneath her. She could see the walls bending, and cracks forming in the bricks.

And then the noise rose to a constant, deafening scream, and the whole outside wall sagged, dissolved into bricks and broken wood, and disappeared. The ripped, torn fabric around the room took flight like startled birds, whipping wildly through the air and getting shredded into ever-smaller sections by the wind and debris.

The storm was screaming as if it had gone insane.

Broken furniture and shards of mirrors flew around, smashing into the walls, hitting the blankets.

Claire heard a heavy groan even over the shrieking wind, and looked up to see the roof sagging overhead. Dust and plaster cascaded down, and she grabbed Shane hard.

The roof came down on top of them.

Claire didn't know how long it lasted. It seemed like forever, really—the screaming, the shaking, the pressure of things on top of her.

And then, very gradually, it stopped, and the rain began to hammer down again, drenching the pile of dust and wood. Some of it trickled down to drip on her cheek, which was how she knew.

Shane's hand moved on her shoulder, more of a twitch than a conscious motion, and then he let go of Claire to heave up with both hands. Debris slid and rattled. They'd been lucky, Claire realized—a heavy wooden beam had collapsed in over their heads at a slant, and it had held the worst of the stuff off them.

"Eve?" Claire reached across Shane and grabbed her friend's hands. Eve's eyes were closed, and there was blood trickling down one side of her face. Her face was even whiter than usual—plaster dust, Claire realized.

Eve coughed, and her eyelids fluttered up. "Mom?" The uncertainty in her voice made Claire want to cry. "Oh God, what happened? Claire?"

"We're alive," Shane said. He sounded kind of surprised. He brushed fallen chunks of wood and plaster off Claire's head, and she coughed, too. The rain pounded in at an angle, soaking the blanket that covered them. "Richard?"

"Over here," Richard said. "Dad? Dad—"

The flashlight was gone, rolled off or buried or just plain taken away by the wind. Lightning flashed, bright as day, and Claire saw the tornado that had hit them still moving through Morganville, crashing through buildings, spraying debris a hundred feet into the air.

It didn't even look *real*.

Shane helped move a beam off Eve's legs—thankfully, they were just bruised, not broken—and crawled across the slipping wreckage toward Richard, who was lifting things off his mother. She looked okay, but she was crying and dazed.

His father, though . . .

"No," Richard said, and dragged his father flat. He started administering CPR. There were bloody cuts on his face, but he didn't seem to care about his own problems at all. "Shane! Breathe for him!"

After a hesitation, Shane tilted the mayor's head back. "Like this?"

"Let me," Eve said. "I've had CPR training." She crawled over and took in a deep breath, bent, and blew it into the mayor's mouth, watching for his chest to rise. It seemed to take a lot of effort. So did what Richard was doing, pumping on his dad's chest, over and over. Eve counted slowly, then breathed again—and again.

"I'll get help," Claire said. She wasn't sure there *was* any help, really, but she had to do something. When she stood up, though, she felt dizzy and weak, and remembered what Richard had said—she had holes in her neck, and she'd lost a lot of blood. "I'll go slow."

"I'll go with you," Shane said, but Richard grabbed him and pulled him down.

"No! I need you to take over here." He showed Shane how to place his hands, and got him started. He pulled the walkie-talkie from his belt and tossed it to Claire. "Go. We need paramedics."

And then Richard collapsed, and Claire realized that he had a huge piece of metal in his side. She stood there, frozen in horror, and then punched in the code for the walkie-talkie. "Hello? Hello, is anybody there?"

Static. If there was anybody, she couldn't hear it over the interference and the roaring rain.

"I have to go!" she shouted at Shane. He looked up.

"No!" But he couldn't stop her, not without letting the mayor die, and after one helpless, furious look at her, he went back to work.

Claire slid over the pile of debris and scrambled out the broken door, into the main apartment.

There was no sign of François or Bishop. If the place had been wrecked before, it was unrecognizable now. Most of this part of the building was gone, just—gone. She felt the floor groan underneath her, and moved fast, heading for the apartment's front door. It was still on its hinges, but as she pulled on it, part of the frame came out of the wall.

Outside, the hallway seemed eerily unmarked, except that the roof overhead—and, Claire presumed, all of the next floor above—was missing. It was a hallway open to the storm. She hurried along it, glad now for the flashes of lightning that lit her way.

The fire stairs at the end seemed intact. She passed some people huddled there, clearly terrified. "We need help!" she said. "There are people hurt upstairs—somebody?"

And then the screaming started, somewhere about a floor down, lots of people screaming at the same time. Those who were sitting on the stairs jumped to their feet and ran up, toward Claire. "No!" she yelled. "No, you can't!"

But she was shoved out of the way, and about fifty people trampled past her, heading up. She had no idea where they'd go.

Worse, she was afraid their combined weight would collapse that part of the building, including the place where Eve, Shane, and the Morrells were.

"Claire?" Michael. He came out of the first-floor

door, and leaped two flights of stairs in about two
jumps to reach her. Before she could protest, he'd
grabbed her in his arms like an invalid. "Come on. I
have to get you out of here."

"No! No, go up. Shane, they need help. Go up;
leave me here!"

"I can't." He looked down, and so did she.

Vampires poured into the stairwell below. Some of
them were fighting, ripping at one another. Any human
who got between them went down screaming.

"Right. Up it is," he said, and she felt them leave
the ground in one powerful leap, hitting the third-floor
landing with catlike grace.

"What's happening?" Claire twisted to try to look
down, but it didn't make any sense to her. It was just
a mob, fighting one another. No telling who was on
which side, or even why they were fighting so furiously.

"Amelie's down there," Michael said. "Bishop's trying to get to her, but he's losing followers fast. She
took him by surprise, during the storm."

"What about the people—I mean, the humans?
Shane's dad, and the ones who wanted to take over?"

Michael kicked open the door to the third-floor
roofless hallway. The people who'd run past Claire
were milling around in it, frightened and babbling. Michael brought down his fangs and snarled at them, and
they scattered into whatever shelter they could reach—
interior offices, mostly, that had sustained little damage except for rain.

He shoved past those who had nowhere to go, and
down to the end of the hall. "In here?" He let Claire
slide down to her feet, and his gaze focused on her
neck. "Someone bit you."

"It's not so bad." Claire put her hand over the
wound, trying to cover it up. The wound's edges felt
ragged, and they were still leaking blood, she thought,
although that could have just been the rain. "I'm
okay."

"No, you're not."

A gust of wind blew his collar back, and she saw the white outlines of marks on his own neck. "Michael! Did you get bitten, too?"

"Like you said, it's nothing. Look, we can talk about that later. Let's get to our friends. First aid later."

Claire opened the door and stepped through . . . and the floor collapsed underneath her.

She must have screamed, but all she heard was the tremendous cracking sound of more of the building falling apart underneath and around her. She turned toward Michael, who was frozen in the doorway, illuminated in stark white by a nearby lightning strike.

He reached out and grabbed her arm as she flung it toward him, and then she was suspended in midair, wind and dust rushing up around her, as the floor underneath fell away. Michael pulled, and she almost flew, weightless, into his arms.

"Oh," she whispered faintly. "Thanks."

He held on to her for a minute without speaking, then said, "Is there another way in?"

"I don't know."

They backed up and found the next office to the left, which had suspicious-looking cracks in its walls. Claire thought the floor felt a little unsteady. Michael pushed her back behind him and said, "Cover your eyes."

Then he began ripping away the wall between the office and Amelie's apartments. When he hit solid red brick, he punched it, breaking it into dust.

"This isn't helping keep things together!" Claire yelled.

"I know, but we need to get them out!"

He ripped a hole in the wall big enough to step through, and braced himself in it as the whole building seemed to shudder, as if shifting its weight. "The floor's all right here," he said. "You stay. I'll go."

"Through that door, to the left!" Claire called. Michael disappeared, moving fast and gracefully.

She wondered, all of a sudden, why he wasn't downstairs. Why he wasn't fighting, like all the others of Amelie's blood.

A couple of tense minutes passed, as she stared through the hole; nothing seemed to be happening. She couldn't hear Michael, or Shane, or anything else.

And then she heard screaming behind her, in the hall. *Vampires,* she thought, and quickly opened the door to look.

Someone fell against the wood, knocking her backward. It was François. Claire tried to shut the door, but a bloodstained white hand wormed through the opening and grabbed the edge, shoving it wider.

François didn't look even remotely human anymore, but he did look absolutely desperate, willing to do anything to survive, and very, very angry.

Claire backed up, slowly, until she was standing with her back against the far wall. There wasn't much in here to help her—a desk, some pens and pencils in a cup.

François laughed, and then he growled. "You think you're winning," he said. "You're not."

"I think you're the one who has to worry," Michael said from the hole in the wall. He stepped through, carrying Mayor Morrell in his arms. Shane and Eve were with him, supporting Richard's sagging body between them. Mrs. Morrell brought up the rear. "Back off. I won't come after you if you run."

François' eyes turned ruby, and he threw himself at Michael, who was burdened with the mayor.

Claire grabbed a pencil from the cup and plunged it into François' back.

He whirled, looking stunned . . . and then he slowly collapsed to the carpet.

"That won't kill him," Michael said.

"I don't care," Eve said. "Because that was *fierce.*"

Claire grabbed the vampire's arms and dragged him out of the way, careful not to dislodge the pencil; she wasn't really sure how deep it had gone, and if it slipped out of his heart, they were all in big trouble. Michael edged around him and opened the door to check the corridor. "Clear," he said. "For the moment. Come on."

Their little refugee group hurried into the rainy hall, squishing through soggy carpet. There were people hiding in the offices, or just pressed against the walls and hoping not to be noticed. "Come on," Eve said to them. "Get up. We're getting out of here before this whole thing comes down!"

The fighting in the stairwell was still going on— snarling, screams, bangs, and thuds. Claire didn't dare look over the railing. Michael led them down to the locked second-floor entrance. He pulled hard on it, and the knob popped off—but the door stayed locked.

"Hey, Mike?" Shane had edged to the end of the landing to look over the railing. "Can't go that way."

"I know!"

"Also, time is—"

"I know, Shane!" Michael started kicking the door, but it was reinforced, stronger than the other doors Claire had seen. It bent, but didn't open.

And then it did open . . . from the inside.

There, in his fancy but battered black velvet, stood Myrnin.

"In," he said. "This way. Hurry."

The falling sensation warned Claire that the door was a portal, but she didn't have time to tell anybody else, so when they stepped through into Myrnin's lab, it was probably kind of a shock. Michael didn't pause; he pushed a bunch of broken glassware from a lab table and put Mr. Morrell down on it, then touched pale fingers to the man's throat. When he found nothing, he started CPR again. Eve hurried over to breathe for him.

Myrnin didn't move as the refugees streamed in past

him. He was standing with his arms folded, a frown grooved between his brows. "Who are all these people?" he asked. "I am not an innkeeper, you know."

"Shut up," Claire said. She didn't have any patience with Myrnin right now. "Is he okay?" She was talking to Shane, who was easing Richard onto a threadbare rug near the far wall.

"You mean, except for the big piece of metal in him? Look, I don't know. He's breathing, at least."

The rest of the refugees clustered together, filtering slowly through the portal. Most of them had no idea what had just happened, which was good. If they'd been part of Frank's group, intending to take over Morganville, that ambition was long gone. Now they were just people, and they were just scared.

"Up the stairs," Claire told them. "You can get out that way."

Most of them rushed for the exit. She hoped they'd make it home, or at least to some kind of safe place.

She hoped they had homes to go back to.

Myrnin glared at her. "You do realize that this was a *secret* laboratory, don't you? And now half of Morganville knows where it is?"

"Hey, I didn't open the door; you did." She reached over and put her hand on his arm, looking up into his face. "Thank you. You saved our lives."

He blinked slowly. "Did I?"

"I know why you weren't fighting," Claire said. "The drugs kept you from having to. But . . . Michael?"

Myrnin followed her gaze to where Eve and Michael remained bent over the mayor's still form. "Amelie let him go," he said. "For now. She could claim him again at any time, but I think she knew you needed help." He uncrossed his arms and walked over to Michael to touch his shoulder. "It's no use," he said. "I can smell death on him. So can you, if you try. You won't bring him back."

"No!" Mrs. Morrell screamed, and threw herself over her husband's body. "No, you have to try!"

"They did," Myrnin said, and retreated to lean against a convenient wall. "Which is more than I would have." He nodded toward Richard. "He might live, but to remove that metal will require a chirurgeon."

"You mean, a doctor?" Claire asked.

"Yes, of course, a doctor," Myrnin snapped, and his eyes flared red. "I know you want me to feel some sympathy for them, but that is not who I am. I care only about those I know, and even then, not all that deeply. Strangers get nothing from me." He was slipping, and the anger was coming back. Next it would be confusion. Claire silently dug in her pockets. She'd put a single glass vial in, and miraculously, it was still unbroken.

He slapped it out of her hand impatiently. "I don't need it!"

Claire watched it clatter to the floor, heart in her mouth, and said, "You do. You know you do. Please, Myrnin. I don't need your crap right now. Just *take your medicine.*"

She didn't think he would, not at first, but then he snorted, bent down, and picked up the vial. He broke the cap off and dumped the liquid into his mouth. "There," he said. "Satisfied?" He shattered the glass in his fingers, and the red glow in his eyes intensified. "Are you, little Claire? Do you enjoy giving me orders?"

"Myrnin."

His hand went around her throat, choking off whatever she was going to say.

She didn't move.

His hand didn't tighten.

The red glow slowly faded away, replaced by a look of shame. He let go of her and backed away a full step, head down.

"I don't know where to get a doctor," Claire said, as if nothing had happened. "The hospital, maybe, or—"

"No," Myrnin murmured. "I will bring help. Don't let anyone go through my things. And watch Michael, in case."

She nodded. Myrnin opened the portal doorway in the wall and stepped through it, heading—where? She had no idea. Amelie had, Claire thought, shut down all the nodes. But if that was true, how had they gotten here?

Myrnin could open and close them at will. But he was probably the only one who could.

Michael and Eve moved away from Mayor Morrell's body, as his wife stood over him and cried.

"What can we do?" Shane asked. He sounded miserable. In all the confusion, he'd missed her confrontation with Myrnin. She was dimly glad about that.

"Nothing," Michael said. "Nothing but wait."

When the portal opened again, Myrnin stepped through, then helped someone else over the step.

It was Theo Goldman, carrying an antique doctor's bag. He looked around the lab, nodding to Claire in particular, and then moved to where Richard was lying on the carpet, with his head in his mother's lap. "Move back, please," he told her, and knelt down to open his bag. "Myrnin. Take her in the other room. A mother shouldn't see this."

He was setting out instruments, unrolling them in a clean white towel. As Claire watched, Myrnin led Mrs. Morrell away and seated her in a chair in the corner, where he normally sat to read. She seemed dazed now, probably in shock. The chair was intact. It was just about the only thing in the lab that was—the scientific instruments were smashed, lab tables overturned, candles and lamps broken.

Books were piled in the corners and burned, reduced to scraps of leather and curling black ash. The whole place smelled sharply of chemicals and fire.

"What can we do?" Michael asked, crouching down on Richard's other side. Theo took out several pairs of latex gloves and passed one set to Michael. He donned one himself.

"You can act as my nurse, my friend," he said. "I would have brought my wife—she has many years of training in this—but I don't want to leave my children on their own. They're already very frightened."

"But they're safe?" Eve asked. "Nobody's bothered you?"

"No one has so much as knocked on the door," he said. "It's a very good hiding place. Thank you."

"I think you're paying us back," Eve said. "Please. Can you save him?"

"It's in God's hands, not mine." Still, Theo's eyes were bright as he looked at the twisted metal plate embedded in Richard's side. "It's good that he's unconscious, but he might wake during the procedure. There is chloroform in the bag. It's Michael, yes? Michael, please put some on a cloth and be ready when I tell you to cover his mouth and nose."

Claire's nerve failed around the time that Theo took hold of the piece of steel, and she turned away. Eve already had, to take a blanket to Mrs. Morrell and put it around her shoulders.

"Where's my daughter?" the mayor's wife asked. "Monica should be here. I don't want her out there alone."

Eve raised her eyebrows at Claire, clearly wondering where Monica was.

"The last time I saw her, she was at school," Claire said. "But that was before I got the call to come home, so I don't know. Maybe she's in shelter in the dorm?" She checked her cell phone. No bars. Reception was usually spotty down here in the lab, but she could usually see something, even if it was only a flicker. "I think the cell towers are down."

"Yeah, likely," Eve agreed. She reached over to tuck the blanket around Mrs. Morrell, who leaned her head back and closed her eyes, as if the strength was just leaking right out of her. "You think this is the right thing to do? I mean, do we even know this guy or anything?"

Claire didn't, really, but she still wanted to like Theo, in much the same way as she liked Myrnin—against her better sense. "I think he's okay. And it's not like anybody's making house calls right now."

The operation—and it was an operation, with suturing and everything—took a couple of hours before Theo sat back, stripped off the gloves, and sighed in quiet satisfaction. "There," he said. Claire and Eve got up to walk over as Michael rose to his feet. Shane had been hanging on the edges, watching in what Claire thought looked like queasy fascination. "His pulse is steady. He's lost some blood, but I believe he will be all right, provided no infection sets in. Still, this century has those wonderful antibiotics, yes? So that is not so bad." Theo was almost beaming. "I must say, I haven't used my surgical skills in years. It's very exciting. Although it makes me hungry."

Claire was pretty sure Richard wouldn't want to know that. She knew she wouldn't have, in his place.

"Thank you," Mrs. Morrell said. She got up from the chair, folded the blanket and put it aside, then walked over to shake Theo's hand with simple, dignified gratitude. "I'll see that my husband compensates you for your kindness."

They all exchanged looks. Michael started to speak, but Theo shook his head. "That's quite all right, dear lady. I am delighted to help. I recently lost a son myself. I know the weight of grief."

"Oh," Mrs. Morrell said, "I'm so sorry for your loss, sir." She said it as if she didn't know her husband was lying across the room, dead.

Tears sparkled in his eyes, Claire saw, but then he blinked them away and smiled. He patted her hand gently. "You are very generous to an old man," he said. "We have always liked living in Morganville, you know. The people are so kind."

Shane said, "Some of those same people killed your son."

Theo looked at him with calm, unflinching eyes. "And without forgiveness, there is never any peace. I tell you this from the distance of many centuries. My son gave his life. I won't reply to his gift with anger, not even for those who took him from me. Those same poor, sad people will wake up tomorrow grieving their own losses, I think, if they survive at all. How can hating them heal me?"

Myrnin, who hadn't spoken at all, murmured, "You shame me, Theo."

"I don't mean to do so," he said, and shrugged. "Well. I should get back to my family now. I wish you all well."

Myrnin got up from his chair and walked with Theo to the portal. They all watched him go. Mrs. Morrell was staring after him with a bright, odd look in her eyes.

"How very strange," she said. "I wish Mr. Morrell had been available to meet him."

She spoke as if he were in a meeting downtown instead of under a sheet on the other side of the room. Claire shuddered.

"Come on, let's go see Richard," Eve said, and led her away.

Shane let out his breath in a slow hiss. "I wish it were as simple as Theo thinks it is, to stop hating." He swallowed, watching Mrs. Morrell. "I wish I could, I really do."

"At least you want to," Michael said. "It's a start."

They stayed the night in the lab, mainly because the storm continued outside until the wee hours of the morning—rain, mostly, with some hail. There didn't seem to be much point running out in it. Claire kept checking her phone, Eve found a portable radio buried in piles of junk at the back of the room, and they checked for news at regular intervals.

Around three a.m. they got some. It was on the radio's emergency alert frequency.

All Morganville residents and surrounding areas: we remain under severe thunderstorm warnings, with high winds and possible flooding, until seven a.m. today. Rescue efforts are under way at City Hall, which was partially destroyed by a tornado that also leveled several warehouses and abandoned buildings, as well as one building in Founder's Square. There are numerous reports of injuries coming in. Please remain calm. Emergency teams are working their way through town now, looking for anyone who may be in need of assistance. Stay where you are. Please do not attempt to go out into the streets at this time.

It started to repeat. Eve frowned and looked up at Myrnin, who had listened as well. "What aren't they saying?" she asked.

"If I had to guess, their urgent desire that people stay within shelter would tell me there are other things to worry about." His dark eyes grew distant for a moment, then snapped back into focus. "Ibid nothing."

"What?" Eve seemed to think she'd misheard.

"Ibid nothing carlo. I don't justice."

Myrnin was making word salad again—a precursor to the drugs wearing off—more quickly than Claire had expected, actually, and that was worrying.

Eve sent Claire a look of alarm. "Okay, I didn't really understand that at all—"

Claire put a hand on her arm to silence her. "Why don't you go see Mrs. Morrell? You too, Shane."

He didn't like it, but he went. As he did, he jerked his head at Michael, who rose from where he was sitting with Richard and strolled over.

Casually.

"Myrnin," Claire said. "You need to listen to me, okay? I think your drugs are wearing off again."

"I'm fine." His excitement level was rising; she could see it—a very light flush in his face, his eyes starting to glitter. "You worry over notebook."

There was no point in trying to explain the signs; he never could identify them. "We should check on the prison," she said. "See if everything's still okay there."

Myrnin smiled. "You're trying to trick me." His eyes were getting darker, endlessly dark, and that smile had edges to it. "Oh, little girl, you don't know. You don't know what it's like, having all these guests here, and all this"—he breathed in deeply—"all this blood." His eyes focused on her throat, with its ragged bite mark hidden under a bandage Theo had given her. "I know it's there. Your mark. Tell me, did François—"

"Stop. Stop it." Claire dug her fingers into her palms. Myrnin took a step toward her, and she forced herself not to flinch. She knew him, knew what he was trying to do. "You won't hurt me. You need me."

"Do I?" He breathed deeply again. "Yes, I do. Bright, so bright. I can feel your energy. I know how it will feel when I . . ." He blinked, and horror sheeted across his face, fast as lightning. "What was I saying? Claire? What did I just say?"

She couldn't repeat it. "Nothing. Don't worry. But I think we'd better get you to the cell, okay? Please?"

He looked devastated. This was the worst part of it, she thought, the mood swings. He'd tried so hard, and he'd helped, he really had—but he wasn't going to be able to hold together much longer. She was seeing him fall apart in slow motion.

Again.

Michael steered him toward the portal. "Let's go," he said. "Claire, can you do this?"

"If he doesn't fight me," she said nervously. She remembered one afternoon when his paranoia had taken over, and every time she'd tried to establish the portal, he'd snapped the connection, sure something was waiting on the other side to destroy him. "I wish we had a tranquilizer."

"Well, you don't," Myrnin said. "And I don't like being stuck with your needles, you know that. I'll behave myself." He laughed softly. "Mostly."

Claire opened the door, but instead of the connection snapping clear to the prison, she felt it shift, pulled out of focus. "Myrnin, stop it!"

He spread his hands theatrically. "I didn't do anything."

She tried again. The connection bent, and before she could bring it back where she wanted it, an alternate destination came into focus.

Theo Goldman fell out of the door.

"Theo!" Myrnin caught him, surprised out of his petulance, at least for the moment. He eased the other vampire down to a sitting position against the wall. "Are you injured?"

"No, no, no—" Theo was gasping, though Claire knew he didn't need air, not the way humans did. This was emotion, not exertion. "Please, you have to help, I beg you. Help us, help my family, please—"

Myrnin crouched down to put their eyes on a level. "What's happened?"

Theo's eyes filled with tears that flowed over his lined, kind face. "Bishop," he said. "Bishop has my family. He says he wants Amelie and the book, or he will kill them all."

14

Theo hadn't come straight from Common Grounds, of course; he'd been taken to one of the open portals—he didn't know where—and forced through by Bishop. "No," he said, and stopped Michael as he tried to come closer. "No, not you. He only wants Amelie, and the book, and I want no more innocent blood shed, not yours or mine. Please. Myrnin, I know you can find her. You have the blood tie and I don't. Please find her and bring her. This is not our fight. It's family; it's father and daughter. They should end this, face-to-face."

Myrnin stared at him for a long, long moment, and then cocked his head to one side. "You want me to betray her," he said. "Deliver her to her father."

"No, no, I wouldn't ask for that. Only to—to let her know what price there will be. Amelie will come. I know she will."

"She won't," Myrnin said. "I won't let her."

Theo cried out in misery, and Claire bit her lip. "Can't you help him?" she said. "There's got to be a way!"

"Oh, there is," Myrnin said. "There is. But you won't like it, my little Claire. It isn't neat, and it isn't easy. And it will require considerable courage from you, yet again."

"I'll do it!"

"No, you won't," Shane and Michael said, at virtually the same time. Shane continued. "You're barely on your feet, Claire. You don't go anywhere, not without me."

"And me," Michael said.

"Hell," Eve sighed. "I guess that means I have to go, too. Which I may not ever forgive you for, even if I don't die horribly."

Myrnin stared at each of them in turn. "You'd go. All of you." His lips stretched into a crazy, rubber-doll smile. "You are the best toys, you know. I can't imagine how much *fun* it will be to play with you."

Silence, and then Eve said, "Okay, that was extra creepy, with whipped creepy topping. And this is me, changing my mind."

The glee faded from Myrnin's eyes, replaced with a kind of lost desperation that Claire recognized all too well. "It's coming. Claire, it's coming, I'm afraid. I don't know what to do. I can feel it."

She reached out and took his hand. "I know. Please, try. We need you right now. Can you hold on?"

He nodded, but it was more a convulsive response than confirmation. "In the drawer by the skulls," he said. "One last dose. I hid it. I forgot."

He did that; he hid things and remembered them at odd moments—or never. Claire dashed off to the far end of the room, near where Richard slept, and opened drawer after drawer under the row of skulls he'd nailed to the wall. He'd promised that they were all clinical specimens, not one of them victims of violence. She still didn't altogether believe him.

In the last drawer, shoved behind ancient rolls of parchment and the mounted skeleton of a bat, were two vials, both in brown glass. One, when she pried up the stopper, proved to be red crystals.

The other was silver powder.

She put the vial with silver powder in her pants pocket—careful to use the pocket without a hole in it—and brought the red crystals back to Myrnin. He nodded and slipped the vial into his vest pocket, inside the coat.

"Aren't you going to take them?"

"Not quite yet," he said, which scared the hell out of her, frankly. "I can stay focused a bit longer. I promise."

"So," Michael said, "what's the plan?"

"This."

Claire felt the portal snap into place behind her, clear as a lightning strike, and Myrnin grabbed the front of her shirt, swung her around, and threw her violently through the doorway.

She seemed to fall a really, really long time, but she hit the ground and rolled.

She opened her eyes on pitch darkness, smelling rot and old wine.

No.

She knew this place.

She was trying to get up when something else hit her from behind—Shane, from the sound of his angry cursing. She writhed around and slapped a hand over his mouth, which made him stop in midcurse. "Shhhh," she hissed, as softly as she could. Not that their rolling around on the floor hadn't rung the dinner bell loud and clear, of course.

Damn you, Myrnin.

A cold hand encircled her wrist and pulled her away from Shane, and when she hit out at it, she felt a velvet sleeve.

Myrnin. Shane was scrambling to his feet, too.

"Michael, can you see?" Myrnin's voice sounded completely calm.

"Yes." Michael's didn't. At *all.*

"Then *run*, damn you! I've got them!"

Myrnin followed his own advice, and Claire's arm was almost yanked from its socket as he dragged her with him. She heard Shane panting on his other side. Her foot came down on something springy, like a body, and she yelped. The sound echoed, and from the darkness on all sides, she heard what sounded like fingers tapping, sliding, coming closer.

Something grabbed her ankle, and this time Claire screamed. It felt like a wire loop, but when she tried to bat at it, she felt fingers, a thin, bony forearm, and nails like talons.

Myrnin skidded to a halt, turned, and stomped. Her ankle came free, and something in the darkness screamed in rage.

"Go!" He roared—not to them, but to Michael, Claire guessed. She saw a flash of something up ahead that wasn't quite light—the portal? That looked like the kind of shimmer it made when it was being activated.

Myrnin let go of her wrist, and shoved her forward.

Once again, she fell. This time, she landed on top of Michael.

Shane fell on top of her, and she gasped for air as all the breath was driven out of her. They squirmed around and separated. Michael pulled Eve to her feet.

"I know this place," Claire said. "This is where Myrnin—"

Myrnin stepped through the portal and slammed it shut, just as Amelie had done not so long ago. "We won't come back here," he said. "Out. Hurry. We don't have much time."

He led the way, long black coat flapping, and Claire had to dig deep to keep up, even with Shane helping her. When he slowed down and started to pick her up, she swatted at him breathlessly. "No, I'll make it!"

He didn't look so sure.

At the end of the stone hallway, they took a left, heading down the dark, paneled hall that Claire remembered, but they passed up the door she remembered as Myrnin's cell, where he'd been chained.

He didn't even slow down.

"Where are we going?" Eve gasped. "Man, I wish I'd worn different shoes—"

She cut herself off as Myrnin stopped at the end of the hallway. There was a massive wooden door there, medieval style with thick, hand-hammered iron bands, and the Founder's Symbol etched into the old wood.

He hadn't even broken a sweat. Of course. Claire windmilled her arms as she stumbled to a halt, and braced herself against the wall, chest heaving.

"Shouldn't we be armed?" Eve asked. "I mean, for a rescue mission, generally people go armed. I'm just pointing that out."

"I don't like this," Shane said.

Myrnin didn't move his gaze away from Claire. He reached out and took her hand in his. "Do you trust me?" he asked.

"I will if you take your meds," she said.

He shook his head. "I can't. I have my reasons, little one. Please. I must have your word."

Shane was shaking his head. Michael wasn't seeming any too confident about this, either, and Eve—Eve looked like she would gladly have run back the other way, if she'd known there was any other choice than going back into that darkness.

"Yes," Claire said.

Myrnin smiled. It was a tired, thin sort of smile, and it had a hint of sadness in it. "Then I should apologize now," he said. "Because I'm about to break that trust most grievously."

He dropped Claire's hand, grabbed Shane by the shirt, and kicked open the door.

He dragged Shane through with him, and the door slammed behind him before any of them could react—even Michael, who hit the wood just an instant later, battering at it. It was built to hold out vampires, Claire realized. And it would hold out Michael for a long, long time.

"Shane!" She screamed his name and threw herself against the wood, slamming her hand over and over into the Founder's Symbol. "Shane, *no*! Myrnin, bring him back. Please, don't do this. Bring him *back*. . . ."

Michael whirled around, facing the other direction. "Stay behind me," he said to Eve and Claire. Claire looked over her shoulder to see doors opening, up and down the hall, as if somebody had pressed a button.

Vampires and humans alike came out, filling the hallway between the three of them, and any possible way out.

Every single one of them had fang marks in their necks, just like the ones in Claire's neck.

Just like the ones in *Michael's* neck.

There was something about the way he was standing there, so still, so quiet. . . .

And then he walked away, heading for the other vampires.

"Michael!" Eve started to lunge after him, but Claire stopped her.

When Michael reached the first vampire, Claire expected to see some kind of a fight—*something*—but instead, they just looked at each other, and then the man nodded.

"Welcome," he said, "Brother Michael."

"Welcome," another vampire murmured, and then a human.

When Michael turned around, his eyes had shifted colors, going from sky blue to dark crimson.

"Oh *hell*," Eve whispered. "This isn't happening. It can't be."

The door opened behind them. On the other side was a big stone hall, something straight out of a castle, and the wooden throne that Claire remembered from the welcome feast was here, sitting up on a stage. It was draped in red velvet.

Sitting on the throne was Mr. Bishop.

"Join us," Bishop said. Claire and Eve looked at each other. Shane was lying on the stone floor, with Myrnin's hand holding him facedown. "Come in, children. There's no point anymore. I've won the night."

Claire felt like she'd stepped off the edge of the

world, and everything was just . . . gone. Myrnin wouldn't look at her. He had his head bowed to Bishop.

Eve, after that first look, returned her attention to Michael, who was walking toward them.

It was not the Michael they knew—not at all.

"Let Shane go," Claire said. Her voice trembled, but it came out clearly enough. Bishop raised one finger, and Michael lunged forward, grabbed Eve by the throat, and pulled her close to him with his fangs bared. "No!"

"Don't give me orders, child," Bishop said. "You should be dead by now. I'm almost impressed. Now, rephrase your request. Something with a *please*."

Claire licked her lips and tasted sweat. "Please," she said. "Please let Shane go. Please don't hurt Eve."

Bishop considered, then nodded. "I don't need the girl," he said. He nodded to Michael, who let Eve go. She backed away, staring at him in disbelief, hands over her throat. "I have what I want. Don't I, Myrnin?"

Myrnin pulled up Shane's shirt. There, stuffed in his waistband at the back, was the book.

No.

Myrnin pulled it free, let Shane up, and walked to Bishop. *I'm about to break that trust most grievously,* he'd said to Claire. She hadn't believed him until this moment.

"Wait," Myrnin said, as Bishop reached for it. "The bargain was for Theo Goldman's family."

"Who? Oh, yes." He smiled. "They'll be quite safe."

"And unharmed," Myrnin said.

"Are you putting conditions on our little agreement?" Bishop asked. "Very well. They go free, and unharmed. Let all witness that Theo Goldman and his family will take no harm from me or mine, but they are not welcome in Morganville. I will not have them here."

Myrnin inclined his head. He lowered himself to one knee in front of the throne, and lifted the book in both hands over his head, offering it up.

Bishop's fingers closed on it, and he let out a long, rattling sigh. "At last," he said. "At last."

Myrnin rested his forearms across his knee, but didn't try to rise. "You said you also required Amelie. May I suggest an alternative?"

"You may, as I'm in good humor with you at the moment."

"The girl wears Amelie's sigil," he said. "She's the only one in town who wears it in the old way, by the old laws. That makes her no less than a part of Amelie herself, blood for blood."

Claire stopped breathing. It seemed as if every head turned toward her, every pair of eyes stared. Shane started to come toward her.

He never made it.

Michael darted forward and slammed his friend down on the stones, snarling. He held him there. Myrnin rose and came to Claire, offering her his hand in an antique, courtly gesture.

His eyes were still dark, still mostly sane.

And that was why she knew she could never really forgive him, ever again. This wasn't the disease talking.

It was just Myrnin.

"Come," he said. "Trust me, Claire. Please."

She avoided him and walked on her own to the foot of Bishop's throne, staring up at him.

"Well?" she asked. "What are you waiting for? Kill me."

"Kill you?" he repeated, mystified. "Why on earth would I do such a foolish thing? Myrnin is quite right. There's no point in killing you, none at all. I need you to run the machines of Morganville for me. I have already declared that Richard Morrell will oversee the humans. I will allow Myrnin the honor of ruling those vampires who choose to stay in my kingdom and swear fealty to me."

Myrnin bowed slightly, from the waist. "I am, of course, deeply grateful for your favor, my lord."

"One thing," Bishop said. "I'll need Oliver's head."

This time, Myrnin smiled. "I know just where to find it, my lord."

"Then be about your work."

Myrnin gave a bow, flourished with elaborate arm movements, and to Claire's eyes, it was almost mocking.

Almost.

While he was bowing, she heard him whisper, "Do as he says."

And then he was gone, walking away, as if none of it meant anything to him at all.

Eve tried to kick him, but he laughed and avoided her, wagging a finger at her as he did.

They watched him skip away down the hall.

Shane said, "Let me up, Michael, or fang me. One or the other."

"No," Bishop said, and snapped his fingers to call Michael off when he snarled. "I may need the boy to control his father. Put them in a cage together."

Shane was hauled up and marched off, but not before he said, "Claire, I'll find you."

"I'll find you first," she said.

Bishop broke the lock on the book that Myrnin had given him, and opened it to flip the pages, as if looking for something in particular. He ripped out a page and pressed the two ends together to make a circle of paper, thickly filled with minute, dark writing. "Put this on your arm," he said, and tossed it to Claire. She hesitated, and he sighed. "Put it on, or one of the many hostages to your good behavior will suffer. Do you understand? Mother, father, friends, acquaintances, complete strangers. You are not Myrnin. Don't try to play his games."

Claire slipped the paper sleeve over her arm, feeling stupid, but she didn't see any alternatives.

The paper felt odd against her skin, and then it sucked in and clung to her like something alive. She panicked and tried to pull it off, but she couldn't get a grip on it, so closely was it sticking to her arm.

After a moment of searing pain, it loosened and slipped off on its own.

As it fluttered to the floor, she saw that the page was blank. Nothing on it at all. The dense writing that had been on it stayed on her arm—no, *under the skin*, as if she'd been tattooed with it.

And the symbols were *moving*. It made her ill to watch. She had no idea what it meant, but she could feel something happening inside, something . . .

Her fear faded away. So did her anger.

"Swear loyalty to me," Bishop said. "In the old tongue."

Claire got on her knees and swore, in a language she didn't even know, and not for one moment did she doubt it was the right thing to do. In fact, it made her happy. Glowingly happy. Some part of her was screaming, *He's making you do this!* but the other parts really didn't care.

"What shall I do with your friends?" he asked her.

"I don't care." She didn't even care that Eve was crying.

"You will, someday. I'll grant you this much: your friend Eve may go. I have absolutely no use for her. I will show I am merciful."

Claire shrugged. "I don't care."

She did, she knew she did, but she couldn't make herself feel it.

"Go," Bishop said, and smiled chillingly at Eve. "Run away. Find Amelie and tell her this: I have taken her town away, and all that she values. Tell her I have the book. If she wants it back, she'll have to come for it herself."

Eve angrily wiped tears from her face, glaring at him. "She'll come. And I'll come with her. You don't own jack. This is *our* town, and we're going to kick you out if it's the last thing we do."

The assembled vampires all laughed. Bishop said, "Then come. We'll be waiting. Won't we, Claire?"

"Yes," she said, and went to sit down on the steps by his feet. "We'll be waiting."

He snapped his fingers. "Then let's begin our celebration, and in the morning, we'll talk about how Morganville will be run from now on. According to *my* wishes."

Author's Note

I had an especially great track list to help me through this book, and I thought you might enjoy listening along. Don't forget: musicians need love and money, too, so buy the CDs or pay for tracks.

"On and On" .... Nikka Costa
"Everybody Got Their Something" .... Nikka Costa
"Above the Clouds" .... Delirium & Shelly Harland
"2 Wicky" .... Hooverphonic
"Is You Is or Is You Ain't My Baby" ....
.... Rae & Christian Remix, Dinah Washington
"Enjoy the Ride" .... Morcheeba
"Hate to Say I Told You So" .... The Hives
"See You Again" .... Miley Cyrus
"Fever" .... Sarah Vaughn, Verve Remix
"Peter Gunn" .... Max Sedgley Remix, Sarah Vaughn
"Blade" ....
.... Spacekid & Maxim Yul Remix, Warp Brothers
"Aly, Walk with Me" .... The Raveonettes
"Hunting for Witches" .... Bloc Party
"Cuts You Up" .... Peter Murphy
"Hurt" .... Christina Aguilera
"Run" .... Gnarls Barkley
"Electrofog" .... Le Charme
"Where I Stood" .... Missy Higgins
"Children (Dream Version)" .... Robert Miles
"Grace" .... Miss Kittin
"Walkie Talkie Man" .... Steriogram
"Living Dead Girl" .... Rob Zombie

"Saw Something"...................................... Dave Gahan
"Boy with a Coin" .... Iron & Wine
"Fever".. Stereo MC's
"Kaybettik".. Candan Ercetin
"Playing with Uranium"............................ Duran Duran
"Staring at the Sun" .... TV on the Radio
"The Moment I Said It"........................ Imogen Heap
"This Is the Sound".................... The Last Goodnight
"Juicy"... Better Than Ezra
"One Week of Danger"............................. The Virgins
"Wolf Like Me" .... TV on the Radio
"Poison Kiss" .... The Last Goodnight
"Beat It" .... Fall Out Boy
"Old Enough" .... The Raconteurs
"I Will Possess Your Heart"..... Death Cab for Cutie

Read on for an exciting excerpt
from Rachel Caine's next
Morganville Vampires novel,

CARPE CORPUS

Coming in June 2009 from NAL Jam

"Claire," Bishop said. He didn't sound pleased. "Did I summon you?"

Claire's heart jumped as if he'd used a cattle prod. She willed herself not to flinch. "No sir," she said, and kept her voice low and respectful. "I came to ask a favor."

Bishop—who was wearing a plain black suit today, with a white shirt that had seen brighter days—picked a piece of lint from his sleeve. "The answer is no. Anything else?"

Claire wet her lips and tried again. "I wanted to see Shane, sir. Just for a few—"

"I said *no*," Bishop snapped, and she felt his anger crackle through the room. Michael and a strange vamp both looked up at her, eyes luminously threatening. Myrnin—dressed in some ratty assortment of Goodwill reject pants and a frock coat from a costume shop, plus several layers of Mardi Gras beads—just seemed bored. He yawned, showing lethally sharp fangs.

"Oh, don't be so harsh," Myrnin said, and rolled his eyes. "Let the girl have her moment. It'll hurt her more in the end. Parting is such sweet sorrow, according to the bards. I wouldn't know, myself."

Claire forgot to breathe. She hadn't expected Myrnin, of all of them, to take up her cause—not that he had, really. But he'd given Bishop pause, and she kept very still, letting him think it over.

Bishop finally crossed his arms, and Michael and the other vampire relaxed in their seats, like puppets with their strings loosened. "This will need supervision," he said. "Myrnin, it's your pet. Clean up after it."

Myrnin gave Bishop a lazy salute. "As my master commands." He stood with that unconscious vampire grace that made Claire feel heavy, stupid, and slow, and his bright black eyes locked with hers for a long moment. If he was trying to tell her something, she had no idea what it was. "Out, girl. Master Bishop has work to do here."

Before she could even start to back away, Myrnin crossed the room and closed ice-cold fingers around her arm. She pulled in a breath for a gasp, but he didn't give her time to react; she was yanked along with him down the hall, moving at a stumbling run.

Myrnin stopped only when there were two closed doors, and about a mile of hallway, between them and Mr. Bishop.

"Let go!" Claire spat, and tried to yank free. Myrnin looked down at her arm, where his pale fingers were still wrapped around it, and raised his eyebrows as if he couldn't quite figure out what his hand was doing. Claire yanked again. "Myrnin, *let go*!"

He did, and stepped back. She thought he looked disappointed for a flicker of a second, and then his loony smile returned. "Will you be a good little girl?"

She glared at him.

"Ah. Probably not. All right, then, on your head be it, little Claire. Come. I'll take you to the boy."

He turned, and the skirts of his frock coat flared. He was wearing flip-flops again, and his feet were dirty, though he didn't smell bad in general. Layers of cheap metallic beads clicked and rattled as he walked, and the slap of his flip-flops made him just about the noisiest vampire Claire had ever heard.

"Are you taking your medicine?" she asked. Myrnin sent her a glance over his shoulder, and once again she didn't know what his look meant at all. "Is that a no?"

"I thought you hated me," he said. "If you do, you really shouldn't care, should you?"

He had a point. Claire shut up and hurried along as he walked down a long, curved hallway to a big wooden door. There was a vampire guard at the door, a tall man who'd probably been Asian in his regular life but was now the color of old ivory. He wore his hair long, braided in the back, and he wasn't much taller than Claire.

Myrnin exchanged some Chinese words with the other vampire—who, like Michael, sported Bishop's fang marks on his neck—and the vampire unlocked the door and swung it open.

This was as far as Claire had ever been able to get. She felt a wave of heat race through her, and then she shivered. Now that she was here, actually walking through the door, she felt faintly sick with anticipation. *If they've hurt him . . .*

Another locked door, another guard, and then they were inside a plain stone hallway with barred cells on the left side. No windows. No light except for blazing fluorescent fixtures far overhead. The first cell was empty. The second held two humans, but neither was Shane. Claire tried not to look too closely. She was afraid she might know them.

The third cell had two small cots, one on each side of the tiny room, and a toilet and sink in the middle. Nothing else. There was an old man with straggly gray hair asleep on one of the beds, and it took Claire a few seconds to realize that he was Frank Collins, Shane's dad. She was used to seeing him awake, and it surprised her to see him so . . . fragile.

Shane was sitting on the other bed.

He looked up from the book he was reading and jerked his head to get the hair out of his eyes. The guarded, closed-in look on his face reminded Claire of his father, but it shattered when Shane saw her.

He dropped the book, surged to his feet, and was at the bars in a little under two seconds. His hands curled around the iron, and his eyes glittered wildly until he squeezed them shut.

When he opened them again, he'd gotten himself under control. Mostly.

"Hey," Shane said, as if they'd just run into each other in the hallway. As if months hadn't gone by since they'd parted. "So . . . happy birthday."

Claire felt tears burn in her eyes, but she blinked them back and put on a brave smile. "Thanks," she said. "What'd you get me?"

"Um . . ." Shane looked around and shrugged. "Must have left it at the club. You know how it is, out all night partying, you get baked and forget where you parked the car."

She stepped forward and wrapped her hands around his. She felt tremors race through him, and Shane sighed, closed his eyes, and rested his forehead against the bars. "Yeah," he whispered. "Shutting up now."

She pressed her forehead against his, and then her lips, and it was hot and sweet and desperate, and the feelings that exploded inside her made her shake in reaction. Shane let go of the bars and reached through to run his fingers through her soft, short hair, and the kiss deepened, darkened, took on a touch of yearning that made Claire's heart pound.

When their lips finally parted, they didn't pull away from each other. Claire threaded her arms through the bars and around his neck, and his hands moved down to her waist.

"I'm really sick of kissing you through bars," Shane said. "I'm all for restraint, but self-restraint is so much more fun."

Claire had almost forgotten that Myrnin was still there, so his soft chuckle made her flinch. "There speaks a young man with little experience," he said, yawned, and draped himself over a bench on the far side of the wall. He propped his chin up on the heel of one hand. "Enjoy that ignorance while you can."

Shane held on to her, and his dark eyes stared into hers. *Ignore him,* they seemed to say. *Stay with me.*

She did.

"I'm trying to get you out," she whispered. "I can't stand knowing you're in here with *him.*"

Shane's eyebrows rose just a little. "Dad? Yeah, well . . . He's okay."

And that, Claire realized, was what she was afraid of—that Shane had forgiven his father for all his crazy stunts. That the Collins boys were together again, united in their hatred of Morganville.

Shane read it in her face. "Not like that," he said, and shook his head. "We had to either get along in here, or kill each other. We decided to get along, that's all."

"Yeah," said a deep, scratchy voice from the other bunk. "It's been one big, sloppy bucket of joy, getting to know my son."

"Shut up, Frank," Shane said.

"That any way to talk to your old man?"

"This is the two of you getting along?" Claire whispered.

"You see any bruises?"

"Good point." This was not how she'd imagined this moment to go, except for the kissing. Then again, the kissing was better than her imagination. "Shane—"

"Shh." He kissed her forehead. "How's Michael?" She didn't want to talk about Michael, so she just shook her head. Shane swallowed hard. "He's not . . . dead?"

"Define *dead* around here," Claire muttered. "No, he's okay. He's just, you know."

"Bishop's, yeah." He knew. "What about Eve?"

"She's working. I haven't seen her in a couple of weeks." Eve, like everyone else in Morganville, treated Claire like the enemy these days, and Claire honestly couldn't blame her. Not that she was about to load Shane up with that knowledge, though. "She's busted up about Michael."

"No doubt," Shane said softly. He seemed to hesitate for a heartbeat. "Have you heard anything about us? What Bishop has planned?"

Claire shook her head. Even if she knew—and she didn't, in detail—she wouldn't have told him. "Let's not talk about it. Shane, I've missed you so much."

He kissed her again, and the world melted into a wonderful spinning blend of heat and bells, and it was only when she finally, regretfully pulled back that she heard Myrnin's mocking, steady clapping.

"Love conquers all," he said. "How quaint."

Claire turned on him, feeling fury erupt like a volcano in her guts. "*Shut up*, Myrnin!"

He didn't even bother to glance at her, just leaned back against the wall and smiled. "You want to know what he's got planned for you, Shane? Do you really?"

"Myrnin, don't!"

Shane reached through the bars and grabbed Claire's shoulders, turning her back to face him. "It doesn't matter," he said. "*This* matters, right now. Claire, we're going to get out of this. We're going to live through it. Both of us."

"Both of us," she repeated. "We're going to live."

Myrnin's cold hand closed around her wrist, and he dragged her away from the bars. The last thing she let go of was Shane's hand.

"Hey!" Shane yelled as Claire fought, lost, and was pulled through the door. "Claire! We're going to live!"

Myrnin slammed the door, rolled his eyes, and said, "Theatrical, isn't he? Come on, girl. We have work to do."

"I'm not going anywhere with you!"

Myrnin didn't give her a choice; he half dragged, half marched her away from the first vampire guard, then the second, and then pulled her into an empty, quiet room off the long hallway. He shut the door with a wicked boom and whirled to face her.

Claire grabbed the first thing she saw—it happened to be a heavy candlestick—and swung it at his head. He ducked, rushed in, and effortlessly took it away from her. "Girl. *Claire!*" He shook her into stillness. His eyes were wide and very dark. Not at all crazy. "If you want the boy to live, you'll stop fighting me. It's not productive."

"Why should I help Bishop?" she said, and twisted to throw him off. It was like trying to throw off a granite statue.

"Who says you would be?" Myrnin asked, very reasonably. "Who says I work for him?"

She wouldn't have believed him, not for a second, except that a section of the wall opened, there was a flash of white-hot light, and a woman stepped through, followed by a long line of people.

Amelie, though she didn't look anything like the perfect white queen whom Claire had always seen. Amelie had on black pants, a black zip-up hoodie, and *running shoes.*

And behind her was the frickin' vampire army. Led by Oliver, all in black, looking scarier than Claire could remember having ever seen him—he usually at least tried to look nondangerous, but today he obviously didn't care.

He crossed his arms and looked at Myrnin and Claire as if they were something slimy on his coffee-shop floor.

"Myrnin," Amelie said, and nodded graciously. He nodded back, as though they were passing on the street. As if it were a normal day. "What's the girl done?"

Myrnin looked at Claire, grinned, and let go of her.

"Oh, she's been quite difficult," he said, "which helped convince Bishop that I am, indeed, his creature. But I think it's best if you leave us behind now. We have more work to do here, work that can't be done in hiding."

Claire opened her mouth, and then closed it without having thought of a single coherent question to ask. Oliver dismissed both of them with a shake of his head and signaled for his vampire shock troops to fan out around the room on either side of the door to the hallway.

"Can you protect her, Myrnin?" Amelie asked, and her pale gray eyes bored into his, colder than marble. "I will hold you to your answer."

"With my last breath," he promised, and clasped his hand dramatically to his ragged frock coat. "Oh, wait. That doesn't mean much, does it? Sorry. I mean, yes. Of course. With what's left of my life."

"I'm not joking, jester."

"And I'm not laughing, my lady."

Claire's head was spinning. She looked from Myrnin to Amelie to Oliver, and finally thought of a decent question to ask. "Why are you here?"

"They're here to rescue your boyfriend," Myrnin said. "Happy birthday, my dear."

ABOUT THE AUTHOR

In addition to the Morganville Vampires series, **Rachel Caine** is the author of the popular Weather Warden series, which includes *Ill Wind*, *Heat Stroke*, *Chill Factor*, *Windfall*, *Firestorm*, *Thin Air*, and *Gale Force*. Rachel and her husband, fantasy artist R. Cat Conrad, live in Texas with their iguanas, Popeye and Darwin; a *mali uromastyx* named (appropriately) O'Malley; and a leopard tortoise named Shelley (for the poet, of course).

Please visit her Web site at www.rachelcaine.com and her MySpace, www.myspace.com/rachelcaine.